DAMNED IN HEAVEN

■ ■ ■ ■ ■ ■ ■ ■ ■ ■ ■ ■

On the screen the rings of Discus edged into view, eclipsing the night; twenty bands of utter blackness and moon-white, the setting for the rippling red jewel of gas that was the central planet. Her eyes burned with brightness. She shut her eyes...

They still sat at the table, Eric and Sean and Nikolai, Lara and Claire; they looked up at her, laughing, breathing, looked out through the dome at the glory of Discus.... She opened her eyes. And saw empty night. *Oh, God,* she thought. The room was empty; they were gone. *Oh, God,* only stars, gaping beyond the shattered plastic of the dome, crowding the blackness that had swallowed them... She didn't scream... lost in the soundless void...

"They're all—gone. All of them. That warhead... it shattered the dome."

"MS. VINGE HAS ONE OF THE MOST WISHED-FOR GIFTS ANY WRITER CAN HAVE—THE ABILITY TO MAKE THE STRANGE COME WHOLLY ALIVE."
—**Andre Norton**

Also by Joan Vinge

SNOW QUEEN
CATSPAW

JOAN D. VINGE

HEAVEN CHRONICLES

WARNER BOOKS

A Time Warner Company

WARNER BOOKS EDITION

Part of this book was serialized in slightly different form in *Analog* and *Galileo* magazines.

Questar® is a registered trademark of Warner Books, Inc.

This Warner Books Edition is published by arrangement with the author.

Cover design by Don Puckey
Cover illustration by Donald Clavette

Warner Books, Inc.
666 Fifth Avenue
New York, NY 10103

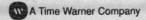A Time Warner Company

Printed in the United States of America

First Warner Books Printing: August, 1991

10 9 8 7 6 5 4 3 2 1

To Barb, my friend of a lifetime
■ ■ ■ ■

Two are better than one; because they have
a good reward for their labours. For if they
fall, the one will lift up his fellow:
but woe to him that is alone when he falleth;
for he hath not another to help him up.

—ECCLESIASTES

TABLE OF CONTENTS

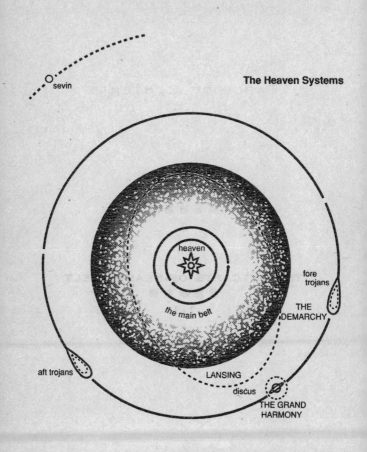

The Heaven Systems

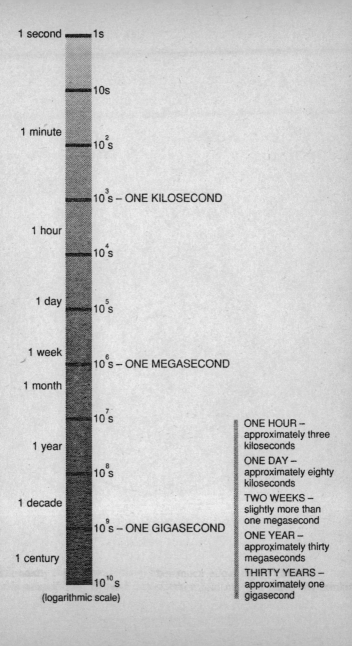

LEGACY

■ ■ ■ ■ ■

The sound of silence filled the black and silver vacuum of the Mecca docking field, echoed from the winking distillery towers, the phosphorescently-glowing storage sacks of gases, the insectoid forms of the looming cargo freighters. But it only filled the helmet of Chaim Dartagnan's suit by an effort of will, as his mind blocked the invidious clamor from the helmet's speakers:

"Demarch Siamang. Demarch Siamang—!"

"—true that you're going to—"

"What will you be bringing back?"

"—rescue the stranded—?"

"Hey, Dartagnan, c'mon, Red, give your ol' buddies a break!"

Dartagnan smiled and released the mooring rope to casually readjust his camera strap against his shoulder. *Eat your hearts out, bastards. Any one of you'd break my neck to be here instead of me.* He glanced back across the glaring, pitted gravel of the field. At the very front of the crowd beyond the gate he saw the elbowing desperation of his fellow mediamen, cameras draped across the barrier; the security guard shoved them back with what looked like relish. Independents all, crawling all over each other to get at the big story, or the unique pitch, that would win the attention of a corporate head and earn them a place in the ranks of a corporation's promotional crew. *There but for the grace of Siamang and Sons go I. . . .* He had won, by flattering the hell out of Old Man Siamang; won the chance

3

to prove his reporting and image-hyping skills as the only mediaman along on this (he saw it in rhetoric) History-Making Journey, a Daring Rescue by a Siamang Scion, a Philanthropic Family's Mission of Mercy... *my ass,* Dartagnan thought. He saw the two corporate cameramen filming his passage, the colored armbands that made them Siamang's men. His stomach constricted over an unexpected pang of hope.

He glanced up, at the purity of blackness unmarred by atmosphere, at the stars. Somewhere below his feet, through kilometers of nearly solid rock, was the tiny, pale spinel of the sun Heaven. He would be seeing it again, soon enough—he focused on the looming grotesqueness tethered at the end of the mooring cable, bifurcated by the abrupt edge of the asteroid's horizon: the converted volatile freighter that would take them across the Main Belt and on in to Heaven's second planet, to pick up one man... and a treasure. The three jutting booms that kept its nuclear electric rockets suspended away from the living quarters clutched rigid cylinders instead of the usual flimsy volatiles sack; it carried a liquid fuel rocket for their descent to the planet's surface.

The rest of the party was clustering now beneath the ship. He pulled himself along the final length of cable, unslung his camera and checked its pressure seal, plugged the recording jack into his suit's radio. He began to film, identifying one figure from another by the intricately colored geometric patternings on their suits. There was Old Man Siamang, praising the nobility of a single human life, no effort should be too great to save this man—and a salvage find that could benefit all the people of the Demarchy.... Dartagnan shook his head, behind his shielding faceplate. The Demarchy was an absolute democracy, and its philosophy was every man for himself, unless he got in the way of too many others... or he happened to have something too many others wanted.

Chaim knew, because it was his business to know, that a prospector had gotten himself stranded on Planet Two when his landing craft broke down. The prospector's radioed distress calls had been monitored; and knowing, like everyone else, that no one would come after him unless it was worth their while, he had revealed that he had found a considerable cache of prewar salvage items, including computer software that could streamline any distillery's volatile processing.

The distilleries were among the few of the small, independent corporations of the Demarchy to have the resources to send a ship in after him, and his discovery provided them with the motivation. Siamang and Sons had as much motivation as anyone, but they also had one crucial additional asset: they alone had the rocket engines available for a landing craft. And so Siamang and Sons would be the first to reach Planet Two, making them most likely to get the rights to the prize as well.

Old Man Siamang had finished his speech, and the handful of representatives of other distilleries responded with all the sincerity their silent applause implied. Sabu Siamang, the old man's son and heir, added a few words, equally insincere. *But great copy.* Siamang was sending his own son on a journey into the unknown, a landing on a world with not only a substantial gravity well, but also the unpredictability of an atmosphere. Maybe there was no one else Old Siamang would trust: but Dartagnan had heard it rumored that there were other reasons why the old man might want the future corporate head to face a little reality and responsibility. Young Siamang said good-bye to his father—any resentment well disguised under a gracious respectfulness—and to his wife. Dartagnan felt surprised that a woman of her position had come out onto the surface, even for this short a time. Her voice was calm, self-assured, like her husband's. Chaim wondered whether she did it for appearances, or if she'd wanted to come. He felt another sharp, sudden emotion; ignored it, unsure even of what it was.

He filmed the ritual of cordial bowing, the leave-taking, the others going back across the field: filming and being filmed, he followed Sabu Siamang up into the waiting ship.

Dartagnan kicked free of his suit in the cramped alcove with the unconscious grace of a man who had spent his whole life on planetoids where gravity was almost nonexistent. He pulled himself through the doorway into the control room, took in the instrument panels: Siamang leaned lightly against one, probing carelessly among the rows of displays.

"Don't touch those!... please, Demarch Siamang." The

soft, almost girlish voice had a cutting edge of irritation, which dulled abruptly with remembered deference.

Dartagnan looked past Siamang in the dim half-light: saw the pilot, the third and final member of their expedition. *Just a kid,* he thought, startled: a slim boy in a dark, formless jumpsuit, with short sky-black hair: average height, his own height, maybe two meters. Epicanthic folds almost hooded the bad temper in the boy's dark, upturning eyes.

Siamang looked around, startled at the tone; an expression of not-quite-apology formed on his face. "Oh, sorry." A broad expanse of smile showed against his dark skin, darker hair. Dartagnan irrelevantly remembered animal faces frescoed on an antique table. (He had never seen any real animal larger than an insect; they were extreme rarities since the Civil War.) Chaim was never sure of the color of Siamang's eyes, but only that they struck with the building intensity of a spotlight. He saw the pilot falter and look down. Siamang looked back at Dartagnan, relaxing. Chaim faced the blinding gaze easily, used to not-seeing a face. Siamang was in his mid-thirties, perhaps ten years older than Dartagnan himself, and the rich embroidery of his loose jacket, the precise tailoring of his tight breeches, the shine on his boots, were blinding in their own right. *The well-dressed demarch* . . . "You haven't met our pilot, have you? Mythili Fukinuki. . . Our token mediaman, Mythili—"

Something in Siamang's voice made the pilot's surname into a double double-entendre. Dartagnan looked back at the pilot, stared, as suspicion became realization. *My God, a woman—?* He didn't say it aloud; was grateful, as her eyes snapped up, burning with hostility. He had never seen a female pilot, they were as much a rarity as a living animal. He realized belatedly that Siamang had not introduced him, apparently wasn't planning to. He wondered if Siamang had already forgotten his name. "Uh—my name's Chaim Dartagnan. My friends call me Red." He raised a hand, gestured at the auburn friz of his hair above his own faded-brown skin.

The pilot categorized him with a look he had grown used to.

Siamang's easy laughter filled the uneasy space between them. "'I didn't think mediamen had any friends."

Dartagnan matched the laughter, added a careful note of self-deprecation. "I guess I should've said 'acquaintances.'"

"Red, here, is up from the media ranks, Mythili. If he does a good job, Dad's going to hire him permanently. So be nice to him; you may have to be seeing a lot more of him." He winked, and the pilot's expression changed slightly. Chaim estimated that the temperature in the room dropped ten degrees. "How does it feel, Red, to be up here now, instead of down there with the rest of the coprophage-corps?"

Dartagnan laughed again, meaning it. "Real good, boss. Just fine. I plan to make a habit of it."

"We're scheduled for departure in one kilosecond. Demarch Siamang," the pilot said. "Maybe you ought to check your cabin to make sure all your belongings are aboard. Just down the passageway—" She pointed at the hole in the middle of the floor, ringed by an aluminum guardrail.

"Good idea." Siamang pushed himself away from the panel, moving by her as he half-drifted toward the well. "Good to be aboard, Fukinuki . . ." His hand slid down over her buttocks in passing.

If looks could kill, we'd be dead men. Dartagnan studied the floor, waiting to be turned to stone.

"Well?"

He glanced up, not focusing.

"You have the crew's dormitory all to yourself. Do you want to check out your belongings or not?" She pointed again. She had moved out of range of the exit well.

He waved at his camera and sack of gear, at his own threadbare, unembellished jacket. "This's it; I travel light." He grinned ingratiatingly at nothing, got no response. "You know . . . uh . . . I have the same problem with my name. Everybody's always asking me, 'Where's the Three Musketeers?'" It was a subject of morbid fascination to him that the most stupid and illiterate of men seemed somehow to have heard of that obscure Old World novel.

"I don't know what you're talking about." She drifted to the control panel, caught hold of a stabilizing strap, began to check readings.

"What's—"

"And before you ask, 'What's a nice girl like me doing in a job like this?' I'll tell you. It's because I want to be here. And yes, no, no, and no. Yes, I am sterile. No, I wasn't born that way. No, I'm not sorry I did it. And no, I did not get the job by agreeing to put out for my passengers—I got it because I'm a damn good pilot! . . . Any more questions, mediaman?''

"No . . . I guess that about covers them all." He raised his hands, palms out in surrender. "But actually," he lied, "I was only planning to ask if you'd mind my filming our departure on your screen.''

"I do mind. The control room's a restricted area as far as the passengers are concerned.''

"It's my job—''

"It's *my* job. Keep your lens out of it.''

He shrugged, and bowed, and stepped into the well.

Supplies and equipment had been stored in the crew's quarters, filling most of the space from ceiling to floor, wall to wall. Dartagnan found the one remaining bunk halfway up a wall and strapped himself onto it, comforted by the feeling of closeness, used to it. *My God, is it really happening. . . ?* He shut his eyes, hands under his head; relaxed his body abruptly, thoroughly, like switching off a machine. Memories from the time when he had piloted his father's ship showed him the images he would have seen on this ship's viewscreen, as they rose almost silently, almost without sensation of movement, from Mecca's surface. . . . His imagination expanded, for a vision of the entire Heaven system, circling in a sea of darkness:

The Heaven system consisted of a G-class star orbited by four planets. The two inner worlds, nameless, were essentially uninhabitable, one too hot, one too cold, with nearly nonexistent atmospheres. The two outer worlds were gas giants: Discus, a carnelian scarab set within twenty separate bands of sun-silvered dust and frozen gases; Sevin, dim green, and unreachable since the Civil War. Both of those worlds were also uninhabited.

But between Planet Two and Discus lay an asteroid belt, the Heaven Belt, which at one time had held a thriving human colony richer even than its parent Earth. But the Civil War had destroyed Heaven Belt, bringing death to nearly a hundred million people, most of its population; and now the Belt was for the most part a vast ruin, where the still-living preyed on the artifacts of the dead in order to keep on living. Among the small isolated pockets of humanity that still continued, the Demarchy had survived almost intact, due to its location. The Demarchy lay in the trojan asteroids, a 140,000-kilometer teardrop of planetoids trapped forever sixty degrees ahead of Discus in its orbital path. The Demarchy had been able to continue trade within itself, and with another surviving subculture, the inhabitants of the ice-bound debris that circled just beyond the rings of Discus proper. The Ringers supplied the volatiles—oxygen, hydrogen and hydrocarbons—necessary to life, as they had once supplied them to the whole of Heaven Belt. In return, the Demarchy provided the Rings with the pure minerals and refined ores that it had in plenty.

Even before the war, the corporations that dominated the Demarchy's economy and its trade had been primarily small and fragmented. The self-interested nature of the Demarchy's town-meeting style of government discouraged monopolies, and so the inherent competitiveness of capitalism had gone to an extreme. The same sophisticated communications network that kept the Demarchy's radical democracy functioning also provided a medium for the expression of corporate competition, and as a result the citizens of the Demarchy were dunned by a constant flow of news disguised by promotion, promotions disguised as news. The need for an ever-slicker, more compelling distortion of the truth had created a new ecological niche in Demarchy society, one that had been filled by the pen-for-hire, the mediaman, willing to say anything, sell anything, without question, for the highest bidder. Willing to do anything at all to impress a corporate head...

Dartagnan grew rigid unconsciously; pain knifed him in the stomach. He pressed his hands down over the pain, sighed, remembering the bribes, the lies, the haunting of offices and corridors, the long, long megaseconds it had taken to catch Old Man Siamang's ear at last, in a public washroom...the obsequious flattery it had taken to win an interview, and in his office, the careful camera angles, the fulsome praise. Sabu

Siamang had been there, too, easy, gracious, charming, the complete gentleman. Dartagnan had used the same fawning approach on him, with mixed results. Sabu had asked his name, bemused, and asked, "What happened to the Three Musketeers?" Dartagnan had laughed too loudly.

Dartagnan winced mentally, opened his eyes, staring at the wall. . . . But Old Siamang had liked his work, had offered him this bizarre journey as a reward: ten megaseconds away from civilization, putting him out of touch with everything he needed to know. But if he did his job well, that wouldn't matter; when he returned to Mecca City he would be Siamang's man, and his life would be secure at last.

He thought about Mythili Fukinuki, Goody Two-Shoes, I-don't-put-out-for-the-passengers, wondered how the hell she'd ever won the old man's alleged heart. A woman pilot, for God's sake—one of those women who put selfish interests and personal ambition above their own biological role as women, as childbearers, as the preservation of mankind's future.

Before the Civil War there had been no reason why women could not work or travel in space; but the war had changed many things, even for the Demarchy. The Demarchy still had the resources to preserve sperm, but not ova; because of the high shipboard radiation levels men were exposed to—both from solar storms and from the dirty atomic fission batteries of their own ships—they were usually sterilized, and a supply of undamaged sperm was put aside for the time when they were ready to raise a family. Sound, fertile women had no similar recourse, and so they were encouraged, even forced, to remain in the relative safety of the cities, protected by walls of stone, supported by their men. But with the comparatively high background radiation from the dirty postwar power sources, even in the "protected" cities, the percentage of defective births was on the rise. Women who could produce a healthy child were considered to be one of the Demarchy's prime assets. But to some of them, that still wasn't enough. . . . *She had contacts. That's the only way anybody ever gets anything.*

He heard someone moving in the commons on the next level; he got up, taking his camera with him. Mythili Fukinuki was heating containers of food in the pantry. He drifted up behind her, looked over her shoulder.

"Lunchtime?"

She twisted to face him, startled; light danced along the tines of the fork in her hand.

Chaim jerked back, awkwardly, through half a somersault. He righted himself, hands raised. "Hey, all I want is lunch!"

Her face eased into a mocking smile; he wondered who was being mocked. "There are the bins, pick out what you want. Remember to close the lids tightly. This is an infrared heater, there's the trash. Eat when you want to, clean up after yourself." She turned back, fixed her containers with a *clack* onto the magnetized tray, and moved away to the table.

He joined her with his own tray, half-sitting on air in the near-normal gravity of the ship's constant acceleration. She frowned faintly, went on eating, in silence. Uncomfortable, he began, "I'm impressed. This is a hell of a nice ship, I—"

"Well it looks like the two of you are getting along even better than I imagined." Siamang drifted down through the ceiling well. "Put in a good word for me, Red; if you get any further—"

Dartagnan looked up, feeling the edge on Siamang's voice. He offered a grin. "I sure will, boss . . . if I get any further."

The pilot picked up her tray wordlessly, made a wide circuit upward to the entry well, and disappeared. Chaim heard the door of her cabin slam to, and, in the silence, the click of a lock. This time it was Siamang who laughed too loudly. Siamang glanced at the pantry, the empty table, the fork spearing a sticky lump of vegetable-in-sauce halfway to Dartagnan's mouth. Siamang raised his eyebrows, used his eyes.

Dartagnan lowered the fork, noticed something new and peculiar about the eyes. "I just started, boss, if you want to take mine. I can heat up some more." He offered with his hands, pushed himself away from the table.

"You're sure you don't mind? thanks, Red." Siamang moved complacently in toward the table as Chaim moved away. His voice slurred, barely noticeable. "One thing you must have that I don't is a way with women . . . if you could call that one a woman. Must come from all the lies you tell." He picked up the fork. "You impress me, Red. How can you mediamen tell so many lies, so convincingly? Are you born that way?"

Chaim focused on Siamang's eyes for half a second, trying to be certain of what he saw; Siamang's eyes probed the private darknesses of his mind like a spotlight. He looked away, unfocused. *An aggressor* . . . The disjointed word burned on his eyelids like an afterimage. But the eyes were too bright, glassy, the pupils dilated until he couldn't see an iris. Siamang was high on something; Dartagnan didn't know what, didn't want to know. He smiled inanely. "No, boss, nobody's born that way. It takes practice; a hell of a lot of practice." He flipped the cover casually down over his camera lens, drifted toward the pantry. He had the sudden unhappy thought that there wouldn't be many scenes worth recording during their transit to Planet Two. He said a quick, silent prayer to no one in particular that Siamang would give him some decent footage when they got there.

"Tell me something else, Red—" Siamang's voice went on, teasing, vaguely condescending.

Dartagnan grinned, not seeing Siamang, or the room, or even the ship, but only the starry void beyond. *It's going to be a long trip. It better be worth it.*

After the first few hundred kiloseconds, Dartagnan stopped carrying his camera, stopped doing almost everything that brought him into contact with the others. Siamang stayed closed in his room, passing the time in a world that Chaim was not interested in visiting; he came out only for meals, for an occasional, teasing attack on Dartagnan's scruples, or a casual pass at the pilot. The pilot stayed locked in her own cabin, doing what, Dartagnan didn't know, didn't care; she came out only to eat and check readings in the control room, avoiding them both.

But he used the opportunity of her absence, eventually, to ignore her arbitrary restrictions and get into the control room himself. He filmed the view of stars that showed on the screen; stayed, watching the screen in the comfortable, clicking silence, escaping from the blank-walled boredom of his cluttered quarters below.

His eyes began to drift from the central viewscreen, studying the projected strings of numbers, the intricate geometric filigrees that showed on the peripheral screens. He frowned absently at the angle of the sun, the position of the lightweight screen beyond the ship's hull that kept sunlight from striking directly on the landing module. He murmured an inquiry to the computer, watched as the string of figures changed on the screen, began to flash, on and off.

"What do you think you're doing?"

He jerked guiltily, caught hold of the panel as the pilot rose up into the room. "I think one of the propellant tanks on the landing module is heating up; you might want to adjust the sunshade—"

"Get away from there. I told you the control room was off limits! What have you done...." She pushed off from the rungs that circled the well's perimeter, came up to the panel. "Of all the stupid—" Her eyes went to the flashing figures on the screen, back down to the panel. She queried, got the same answer. "You're right." She looked up at him again as if she'd never seen him before. "How could you know that?"

"Mediamen know everything." He saw her expression begin to change back. "Well—actually, I'm a qualified pilot."

"*You?*" She blinked. "I didn't think—"

"Funny, I think the same things about women."

She turned back to the panel; he watched her reposition the sunshade. She said, very softly, defensively, "I don't usually make those mistakes. But I haven't been coming up here as much as I should... I shouldn't let him get to me!"

"Siamang?"

She nodded, not looking at him, the soft, shadowed curve of her mouth drawing tight.

"Yeah." He shrugged. "Not exactly what you'd call easy to love, is he?" *But believe me, I've known worse.*

"He's a sadist!" Her voice shook.

Dartagnan felt his throat close, swallowed. "What do you mean? You mean he—"

"No. No, he's too 'civilized' for that. He's a psychological sadist. When he's with his father, with the other corporation men, he's fine, charming, *normal*. But when it's someone he doesn't—respect—he . . ." she broke off, searching for the word, ". . . he . . ."

"He 'teases.'" Chaim nodded. "I'll show you my scars, if you'll show me yours." He hesitated. "Why do you put up with it?"

"I like my job! He—doesn't travel much."

He heard a noise below; his slow smile widened with insincerity as he looked toward the well. "Heads up."

Siamang appeared, pinned them against the panel with his gaze as he pushed upward past the rim of the well. "So here you are," he said, too congenially. He held a drink bulb in his hand, sucked at the straw.

"Hello, boss." Dartagnan bowed. "We were just talking about what a pleasure it is to work for Siamang and Sons."

Siamang laughed in disbelief. "I thought we were supposed to confine our socializing to the lower levels."

"I was just getting a little footage of the stars, a little arty effect: with the pilot's supervision. . . ." He raised his hands apologetically.

"He was just leaving," Mythili said, her voice brittle.

"Good. Don't want to break the rules, do we, Red?" Siamang tossed his drink bulb out into the air. Chaim watched it arc slowly downward toward the cold metal of the floor. "Time for a refill." He sank, like the bulb, disappeared below floor level. His door opened, closed.

"You're always surrendering, aren't you, Dartagnan? Always lying—"

Dartagnan looked back at the pilot's rigid face, feeling her distaste, and down at his hands, still palm-out in the air. He pulled them in against his sides, unexpectedly ashamed, covered the twinge of his stomach. "Yeah." He wiped his hands on his jacket. "Always lying flat on my back, while the whole damned universe fucks my integrity." He stepped into the well.

Mythili Fukinuki caught at the ceiling, stopped herself from drifting on down into the dormitory. Dartagnan looked up, almost surprised.

"Do you mind?"

"Not if you don't." He pushed aside his camera on the bunk. "Make yourself at home. I'm harmless."

She floated down. Her knees bent slightly as she reached the floor, stabilizing. Her short, shining hair moved softly across her forehead; her skin was the color of antique gold in the strong light. Chaim glanced away uneasily.

Her own dark eyes searched the emptiness, avoiding him. "Why do you do it, if it—"

"What's a nice boy like me doing in a job like this?" He grinned, peering down at her, like the Cheshire Cat. She flushed. The grin disappeared, leaving him behind. "Somebody has to do it."

"But *you* don't." She brushed back her hair. "Not if you really hate it so much."

"The voice of experience?" He baited her, smarting with the things she didn't say. "Goody Two-Shoes, female pilot, tell our viewers how you got where you are. And don't tell me it was clean living. It was connections—"

Her mouth tightened. "That's right, it was. My uncle was a freighter pilot, my father got him to use his influence. But they did it because it was what *I* wanted."

"Well, good for them; good for you," he said sourly. "We should all have it so good. If we did, maybe I'd be where you are, instead of where I am."

"There are other jobs. You don't need influence—"

"—to dump fertilizer into a hydroponics tank for the rest of my life? To break up rocks in a refinery? Sure. All the dead-end jobs in the universe, back home on Delhi. . . . Being a mediaman, at least I've got a chance, at money, at making contacts . . . at maybe getting free, getting a ship of my own again, someday. If this's what I have to do to get it—whatever I have to do—I will."

She settled slowly onto a box. "Oh . . . What happened to your ship? What kind of ship was it?"

"It wasn't my ship . . . my father's. He taught me all I know; like they say." He laughed oddly. "He was a prospector, it was a flyin' piece of junk. I never saw it till I was eighteen. I hardly ever saw him. My mother was a contract mother."

"Oh." Almost sorrow.

He nodded. "When I was eighteen my father dropped in out of the black like a meteor and told me I was going prospecting. I spent fifty megasecs learning to pilot a ship, scouting artifacts on rocks with names I'd never even heard of; hardly ever seeing anybody but him . . . and a lot of corpses." He laughed again, not hearing it. "I thought I'd go crazy. Finally he gave up and let me go home, instead. The next thing we heard from him, he claimed he'd made the strike of his life . . . and the next thing we heard, he was dead. He'd smashed up the ship, and smashed himself up, in a lousy docking accident. Some corporation picked up his salvage find, we never got a thing. I had to start doing something then, to support my mother . . . and here I am. I thought I'd enjoy being a mediaman, after fifty megaseconds of prospecting . . . Now, even solitary confinement sounds good."

"Why did your mother let you do it? Doesn't she know—?" Sympathy softened the clear, straight lines of her face.

"What was she supposed to do? Dump fertilizer instead of me?" He shrugged. "She's nice looking, she got married, maybe a hundred megasecs ago. I don't hear from her much now; her husband doesn't appreciate me, for obvious reasons. . . . While my father was alive, she never even contracted to have anybody else's children. Funny—he stayed with us maybe seven times in six hundred megaseconds, never gave her a thing, except me; but she loved him, I think she always hoped he'd marry her someday." He grunted. "Wouldn't that make a great human-interest filler. . . . Sorry, I haven't been filling my quota of compulsive conversation for the last megasecond." And watching her, all at once he was overwhelmingly aware of another need that had not been fulfilled for too long. The fact that she made no effort at all at sensuality made her suddenly, unbearably sensual. He unbuttoned the high collar of his loose, gray-green jacket, shifted uncomfortably above the edge of the bunk, almost losing his balance.

"My father," she said, looking down, unaware, "wanted a son. But he couldn't have one . . . genetic damage. That's why he let me become a pilot; it was like having a son for him. But there's nothing wrong with that—'' her voice rose slightly. "Because piloting is what I always wanted to do."

"Was it? Or was it really just that you wanted to please your father?" He wondered what had made him say that.

She looked up sharply. "It was what I wanted. If a mediaman isn't satisfied to stay in his 'place,' why should I have to be?"

Something in her look cracked the barrier of his invulnerable public face. He nodded. "It's not easy, is it? They never make it easy. . . ."

She smiled, very faintly. "No, Dartagnan . . . they never do. But maybe you've helped, a little."

"Call me Chaim?"

"I thought your friends called you Red."

"I don't have any friends."

She shook her head, still smiling; pushed up from the box, and rose toward the entrywell. "Yes, you do."

Alone, he meditated on stars until his arousal subsided, leaving a warmth in his mind that had nothing to do with sex. He savored it as he listened to her heating food in the commons above his head; heard something else, Siamang's voice:

"How about heating something up for me, Mythili?"

"I'm a pilot, not a cook, Demarch Siamang. You'll have to do it yourself."

"That's not what I meant—"

Dartagnan heard a magnetized tray clatter on the counter, a choked noise of indignation. "Do that for yourself, too!"

More faintly, a door slammed shut. Chaim let her image back into his mind, grinned at it, rueful. *Well, your friendship is better than nothing, poor Goody Two-Shoes. . . .*

But he saw little more of her, as a friend or in any other way, for the next four and a half megaseconds; their mutual dislike of Siamang, and fear of provoking him, still came between them, an impassable barrier.

Until finally Planet Two filled the viewscreen: alien, immense, a painter's palette in sterile grays—gray-blue, gray-green, gray-brown. A castaway's grateful voice filled the speaker static; tracing his radio fix, Mythili put them into a polar orbit, breaking the hypnotic flow of grays with the blinding whiteness of ice caps. For the first time, Chaim saw clouds—pale, wispy streamers of frozen water vapor trapped high in the planet's atmospheric layer. He recorded it all, and was filled with a rare wonder at being one of the few human beings in Heaven system ever to have seen it firsthand. It occurred to him that the clouds seemed more numerous than he remembered from pictures: he managed to make intelligent conversation about it, standing at Mythili's side. And, as they made final preparations to enter the ungainly craft that would take them down out of orbit, she asked him quietly to assist her in the landing.

He sat strapped into the heavily padded seat beside her own in the cabin that seemed cramped even to him. Siamang sat behind him, apparently sober, surprisingly silent. Chaim studied Mythili's movements, saw his own nervousness reflected in her face, but making her movements sharper, more certain, as though it only augmented her skill. She freed them from the grasp of the parent ship, executed the first rocket burn that broke them out of their orbit . . . and began the descent maneuver that neither she nor any living pilot in Heaven system had ever done, with the exception of the man stranded below.

They entered the upper atmosphere; she began the second burn. She would have to maintain a crucial balance: too swift a rate of descent would result in their destruction . . . but too slow a one would exhaust the ship's fuel resources while they were still high above the surface. No ships had been constructed for over two billion seconds in the Heaven system that were capable of using a planet's atmosphere to slow their descent— because since the war there had never been a need for such a ship. Until now: No nuclear electric rocket could produce the acceleration necessary for a planetary landing. And so this ship, which could provide the necessary thrust to slow their descent, had been constructed of makeshift parts and with makeshift technology, in scarcely two megaseconds' time.

Chaim read off their altitude and rate of descent from instruments that had never been calibrated for second-to-second precision at six hundred meters per second; clutched the instrument panel with sweating hands, fighting against his own sudden, unaccustomed weight. Mythili dropped them down toward the signal of the radio beacon, the viewscreen virtually useless, blocked by the intermittent glare of their rockets and the angle of their descent. She bit off a gasp, or a curse, each time they were buffeted or swept from the line of their trajectory by the terrifying force of the unseen atmospheric turbulence.

And at a thousand meters, she began the final burn. Chaim raised his voice as the sound of the rockets reached them, growing: "...six hundred meters, twenty meters per second, five hundred meters—" he felt thrust increase, "—four hundred meters, eighteen meters per second...three hundred meters... two hundred...one hundred meters, ten meters per second..." She cut thrust again, their rate of descent stabilized. "...fifty meters, ten meters per second...forty meters...thirty...twenty meters....Mythili, we're—" She increased thrust to full; ten meters per second squared crushed him down into his seat. The viewscreen was blind with dust. The ship lurched, noise drowned his words, vibration rattled his teeth, "—too fast!"

Impact jarred through him, almost an anticlimax. Mythili cut power; seconds passed before the silence registered. He blinked at the screen, still swirling gray, and pushed up in his seat against gravity's unfamiliar hand. "Congratulations—" he laughed, finding himself breathless, "it's a planet....And I didn't get a single damned shot of the whole descent!"

She drooped, triumphant, laughing with him. "If you'd been filming instead of being my copilot, I don't think we'd be here to worry about it."

He bobbed his head. "Too kind—" touched her with his eyes. She held his gaze, smiling.

"Is it my imagination, or is it getting cold in here?" Dartagnan watched his breath frost as he spoke. He struggled with his spacesuit, feeling leaden and clumsy. He heard Siamang swear in irritation in the cramped space behind him.

"It's not your imagination—the atmosphere acts like water, it's conducting all our heat away right through the hull." Mythili massaged her arms as she studied the viewscreen. "Siamang's engineers predicted something like this."

Chaim saw the dome of the abandoned experimental station, nearly a kilometer away across the flat, subpolar plain; and closer in, the ungainly bulk of the prospector's ship. *Both of us made a better landing than we had a right to. . . .* Beyond them both, along the incredibly distant horizon, he thought he saw a dusting of pale snow pocked with broad, shallow craters: the south-polar icecap of Planet Two. He imagined the incredible volatile resources this world represented; remembered abruptly that they were all at the bottom of a gravity well.

"Come on, Red. Get your camera and let's get going. This is what we came for!" Siamang's voice was good natured, eager. Chaim felt a surge of relief, hoping Siamang's professional business dealings would be easier to record than his private life.

"Coming, boss . . . Aren't you coming?" He looked back at Mythili. "Walking on a planet isn't something everybody's done—"

She nodded. "I know. But I have to stay with the ship; it's not very well designed to deal with the effects of an atmosphere. I have to keep the cabin warm enough so that the instruments don't freeze, and enough fuel has to be bled from the tanks so that they don't rupture. And besides," she lowered her voice, "I stay out of corporate business dealings."

"Oh. Well, I'll show you my home movies when I get back." He settled his helmet onto his head, latched it, picked up his camera. He staggered, stunned by its weight. The surface gravity of Planet Two was over a hundred times normal: He suddenly wished he'd accepted the corporation's offer of a lightweight prewar camera, instead of insisting on his own.

"Come *on,* Red!"

He followed Siamang through the lock and down the precarious rungs of the ladder. The atmospheric pressure kept his suit from ballooning; it clutched him as he moved, with hands of ice.

"Damn it!" Siamang stumbled sideways, struck by an invisible blow: wind, Dartagnan realized, as it shoved him roughly back against the side of the ship. His helmet rang on metal. The surface air had been calm when they set down, but the wind was rising now, swirling the blue-gray dust into translucent curtains. Between the gusts he caught sight of a tiny figure starting toward them from the dome.

They struggled out across the shallow, flame-fused dish of the ship's landing area, went on across the fine, loose surface of the dust. "We're real dirt-siders now, boss," he said cheerfully, more cheerfully than he felt. Dust sandblasted his faceplate; he shut his eyes against it, beginning to sweat, already shivering. Siamang didn't answer, as he struggled to keep his footing; his face was grim, barely visible behind his helmet glass. Dartagnan looked up at the sky, the spinel sun grown large against an alien ultramarine blue. He thought of sapphire, the only thing he could remember that possessed the same purity of color. *They should have named it Blue instead of Two . . . Blue Hell.* He looked down again, across the blue-gray plain at the dome, hardly larger, and at the suited figure closing with them now, proof that they were actually making headway. He let his camera slip off of his stiffening shoulder, wrapped the strap around a numb, gloved hand.

"If you aren't a sight for sore eyes!" A stranger's voice burst from his helmet speakers: the prospector, castaway, welcoming committee of one. The man held out his hands as he reached them, caught one of their own in each, shook them, bowing, all at once. He moved almost easily, Chaim noticed, envious.

"That's not all that's sore," Siamang said, his congeniality sounding strained. "Let's get in out of this damned atmosphere."

"Sure, of course. Let me take that for you, I'm used to this—" The man reached for Dartagnan's camera.

Chaim waved him off, recalling his duty. "No, thanks, I'm with the media . . . let me get a shot of this. . . ." He moved out, hefting the camera, plugged in, focused, pressed the trigger, tripping over his own feet. *Historic Moment, Historic Rescue, Historic Setting . . . Cameraman Busts His Ass. . . .* They were passing the prospector's stranded ship. Siamang's voice reached him. "Get a shot of that, Red—"

"Right, boss." He did a close-up of the name painted on the hull, and the silhouette of an insect. "The *Esso Bee*?" He laughed incredulously, heard the others laugh, in amusement, and in startled recognition. He looked back toward the prospector's shadowed face, "Kwaime Sekka-Olefin, I presume?" He remembered the details of the original news broadcast. Their stranded man was an heir to a distillery fortune, but the actual corporation had been destroyed during the Civil War: Sekka-Olefin Volatiles, Esso for short, and this "secret" experimental station had been run by them before the war.

"That's right; and damned glad to meet you!" The man laughed again. "My God—it's wonderful!"

"Our pleasure," Siamang said easily, "our pleasure to be of service, to one man or all mankind."

They reached the low dome at last. Dartagnan recorded it for posterity, set in the desolation of wind and dust and snow, tried to keep his chattering teeth from recording on the soundtrack. Breathing hard, he trudged ahead to film their arrival, found the dark, welcoming entrance of the shelter. A passageway led steeply down, he noticed, as they passed through the airlock; he realized the main part of the installation must be underground, to help maintain an even interior temperature. He noticed that one wall of the passage was oddly serrated. He backed slowly toward it, filming, as the others entered the hall; stared, through the lens, as Sekka-Olefin suddenly lunged toward him. "Look out—!" Olefin's voice rattled in his helmet. Olefin's glove caught at his arm, missed, as Dartagnan stepped out onto the air.

The air let him down, and with a yelp of surprise he fell backwards down the stairs. The camera landed on his stomach. He lay dazed and battered, gasping for breath, seeing stars without trying. The others reached him, somehow managing not to land on top of him. They lifted the camera off of him, hauled him to his feet.

"You all right, Red?"

"Say, didn't you see the steps there—?"

"Steps?" he mumbled. "What do you mean—uh!" His right ankle buckled under a fraction of his mass, pain shot up his leg, on up his spine like an electric shock. "My leg . . ." He pressed back against the corridor wall, balancing on one foot. "Hurts like hell."

"Hell's what this place is," Siamang muttered, disgusted. "How about your camera?" He dropped it into Dartagnan's arms.

Dartagnan lost his balance; Olefin reached out and caught

him. He shook the sealed case, probed it, turned it over, and peered through the lens. His chest hurt. He replugged the recording jack. "Looks okay... Ought to be a great shot of the ceiling as I went over backwards." He tasted blood from his split lip. "I think the damned thing landed on top of me on purpose."

"Good thing it's tougher than you are," Siamang said, "or you might be out of a job, Red."

Dartagnan laughed, weakly. He looked back up the passageway. The purpose of the serrated wall was appallingly obvious to him, in hindsight; steps, a series of plateaus for breaking downward momentum under high gravity. *That's adding insult to injury....* He grimaced.

The prospector offered him a shoulder to lean on, and they went on along the hall.

"How about a drink to celebrate the occasion? To celebrate my not having to drink alone—" Olefin picked a bottle up off of the floor in the littered cubicle that had been his home for the past ten megaseconds. Dartagnan noticed a pile of other bottles, mostly empty.

"Sounds good. I could use some antifreeze; this place is instant death. How cold does it get here, anyway? It must be zero degrees Kelvin...." Siamang rubbed circulation back into his fingers. They had taken off their suits, at Olefin's urging; the air would have been uncomfortably cool under other circumstances.

"No... no, it only gets down to about 230 degrees Kelvin after the sun sets. Of course, that's not counting the wind chill factor." Olefin grinned.

Dartagnan sat on the bare cot, his leg up, his ankle swelling inside his boot. Olefin glanced back at him, questioning. Chaim noticed that the eyes were green, freckled with brown, under the heavy brows, brow-ridges. Olefin was in his fifties and well preserved for a man who had spent most of his life in space. His unkempt, uncut hair was receding, silvering at the temples, a startling brightness against his brown skin. *Distinguished Scion of Old Money... didn't know any of 'em were real people*. Dartagnan shook his head. "No, thanks . . . I'm a teetotaler."

Siamang looked surprised.

"Medicinal purposes?" Olefin asked, gestured with the bottle.

"That's why I don't." He shook his head again, sincerely remorseful. "I can't drink. Got an ulcer." He wiped his bloody lip.

Siamang's surprise burst out in laughter. "An ulcer? What've *you* got to worry about, Red?"

Dartagnan sighed. "I worry about having to refuse a free drink. I could sure use one."

Olefin poured vodka into hemispherical cups; the clear liquid stayed level and didn't ooze back up the sides as he poured. Afraid to start feeling sorry for himself, Dartagnan reached for his camera. "Would you say you were lucky in finding so much intact here, Demarch Sekka-Olefin? It looks like all the life-support systems are still functional. Did that save your life? What happened to the researchers stationed here, after the war?" It almost felt good to him, after seven megaseconds of enforced silence.

Olefin leaned forward on his stool, sharing the eagerness for the sound of his own voice. "Yes, I sure as hell was lucky. Would've been damned fatal on board the *Esso Bee*. But nothing actually happened to damage this station during the Civil War; nobody knew it was here except Esso. After the war nobody was in a position to come here at all. . . . From the looks of things, the crew must have starved to death."

Dartagnan swallowed. *God, the public will love this. . . .* "But . . . uh, the valuable salvage finds you made will mean that they didn't die in vain? Their discoveries will go to help the living—?"

"Yes . . . yes! In ways I never expected." Olefin's voice took on a vaguely fanatical note. "Did you know that—"

Siamang shifted impatiently, set down his cup. "Demarch Sekka-Olefin; Red. If I'm not imposing—" there was no trace of sarcasm "—I'd like to ask that the interviewing be postponed until we've had the chance to discuss more important matters."

"Oh. Certainly..." Olefin broke off, seemed suddenly almost glad of the interruption. "Anything I can do, considering what you've done for me."

Siamang composed his face as Dartagnan turned the camera on him. "Of course, the most important matter, the basic reason I've come four hundred million kilometers, is—"

—*more money,* Dartagnan thought.

"—to see that you get safely off this miserable hell-world of a planet." He produced something packaged in foam from his thin folder. "This is the replacement unit, complete with the instructions, for the component that was damaged when your ship landed here on Planet Two."

Olefin beamed like a child with a birthday present; but Chaim noted the dark flash of another sort of humor that moved behind the hazel eyes. " 'For want of a chip, the ship was lost!' To think of all the time and money I put in, perfecting the *Esso Bee* and a nuke-electric that could drag home half a planet; the best design possible—to have it all go for nothing, because one single piece of electronics was put on the outside, when it should have been on the inside.... Thank you—I literally can't thank you enough, Demarch Siamang; but I'll do my best." He stood, reached out to shake Siamang's hand heartily. Seated again, he poured himself another drink, raised it in salute, drank it down.

"Well, you can repay us, in a sense..." Siamang paused, poised, disarmingly reticent, "... by giving Siamang and Sons the opportunity to be the first corporation to make an offer on the computer software that you reported finding."

Olefin gave a quick nod, barely visible, that was not meant to be agreement.

Siamang went on, oblivious. "As you obviously know, it would be vital in streamlining our distilling processes—"

"And in streamlining the processing of a lot of other distilleries." Olefin interrupted with unexpected smoothness. "What I had in mind, Demarch Siamang, was to call a public auction on the media for all the salvage, when I return to the Demarchy. I planned to offer to you, or whomever came after me, a substantial percentage of the take as a reward—"

Siamang's expression tightened imperceptibly. "What we

had in mind, Demarch Sekka-Olefin, was more on the order of a flat fee offer on the software. We're not interested in any of the rest, you could bargain however you wanted on that. But it's very important to us—naturally—that Siamang and Sons is the firm to get those programs.''

And a general auction wouldn't guarantee you did. Dartagnan hid a smile behind his camera. He realized suddenly why Siamang and Sons had wanted an edited tape, and not live transmission, on this rescue mission: business transactions were never meant to be public affairs.

''I understand your feelings, Siamang; come from a distillery family myself. But I feel a covert agreement with one firm is too monopolistic, not in keeping with the Demarchy's traditions of free enterprise.... And besides, to be blunt, I've got important plans for the profit I'll be making on this salvage, and I want to get as good a deal on it as possible. That software is by far the most valuable part of it.''

''I see.'' Siamang's eyes flickered to the replacement part safely settled on Olefin's knees. Chaim guessed, without trying, what wish he made. ''Well, then, if you don't mind, I'll make that pleasant trek to our ship one more time and radio the home company about your position on the matter.'' His smile was sunlight on the cold edge of his voice. ''They may give me a little more flexibility in making an offer....'' He bowed.

Chaim stood up, goaded by an indefinable unease: he sat down again abruptly.

Siamang glanced back, pulling on his suit. ''You stay here, Red. Finish your interview. You'd just slow me up. I don't intend to spend any more time out in that open air than I have to.'' He bowed again courteously to Sekka-Olefin, and left the room.

Dartagnan listened to the odd shuffling of unaccustomed footsteps recede, and swore under his breath, with pain and frustration. He lifted the camera again, compulsively, protective coloration. Through the lens he saw Olefin shake his head, hand up, and reach to pour himself another drink. Chaim let the camera drop, irritated, but relieved to see that the prospector wasn't drinking this one down like the others. There was plenty of time for an interview: with the communications time-lag, Siamang wouldn't be back for at least three kiloseconds.

Olefin grinned. "A little loosens tongues, and makes life easier; a lot loosens brains, and makes it hell. I try to draw the line.... Fall was worse than you care to admit, wasn't it? Where does it hurt?... maybe I ought to have a look at that ankle." He stood up.

Dartagnan leaned back against the cold wall, laughed once. "Ask me where it doesn't hurt! Black and blue and green all over.... Thanks, but you'd have to cut off my boot, by now, and it's the only one I've got. Doesn't matter, we'll be back in normal gee soon and it won't give me any trouble. I just have to get the job done now—" He winced as Olefin's fingers probed along his ankle.

"Job comes before everything, even you, huh? So you're a corporate flak...." Olefin's fist rapped the sole of his boot, "Siamang's man?"

"I'm—hoping to be!" Dartagnan muttered, through clenched teeth. "So when he tells me to jump, I don't ask why, or how...I just ask, 'Is this high enough?'"

"You won't be doing much jumping for a while, for anybody. Got a sprain, maybe a fracture." The green-brown eyes studied him, amused; he wondered exactly what was funny. Olefin went back to pick his drink off a dusty shelf. "Don't think I could stand to work for anybody else. Comes from being raised among the idle rich, I suppose...."

"You don't have to be rich, believe me." Dartagnan settled on an elbow, and the cot creaked.

Olefin looked at him, the rough brows rose.

He smiled automatically. "My father was a prospector. Rock poor, to the day he died...just when he'd finally found something big, or so he claimed." Establish a rapport with the subject, get a better interview....

"That right? What was his name?" An encouraging interest showed on Olefin's face.

"Dartagnan—Gamal Dartagnan."

"Yeah, I knew him—" Olefin nodded at his drink. "Didn't know he had a son. Only talked to him four or five times."

"You and me both. He took me out with him, though. Just before the last trip he made."

"That's right . . . heard about his accident. Very sorry to hear it."

Chaim shifted his weight. "They called it an accident."

Olefin sat down, said carefully, "Are you saying you don't think it was?"

He shrugged. "My father'd been prospecting for a long time. He knew enough not to make a mistake that big. And it seemed a little coincidental to me that a corporation just happened to be right there to pick up his find."

"Somebody had to get there first—" Sekka-Olefin shook his head. "I suppose in your line of work you don't see the best side of corporation policy. But not many stoop to that kind of thing; that would be suicide, if it ever got out. Maybe his instruments went out; accidents happen, people make mistakes . . . space doesn't give you a second chance."

Dartagnan nodded, looking down. "Maybe so. Maybe that is what happened. I suppose you'd know the truth if anybody would—you play both sides of the game. . . . He held that damned junkheap together with frozen spit—"

Olefin sipped his drink, expressionless. "What made you decide to quit prospecting to become a mediaman?"

Dartagnan wondered suddenly who was interviewing whom. "Prospecting. Maybe I didn't know when I was well off."

"But now it's too late."

He wasn't sure whether it was a question or a moral judgment. "Not if I make good in this job. . . ."

Olefin nodded, at something. "How'd you like another long-term job instead?"

Chaim sat up, not hiding his eagerness. "Doing what—prospecting?"

"Conducting a media campaign."

Dartagnan slumped forward, oddly disappointed. "That's—a hell of a compliment, from a total stranger. Are you sure you mean it? And what kind of a campaign—what are you planning to sell?"

"Planet Two."

Dartagnan sat up straight again. "What?"

"The colonizing of Planet Two from the Demarchy."

Geez Allah: a job offer from a maniac. A rich maniac. . . . He reached for his camera. *At least this won't be dull—*

"Let's forget about that thing for a while—" Olefin shook his head. "I'll talk to it all you want, if you accept the job. But hear me out, before you type me as a crank."

Chaim grinned sheepishly. "Whatever you say." He toyed with the lens, aiming it where it lay; he jammed the trigger ON. A sound pierced his left eardrum, barely audible even to him, at the extreme upper end of the register. He gambled that Olefin's hearing wasn't good enough to pick it up. *More than one way to get a good interview . . . a job in the hand's worth two in the offing.* "Okay, then, would you care to expand on your reasons for wanting to establish a colony on a hellhole like Planet Two?" He settled back, hands massaging his injured leg.

Olefin laughed, sobered. "How many megaseconds would you estimate Heaven Belt has left?"

Dartagnan looked at him blankly. "Before what?"

"Before civilization collapses entirely; before we all join the hundred million people who died right after the Civil War."

Dartagnan remembered Mecca City, a manmade geode in the heart of the rock, towers like crystal growths in every imaginable shading of jewel color. He tried to imagine it as a place of death, and failed. "I don't know about the scavengers back in the Main Belt, but I don't see any reason why the Demarchy can't go on forever, just like it always has."

"Don't you? . . . No. I suppose you don't. Nobody does. I suppose they don't want to face the inevitability of death. And who am I to blame them?"

"We all have to die someday."

"But who really believes that? Maybe the fact that Esso was wiped out by the war, the fact that I was squandering literally the last of the family fortune, made me see it so clearly: that humanity's existence here has a finite end; and that end's in sight. Speaking of making mistakes, we made a hell of a big one—the Civil War—and one mistake in Heaven and you're damned forever. Damned dead. . . .

"Existing in an asteroid belt depends entirely on an artificial

ecosystem. Everything that's vital for life, we have to process
or make ourselves—air, water, food; everything. But like any
other ecosystem—more than most—you destroy enough of it,
and nothing that's left can survive for long. It has to retreat, or
die. Back in the Solar Belt they had Earth to retreat to, if they
needed it, where everything necessary for life happened naturally. But at the time Heaven was colonized, this hadn't
happened to them, so they didn't foresee the need. When the
old Belters colonized this system, they figured that the raw
elements—the ores and the minerals, the frozen gases around
Discus—were all they had to have. Never occurred to anyone
that sometime they wouldn't be able to process them.

"But that's what happened. Most of the capital industry in
Heaven was destroyed during the war. What we've got left is
barely adequate, and there's no way we can expand or even
replace it. Hell, the Ringers are hardly surviving now, and if
they go under I don't know how our own distilleries are going
to make it. . . . How good are you at holding your breath?"

Dartagnan laughed uneasily. "But—" He groped for a rebuttal, found his mind empty, like his sudden vision of the future.
"But—all right. So maybe you're right, we are sliding down-
hill to the end. . . . If there's nothing we can do to save
ourselves, why worry about it? Just make the best of what
we've got, while we've still got it."

"But that's the point! There is something we can do—
starting now, we can establish a colony here on Planet Two,
against the time when technology fails and the Demarchy can't
support us anymore."

"I don't see the point." Dartagnan shook his head. "It's
even harder to stay alive here than out in space. Even in a suit,
you'd freeze to death! The atmosphere sucks the warmth out of
you, even now, when the sun's up. And the gravity—"

"Gravity here's only a quarter what the human body was
built to withstand. As for the cold—our equipment wasn't
designed to deal with it, but it'd be easy enough to adapt; all
we need is better insulation. This's no worse than parts of old
Earth. Antarctica, for instance. No warmer than this, and snow
up to here; but they didn't mind. The greatest thing human
beings have going for them is adaptability! If those dirt-siders

could do it, a Belter can do it." Olefin's hands leaped with emphasis, his eyes gleaming like agate, lit by an inner vision. "In fact, part of my idea for a media campaign would be to rename this planet Antarctica: 'Return to nature, cast off the artificial environment; live the way man was meant to live'—"

"I don't know. . . ." Dartagnan's head moved again in negation. "You sure this place is no colder than Earth? Besides, the atmosphere's still unbreathable."

"But it's not! That's one of the most crucial points the public has to be made aware of. One of the experimental projects here was a study of the atmospheric conditions—and it proved conclusively that the atmosphere of this world is denser than it was when we first came into the system. The way the various periodicities of its orbit add up right now is causing the polar caps to melt, freeing the gases. The atmosphere's thin and dry compared to what we're used to, but it's breathable. I know; I've tried it."

"For how long?" Dartagnan felt a sudden constricted panic at the thought of trying to breathe an alien atmosphere; his hand rose to his throat. "How's that possible? How could there be enough free oxygen?"

"Don't know. But there is; I've been out two, three kilosecs at a time."

Dartagnan looked down, polishing the polish on the worn vinyl of his boot. "You'd have to live underground, I suppose; help to conserve heat. But we do that anyhow. And solar power—it's a lot closer in to the sun. . . ."

"There, you see!" Olefin nodded eagerly. "You're starting to see the possibilities. It's the answer; we had to find an answer, and this is it. This can make your career! With the money I make off of this salvage sale, we can launch a media campaign that'll convert the entire Demarchy. What do you say, Dartagnan?"

Chaim stopped polishing, kept his face averted. "I want a chance to think over what you told me first, Demarch Sekka-Olefin. I still can't really see this place as the Garden of Allah. . . . I'll give you my answer before we lift off, all right?" He realized that the real question he needed an answer to was whether this was what he wanted to do with the rest of his life . . . or whether he really had any choice. But a kind of excitement rose in him like desire, filling the void Olefin's future had created, with the knowledge that if he sold himself to Sekka-Olefin, he might not be selling out at all.

"Fair enough. . . ." Olefin was saying, smiling, as though he already had his answer. "I expect my numerous blood-sucking relations are going to be prostrate with grief when they hear about my plans for this salvage money. They didn't appreciate my spending what was left of the family inheritance on this project; I didn't name that ship out there; they named it, after me. . . ." He laughed at his own joke. "And my mother-ship up there in orbit isn't called the *Mother* for nothing."

Dartagnan began a grin, heard footsteps in the hall, and felt his face lose all expression again. He drew his aching leg off of the cot, positioned it gingerly on the floor. He stood up, and was suddenly afraid to move.

Olefin leaned past him, pulled a long t-barred pole from under the cot, and held it out. Chaim saw that the ends were wrapped in rags. "Here," Olefin said, "use my crutch. I fell down the goddamned steps in the dark when I first got here."

Chaim finished the grin this time, as Siamang arrived in the doorway, his helmet under his arm. Dartagnan's eyes moved from Olefin's face to Siamang's. He realized suddenly that he had made his decision. He bowed.

Siamang bowed to them in return, his gaze shielded by propriety. "I trust I haven't inconvenienced you, Demarch Sekka-Olefin. I'm sure you want to make your repairs and get off of this miserable planet as soon as possible." He chafed his arms through his suit. "My pilot tells me we'll have to lift off before sunset, ourselves; our storage batteries are getting low from trying to maintain temperatures in the ship. But I've got good news—permission to do whatever's necessary to reach an agreement with you about that software." A gleam like a splinter of ice escaped his eyes. Dartagnan tried to see whether his pupils were dilated, couldn't.

"Good, then." Olefin nodded. "Maybe we can discuss business matters further, after all."

"My hope as well. But first—if you don't mind—I would like to take a look at what we're going to be bargaining for."

Olefin looked vaguely surprised; Dartagnan wondered what Siamang thought he could tell simply by looking at program spools. Olefin shrugged. "If *you* don't mind going back out into the 'weather,' Demarch Siamang. I've got them aboard the *Esso Bee*."

Siamang grimaced. "That's what I was afraid of. But yes, I'd still like to see them."

They made their way across the shifting, slatey dust to the base of Olefin's landing craft. Dartagnan stopped, staring at the ladder that climbed the mass of the solid-fuel module between jutting pod-feet. His muscles twitched with fatigue, his ankle screamed abuse along the corridors of his nerves.

Siamang looked at his upturned faceplate. "You'll never make it up there, Red." Siamang's voice inside his helmet was oddly unperturbed, and slurred, very slightly. "Don't worry about it, you've got plenty of film footage. Just record the audio... and worry about how you'll get back on board our own ship." Siamang's glove closed lightly on his shoulder, good-humoredly, unexpectedly. Startled, he watched them climb the ladder and disappear through the lock.

Dartagnan settled on a rung of the ladder, grateful that for now at least the atmosphere was at rest, and kept its own invisible hands off of him. The sun was dropping down from its zenith in the ultramarine shell of the sky; he noticed tiny flecks of gauzy white sticking to the flawless, sapphire purity of blue, very high up. He realized he was seeing clouds from below. He began to shiver, wondering when the others would finish their business, and whether it would be before he froze to death. Their cautious haggling droned on, filling his ears; he began to feel sleepy under the anesthetic of cold. . . .

He shook his head abruptly, stood up, waking himself with pain. He realized then that the ghost-conversation inside his helmet was no longer either droning or polite; heard Siamang threatening: "This's my last offer, Olefin. I advise you to take it, or I'll have to—"

"Put it away, Siamang. Threats don't work with me. I've been around too long—"

Dartagnan heard vague, disassociated noises, a cry, a *thud*.

And finally, Siamang's voice: "Olefin. Olefin?" Numbed with another kind of coldness, Chaim focused his camera on the hatchway, and waited.

Siamang appeared, dragging Olefin's limp, suited form. He gave it a push; Dartagnan stumbled back as it dropped like a projectile to the dust in front of him, to lie twisted, unmoving. Dumbfounded, he went on filming: the corpse, Siamang's descent of the ladder; the Death of a Dream.

Siamang came toward him across the fire-fused dust, took the camera out of his nerveless hands. He pried the thumb-sized film cassette loose and threw it away. Dartagnan saw it arc downward, disappear somewhere out in the endless blue-gray silt of the plain: His own future, mankind's future, Sekka-Olefin's last will and testament, lost to his heirs—lost to mankind, forever. "That wouldn't have made very good copy, now, would it?" Siamang dropped the camera, stepped on the fragile lens aperture with his booted foot. He picked it up again, handed it back. "Too bad your camera broke when you took that fall. But we don't hold bad luck against a man, as long as he cooperates. I'm sure I can depend on you to cooperate, in return for the proper incentive?"

Dartagnan struggled to reach his voice. "He—he's really dead?" *"No corporation would stoop to murder,"* Olefin had said. . . .

Siamang nodded; his hand moved slightly. Dartagnan saw the dark sheen of metal. Siamang was armed. A dart-gun; untraceable poison. "I *can* depend on you, can't I, Red? I'd like to keep this simple."

"I'm your man, boss . . . body and soul," Dartagnan whispered. Thinking, *I'll see you in hell for this; if it's the last thing I ever do.*

"That's what I figured. . . . It was an accident, he fell; he was too damned fragile, he'd been in space too long. I never intended to kill him. But that doesn't make much difference, under the circumstances. So I think we'll just say he was alive when we left him. His body'll freeze out here, nobody can prove he didn't fall after we left—if anybody ever even bothers to investigate. Anybody could see he drank too much."

"Yeah . . . anybody." The wind was rising, butting against

Dartagnan's body; the dust shifted under his feet, eroding his stability.

"I'm sure you can construct a moving account of our mission, even without film—a portrait in words of the grateful old man, the successful conclusion of our business transaction. . . ." Siamang brushed the metal container fixed at the waist of his suit. "Do a good, convincing job, and I'll make it more than worth your while." Dartagnan felt more than saw the aggressor's eyes assess him, behind Siamang's helmet-glass. "What's your fondest wish, Red? Head of our media staff? Company pilot? Maybe a ship of your own? . . . Name it, it's yours."

"A ship," he mumbled, startled. "I want a ship," thinking wildly, *The smart businessman knows his client.*

"Done." Siamang bowed formally, offered a gloved hand. Chaim took the hand, shook it.

Siamang's heavy boot kicked the bottom of his crutch, it flew free. Dartagnan landed flat on his back in the dirt.

"Just remember your place, Red; and don't get any foolish ideas." Siamang turned away, starting back toward their ship across the lifeless plain.

Dartagnan belly-flopped into the airlock, lay gasping for long seconds before he pulled himself to his feet and started it cycling. He removed his helmet, picked up his crutch, started after Siamang into the control room. The vision of Mythili Fukinuki formed like a fragile blossom in the empty desolation of his mind; he forced his face into obedient blankness, hoped it would hold, as the image in his mind became reality.

She stood at the panel, arms folded, listening noncommittally to Siamang's easy lies. Chaim entered the cramped cabin, she glanced at him as Siamang said, "Isn't that about all, Red?"

"I guess so, boss." He nodded, not sure what he had agreed to. He stopped, balancing precariously, as her eyes struck him like a slap.

"I'm afraid that's not all, Demarch Siamang." Mythili pushed away from the panel, set her gaze of loathing hatred against Siamang's own impenetrable stare. A small knife glittered suddenly in her hand. "There's the matter of a murder." She gained the satisfaction of seeing Siamang's self-confidence suddenly crack. "I didn't like what I heard when you talked to your father, and so I monitored your suit radio. I heard everything." She looked again at Dartagnan, and away. "And I intend to tell everything, when we get back to the Demarchy. You won't get away with it."

"Never underestimate the power of a woman." Siamang smiled sourly, flexing his hands. "I don't suppose it would do any good to point out that if you turn me in you'll be out of a job; whereas if you were willing to play along, you could have any job you wanted?"

"No," she said, "it wouldn't. Not everybody has a price."

"I didn't expect you would, in any case. But I expect you're getting a great deal of pleasure out of doing this to me, Fukinuki. . . . Unfortunately, there's another old saying, 'Never underestimate your enemy.' I'm terminating your services, Mythili. You're not getting a chance to talk." Siamang produced the gun, raised it.

She stiffened, lifting her head defiantly. "You won't kill me. I'm your pilot, you need me to get you home."

"That's where you're wrong. As you pointed out to me, Red here is a qualified pilot. So I don't really need you anymore. You've made yourself expendable. Drop the knife, Mythili." His hand tightened. "Drop it or I'll kill you right now."

Slowly her fingers opened; the knife clattered on the floor. Siamang picked it up.

Dartagnan swore under his breath. "But, boss, I'm not qualified to pilot anything like this—"

"A ship's a ship." Siamang frowned. "You'll manage."

"Chaim—" she turned to him desperately, "help me. He won't kill us both, he'd never get back to the Demarchy if he did! Together we can stop him; don't let him get away with this—"

"I'll kill you both if I have to, and pilot the ship myself." Siamang's eyes turned deadly; Dartagnan saw the dilated pupils clearly now—and believed him.

"He's bluffing," Mythili said.

Chaim caught her gaze, pleading. "Mythili, for God's sake,

change your mind. Tell him you'll keep your mouth shut. Go along with him, it isn't worth it, it's not worth your life."

She looked away from him, deaf and blind.

"Save your breath, Red. I wouldn't trust her anyway ... she's got too much integrity. And besides, she hates me too much; she'd never change her mind. She's just been waiting for a chance like this, look at her—" Anger strained his voice. "No. I think we'll just drop her off somewhere between here and the Demarchy, and let her walk home. And in the meantime—" he moved toward her suddenly, "—we might as well have a little fun." He blocked her as she tried to escape, threw her back against the instrument panel, ripping open the seal of her jumpsuit.

"No!" Dartagnan cried.

Siamang turned; held her, struggling, against the panel. Dartagnan glimpsed her face beyond him, the loathing and the fresh, sudden terror; her shining, golden skin. Siamang pulled her away from the board, twisting her arm behind her. "Okay, Red, if you want her first. She's sweet on you anyway. . . ." He pushed her at Dartagnan.

Chaim caught hold of her, dropped his crutch, fighting to keep his balance. "Mythili . . ."

She spat in his face, pulling her jumpsuit closed. Siamang laughed.

Chaim let anger show. "Forget it; I'm not interested."

"Don't do me any favors, mediaman—" She was flint-on-steel against him, her outrage burned him like a flame.

He let her go, wiped his face; he said roughly, "Believe me. I'm not doing you any favor." *But, God help me, maybe I'm saving your life—and mine.* He looked back at Siamang, leaned down to pick up his crutch, covering sudden inspiration. "I've got a better idea. Instead of spacing her later, put her out here, now, in a suit with the valve jammed. The sun's going down ... she'll suffocate or freeze ... and we can watch, to make sure she's dead. A tragic accident." He felt her anguish, her helpless rage; felt a hot, stabbing pain in his stomach.

Siamang smiled as the possibilities registered. "Yes, I like it. . . . All right, Red; we'll do it your way. But there's no reason why I still can't have some fun with little Fukinuki, first. . . ." He reached up, began to unbutton his jacket.

"Yes, there is."

Siamang looked at him. "Oh?"

"It's getting late, the ship's batteries are running down. And besides, the wind's rising. If you expect me to get us up out of here safely, I don't want to wait any longer. . . . Won't you get enough pleasure watching her die out there—?" Dartagnan's voice rose too much.

Siamang smiled again, slowly. "Okay, Red, you win. . . . Get into a suit, Mythili, before I change my mind."

She walked wordlessly past Dartagnan, clinging to the shreds of her dignity; he watched her put on a suit. She fumbled, awkward, made clumsy by gravity and nervousness. Wanting to help her, Chaim stood motionless, turned to stone.

She turned back to them at last, waiting, the helmet under her arm. "All right," she murmured, barely audible. "I'm ready. . . ."

Siamang crossed the cabin to her side, reached behind her head to the airflow valve at her neck. She shuddered as he touched her. Dartagnan watched him tighten the knob that shut off the oxygen flow, watched his body tighten with the effort.

"Put on your helmet."

She took a deep breath, put it on. Siamang latched it in place, motioned her toward the lock. She went to it, stepped inside, jerkily, like a broken doll.

"Red." Siamang gestured. "You do the honors."

Dartagnan hobbled to the control plate, counting seconds in his mind. He could barely see her face, staring back at him, saw her mouth move silently: *Damn you, damn you, damn you!* . . . He thought there were tears in her eyes, wasn't sure.

He nodded, whispering, "Goodbye, Goody Two-Shoes. Good luck—" His hand trembled as he reached out to start the lock cycling.

He turned back with Siamang to the control panel, watched the viewscreen, waited. The seconds passed, the lock cycled. She appeared suddenly on the screen, stumbled as the wind gusted . . . fell, got up, fell again as she tried to run, trying to reach the sheltering dome, too far away. The shifting, slate-blue dust slipped under her feet; she fell again, tried to get up, couldn't. At last he saw her try to free the frozen valve one final time . . . and then unlatch her helmet. She raised her head, too far away for him to see her face; he dragged a breath into his own tortured lungs. She reached for her helmet again, frantically . . . crumpled forward into the dust, lay coiled like a fetus, lay still.

Dartagnan made himself look at Siamang; looked away again, sick. He sagged down into the pilot's seat, reached for the restraining straps. Siamang turned back from the screen, the obscenity of his pleasure fading to stunned disgust. "Get us out of this graveyard." He moved past Chaim, toward his own padded couch; stopped, turned back. "By the way, this time it was premeditated murder. And you did it, Red. Keep that in mind."

Dartagnan didn't answer, staring at the screen, looking down at the empty seat beside him.

He took the ship safely up through the atmosphere, learning that getting up off a planet's surface was much simpler than getting safely down. He rendezvoused, docked the shrunken landing module at last within the stretched, arachnoid fingers of the parent ship; he heard his father's voice directing, guiding, encouraging . . . knowing with a kind of certainty that after what he had seen and done on the world below, he couldn't make a mistake now.

On board the main ship again, he moved through the levels to the control room, found their flight coordinates already in the computer. Mechanically he took the ship out of orbit, barely conscious of what he did; as he turned away from the panel Siamang congratulated him, with apparent sincerity. Dartagnan pushed on past, wordlessly, and ducked into the aluminum-ringed well. He reached Mythili Fukinuki's cabin door, stopped himself, and with a sudden masochistic urge, opened it and went inside. He slid the door shut, drifted to the bed, pulling off his jacket, his shirt, one boot. He forced his aching body into the sleeping bag, settled softly, mumbling, "Good night, Goody Two-Shoes. . . ." And finally, thankfully, he slept.

When he woke again his face burned under his touch, his

ankle was hot and swollen inside his boot. He went down into the commons, forced himself to eat, found a bottle of antibiotics and swallowed a handful of pills heedlessly. Then he went back to the cabin, locked the door, and slept again.

He repeated the cycle four more times, avoiding Siamang, before his fever broke and he remembered to check the ship's progress. He made minor alterations in their course, lingered at the screen for long seconds, searching the darkness for something he would never find. Then he tried to use the radio, and was deafened by a rush of static. He realized that Siamang had done something to the long-range antenna while he slept; there would be no more radio contact until they were back within Demarchy space. He checked the chronometer: Less than half a megasecond of flight time had elapsed; even without the added mass of the propellant tanks they had carried on the way out, more than three megaseconds still remained.

"How's our progress?"

He turned and found Siamang behind him. "Fine, as far as I can tell." His own voice startled him, unexpected.

"And how's your conscience?"

Dartagnan laughed sharply, nervously. "What conscience?"

Siamang smiled. Dartagnan risked a look straight into his eyes. They were clear, the pupils undilated; he wondered whether that was good or bad. "I wondered whether you might be suffering the pangs of remorse; you're not looking too well." Faint mockery, faint disapproval . . . faint suspicion.

Chaim scratched an unshaven cheek, cautiously expressionless. "Only the pangs of a fall down stairs." He glanced down at his unbuttoned jacket, the cheap bedraggled lace on his half-tucked-in shirt. He looked back at Siamang, flawlessly in control, as always. He raised his hands. "I was just going to go clean myself up," he muttered, and retreated.

Seconds sifted down through the hourglass of time; the ship moved through the darkness, slowly gaining speed. The casual persecution Siamang had inflicted on the trip out grew more calculated now, and more pervasive; until Dartagnan began to feel that Siamang only lived for his personal torment, a private demon sprung from his own private hell. He lived on soy milk, as the chronic tension exacerbated his ulcer; he began to lose sleep, as Siamang's probing found the hidden wounds of his guilt. He felt the armor of his hard-won, studied indifference wearing thin, and wondered how much more he could stand. And he wondered what pathology drove Siamang to methodically destroy the loyalty of the only "witness" in his own defense. . . .

Until suddenly Dartagnan saw that it was no pathology at all, but a coldly rational test. In spite of what he was, in spite of everything, Siamang didn't trust him . . . and unless Siamang was completely convinced of his cowed submission, and his totally amoral self-interest, there might be a third Tragic Accident before the end of this Odyssey of Lies and Death. They were safely on a homeward course; he was entirely expendable again. Three deaths might be hard to explain, but Siamang had the means to sway public opinion at any trial—as long as there was no one to testify against him.

His sudden comprehension of his danger steadied Dartagnan on the tightwire he walked above the abyss of his desperation: He would endure anything, do anything he had to do; there were only two things that mattered now—his own survival, and the reward that he would have earned a thousand times over. . . . Not a ship, not his freedom, but the knowledge that Siamang and Sons would pay. They would pay to bring Mythili Fukinuki back to the Demarchy; they would pay for Sekka-Olefin's death . . . they could never even begin to pay enough, for what they had done to Heaven's future.

And so he endured, ingratiating, obedient, and smiling—always smiling. He lived for the future, the present was a darkness behind his eyes; he was a man on a wire above the starry void between the past and their destination. And in the refuge of his cabin, he found the private world of Mythili Fukinuki, in a chest filled with books and papers. Ashamed at first, he rummaged through them, finding the precise impersonalities of astrogation manuals . . . and books on poetry and philosophy, not only recent but translations into the Anglo from all the varied cultures of their heritage on Earth. Passages were marked with parentheses, question marks, exclamations; her own thoughts held communion in the margins of the shining plastic pages or spilled over, filling notebooks.

He began to read, as she had read, to fill the empty stretch of time. He felt her presence in everything he read, in each small discovery; beyond anger or bitter grief, she gave him comfort, brought him strength. . . . And he understood at last that he had hated prospecting because he hated loneliness; that because of his resentment, being with his father had been the same as being alone. But he saw himself on his own ship, imagined Mythili Fukinuki as his partner—and knew he would need nothing more, need no one else, to be content. . . . A much-opened book of poems fell open again in his hands, and he saw her plain, back-slated writing in the margin: *It will be lonely to be dead; but it cannot be much more lonely than it is to be alive.* . . .

He found a grease pencil in the sack of his belongings, and slowly, as though there was no strength left in his hand, wrote *Yes, yes, yes* . . . The vision of her motionless form, the swirling dust of Planet Two, choked his memory; he snapped the book shut. *No, I wasn't wrong!* He put the book carefully into his sack, and after that he stopped reading.

But he realized then that if he was wrong, if he was as guilty as Siamang himself . . . if Mythili Fukinuki had died because of him, then even if he survived to give testimony, it would only be his own word against Siamang's, and that might not be enough. Siamang had influence; he had nothing—he had no proof, without Mythili. And if she was dead, he had to be certain that Siamang would never get away with it. Somehow he had to find a way to make Siamang incriminate himself. But his camera was ruined, the radio was out; he didn't even have a tape recorder on him . . . or did he?

He got up silently, and slipped out of the room.

They were well within Demarchy space; a hundred kiloseconds remained before they would dock at Mecca. Dartagnan made radio contact at last, as Siamang looked on, and set up a media conference for their arrival. A hundred kiloseconds . . . and still he had no proof.

"Come on, Red, let's celebrate our impending return to civilization." Siamang gestured, smiling openly, without sarcasm. "God, it'll be a relief to get back to the real world! This whole damned thing is an experience I only want to forget."

"The same here, boss. The sooner the better." Dartagnan followed him below, humoring his apparent good humor. Chaim drank soy milk cut with water, trying to lull the chronic spasms of his stomach; Siamang drank something that he assumed was considerably stronger. But Siamang's mood stayed easy and congenial, his conversation rambled, innocuous, clever, only slightly condescending. "... join me in one drink at least, Red—" Siamang slid one of the magnetized drink bulbs across the metal surface of the table. "How much can it hurt?"

"It hurts plenty, believe me, boss. I'd like to, I would; but I just can't take liquor."

"It's not vodka." Siamang's tone turned conspiratorial, and sharpened slightly. "I want you to have a drink with me, Red. I won't take no for an answer."

"No, I'm sorry. . . ."

"Drink it." Siamang laughed; Chaim felt his stomach tighten. "Do it—as a favor to me."

Dartagnan hesitated, toying absently with the metal band that circled his throat beneath the high collar of his jacket. "All right, boss; just one . . . if you'll do me a favor in return?"

Siamang started. "What did you have in mind?"

"I want my payoff now. I want you to give me a corporate credit voucher for the value of my scoutship."

Siamang frowned. "I'm willing to transfer the credit to your account directly—"

He shook his head. "Sometimes direct credit transfers don't— get registered. I want it in writing before I do my part to keep you clear of that murder."

Siamang's frown deepened, lifted slowly. "All right. Red . . . I'll humor you. I don't expect you'll let me down if I do; since you're in this as deep as I am, and you'll go right down with me—" He went out of the room.

Dartagnan sat staring uneasily at the cup. *What the hell; it hasn't done anything to Siamang. . . .* He turned the metal collar slowly around his neck. *Damn it, it's worth a bellyache; it's worth anything, to be sure I get what I need.*

Siamang returned, passed the voucher across the table to him. "Is that satisfactory?"

Dartagnan took it in his hands, like a starving man holding food. For a second the realization of what that money could mean to his own future rose into his mind, and made him dizzy. "Yeah," he said hoarsely, "that's just perfect." He folded it and stuck it into his boot. He lifted the drink bulb from the table, "I'll drink to that." He pulled up on the straw, and drank.

He tasted nothing, only the bland sweetness of pear juice; he went on drinking, surprised, finished it.

Siamang drank with him, smiled. "What are you going to do with a ship, Red? You mean you really don't enjoy being a garbage man to humanity?"

"I've recycled just about all the shit I ever want to face, boss. Just about all I can stand. . . ." He squinted; the light glancing up from the table top hurt his eyes: *Come on, that's impossible* . . . suddenly afraid that it wasn't.

"Going to be a prospector, like Sekka-Olefin?"

He looked back at Siamang. "Not like Sekka-Olefin. He—made a mistake." Siamang's voice set his teeth on edge, his skin prickled, he began to feel as though his body was strung together on live wires. "Just like my old man . . . I'm not going to make that mistake." *Shut up!* He shook his head, the light broke up into prisms.

"What mistake was that, Red? What mistake could there be that a man who'd go into your profession hasn't made already?"

Chaim almost shouted it, shaking with uncontrollable rage. He choked back the words, gagged on sudden self-loathing. . . . *Why isn't Siamang feeling it?* And then he realized that Siamang hadn't been drinking anything at all, except fruit juice. Siamang was entirely sober; and he had been given one last test. . . .

Mecca City opened around him, vibrant, brilliant, beautiful, an alien flower . . . his mind sang, a choir of voices, the voice of the city, eternal life. He cupped life in his hands and drank . . . life streaming through the prism of his fingers in rainstars of light. He was eternal, he laughed, inhaling the city fragrance of sound, chords of cinnamon and cloves, leitmotif of gardenia . . . of corruption . . . a fragrance growing, that deafened him, shattering his ears, shattering his soul like crystal, shattering the crystal city. . . . A cloying stench of decay clogged his nose, his mouth, his lungs, like slatey dust; the fragile towers withered, fading, shriveling around him; like bodies decaying, betrayed . . . death was eternal, only death; and her face, all their faces turned to him, turned to ruin, worm-eaten, rotting, decayed . . . *I know you . . . Mythili, I know you . . .* he had no voice . . . *I know you aren't!* . . . *I know you . . .* He heard her sobbing, like flowers, crystal acid-drops eating away his viscera like decay, *I don't want to! I don't want to die . . . I want to live . . . I have to . . . want to live.* . . . Cradled in the arms of death, worm-riddled, he saw his flesh rotting, falling from his bones . . . and it was the end, the end of the world. . . .

Dartagnan woke, moved feebly on the floor in the bathroom of his private cabin, trying to remember how he had gotten here, why he had eaten hot coals . . . why he was crying. He lay still, too weary to move, listened to the grating whine of a fan . . . the exhaust fan. He remembered, then, being sick to his stomach. He touched his face, filmed with wetness, sweat and tears—and vomit; God, he hadn't done a very clean job of it. He pushed himself up, drifted to the wash basin to shut off the fan. He saw himself in the mirror, shut his eyes instead and swore in a fury of humiliation—

Siamang. He reached down, dragged his boot off, swearing again as he wrenched his still-swollen ankle. But he laughed in satisfaction as his hand closed over the crumpled, drifting prize, the credit voucher. *Still there* . . . He tried again futilely to remember what else had happened; knowing that Siamang had drugged him for a reason, and that he could have said anything, *would* have said anything, and anything could have been the wrong thing. But he had the voucher; and he was still alive—A flicker of nightmare, a discontinuity, shook him; he ran his hands down his body in sudden fear. He was still alive. The metal collar was still around his neck; he had what he needed. Maybe, just this once, something was going to come out right. . . .

He stripped, went to the shower, sealed himself in along with his ruined clothes, and turned on the water. He let it run, heedless of the waste, through three full shower cycles, an entire kilosecond, until he finally began to feel clean. Life, and—almost—self-respect, stirred sluggishly in him again as the heat lamp dried the sheen of water from his skin, baked the shame and the last of the stiffness out of his mind and body. He shaved, did what he could with his clammy clothes, put on the one fresh shirt he had saved for their return to Mecca. Appearance was everything; he had to present a good appearance when he faced himself in the eyes of the media cameras. . . . He investigated his ankle. The brown skin was still splotched with ugly bruises, but it was healing, slowly, with the passing of time. He forced it back into his boot, polished both boots with his dirty shirt. He thought about other wounds, and wondered how much time he would need before those were healed as well.

"Dartagnan—"

He heard Siamang rap on his door, quietly, and then more loudly. He went to it, opened it, his face set. Siamang stared; Chaim wondered whether he was staring at the neatness of his clothes, or the haggardness of his face. "What do you want?"

Almost diffidently, Siamang held out a drink bulb; Dartagnan grimaced. "It's just milk; you can believe it. Look, I'm sorry about what happened to you, Red. I shouldn't have given you that big a dose, I didn't think about your not being used to it—"

The hell you didn't, Dartagnan thought.

"—I want you to know I'm sorry. How do you feel?"

"Like I'll be glad when I can forget it. How much time's left before we reach Mecca?"

"That's why I knocked—only five kiloseconds. Are you going to be able to bring us in all right?"

Dartagnan almost smiled, realizing the reason for Siamang's sudden solicitude. "I think so. I hope so." He moved out into the hall, hesitated, trying to make it sound casual: "I hope I didn't—say anything I shouldn't have, boss. I . . . don't remember much about it."

"You told me you hated my stinking guts, Red."

He froze. "I'm sorry, boss, I didn't mean it, I didn't know what I was—"

Siamang grinned forgiveness. "It's all right, Red. I don't blame you at all. In fact it's just what I wanted to hear...I wanted to hear you say what you really thought, just once. Because you also said that I'd given you what you wanted, and that was all that mattered. I know I can trust you now, Red; because I'm sure we understand each other. Isn't that right?" Mockery traced the words. His hand struck Chaim's shoulder lightly.

Dartagnan smiled. "Sure boss. Anything you say."

Dartagnan watched the elongated crescent of the asteroid Mecca grow large on the viewscreen, and gradually eclipse as he maneuvered them into its shadow. Siamang hung behind him, watching; oblivious, Chaim watched only the intricate, expanding pattern of strangely familiar ground lights below them. He began to pick out ships—the tankers like gigantic ticks, bloated or empty; the small, red-blossoming tows. He listened to the disjointed, disembodied radio communications, almost thought he could see the ships making way for him. He spoke calmly to the ground controller, explaining who he was, and boosted the response for Siamang to hear: the encouragements, the welcomings—interspersed with the terse, anxious coordinates to guide an inexperienced pilot down to the bright, scarred surface of the docking field. Their ship closed with the real world; Dartagnan felt the slight, jarring impact of a perfect landing rise through its structure. In his mind he compared the slow ceremony of docking to the terrifying urgency of their descent to the surface of Planet Two...remembered sharing the pride of a job well done. For half a second, he smiled.

The field was curiously empty, their helmet speakers strangely silent, as they disembarked at last and made their way along a mooring cable toward the exit from the field. One guard met them, greeting Siamang with deference, cleared them to pass downward through the airlock into the asteroid's heart.

"Where the hell is everybody, Red? My father should be

here, where's our media coverage?" Siamang's voice frowned.
"I thought you radioed ahead about our arrival."

"I did, boss; you heard me. They must be waiting for us
inside." *They've got to be. . . .*

They were: Dartagnan followed Siamang along the corridor
that dropped them inward from the surface, his broken camera
floating at his shoulder, and saw his fellow mediamen clustered
in wait on the platform at the city's edge. A surprisingly sparse
crowd of curious onlookers, surprisingly quiet, bumped and
drifted among them. *Awed . . . ?* he thought. He wondered if
Siamang's rivals among the distilleries had kept their workers
away. The irony pleased him; but not, he noticed, Siamang.

He watched the crowd flow forward to meet them, let it
surround him, letting the mediamen get it out of their systems.
"Demarch Siamang . . . Demarch Siamang . . . Hey, Red—?" He
glimpsed the city, past and through them . . . a kilometer in
diameter, towers trembling faintly, glittering in the shifting
currents of air. Colored plastic stretched over fragile frames
filled every square meter of ceiling, wall, floor, here where
gravity was barely more than an abstraction: A manmade
tribute to the magnificent generosity of nature, and the splendor
of the Heaven Belt. The splendor made sterile because nature
had turned its back on man; man the betrayer, who had
betrayed himself. Chaim saw Sekka-Olefin's future, in a sudden, strobing nightmare of horror overlying every crystal-facet
wall, every stranger's face that closed in on his own. . . . *My
God . . . my God . . . And I'm the only one who knows!* He
steadied himself, inhaling the spices of the scented air, summoning
strength and resolution.

And then he raised his hands, raised his voice into the
familiar singsong of a media hype. "Ladies and gentlemen . . . my
fellow Demarchs . . ." Silence began to gather. "I'm sure you
all know and recognize Demarch Siamang. But there's a side of
him that none of you really knows—" he stretched his silence
until the silence around him was absolute; every eye, every
pitiless camera lens was trained on him where he stood, with
Siamang complacently at his side. He took a deep breath.
"This man—is a murderer. He went four hundred million
kilometers to Planet Two, to save Kwaime Sekka-Olefin, and

wound up killing him instead, over that box of—stolen—computer software you see there in his hand." He turned, bracing, saw Siamang's face, the perfect image of incredulous amazement.

Siamang's eyes were blank with a fury that only he could read. "This man is a psychotic. I don't have any idea what he's talking about. I obtained this salvage from Sekka-Olefin in a legitimate business transaction: and he was perfectly alive when we left him—"

A stranger pushed forward, touched Dartagnan's arm; golden-brown eyes demanded his attention, assured, analytical. "Are you Chaim Dartagnan?"

Chaim nodded, distracted; Siamang broke off speaking abruptly, "Who the hell are you?"

"My name's Abdhiamal; I'm a government negotiator... Demarch Dartagnan, what evidence do you have to support your charge?"

"Now, listen, Abdhiamal—" Siamang interrupted, indignant. "No one needs any government interference here, this is simply a—"

"Demarch Dartagnan has the floor," Abdhiamal said evenly, his eyes never leaving Chaim's face. "You'll be permitted to speak in turn. Dartagnan?"

Dartagnan almost laughed; triumph filled him, overwhelming gratitude made him giddy. He kept his own eyes on the media cameras—his damnation, his salvation, his weapon. . . . "He got hold of my camera. I don't have the recording of the murder. But he bribed me, to cover the whole thing up. . . . This's the corporation credit voucher, made out to me—" He spread it between his hands, held it out to the thousands of hungry eyes behind every camera lens.

"That's a forgery."

"And this—" Dartagnan pulled open the collar of his jacket, "is a recording of the transaction." He twisted the jury-rigged playback knob on the note recorder he had ripped out of his spacesuit; he heard his own voice, ". . . I want it in writing, before I do my part to keep you clear of that murder." And Siamang's, "All right, Red."

"That was an accident!" Siamang's voice slipped out of control. "I didn't mean to kill Olefin, it was an accident—But ask him about Mythili Fukinuki, ask him about our pilot: That was no accident. He murdered her in cold blood; there was nothing I could do to stop him. He's a madman, a homicidal maniac—''

"Mythili Fukinuki's not dead." Dartagnan turned to watch for the second it took to register on Siamang's face. He smiled; he turned back again to Abdhiamal, was surprised at the surprise he found in the amber-colored eyes. "At least . . . I don't think she is. When I was alone with Sekka-Olefin he claimed a human could survive in Planet Two's atmosphere; he said he'd breathed it himself. Siamang wanted to space her, because she overheard Olefin's murder . . . I told him to put her out on the surface instead. He was on drugs, I couldn't stop it or he would've killed us all. It was the only thing I could think of. . . .'' Ashamed, he looked down, away from the memory of her face: "*Damn you, damn you . . .*" "If I was wrong, if she died, then I'm just as guilty as he is; the Demarchy can do anything they choose to me, I deserve it. All that matters to me now is that somebody made it back, to tell the truth. And to see that Siamang and Sons pays to get her home—because I don't believe that she is . . . dead. . . .'' A sudden reaction took away his voice. "Has there . . . have you heard of any radio messages being received? Is there any word?''

"Better than that, as far as you're concerned." Abdhiamal smiled, without amusement. "Mythili Fukinuki returned to the Demarchy before you did, in that prospector's ship. She reported everything that happened . . . except the fact that you weren't actually trying to kill her, Dartagnan.''

Dartagnan laughed incredulously. "My God, she would . . . she would!''

Abdhiamal smiled again, at something he saw in Dartagnan's face. "As far as the Demarchy's concerned, your testimony leaves it up to her whether she wants to press her charges of attempted murder against you. But with a confession, and both your evidence and hers, I'd say the case against Demarch Siamang is a little more clear-cut. . . . You see, Demarch Siamang,'' he looked back, "this isn't a news conference; consider it more of a preliminary hearing. The Demarchy had already been informed of Demarch Fukinuki's testimony and evidence before you arrived; your father is being considered an accomplice, pending further questioning. All we needed was your version; and we have that, now."

Never underestimate the power of a woman. . . . Dartagnan grinned, weak in the knees. He noticed that Siamang was ringed in now by "spectators": vigilantes, volunteer police requested for the occasion. Siamang's eyes raked them with disdain. "This is an outrage. This is entrapment—" He looked back at the cameras. "People of the Demarchy, are you going to stand by while a fellow Demarch is persecuted by the government?"

"The people asked me to come here, Siamang. Save your rhetoric for your trial; in the meantime, consider yourself confined to your home. . . . And I'll take charge of the software—" Abdhiamal held out his hand. Chaim recognized a kind of gratification on the government man's face; realized that Abdhiamal was hardly older than himself, behind the mask of his self-assurance. In the Demarchy, a government agent earned less respect than a mediaman; and had considerably less influence.

Siamang passed the container to him, entirely in control once more. He faced Dartagnan again, at last; Dartagnan tried to read the expression behind his eyes, couldn't. Siamang reached out abruptly, caught Dartagnan's arm, jerked the voucher out of his hand. Chaim watched him tear it up, watched the pieces drift as they sought the lines of gravitational force. "You'll never have a ship now, Red." A final mockery showed in Siamang's eyes, edged his voice. "But I hope you never stop wanting one, so you'll never stop hating yourself for this."

Dartagnan smiled, filled with a terrible pride; smiled with a sincerity he didn't know he still had in him. He shook his head, met the aggressor's eyes at last. "Believe me, boss, I never wanted a ship, or anything, half so much as I wanted to see this happen . . . to see truth win out in this lousy business, just once, because of me." He turned the smile on the cameras, and on the men behind them.

Siamang's escort led him away, to the rim of the ledge where an airbus waited. The handful of mediamen swarmed after them, onto the bus, into air taxis; Dartagnan stared at the bobbing mass of striped canopies, whirring propellers. The remaining crowd of strangers around him began to disperse, drifting over the ledge into the city, leaving him alone with Abdhiamal. "What about me?"

Abdhiamal shrugged. "You're not going anywhere, are you? Your further testimony will be needed when they call a trial; somehow I expect you'll want to be there. I'd hate to see Siamang promo his way out of a guilty verdict now."

Dartagnan frowned. "He won't, will he—?"

"I doubt it. Public opinion's had too much time to build against him. His father couldn't do much to help him, because he didn't know enough about the situation. . . . You know, your fellow mediamen seem to be a lot more interested in the murderer than in your having exposed him." Abdhiamal looked at him.

Dartagnan grinned weakly. "It figures . . . I just paid 'em the biggest insult I could think of. Besides, a mediaman follows the smell of power . . . it smells like money, in case you're interested." He leaned down, picked up a corner of the ruined credit voucher. The full impact of what he had given up caught him like a blow. "Easy come, easy go." He laughed, painfully, embarrassing himself. "That reminds me—what about the software, the salvage; what happens to Sekka-Olefin's money, now?"

"The artifacts will be sold at a public auction; Siamang and Sons being disqualified from bidding, of course. Sekka-Olefin's relatives have put in claims against it; the money will be distributed among them, since he didn't leave any will stating what he wanted done with it."

"But he did! He told me what he wanted done with it. He didn't want it to go to his relatives; he wants it used to establish a colony on Planet Two, against the time when the Demarch's not habitable anymore—" Chaim broke off, realizing how it sounded.

Abdhiamal looked at him, tactfully noncommittal. "Do you have any proof of that?"

"Yeah. Every word of it, on film . . . at the bottom of a well. A gravity well—" He swore. "His goddamned relatives'll never listen. He was right! And it all went for nothing, because of Siamang." He saw the crystal city through a haze of death, knew he would have to see it that way for the rest of his life: the towers decaying, the fragile thread of life coming apart. "That stinking bastard... I hope they vote to space him. Because that's what he's done to their future, and they'll never even know...." His voice shook, with bitterness and exasperation.

"At least you've done something to try to make it up to him." The voice wasn't Abdhiamal's.

He turned back, incredulous. "Mythili?" She stood beside him, materializing out of the diminished crowd; Abdhiamal had moved away, discreetly. "Mythili." He started toward her. She pushed away, out of his reach. He stopped, pulled in his hands. "Sorry... I'm just... I'm glad. Just glad to see you." He noticed the patches of pink, healing skin on her cheeks and nose. "Are you all right?"

She nodded. "Some frostbite. Some burns, from the cold. I was a mess for a while. But I'm fine."

He nodded too, unthinking. "I'm glad. The old man was right, then—Sekka-Olefin. He told me that it was possible to live—"

"I know." She looked down abruptly, rubbed her eyes with the back of her hand. "I heard you."

"Do you believe it?"

She still looked down. "Yes... yes, I believe you, now, Chaim. But why did you do it? We could have stopped him; you could have—"

"—gotten us both killed?" Shame kindled anger. "Why didn't you just keep your mouth shut, like I did? Everything would've been okay."

Her eyes flashed up. "Because I'm not like you!... I know, it was stupid. I know that now.... But I couldn't have hidden it anyway; he would have known. I'm not good at hiding what I feel—" She bit her lip. "I'm not like you, Dartagnan."

He let his breath out slowly, said stupidly, again, "I'm just glad you're all right... I saw you, on the viewscreen, saw you take off your helmet. And then I thought I'd been wrong, that you—"

"I thought so, too." She laughed, tremulously, at the ghost of memory. "The air was so thin, so cold, I thought I couldn't breathe. I panicked, and I blacked out. The noise and heat

when you lifted off saved me, it woke me, or I would have
frozen to death instead. I almost didn't get up again...I
thought I'd already died."

"You repaired Olefin's ship?"

"Yes...It's a good ship, and the *Mother* is a fantastic ship;
he must have spent a fortune—"

"He did. Literally. On a dream."

"I brought his body back; a pleasant companion, for a trip of
three-plus megaseconds." She shuddered. "Three and a quarter
megaseconds, with a dead man, and frost-burned lungs, and
memory....God, how I hated you, Chaim! How I hated
you...and yet—" She wouldn't look at him.

"I know," he said. "I know. Three and a half megaseconds
with Siamang, and memory; wanting to kill him, and afraid
he'd kill me. But you were there. I could feel you, helping me
get through. Helping me survive to make it right. I always
planned to tell the truth, Mythili, I never meant to do anything
else."

"So the end justifies the means, then?" Her voice teetered
on the edge of control.

He didn't answer, couldn't.

"I won't press charges against you." She turned away.

"Mythili. Don't go yet—" She looked back at him, he
groped for words. "What...what will you be doing now? Are
you still working for Siamang and Sons?"

"No. Siamang, senior, fired me, after I made my accusa-
tions." She almost smiled, not meaning it, "I'm hoping one of
his competitors will offer me a job...." hopelessly. "So you
won't have a ship of your own, now, either—?"

"No." He looked down, at the torn corner of the voucher
still wadded in his hand. "Not now...but someday, I will.
And when I get it, I want you to be my partner. I want you
to—to—" *To stay with me*. His mind, his eyes, finished it,
uselessly.

"Good-bye, Goody Two-Shoes," she whispered. She shook
her head. Her own eyes were mirrors of memory, for the face
of a man who had tried to kill her; a man who had lied too well.
"I might forgive you...but how could I ever forget?" An

anguished brightness silvered the mirror of her eyes, she turned away again.

"Mythili, wait!" He fumbled in the sack of his belongings, pulled out the book of poetry. "Wait; this belongs to you." He held it out.

She came back, took it from his hand without touching him. Confused anger startled her face as she recognized the title. "What are you doing with this?" pain and grief, "Shiva, isn't there anything that you wouldn't pry into? You'll never have a ship! You'll be a mediaman all your life, because that's all you were ever meant to be." She might have said "whore."

"I will get a ship. If it takes me the rest of my goddamned life, I will. . . . And when I do, I'll find you! Mythili—"

She didn't turn back, this time. He saw her hail a taxi, get in; watched it fall out and down into the vastness of the city air. Pain knotted his stomach, he clenched his teeth.

"Dartagnan—" Abdhiamal came up beside him, eyes questioning, sympathetic. "No?"

"No." Chaim produced a smile, pasted it hastily over his mouth. "But that's life. The only reward of virtue is virtue . . . the hell with that." He picked up his sack, readjusted his camera strap. "You can't afford it, in my business. . . . Good thing my camera's already broken; one of my good buddies will probably smash it over my head when I get back to work. Nobody likes an honest mediaman; you can't trust 'em."

Abdhiamal smiled. "I disagree."

Dartagnan laughed, still looking out into the city. "Everybody knows you've got to be crazy to work for the government." His eyes stung, from too much staring.

"You look like you could use a drink. On me?" Abdhiamal gestured toward the city.

"Why not?" Dartagnan nodded, hand pressing his stomach. "Yeah . . . that's just what I need."

"Excuse me . . . pardon me—"

"Wait your turn, pal. We got plenty of work for everybody."
The clerk snatched permission forms out of the air as the
stranger's approach pulled them loose from gravity's feeble
hand. He stuffed them into a mesh container on the cluttered
table top. His expression ate holes in the amorphous mass of
faces drifting in line before him; he fixed a steel-hard stare on
the man who had upset their equilibrium.

"My name is Wadie Abdhiamal, I'm a government negotiator."

"No wonder you're in a hurry. But you got to wait your turn
like everybody—"

"I'm here officially." Abdhiamal raised his voice without
seeming to. "I'm looking for a man named Dartagnan."

"Take your pick." The clerk frowned at Abdhiamal's elegantly
embroidered jacket, away from the bare civility of his face.

"I was told he'd be here, but he's not. Where would he go
next?" Abdhiamal's impatience seized the clerk by his own
unbuttoned jacket-front.

"To suit up. That way—" The clerk waved left-handed,
brushing him off.

Abdhiamal pushed off from the table, scattering the drift of
derelict humanity as his arrival had scattered paper. His trajectory angled him toward the corridor entrance the clerk had
indicated. He caught at a hand-hold and readjusted his course,
pushed off again with undecorous force.

The tunnel let him out into another room as devoid of

56

personality as the waiting room, and as crowded with bodies. Abdhiamal pulled himself up short, searched the shifting mass for a glimpse of remembered red hair, the brown face of Chaim Dartagnan. He saw a dozen strangers already in suits, helmets in hand, lining up before the small hatch in a ponderous steel wall—which he recognized suddenly as a much greater entrance on the unknown. All were strangers to him. One was a woman, and the thought of what she waited to do made his stomach turn over . . . what they all waited to do to themselves.

He looked on around the room, away from the hatch, into the mass of half-suited workers awaiting the next shift. A man he recognized instinctively as an authority figure—a man who belonged here, one who would never pass through that lock— was peering back at him across the broken line of sight. And half-standing, half-drifting at his side—

"Dartagnan!" Abdhiamal raised a hand, his voice echoing; signalling the distant lifted face, the suddenly motionless body, toward him.

Dartagnan came across the vast room, trailing an insulated pressure suit, clouded with uncertainty. "Abdhiamal?" He caught a wall brace as he reached Abdhiamal's side, staring at him. He laughed once, rubbing his head. "What the hell? Working for the government finally drive you to this?"

Abdhiamal studied his face unobtrusively. Dartagnan looked thinner than he remembered; tighter, harder . . . older. It had been barely six megaseconds since he first laid eyes on Chaim Dartagnan; since he had watched him give up his chance for a decent future—watched him lose everything, under the pitiless gaze of the media cameras—because he had put honesty and justice above his own self-interest. But justice was blind, and the only reward society had given him was the back of its hand. Abdhiamal shook his head. "Even my job is better than this. I came for you, in an official capacity—about the Siamang affair."

Dartagnan's face aged further. "Why?" He glanced away at the waiting wall of steel, and back. "The trial, the judgment. I thought all that was over. Did she decide to press charges— Mythili, I mean?" His hands pressed his stomach; the suit drifted down out of his grasp.

"No. She didn't change her mind. That part is over."

"Over." Dartagnan's mouth pulled. "Then what?"

"What the hell are you doing here?" Abdhiamal said suddenly, unable to keep it in. "For God's sake, man—"

Dartagnan shrugged, looking away again. "It's a year's pay for an hour's work."

"And a lifetime dose of radiation!" Abdhiamal's disgust broke through. "You know why they pay you so well." He pointed toward the steel wall/door.

"Sure I know." Dartagnan leaned over, his feet lifting in equilibrium as he picked up the suit. "They gave us the whole hype: Their waldoes broke down, and without this plant there's only one factory left to make nuclear batteries for the whole of the Demarchy. They're trying to get them functional again, but in the meantime there's a lot of work only a human can handle. It's all very patriotic." His eyes were as bleak as death. "And somebody has to do it."

Abdhiamal shifted uncomfortably. "You don't. This is for losers, not an able-bodied, healthy man."

Dartagnan laughed again; his laughter was like tar. Abdhiamal failed to see the joke. "I've had this conversation before. What else can I do? I haven't got a chance in hell of getting a media position with a corporation after I sold out Siamang and Sons—"

"After you brought a murderer to justice," Abdhiamal cut him off.

Dartagnan smirked. "It all depends on your point of view. But I'll never make it as a mediaman. If I learned anything I learned that, the hard way, these past megasecs. And I'm no damn good at anything else; at anything that takes any brains or guts or talent. . . ." The suit twisted in his hands, the reflected image of his face tearing apart.

Abdhiamal thumped the slick wall surface beside them with a hand. "If you need to suffer that much, Dartagnan, why don't you knock your head against a wall? It makes as much sense."

Dartagnan looked up, expressionless. "It doesn't pay as well."

"At least when you've stopped punishing yourself, your body won't have to go on paying for the rest of your life."

"It's too late for that." His hands pressed his stomach again.

He watched the cluster of suited workers across the room fasten helmets; watched the air lock hatch unseal, open, release a cloud of spent strangers and swallow up a new sacrifice. Another line began to form; his line. Beyond the meters-thick seal of metal the actual manufacturing area lay in the open vacuum of Calcutta planetoid's dead and deadly surface. Since the Civil War the factory's production capacity had steadily deteriorated, and the amount of radiation it spewed into space had climbed correspondingly. The war had destroyed the critical symbiosis of technologies that produced sophisticated microprocessor replacement parts for plants like this one; the resulting jury-rigged repairs had eaten away at its efficiency.

"What do you want from me, Abdhiamal?" Dartagnan began to pull open the seal on the radiation suit, impatiently, nervously. "Or did you just come here to kick me when I'm—"

Abdhiamal reached out, stopped him from pulling the suit on. "I came to make you a better offer. I've been in contact with Kwaime Sekka-Olefin's relatives about the settling of his estate."

Dartagnan's arm stopped resisting his grip. Blinking too much, he said, "And—"

"And they feel you deserve some consideration for bringing his murderer to justice. Since I knew you were interested in prospecting—"

"The *Mother*? They're going to give me his ship?" Dartagnan's intensity jerked them off-balance.

Abdhiamal clutched at the wall-brace. "No," he said gently. He let Dartagnan go. "Not exactly. They're offering you first chance to buy it."

"*Buy* it?" Dartagnan's free-drifting hand became a fist, and Abdhiamal thought for a split second that it would hit him in the face. But something in his expression stopped it; Dartagnan's body sagged. "Thanks for letting me know."

"They know you don't have the money, Dartagnan. That's why they're not asking for payment up front." Dartagnan's head rose slowly. "They're only asking half what the ship's really worth. And they'll give you a certain amount of time before you have to pay them anything. You can use the ship to hunt salvage in the meantime. If you're any good as a prospector, you'll be able to pay it off." He made it sound as fair and reasonable as he could, drawing on his years of experience as a negotiator. He didn't say how hard he had had to pressure Sekka-Olefin's relatives to wring even that concession from them.

Dartagnan let the radiation suit slip from his hand again. He looked away, aware once more of the space beyond their own small cone of contact, the heavy, murmuring despair that filled the room. He studied the new line forming for work. And then he kicked the suit aside. "Let's get out of here."

III

■ ■ ■ ■ ■

Mythili Fukinuki stood before the instrument panel on board the *Mother,* her feet barely resting on the floor in Mecca planetoid's slight gravity. She held her concentration on inventorying the ship's functions; trying to hold back the memories that the sight of the control room raised in her. This was not the first time she had worked at this panel; not the first time she had moved silently and alone through the levels of this immense spider-legged ship's belly. But not entirely alone, the last time....

She blinked convulsively, dissipating the glistening film of double-vision; the golden skin over her knuckles whitened as she clenched her hands. She would never forget that she had shared this ship with Sekka-Olefin's corpse on the journey back from Planet Two. She could not stop reliving the nightmare that had preceded it, or the grueling sideshow of a trial that had followed. No matter that Sabu Siamang had been declared guilty and sent into exile on an uninhabited rock—he had still ruined her career and contaminated her entire life, and no punishment would ever be enough to repay that wrong.

Or to repay her for the way he had destroyed the fragile net of trust and—and—(her mind would not shape the word) *feeling* (inadequately), that had formed between herself and Chaim Dartagnan. She saw Dartagnan suddenly in her mind's eye, his hands upraised in habitual apology, begging the forgiveness she could never really grant him in her heart. She shut her eyes tightly, setting his image on fire, burning it away.

Siamang had stripped that image of illusions; had proven that at
his core Dartagnan was only a self-serving coward after all,
willing to do anything to save his own life. And although he
had done all he could to bring Siamang to justice, still she
could never forget. . . .

She looked up sharply from the panel's glowing displays at
the sound of someone entering the ship down below. She pulled
her face back into an acceptable cypher, smoothed her hands
along the cloth of her utilitarian flightsuit. This must be Wadie
Abdhiamal's arrival. She had agreed to meet him here, to
discuss the specific terms under which she could make this ship
her own. *Could they spare it?* Resentment made her face
twitch. She had lost her job as a Siamang company pilot
because she had testified against Sabu; and all Sekka-Olefin's
relatives were offering her in return was an impossible dream.
She was no prospector—and yet she would have to somehow,
miraculously, shape-change into one if she was going to meet
the price they were asking for this ship. And this ship was her
only chance at a life with any dignity or freedom, now that her
job as a pilot was gone forever. No one else in this damned,
twisted society would let her do the job she was trained for, and
because she was unmarried and sterile, her only alternatives
were deadly or degrading. She had to succeed; she *had* to. . . . Her
hands knotted.

"Demarch Fukinuki." Wadie Abdhiamal appeared abruptly,
rising up through the concentric railings of the drift-well at the
control room's center. He had left his pressure suit down
below; he was faultlessly dressed, as always. "I'm glad you're
punctual."

Mythili nodded, managing a strained smile of welcome.
"Demarch Abdhiamal. You're late." Her smile broadened
barely, fell away again all at once as she saw that he was not
alone.

Abdhiamal pushed off from the railing, drifted to one side of
the well and settled, leaving the opening clear. She watched
another head materialize in his place, shoulders, arms, body . . .
Dartagnan. Dartagnan. The word repeated over and over in
her mind as she tried to believe what her eyes showed her.
"Dartagnan!" Surprise shouted it, and anger, and betrayal as

she realized what his presence here must mean. "What's he doing here?" She turned toward Abdhiamal furiously; knowing the answer, making the question an accusation.

"Mythili?" Chaim caught himself on the well-railing, jerked his rising body to a halt.

She glanced at him: a split second of the incredulous look on his face told her that he was no more a party to this than she was. She looked back at Abdhiamal before Chaim's eyes could catch and hold her own. "You had no right to do this to—to us! I won't work with him—" Her hand shot out.

"I'm afraid you'll have to, if you want this ship." She heard the vaguely condescending tone that Abdhiamal could never quite keep out of his voice when he spoke to her. "Sekka-Olefin's relatives agreed that the ship should go to both of you, since you had an equal share in bringing his murderer to justice."

"Equal—?" She choked back the rest, looking from face to face again, feeling a cage close her in. "Whose idea was that? I suppose you think this is all terribly clever, Abdhiamal, setting me up like this—"

"Wait, wait," Chaim put his hands up, palm-out, in the placating gesture that set her memory on edge. He finished his ascent into the room, dressed in a drab gray-white jumpsuit like her own, with no mediaman's camera slung at his shoulder. "Abdhiamal, what is this? You mean we share in this—?" His hands spread, taking in the ship around them, but his eyes stopped at her face. "Why the hell didn't you say something?"

Abdhiamal smiled, smugly omniscient. "If I had, would you both be here now?"

"Yes."

"No." Her refusal went directly to Dartagnan.

"That's why I didn't tell you." Abdhiamal shrugged slightly, tugged the hem of his loose jacket back under his belt. "Listen—the two of you tried to do something worthwhile, the right thing. And you weren't rewarded for it, you were punished. I'm only trying to do my job, which is to see that things are settled fairly. This is the best I could do. It's up to you from here on."

"Thanks, Abdhiamal," Chaim said, as though he meant it.

"Even if we can't keep this ship, I'll always appreciate this," looking back at her again.

Abdhiamal nodded. "I appreciate the appreciation."

"I hope you'll do us one more favor, then, Abdhiamal." Mythili pressed her hands together fitfully, avoiding both their gazes. "Get out of here, and leave us alone—"

Abdhiamal bowed his acquiescence, and glancing up she couldn't detect any change in his expression. He moved toward the exit well.

Chaim threw an apologetic glance after him. "Thanks again, Abdhiamal."

"Let me know what you decide." Abdhiamal disappeared into the well.

Mythili turned back to the control panel, listening to the echoes recede through the ship, filled with sudden claustrophobia. To be alone in this place with one man—this one man— was to feel the hull close around her in a way that it had not when she shared it with the two of them. She punched in a sequence on the panel, clumsy with haste, opening the segment of wall that became a port above the viewscreen.

She looked out on the docking field abruptly: on the ungainly insectoid forms of volatiles tankers clutching the flaccid sacs in which they transported unrefined and semi-refined gases to the Demarchy's distilleries. Immense ballooning storage tanks ringed the eternally eclipsed field, obscuring the light-hazed horizons of Mecca planetoid. Beyond the field's fog of artificial light she knew that a starry black infinity of space lay on all sides, and that she was not a prisoner. . . .

Dartagnan came toward her from the hub of the cabin; she sensed his movement more than heard it, and turned to meet him. "Don't come any closer. Please." She brushed her night-black hair back from her face irritably. He stopped himself, wavering as he regained his balance; his open disappointment reached across the space between them.

"Mythili, I didn't know about this. . . ."

"I know you didn't." She cut him off. In his eyes lost images were rising; something between disgust and terror would not let her see them. "You don't need to fawn on me,

Chaim. I'm not working for a corporation anymore. And neither are you, from the looks of it."

"No." His head stayed down; he stared at his own long-fingered brown hand clenched over a seat-back before the panel. "Sorry," he said, still apologizing, compulsively, for something beyond words. "But maybe we've bottomed out, Mythili. Maybe we've changed our luck." He lifted his head slowly. "This ship—look at it! It's all ours; it's giving us a chance to start over again, to prove we've got the guts to live by our own rules, this time. This is a dream come true—" His wide mouth stretched wider in a hopeful grin.

"Your dream, not mine!" She rebelled against the part of him that had included her without asking; against the part of herself that might have been glad. "I never wanted to be a prospector, I don't know a damn thing about it. I don't want to spend the rest of my life as a junker, living on the edge of starvation. And I don't want to spend it sharing this ship with you, Dartagnan!"

His whole body tautened visibly. "I see." He sagged, as though the unseen tensions had let him go again abruptly, leaving him more formless than before. But the yielding softness had gone out of his eyes, and he looked at her without hope or apology. "So it's not your dream. Have you got anything to put in its place? No—or you wouldn't be here. You don't know a damn thing about prospecting; but I do. Only I can't pilot a ship this size well enough to get it into the places a prospector has to go. You can. Maybe we don't want each other," he said with spiteful satisfaction, "but we sure as hell *need* each other. I want this ship; I want this chance at a real life. And even if you don't want it, you want a chance at some kind of life, and this's your last one. I can stand it if you can." His free hand clutched the arm that anchored him to the chair.

Mythili bit the inside of her mouth until she felt sharp pain, until the first response died in her throat. "All right. I agree with everything you say. I'll work with you, because I have to. We'll share whatever we find fifty-fifty. But that's all—" words escaping again in spite of her.

"That's all I expected." Chaim moved his mouth, imitating

a smile sourly. "And I think there's one more thing we can agree on: Abdhiamal really screwed both of us."

In the artificial brightening of a new day, Mythili left her tiny rented room and took an air taxi out across the kilometer-wide vacuole that held Mecca City. The towers of the city clustered on every side, their colored surfaces shimmering with faint movement as she looked outward and ahead. The sight did not touch her with wonder as it once had; today she scarcely saw them at all.

She had agreed to share a ship and a gamble with Chaim Dartagnan, and now she was about to back it up, taking all that was left of her life savings to buy the equipment and supplies they needed to make their trip. It was insane . . . but what other choice was there? She felt the tension that had shocked her awake after a night of depression-drugged sleep winding still tighter in her chest. She swallowed and sighed; but the tightness came back, and the taxi closed inexorably with her destination.

She made her way down the central core of the Abraxis commercial building, settling like a feather into gravity's soft well of suction. The skin of the building walls was golden, and she felt herself suffocating, sinking through honey. Workers and customers moved past her, propelling themselves like swimmers from the corridor's wall. She let them pass, letting her own slow sink-rate remain undisturbed.

The ship-outfitter's business, with its massive displays, occupied the two bottom-most levels of the building. Grimly she pushed aside the flaps of the upper-level entrance, found herself in a catacomb of stabilized boxes and closed mesh containers. She moved cautiously through the narrow aisles, where a handful of desultory strangers inspected navigation equipment she identified at a glance and prospector's gear she could not recognize at all. They stared as she passed, herself an unclassifiable oddity in this male domain.

She emerged finally into a large, less cluttered area; saw Chaim at last, gesturing over an equipment list, a pile of potential purchases growing at his feet. He glanced up, as though her tension radiated like cold, and broke off his conversation with the shopman. But his face stayed flatly expressionless, unlike her own; the gift of his career as a professional liar. "This is my partner. She'll fill you in on anything else we need."

She moved across the open space, joined the two men beside the counter where a small screen recorded the growing cost of their journey. The shopman regarded her with mixed emotions; she ignored him for the pile of supplies. She stared at the screen again, tallying the list in her mind, feeling a resentment rooted in something deeper than her ignorance of a prospector's needs: "Do we really need all that, Dartagnan?"

"We need more. But we can't afford it." He glanced uncomfortably at the shopman.

"What about that spectroscope? The ship already has one." She touched the one word on the screen that she really recognized, her fingers rigid.

"Not good enough. Sekka-Olefin already knew what he was looking for, and where to find it. We don't. We need all the help we can get."

She shrugged, her mouth pulling down. "All right."

"What about navigation equipment?"

"I checked the ship's system over again. It's in fine shape. There's nothing we can afford to add to it that would make a real difference."

He looked relieved, the first genuine expression she had seen on his face. "Then I guess we can afford to eat, after all."

"You want me to go ahead and fill the rest of your order, then?" The shopman addressed Chaim.

"Yeah." Chaim passed him the list, glancing her way. "Go ahead."

She looked away from him, becoming aware of the man in worn coveralls who waited, listening, at the edge of her sight. He moved forward at her glance, intruding on their circle of consciousness. Another prospector, she guessed, and not a very successful one; a heavyset man who looked old, older than he was, because a lifetime spent exposed to shipboard radiation aged the body badly. His dark brown, graying hair was clipped close along the sides of his bald head, and his broad, gnarly face was seamed with lines that could have been good-humored. As if to prove it, he smiled when she looked at him. She did not smile back. Undaunted, he cracked open their privacy and included himself in it.

Chaim turned at his approach, ungraceful with surprise.

The prospector squinted. "Aren't you . . . yeah, you must be! Gamal Dartagnan's kid? I'll be damned! Imagine runnin' into you, after all this time."

Chaim stared, mildly disbelieving. "You knew my old ma— uh, my father?" he said, groping for a civil response.

"Yeah, I sure did. We were great friends, him and me. Almost partners."

Mythili felt her face pinch at the falseness of the tone. Chaim's own face had become a vacant wall again; a defense, against what she wasn't sure. "What's your name?"

"Fitch. He must've mentioned me—"

"No." Chaim's boot nudged the pile of supplies; containers stirred sluggishly and resettled. "How'd you know me? . . . We didn't look much alike."

Fitch laughed, unaffected by the lack of positive response. "The hair. Anybody'd know that hair. And he talked about you all the time."

Chaim's expression became slightly more expressionless.

"And you're kind of a celebrity, you know—all the media about old Sekka-Olefin's murder, and how you brought the killer in, with the help of the little lady, here."

Mythili considered silently the fact that she stood half a head taller than Fitch, and wondered why she couldn't find the irony even slightly amusing; wondered whether she had lost her sense of humor permanently.

"And now word has it that you've got yourself Sekka-Olefin's ship. Word must be right, or you wouldn't be here outfitting. Following in the old man's footsteps, huh? Got a damn fine ship for it, from what I hear. . . . You know much about prospecting?"

"Only what I learned by doing it, with my old man." A controlled sarcasm oiled the words.

"Oh, yeah?" Fitch laughed again; a trace of self-consciousness weakened it this time. "Well, he was a damn shrewd man. But still, you couldn't have spent much time out there. It takes a lifetime of experience—"

"A lifetime wasn't enough to keep my old man from killing himself." Chaim's frown broke through. Mythili saw Fitch's face begin to lose hope, struggle to hold on to it. "What do you want, Fitch? You want something."

"I just wanted to meet Gamal Dartagnan's son. Gamal was a man with a big heart and some big ideas, and I figured you might share them . . . I wanted to know if maybe you could use some help." He threw the words out with too much energy. "I mean, I've got a ship of my own and all—I've spent my whole life searching salvage. But my ship can't do anything like what that one of yours could do; she just doesn't have the reach. Just like your old man—if he'd had a better ship, he could've made a million, I'm sure of it. I've got the experience, I know where to look . . . I've got a lot to offer a partner." He craned forward.

"He has a partner," Mythili said abruptly. "We can't afford another one."

"She's right. There's already one too many." Chaim grimaced. "The ship belongs to the two of us, Fitch. We'll make it on our own, or not at all. We don't need any more 'help.' We're up to our necks in it." His hand chopped the air like a headsman's blade, cutting off the conversation.

Fitch withdrew, deflated, shriveling. "Well . . . I'm sorry you feel that way, but I guess I can understand it," he said thickly. "It's a loner's trade, prospecting. You got to think of yourself first, and make your own chances. But just to show you I understand, I want you to have this signal separater." He held it out, packaged in plastic foam. "It'll stretch the range of your equipment. Maybe it'll bring you luck. I was going to put it in my ship, but there's nothing much it'll change for me. Maybe when I see you again, you'll remember I gave you this, and reconsider taking on a partner."

Mythili opened her mouth to refuse it, hearing the same hollow hypocrisy in his humility that she'd heard in his bluster. But Chaim reached out before she could speak and took the package from Fitch's hands with a small, stomach-tight bow of acknowledgment. "Thanks. We appreciate it." The hostility had disappeared from his eyes, and he actually seemed sincere. Mythili closed her mouth without saying anything, surprised into silence.

"And maybe...maybe you'd take this on, too..." Fitch reached behind him, and produced something else, a mesh container.

Ah, she thought, her tension suddenly loosening. *Here it comes—I knew there was more. The catch.*

But the thing he pressed into her unwilling hands was totally unexpected—a small cage, containing a live animal. She stared at it incredulously. She had never been this close to an animal before; never held one in her hands, even caged. "What is it—?" she murmured, resisting her urge to push it back at him.

"Some kind of lizard." Fitch shrugged. "I won it in a card game. It only eats insects; I can't afford to feed it any more...." He looked down at the cage, and what looked like genuine regret filled his eyes. "I got real attached to him. You would, too. He changes colors, see—? Reacts to light or heat." He pointed at the creature in the cage. "I call him Lucky."

Mythili peered in at the lizard, feeling her refusal die stillborn as it gazed back at her, its skeptical eye encased in a turret of beaded flesh. Its pebbly, hairless green skin was changing hue as she watched, taking on a speckled pattern of light and shadow like a photograph. She stared at it, unable to tear her gaze away.

"Sure," Chaim said. "We'll take good care of it."

"I'm grateful to you." Fitch bobbed politely, and disappeared into the maze of piled supplies as unexpectedly as he had come.

The shopman shook his head, one hand hugging the inventory terminal. "Who can figure junkers? That signal separater is the first thing he's paid for up front in half a gigasec—and he gives it away." His drooping black mustache twitched as he twisted his mouth. "Speaking of insects: I'd check that device for bugs, if you know what I mean...." He gestured.

"I intend to." Mythili looked back at Chaim, still holding the signal separater in his hands. She glanced down at the lizard again. *A chameleon:* that was what it was called. She had read about them, once. She wondered just how Chaim expected to pay for its food, when they could barely afford their own. Insects were restricted to the hydroponic gardens; it wasn't like they were plentiful or cheap. "Why do you want to be bound to a sleazy piece of quartz like Fitch?'' she asked, as much curious as disapproving. ''He looked like he's never made enough scavenging junk to pay for a cup of water. Why did you let him give you that?'' She bent her head at the separater. *Or this.* But her eyes went to the lizard's motionless form again, in unwilling fascination. It balanced like a dancer on a single slender branch inside its cage. Its combination of alienness and astonishing grace held her spellbound.

''Because we can use a signal separater. That's Rule One.'' Chaim looked at her steadily, forcing her to acknowledge him. ''And because if we don't get lucky, we'll end up a gigasec from now just as lousy as he is.'' He let the signal separater go, watched it drift down and impact dully in the pile of supplies, before he turned away.

''Lifting.'' Mythili flicked the final switch of the sequence, felt the almost imperceptible shudder of the ship's transformation from stasis to motion. They began to move slowly—like a pageant starting, she thought—outward and away from the docking field. Watching through the unshielded port, she felt the shackles fall from her own existence as she left behind the prison that Mecca had become in these past megaseconds. Elation swelled inside her, unexpectedly, a soft explosion of heart-music spilling into her veins as she looked out on the infinite night, the star Heaven rising like a promise of new beginnings past Mecca's shrinking horizon.

She glanced sideways at the small intrusion of someone else's sigh, saw Chaim Dartagnan pressed intently against the panel just beyond reach. Her elation fell inward, became a tight compression aching at her core. Her freedom was illusory, uncertain, as ephemeral as the life of the insects they had purchased to feed their new pet. There was no promise that there would ever be another journey, if this one failed. And whether this journey succeeded or not, she would have to endure *his* presence; the dark, turbid waters that every glimpse of him eddied in her mind. She felt her mind replay images of the past on the screen of the present, as it had done over and over on the empty walls of her rented room . . . the last time she had piloted a ship with Chaim Dartagnan on board; the humiliation, the suffering, the death of Sekka-Olefin—the death that had almost been her own, because of Chaim Dartagnan's weakness.

Chaim looked over at her, away from the widening blackness of the sky, as if the intensity of her stare were something he could feel. He shook his head slightly, almost unconsciously; she didn't know whether he was reorienting his own reality or making a denial.

Mecca had dropped completely from sight below them; the distant diamond-chip sun was centering in the port and on the display screens. She looked back at the panel without comment. The barely perceptible thrust of the ship's nuclear-electric rockets was slowly but constantly increasing their speed, beginning their long journey in toward the desolate torus of drifting worldlets that was the Main Belt; where before the Civil War the majority of Heaven system's population had lived—where the majority of it had died.

The Civil War had turned the Main Belt into a vast cemetery, its planetoids into gravestones for a hundred million people. The Demarchy, in their own postwar struggle to survive, had already stripped it clean of its most obvious technological artifacts; but individual scavengers still picked through the ruins, hoping for some fortunate oversight that would make them rich, or at least let them go on searching.... "What happens when we reach the Belt? Where do we start?" She begrudged having to ask, tried to keep it from showing in her voice.

"We start as soon as we're close enough to the first rock we meet to scan it. My old man never overlooked anything, even if it wasn't on the charts. Every other prospector who's ever been in to the Main Belt has the same set of charts on file that we do, and they've been picking it over for a couple of our lifetimes." He input a sequence on the panel almost roughly, and a navigation chart flashed onto the middle screen between them. "Of course, it never did him a damn bit of good, in all the time I was with him. He had 'big ideas,' like Fitch said, and nothing else. He was always sure he could've found some battery plant that disappeared during the war, or a lost starship orbiting the sun—or complete happiness in a goddamn hydro tank, for all I know—if he just had a better ship, or more supplies, or an even break . . . They're all alike, the damn fools; looking for fool's gold." He struck another contact point, and the screen went blank. He sighed, letting go of his anger. "But then . . . one of his crack-brained ideas finally paid off for him, in the end."

She half-turned in surprise. "It did? Then why aren't you—"

"—rich?" He laughed the way he had input commands. "Because he had an accident that killed him before he could collect. His luck ran true to the end; all bad. A corporate scout filed on his claim and they got it all."

"What went wrong? What happened to him?" she asked, in spite of herself.

"I don't know." Chaim's arms crossed his stomach, his hands pulled restlessly at his coveralls. Mythili felt her own stomach clench and turn, remembering what had happened to Sekka-Olefin. "But it doesn't matter to him anymore. And it probably won't matter to anybody before much longer; not even to me." He pushed off from the panel, reached the rim of the well to the lower levels and sank into it.

She watched him go, uncomprehending; feeling words rattle against her teeth like pebbles, cold and heavy. But she turned back to the board, watching the chronometer tick off seconds like a census of stars.

The census mounted. As seconds piled up into kiloseconds and megaseconds, Mythili wove patterns of behavior that avoided Chaim Dartagnan as completely as possible, keeping her mind as empty of his presence on board as the night they moved through was empty.

Yet even the emptiness turned against her; not bringing her peace of mind, but only leaving room for memories to grow wild, spiny and bitter. She could deny the present or deny the past, but not both together: more and more she could see only the resemblance of this voyage to the last one she had made, with Dartagnan the mediaman, and Sabu Siamang the killer. There was no solace in silence, no comfort in avoidance, no escaping from the gray limbo of her own mind.

She forced herself to perform the routines of her normal

shipboard duties—although until they reached the Main Belt her responsibilities were few and unchallenging. She had found herself unconsciously competing with Dartagnan even for the simple activity of feeding their pet; until one day, unused to the behavior of insects, one of them had accidentally set the supply of live crickets free. The creatures had scattered, escaping into all parts of the ship, filling its crannies with their unexpected, chirping song. And so she had set Lucky free as well, to wander the ship at will, capturing crickets with a tongue of impossible length and quickness.

From time to time she was aware of a brief, random fluctuation in the ship's energy levels; but her cursory attempts to trace the source came to nothing. She had checked out the signal separater that Fitch had given them, using every imaginable test, until she was certain it hid no unwelcome secrets. There was nothing else that she could discover a hidden glitch in, and so the problem drifted out of her thoughts again. She did not bother to mention it in her brief exchanges with Chaim—she spoke with him only when she could not avoid it.

She ate listlessly, alone in her cabin; slept badly, dreaming dreams filled with vivid terror which hung on into her waking. She tried to read the books that lay in her private trunk, that had always been her solace; but even they were corrupted by the knowledge that Dartagnan's hands had violated them, that his mind had shared the intimacy of their pages and intruded on her innermost thoughts. She put them back in her trunk again, hating him, hating all men. Hating even her father, who in his own weakness, unable to produce the son he wanted, had given those books to her and encouraged her to act a man's role in a world that would never accept it. And she felt herself sliding further down the yielding walls into a formless blackness where nothing had meaning; knowing that she needed something, anything, to hold on to, but lacking the strength to reach out and find it.

She gathered enough strength, wearily, to perform the functional act of feeding herself one more time; even though her stomach was a shrunken, hard lump of denial. She slipped out of her cabin, confident that Chaim was not outside his own across the well, and let herself fall downward into the eating area. The *Mother*'s living quarters were spacious for two people, the ship having originally carried a crew of eight, and she recoiled from the emptiness of the commons after the womb-small security of her own cabin.

But as her eyes readjusted their scale she realized that she was not alone this time. Chaim balanced lightly on a seat at the near side of the wide, dull-metal table in the room's center. He turned as she entered, his face almost eager. She looked away from it quickly, not quickly enough, as her feet settled with a click onto the mirroring floor.

"Mythili—"

She moved away from him stubbornly, toward the food lockers. She pulled a can out of one and pushed it into the warmer without even looking at the label. "What are you doing here?" she said resentfully. She had redesigned her days almost unconsciously so that she ate and slept at nonstandard times, the better to avoid even the sight of him.

"Waiting for you."

"Why? Is there some problem with the ship?" She half-turned, glancing back; the small, elusive fluctuation of energy intruded on her memory.

"Yes." He straightened, balancing against the table, searching her face for a response. "With the crew, damn it!"

"What do you mean?" She flinched away from the anger in his voice.

"*Who* do I mean. I mean us, for God's sake. You see anybody else on this ship?" He gestured, almost losing his balance. "It won't work like this. We can't go on pretending there's no one else on board. I can't, anyway. We're partners, like it or not; and we've got to face it or we won't survive. It won't work like this."

"I know," she murmured, almost inaudibly. The heated container of food popped out at her and she jerked back.

"Do you want it to fail? Don't you care whether we make it or not?"

"I don't know."

"What?" he said, demanding, not asking.

She bit her suddenly quivering lips, held her face and body

rigid against the counter. "Yes, I care." Some part of her shouted silently that it was a lie, *No, God, I don't give a damn; it's all useless*— Her hand groped the air, reaching out to something nameless.

"Mythili . . . are you all right?" His anger faded as suddenly as it had come; his voice gentled, his concern reached toward her uncertainly, brushed her straining fingertips like a touch. "Can I help? Let me help, if I can . . ."

She pulled her hand in, pulled her voice together. "I'm fine!" The past and present fused into one inescapable cage of hot steel.

His silence lay as loudly as speech in the space between them. "I'm not fine," he said at last, confessing almost defiantly to the weakness she would not admit. "It's like I've been on this ship all alone!" She didn't understand the peculiar vehemence of the words, didn't want to. "I see more of that damn lizard than I see of you! I know you've been avoiding me. But damn it, I haven't given you any reason to, have I?"

"No reason? What reason do I need except the sight of you!" She turned to look at him finally, brushing back her disheveled hair.

"What the—? What's that supposed to mean, for God's sake?" His face clenched.

"It means that every time I see you I remember what happened on Planet Two." Feeling Siamang's rough hands tearing at her clothing; what he had wanted to do and almost done to her, before they had abandoned her on the lifeless surface. . . . "That it happened because you wouldn't help me, because you didn't have the guts to stand up to Siamang. You used me as a pawn to save your own life, and every time I see you I remember that!"

"Well, what the hell do you want me to do about it?" He held out his hands, but they were knotted into fists. "Do you want me to mutilate myself, so you don't have to see this—?" One hand leaped at his face, as if he really meant to dig his fingers into his flesh. "Do you want a stick to beat me with? Is that what you want from me? God damn it, Mythili, do you think there's anything you could do to me, say to me, think about me that I haven't done myself?" His hands dropped away. "But it doesn't change anything. . . . What happened on Planet Two happened. Yes, I was scared, I didn't want to die. I did the best I could—it wasn't good enough. I'd do anything to make it right; but there's nothing I can do! I wish to God you'd pressed the charges against me, and gotten it over with!"

"I don't know why I didn't!" Her voice broke under the weight of the lie, the knowledge of why she had never pressed charges, and why she could never let it go. She shook her head. "But I didn't. And if I didn't, I—I have to live with the consequences, I suppose. I have to face the fact that we are on this ship—together." She clasped her hands around the food can like a holy offering refused, a useless prayer for understanding. She moved it stiffly to a magnetized tray and felt it click down on the surface; aching to feel the same stability seize her own life and hold it fast. "What do you want changed, then?"

His mouth worked. "I need to see a human face once in a while—yours will have to do, since it's the only one here besides my own. I'm not asking to share your body, for God's sake—" expecting a protest as her mouth opened, "—just to share my meals with you. That's all I want. You don't even have to talk if you don't have anything to say to me."

"All right." She nodded, surprised to feel an immense and inexpressible relief filling her. "I suppose that's fair enough," knowing that it was both less and more than that. She carried the food she had heated to the table and settled there with it, not close to him, but not pointedly far away. Peeling back the plastic, she discovered a serving of unflavored green beans, and nothing more. She ate them in silence, feeling his eyes track every bite. A cricket began to chirp somewhere, reassured by the quiet. The sound filled her with a nameless longing. She took the container to the disposal when she finished, with no appetite left to make her heat up something more. Nodding selfconsciously, she pushed off, rising up like a bird, seeking freedom in flight.

"See you at dinner."

She saw him at dinner, and three times a day-period from then on; oftener, sometimes, when he joined her in the control room as she fitted their trajectory to the Main Belt's fluid ballet. She brought a book with her to the commons, a shield against contact; although she only stared blindly at the pages while she ate her tasteless, haphazard meals. Dartagnan often brought the lizard, wearing it like jewelry, letting it creep slowly, impossibly, over his shirt. She tried not to watch it, to give him any unnecessary attention at all.

But somehow she found herself offering the book to him, to deflect his staring curiosity; and then, because she had, forced to discuss the implications of its tedious Old World essays on ecological adaptation. Although she was never certain whether he had any more real interest in the subject than she did, her appetite gradually returned, along with something like her old ability to speak without effort.

But still she found no enthusiasm or pleasure anywhere in herself, no more than a weary acceptance of things she could not change. And Dartagnan's appetite dwindled until he seemed to live on soy milk, and she saw him surreptitiously swallowing nameless pills. His face grew hollow; bitter brackets tightened at the corners of his mouth. She wondered whether he was sick, got an irritable denial when she tried to question him about it. She didn't ask again, but nursed a fresh resentment.

They reached the perimeter of the Main Belt at last, and she altered their course to intersect the orbit of the first planetoid they encountered. But their scans showed them nothing of any value, no sign that a human being had ever even visited that tumbling spark of sun-washed rock. They encountered another, and another, as they pushed deeper into the riverflow of stone, but none of those showed any signs of life or profit. They changed course again, tracking down the first of the planetoids on their charts that had a name—one that had actually held a population—only to find a blasted drift of rubble screaming with radiation.

They went on from there, moving further in across the Main Belt's track of desolation, moving further upstream against its flow, further and further from their origin and ultimate destination. They intercepted more worldlets, named and nameless, each encounter becoming a new defeat.

But still they went on searching, letting the ship hope for them as their supplies of food and faith dwindled. Until at last the empty ritual scan for manmade materials, performed on one more featureless, nameless piece of rock, began to read out in positives. They looked on in silence as the vital signs spilled onto the screen; Mythili felt Chaim catch her own fear of shattering the moment's reality with a word. She moved past him along the panel's grips, still without speaking, and began to set their course to match speed and trajectory with #5359. The chameleon drifted in the air near her face, its prehensile tail hooked around a handhold above the panel. *Lucky....* she thought, glancing at it, feeling the random motion of its turret eyes fixed on her in turn. She didn't let herself finish the thought.

The kiloseconds passed, and she brought the *Mother* into position above a silver-lit, artificially smooth docking surface. She matched the stately rotation of the tiny planetoid's surface, until its pitted antisilhouette seemed to stand still beneath them while the universe revolved in another plane of existence. And then she set the gentle motion free that closed the final kilometer separating them from their destination. The ship settled toward the stone, touched down with the fragile impact of a dragonfly settling on water.

She felt Chaim smile beside her in unconscious appreciation, felt it color with envy as he watched without sharing in her skill. She had denigrated his attempts to participate in the operation of the ship, undermining his confidence in his ability as a pilot; attempting to keep her own position secure against his claim of prospecting expertise. Although it kept her from sharing his knowledge, still she would not risk the vulnerability that an exchange of powers would open to her. And now she savored the triumph, however momentary, of her own skill over his. Chaim pinned his restless hands under his belt; his eyes were still on her, although she kept her own stubbornly on the viewscreen filled with gravel and stars.

"Good job," he said at last, trying to keep his voice noncommittal. The canvas of his belt twisted.

"A little rough." She lied, knowing that no one could have done it more cleanly, knowing that he would know it too.

They pulled on their pressure suits wordlessly. She considered the different qualities of mood that she had come to recognize in the megaseconds of silence between them . . . and that none of those silences had ever been an easy one, and that this one was coiling ever tighter around the mystery of what lay waiting. She put her helmet on with an abrupt movement, locking it in place almost frantically; straining for the sound of oxygen feeding into her suddenly self-contained universe from the pack on her back. Still she remembered Siamang's hard strength jamming shut the feed-valve that cut off her air, before he had forced her into the lock and out onto Planet Two's blue-dust plain to suffocate and die. . . . Every time she closed herself into her suit again, the memory came crowding in to share it. But air fed smoothly into her suit and cooled her sweating face as she followed Chaim into the airlock. The silence expanded while vacuum formed around them.

They trailed the mooring rope down in a slow arc to the bright gravel, dropping through the pelting drizzle of pebbles still settling out of the hailstorm their landing had dislodged. There was no evidence that she could see of anyone having been here since the Civil War, over three gigaseconds before. But even if no one had scavenged here since, there was no promise that there would be anything worth their taking, no reason to believe that this would be anything more than another milestone on the road to ultimate failure. . . . Desire and need shouted down the dark voice of reason, shouted to the sun and stars that this time, *this* time—

They found the sealed hatch that gave access to the dwelling-vacuole of this private estate, a miniature of the city planetoids where she had spent all of her life. Chaim pressed the plate that would cycle the lock. There was no response: the lights set into the door's surface did not even flicker red or green, but stared up at them blindly, dust-filmed, like the eyes of the dead. He grunted, braced his boots against the footholds in the doorframe and leaned over to operate the manual hatch release—the wheel *oh*ing like a mouth below blind eyes.

The hatch popped at last, exhaling a final, long-held breath of fossil air. Chaim glanced back at her. She heard him breathing heavily in her helmet speakers, but he said nothing as he finished pulling the hatch outward and moved down into the throat of stone beneath it. Mythili looked up and out once more, at the heavens wheeling in slow majesty above them, before she followed him down.

They resealed the hatch laboriously, opened the valve that bled a new mouthful of interior air into the claustrophobic darkness of the dead lock-space. At last, as pressure equalized, they pushed open the inner hatch and entered the tunnel beyond; entered into utter blackness.

"Shiva—there's no light!" The protest burst out of her before the conscious thought could form or answer itself. She had never been in an unlit vacuole, never thought that without manmade light...

Chaim switched on his belt lantern, flooding the long tube with technology's inconstant illumination. "Their atomic batteries must've died long since. These places are almost all like this, now."

"I never thought . . . never thought about how it really was," she said stupidly, still realizing that she had only begun to grasp the enormity, the totality of death and destruction that civil war had brought to the Main Belt.

"How it will be. That's the future you're looking at, not the past. We're the past—we've run out of time."

"What are you talking about?" she snapped, trying to recover her own sense of equilibrium. "This all happened before we were born."

"But it doomed us—all of us. Sekka-Olefin knew, that's why he wanted the money from that software he found on Planet Two so much. He knew we were all dying, because we can't keep our technology going, and we can't live without it. While he was stuck on Two he found out about its atmosphere being breathable, and he wanted to start a media campaign to get people to move there, before it was too late."

"Move there?" Her mind moved back through time and space to the final moment when she had clawed off the suffocating helmet of her suit, on her knees in the blue-gray dust, and sucked in the lungful of impossibly thin, searingly cold free air of Planet Two; the breath she had thought would be her last. . . . "He was crazy! And so are you."

Chaim frowned. "Then tell me what we're doing here,

picking the bones of the dead. And tell me what the Demarchy's going to do when there's nothing left on them.''

She felt the cold grip of his doomsaying close on her flesh unexpectedly, threw it off in anger. ''You sound like you're afraid of the dark.''

''You're damn right I am,'' he muttered. But she knew it was not the darkness of this place he was afraid of. He gathered himself and pushed on along the tunnel, his light battering the walls and forcing open the way ahead.

She followed sullenly, overlapping his light with her own.

''Geez Allah!'' His curse rattled inside her helmet as she caught up with him where the tunnel ended. ''What the hell is this place?''

Peering past him she saw not an opening-out into a larger room or rooms, but an abrupt barricade of some striated material. The passageway funneled down into a narrow worm-hole of access. She reached out past his shoulder, running a glove over the wall of unidentifiable material; feeling its solid mass resist her, yet feeling individual striations give under her pressure. She felt a sudden charge build in her as her brain cross-referenced. . . . ''Print-outs! It's all print-outs—kilos and kilos of them.''

''More like tons and tons.'' Chaim braced his feet and threw his weight against the wall of paper, but there was no give to the greater mass. ''All piled up for the recycler that never came back.''

''No.'' She shook her head. He looked at her. ''There's way too much here. Even if they saved every news report and corporate hypesheet from the whole of the Main Belt, there must be half a gigasec's worth here. It couldn't be just the postwar breakdown.''

''But why? Why would anybody save old hypesheets, when everything was in info storage anyway?''

She shrugged inside her suit. ''Maybe it was a hobby. Are we going on through?''

He bent over, throwing light into the paper-walled tunnel. ''I don't know. I can't see anything, if it even ends. . . . God, what if the whole damn rock's stuffed full of this, and we get stuck with nowhere to turn around?''

"Somebody lived here.. There must be something else in there besides paper," she said impatiently. "I'll go first, if it bothers you." *Coward.* She refused to let herself even begin to shape a mental image around his words. She reached up to loosen her helmet. "If we take off our suits we'll have more room to move—"

"Wait." He caught her hand, freezing it in mid-motion. "Leave that on. The purifier's dead. You don't know what these places can smell like. Or look like.... I'd better go in first." She saw his face through the dark reflection of her own, helmet to helmet; saw the strain-sharp line of his mouth that bit the words off raw-edged. "Wait here."

Remembering that he did know—and that most of the Main Belt had died of slow starvation or thirst—she dropped her hands and waited. He squirmed like an eel into the depths of the print-out mass. The seconds passed, and more seconds; until the darkness lost its form and grew timeless, until she could not keep the image of suffocating gullets choked by warm human flesh out of her mind—

A small grunt of surprise or disgust came out of her suit speakers; Chaim's voice, from somewhere beyond the wall. "Chaim—?" Her own voice startled her more, squeezed with unexpected tension.

" 'S okay." His reassurance slipped, on uncertain footing. "I'm through. Come ahead, there's a room here. But get ready; there's a couple of bodies, too."

She felt her skin prickle, coldness in the pit of her stomach. But she had spent megaseconds with the frozen corpse of Sekka-Olefin on board his ship, returning to Mecca from Planet Two. She was no stranger to death. She tightened her hands, loosened them again to pull herself into the print-out mass. Clawing with her heavy gloves, thrusting and kicking like a swimmer, she worked her way along the uneven intestine, following the beam of her light. At last she saw the beam spread and diffuse, blinked as it was answered by another light beaconing ahead. Chaim caught her reaching hands to draw her out of the tunnel; unable to avoid it, she let him pull her through.

"Thanks." She freed herself from his grasp as quickly as she could, looking away. The glancing brightness of her belt lamp showed her a haphazard plastic meshwork crisscrossing the inner surface of the piled print-outs, to keep them from collapsing in slow inevitability toward the iron-rich asteroid's feeble gravitational heart. *This is all of it, then*. But as she kept turning, following the line of the room's inner surface, she saw more piles of print-out, and heaps of plastic packing crates broken down, immense bags bulging with unnameable contents, heaps of old clothing or rags.

In the center of this carefully filled space a small living area barely survived: a tiny metal table and chairs disorientingly bolted to the far wall—following gravity's lines as she did not—and a wide mat of foam heaped with more piles of rags. . . . *Bodies*. He had said there were bodies. Her eyes fixed on the shapeless rag piles with horrible fascination. She drifted out into the open center of the room as her staring and the harsh light of her lamp began to pick out protruding ends of bone, the pitiless white dome of a skull, the glaring black hollows of its sockets.

She twisted suddenly in the air, trying to stop her forward motion with nothing to stabilize her; banged into the metal table top with a curse. The echoes of her collision and her shout seeped into the soft detritus along the walls, the room closed its silent disapproval around them again. Chaim still hung at the far side of the room, as though he couldn't force himself to get any closer to the corpses.

She righted herself to the table's axis, watching the slow dance around her of things she had dislodged—empty containers with crusts of dried food at their lips, a stain-dulled knife, a long slender bone . . . she thought it looked like an ulna. She caught the drifting knife and jerked it out of the air. "What do . . . what do you think killed—did they die from?" Hating herself as she asked it.

"Starved, probably," he said. "That's what it usually is." The words were very soft. His arms folded over his stomach in what she took for empathy. She remembered that he must have seen this sight over and over while he had prospected with his father. He didn't say anything more; she watched him track the rising arc of the pale bone's dance, end over end in the air.

"Who were these people, anyway? Who would live in a—a garbage dump like this, never throwing anything away? Were they insane?" Still trapped in the fascination of the bizarre, she was dismayed by her own inability to close her eyes or look away.

"Of course they were. What the hell else would they be?" His voice was thin and hard, a drawn wire. "Just like we were for coming here. There's nothing here. Let's go."

She glanced back at him, surprised. "But we just got here. Look, there are other rooms—" She gestured toward the walls of rubbish, other dark, narrow mouths opening on other unknowns.

"Forget it. They won't be any different. There's nothing in this hole but death and garbage." He began to pull himself toward the entrance.

"Damn it, I worked my butt off getting us here! We're not leaving until I'm sure there's nothing else." She brandished the knife, forgetting she still held it.

His body whiplashed with angry surprise, or maybe with fear. She let go of the knife, pushing it away from them both, embarrassed. She moved off in another direction, toward the first of the openings. Looking back as she reached it, she saw him still motionless where he had been. "Well, are you going to help me?"

He shook his head, his helmet winked in her light. His arms still pressed his stomach. "No. If you want to wallow in it, go ahead. Not me."

She turned wordlessly and pulled herself into the opening.

The room beyond was crammed with more print-outs, leaving her only enough space to turn around with claustrophobic eagerness and push her way out again. Chaim drifted, watching, as she moved without comment to the next hole. Beyond it was more paper, but she also found numberless copies of prewar pictorials neatly stacked in boxes. She tried to pull one free, wondering whether they might have historical value; only to find that the pages had fused together from some chemical reaction between the synthetic paper and the ink.

She dropped it in disgust, a memory stirring in her mind like dust disturbed: *Recluse*. She had read about people like this, and that was what they were called; people who withdrew physically as well as mentally into their own private world. The terrible exhilaration of that crippling fear tingled her skin—the ultimate in freedom, the ultimate in security, the ultimate womb of this place. . . . She kicked off from the side of a box, diving back into the narrow exit-hole.

She passed Chaim still silently waiting, pulled herself through the last of the dark holes into the last claustrophobic room. This one was not as crowded as the others; there was still enough room for her to move a few meters through a sphere around its perimeter. Its quality was different, too: a wilderness of tangled, broken furniture, stuffed with rags of ancient clothing, jammed with trunks and boxes. She pried the boxes open desultorily, poked among the furniture legs for anything that might have some real value.

Light leaped back at her unexpectedly, prisming with color, as she opened a small trunk crammed beneath a desk. Her breath caught, her fingers dug into the color, droplets of congealed rainbow, gold and silver made molten by her violence. She brought up a necklace set with sapphires the size of peas, a ruby as big as her thumbnail, diamonds . . . *glass*. They had to be glass, paste, imitation. Her scintillating joy went out, leaving her empty and dark again. Find a treasure, in this squalid midden? She could as soon expect to find the sun shining. Dartagnan was right, there was nothing here worth wasting their time on; it was only her own stubbornness that had kept them here this long.

But her hands moved through the jewelry again, making it float and spiral, winking at her with secret knowledge as she set her fantasies free and dreamed for one brief second that all of it was real. At last she chose two favorites out of the dance; the time-stained, gem-hung necklace, and a golden man's ring, studded with fake rubies and far too massive for the fingers that closed around it. She carried them with her, leaving the rest to resettle into stasis as she left the final room, defeated.

"Find anything?" Chaim's voice was too weary to carry sarcasm.

"Junk jewelry." She held the pieces up in her fist, defiantly. "My claim. There's more in there if you want to pick it over."

"I just want to get the hell out of here." He disappeared into the glacier mass of print-outs.

She followed him through, and back along the corridor of dark stone; he was already waiting in the lock when she reached its end. They went through it together, and she watched him throw himself against the wheel like a man with death at his heels. He reached the *Mother* ahead of her in a reckless outward leap, almost closing her out of the ship's lock in his impatience.

He peeled off his suit and left it hanging in midair, slamming away and up through the levels of the ship before she could get out of her own. Following him upward, half curious and half concerned, she listened in the emptiness outside the closed door of his cabin, and heard very clearly the sounds of his retching.

She waited until there were no more sounds, and rapped on the door. "Chaim?" There was no answer. She pulled the door open, and entered his cabin for the first time. "Chaim?"

He looked up at her from across the room, where he clung to the doorframe of the bathroom entrance, doubled over in what looked like prayer. But one look at his face told her that it was pain, not worship, that humbled his flesh.

"What's wrong?" She was suddenly frightened for them both. "Can I help you?"

"Pills . . . in that drawer." He stretched out his hand, a gesture and a plea.

She moved across the room and opened the top drawer of the cupboard, hearing the magnets snap. Inside, drifting up from a nest of clothing, she found a large, half-empty bottle of pills, plucked it out. "Antacids? There are just antacids—"

"Give them to me!" His hand flagged her frantically.

She carried them to him; he fumbled for a handful, spilling them out into the air. He ate several at once, chewing, grimacing, swallowing. "Damn! Damn . . ." He pressed his ash-colored face against a rigid arm. "God, I don't want to start bleeding—"

"What is it? For God's sake, Chaim, tell me what it is!" She shook him.

"My gut. My ulcer."

"An ulcer?" She let him go. "You have an ulcer?"

He nodded.

"Shiva! Why didn't you tell me!"

"Why?" he gasped, not looking at her. "What was the point?"

"Because it's a danger—to both of us!" Her hands closed over the cloth of her jumpsuit in sudden empathy. "Don't you have anything stronger than that?" The antacid pills and bottle were searching for the floor.

"I couldn't afford it."

She bit her tongue; said, as quietly as she could, "Do you think it's bleeding now?" She had read only a little about ulcers, enough to understand his fear: A perforation could be fatal without medical treatment.

He shook his head. "No sign when I . . . No. But it gets worse and worse. I never hurt this bad before."

"What we just saw in there: I didn't know it bothered you so much. I thought you saw a lot of that kind of thing, before—" breaking off, totally uncomprehending.

"And I always hated it! I still hate it. I hate going on and on, never finding anything worth a damn. And always alone—" Tears welled in his eyes; she watched incredulously as they overflowed, spreading across his face in a shining film. "Like those crazy bastards down in the rock, drowning in garbage, dying by centimeters—just like this goddamned system!" His body spasmed with pain and frustration.

"But we're not like them." She remembered abruptly the strange emotion that had caught her soul there in the dark entrails of the rock.

"We're worse. We had a chance to be a team; more than a team, a—" He looked up again at her, and she stopped the word with her eyes, as she had stopped it once before.

"No. Never." Her own words shivered and paled abruptly. She shook her head, needing her whole body to force the motion. "Not after what happened." She turned her back on him, no longer able to keep her eyes shielded. The bare, ivory-colored walls of his cabin seemed to blur into infinity. "You knew that."

"You 'knew' it! You wouldn't give me a chance. That's why this could never have worked, even if we'd found something—"

His breath hissed between his teeth. "Get the hell out of here.
Let me be alone by myself."

She went out of the room, slamming the door to, and fled
across the narrow well into her own cabin. She huddled there,
eyes closed, clinging to the brace beside the door; burying
herself in the deeper blackness of her mind until she lost all
track of time. But still the light was waiting for her, she knew
that it waited—in this room, or beyond its door, or among the
million stars burning endlessly in the depths of night. She was
alive, she could not escape it, she had only to open her eyes to
see the light, acknowledge it, commit an act of faith. And to
open them was in the end easier than keeping them closed. . . . She
opened her eyes, blinking painfully in the glare.

She released her death-grip on the metal, pushed away from
the wall toward the trunk by her bed and bedroll. In it were the
few possessions she was never without, among them the small
trove of her Old World book translations—the keys that had set
her free from the solitary confinement of her life and let her
share other minds, other worlds. She unfastened the lid and
opened it, searching through the shifting, rising contents as
carefully as she could. At last her hand found the one book she
wanted, the one she had not touched since the moment when
Chaim Dartagnan had put it back into her hands during their
reunion on Mecca.

She opened it, watching its pages riffle effortlessly in the
cover's wake. She separated them hesitantly, randomly, hanging in the air. Her eyes caught an old familiar phrase from this
essay, a paragraph of that one, the notes she had scrawled in
answer in the margins. She pressed aside one more page, and
her eyes fell to the lodestone of a stranger's writing below her
own. She had written, *It will be lonely to be dead; but it cannot
be much more lonely than it is to be alive*. And answering her,
the stranger had written, *Yes, yes, yes*. . . .

The book drifted out of her strengthless hands; she felt her
own face grow slick and warm with tears. She cried as she had
not cried in longer than she could remember, filling the empty
room with lamentation, for all the times that she had held life at
bay, taking the world's contempt into herself and letting it
wound her. She wept herself to exhaustion and beyond it,

knowing as she wept that she would never wash away the last grain of her regret.

But at last her body grew light enough to overcome its own inertia; she went out of her room and crossed the hallwell again. A single cricket chirped somewhere in the commons down below. She tapped softly, and then more loudly, on Chaim's still-closed door, getting no answer. She pushed the door aside. At first she thought the room was empty; until she saw him buried in the cocoon of his sleeping bag, tethered on the frame of his bed. She crossed over to his bedside, making certain that he was only deeply asleep. The chameleon, which hung suspended from a grip on the wall above him, pale with sleep, opened one eye to look at her. Its color began to change, darkening and brightening as it woke, adjusting instinctively to new conditions, as it always did. *Two of a kind . . .* she thought, looking back at Chaim, but there was no bitterness in the thought.

Settling back in the air, her arm loosely through a handhold, she watched him sleeping; able to observe him without being observed, laying down her shield at last in the face of his defenseless sleep. Able to see that the past was past: the mistakes paid for, the wrongs righted, as far as humanly possible. She had let the past fill up the present until there was no room left for a new life, for tomorrow. . . . Who was she punishing besides herself? And why? And when would she have suffered enough . . . *Oh God, is there anyone alive who doesn't hate herself—himself* (looking down at Chaim's sleeping face)—*in their deepest heart? Just by living we betray ourselves and are betrayed. . . . And only we can end it.*

Chaim stirred toward waking; the sleeping bag strained against the fastenings that held it immobile.

"Chaim." Her voice shook him gently.

His eyes opened, staring blankly at the ceiling.

"Chaim—"

He turned his head; body and bag revolved toward her. The blank look stayed on his face as he registered her presence. He looked at her, saying nothing; his eyes were red-rimmed.

"How are you?"

He grimaced, at her or at himself, she wasn't sure. "I don't know."

"I'm better." She glanced down. "Better than I've been in a long time, I think."

The incomprehension returned, chill with resentment. And yet somewhere an ember of understanding still strained toward fire. . . .

She breathed on it tentatively, afraid of being left alone in the darkness now. "I found what you wrote in my book."

Slow surprise filled his face. "Yeah?" He pulled himself partway out of the sleeping bag.

A nod. "When you're so lonely, you feel like you're the only one . . ." She twisted her hand around the support bar.

He laughed softly, unexpectedly. "You are."

She let her mouth relax, and found that it began to smile. She put her free hand up, feeling the strangeness of her face, the smile's distortion of it, the puffiness that remained of her grief. "Chaim—I don't hate myself, anymore. Not the way I've hated myself since Planet Two, at least."

He plucked at the seal on his sleeping bag, separating his cocoon. "Does that mean I can stop hating myself, then?"

She blinked. "Yes . . . I suppose it does."

He searched her eyes for affirmation; she met his gaze, no longer afraid. He pushed up from the bed, a man released. "Partners, then?" He reached out to her.

She nodded; took his hand and squeezed it briefly before she let it go. Warmth stayed in her palm.

The chameleon left its perch and began to creep down the wall, moving with extreme deliberation, going in search of its dwindling, ever-moving food supply. Chaim watched its progress for a long moment. He crossed his arms gingerly against the front of his coveralls, looking up at the ceiling as if he could see through it into space. "So where do we go from here? Where do we look, what do we try next?"

She jerked abruptly at the handhold. "Damn it! I'm not ready to face that now, too." She shook her head.

"We've got to face it, sooner or later. It's better if we do it now." He unzipped his pockets and pushed his hands into them. "Everybody in creation's been over the Main Belt with tweezers. We don't have supplies enough to keep random-searching for as long as it'll take to hit a strike. We've got to think of something better."

"There must be something nobody's tried, something everybody's overlooked, for some reason. Like the station on Planet Two that Sekka-Olefin found." She turned, following his drifting motion out into the room. "Chaim, you're the prospector; isn't there something you heard about, some clue?"

"That's the point—I'm not such a damn great prospector, Mythili! Neither was my old man. He had lousy luck; even when he made a strike, it killed him. And I never learned half of what he knew." His eyes grew distant. "Except . . . I do remember something. I told you back at the start, he had a lot of wild get-rich schemes. And there's one that didn't sound as crazy as the rest . . . about that factory rock from the Demarchy, that just disappeared during the war. Nobody ever found a trace of it, they all figured it must've been hit with a nuke barrage that kicked it clear out of the system. But the odds are against that; it takes a lot of energy to give escape velocity to a rock that big. There was a whole atomic battery plant on it. It was . . ." he frowned, concentrating, "let's see . . . my father said that even if it was knocked out of the fore-trojans—and it must've been, since they would have found it by now if it was still there—if it was, then its orbit should still have similar elements. That means it would drift around the Belt over a gigasecond or so, and it should've been spotted again eventually."

She frowned, concentrating. "So either it was completely fragmented or it did leave the system."

"Unless somehow it got trapped in another equilibrium point."

"But the only way that could have happened in so short a time would be if it was hit twice, or collided with some other rock . . ." They looked at each other and she felt their fantasy building, layer on layer.

"The most likely place would be in the other Lagrange points."

"Right, and probably a stable one—"

"The aft-trojans," he finished it for her. "It could be there right now, as good as new." He looked up again at the ceiling as though he actually expected to see it.

"As good as new?" Her face twisted.

He shrugged. "Let's face it—if the factory itself took a hit, the reactor would probably be spilling radiation. You couldn't miss it. But nobody ever reported anything like that from the aft-trojans. If the plant was blown up, there wouldn't be much point going after it; but if it wasn't . . . we could buy the whole goddamn Demarchy with that find!" He rubbed his hands together.

"How would we ever find it, in the whole of the aft-trojans?"

"They were mostly uninhabited, anything with any manmade stuff would stand out in the readings. That signal separater Fitch gave us could be just the edge we need for this."

"But even the core-trojans are spread over a hundred and forty thousand kilometers—" She pictured them in her mind, their tenuous teardrop spread veil-thin through endless vacuum.

"I didn't say it would be easy. It's probably not even there; this whole thing is insane. But you wanted a long shot, and that's the only one I've got. It's either shoot our wad on this or go on the way we have, bleeding to death." He shrugged. "Your choice is mine. What do you say?"

She took a deep breath. "What the hell. Let's gamble, let's throw it all away on the trojans! What the hell have we got to lose?" She raised her arms and swept them down, rising defiantly through the air.

He nodded, his eyes shining. "Only our chains."

"Nothing." Chaim looked up from the read-outs. They had been in the aft-trojans, sixty degrees behind Discus, for more than two megaseconds. And so far they had found nothing that should not have been there; no trace of radiation or any material that had not been formed in the original fusion of stone out of primordial dust.

Mythili sighed, saying nothing because she could not think of anything to say. She finished a handful of nuts, feeling the presence of every hard, broken fragment prick the tight walls of her stomach; they had begun rationing their supplies to stretch their search time. *Wasted time*. She tried not to think it, and failed. She looked away at the chameleon, which clung to the wall beside her with its tonglike toes. It seemed to crave their company more and more; or perhaps there was simply nothing else left for it to do. There did not seem to be a single cricket remaining on the ship, and there was nothing in their own dwindling supplies the lizard would eat. She wondered how long it could survive without food. *Lucky* . . . she thought, and sighed.

"You want to check out the twin?" Chaim twisted to look directly at her. "There *was* something in the long-range scan; I'm not losing my mind—" he murmured, as if he wasn't absolutely certain of it himself.

She shrugged. "We're here; we might as well." The kilometers-long piece of stone below orbited a common center of gravity with a larger mate she could see shining, a spurious star, above the bleak, dead mass they had just close-scanned.

She altered their course again, feeling the delicate mastery of her skills that she had regained and enhanced these past megaseconds. This was something that used her abilities fully, challenged them, honed them. . . . But soon it would all be gone. She didn't regret the decision they had made in gambling on the long shot; but she did regret that it would do them no good—that the satisfaction of this moment would only leave her more hungry, when their last chance and this ship were gone.

They closed with the second planetoid. Chaim put the results of the reconnaissance scan on the screen almost perfunctorily, below the actual view of naked stone framed in the ship's viewing port. A binary . . . it was hopeless, the original factory had not been part of a binary system. Their long-range instruments must be going bad on top of everything else. She watched morosely over his shoulder as the readings began to appear, lining up as she had learned to expect them, high in iron and nickel ores. Anticipating zero on hydrocarbons and metal alloys, she looked out at the barren scape below them before she saw the actual figures. . . . She blinked, and looked again. "Chaim." She reached out, her hand brushed his arm unthinkingly.

He glanced up. "Oh, God," he breathed. "Oh, God. . . ."

His arm knotted and trembled. A pragmatic, colorless dawn was breaking across its surface; the growing light glanced from the bristling discontinuity of towers and domes. She tore her eyes away from the sight of them: The readings continued to come, and looking down she saw that they were not zero anymore.

"Ninety-five," Chaim murmured. "Look at that! Look! We've found it! Geez Allah, we're rich!" He caught her hand, pulling her toward him, sending them out in a spin until they rebounded from the control room's ceiling. "He was right, the old man was right, God damn him . . . he finally did something for me!"

She heard her own laughter echoing through his shouts, echoing through the ship—her own laughter, as alien as a voice out of deep space. Chaim's arms closed around her, she felt suddenly as solid as steel, as ephemeral as bubbles. She pulled his face toward her own and kissed him.

He stared, speechless, as she broke away again. He kissed her back, eyes closed, arms tightening, pressing himself against her with sudden urgency.

She broke away and struggled back toward the panel. "I—I'll take us down." She felt her blood sweep to the ends of her body and recoil through every artery, capillary, vein; dazed by a feeling as strong as terror, that was not. Her hands stumbled over the instruments.

Chaim nodded, clearing his throat. "Sure . . . Let's see what we've got." He settled down to the instrument panel beside her, his voice husky. "Look at that; there's no radiation leaking at all. It must be in perfect shape!" He grinned, abruptly reoriented.

She felt her own excitement change form again as she looked down at the readings beside him. The figures twitched unexpectedly on the screen, still plagued by the random fluctuation that had been with them from the start. It struck her as ironic that after a gigasec this factory was in better shape than their own equipment. Her eyes tracked on across the readings, caught again. "Chaim, look. It looks like there's something in orbit here besides us."

"Another ship?"

She nodded, pointing at the screen.

"Showing any power?" He peered past her.

"No . . ."

"Hm." He let himself drift again abruptly. "Must be a derelict; doesn't look like much. We can check it out later, see what's left of it. But first I want to see that factory!"

She didn't argue.

She brought the ship in as close to the source of their readings as she could, handling the difficult rendezvous perfectly with only half her concentration. They went through the ritual of suiting up, emerging through the lock onto the airless surface of another unfamiliar world, seeming to move through it all for the first time. The planetoid rolled sunward into another fleeting day, and the light of distant Heaven silvered the razed stone surface of the docking field, limned the eerie insect-silhouette of the *Mother* behind them—etched the shining reality of the factory up ahead against the black surface of the sky. It seemed to grow out of the stone itself, an iceberg jutting above a frozen sea, the greater part of its plant buried beneath the surface. Beautiful, incongruous, immense—flawed. Unfamiliar with its form, still she recognized the gaping, unnatural breach along one side: "Chaim, it looks like it did take a hit."

"I know. But there's no radiation." He repeated the reading like a prayer. "The reactor has to be intact. That's still worth a ship and then some . . . it's still worth plenty! And look at the waldoes, they haven't been touched. I know a factory back home that'd pay a mint just for those."

They crossed the distance toward the factory's evaporating shadow in bounds that seemed effortless, her body as light as her spirits. The airlock that faced on the empty docking field gaped open in a cry of perpetual astonishment; but this time the morbid image did not stay in her mind. They passed on through it into the factory's fractured cavern.

Near the entrance their spotlights picked out the broad access tunnel that led down into the planetoid's insulating heart, where the factory's hundreds of workers had lived before the war. Passing it by, they moved on into the plant itself. Dim illumination suffused the interior from the broken wall to their right, and gradually their eyes adjusted to the darkness. Looking up, Mythili saw cranes and unnameable appendages dripping like stalactites from the ceiling high overhead, the shadowy walls and partitions that broke the space into a maze of soundless mysteries through which they drifted like lost souls. "Do you know where we're going?" she asked, suddenly uncertain. "What are we looking for?"

Chaim nodded, ahead of her. "More or less. I almost worked at one of these places; they gave me an orientation. I want to see the reactor, and what kind of damage there's been."

Mythili glanced down at the radiation counter at the wrist of her suit. It still registered nothing; she followed his slow, searching progress without further questions. The light grew stronger as they neared the ragged break in the dome's fragile outer shell. She found herself wondering that a hit which had apparently come so close to the reactor itself had not damaged it enough to cause even a small leakage.

"Watch your step—" Chaim was silhouetted as he bounded up and over the heap of rubble from a collapsed wall. She followed him like a dancer over the shifting surface, saw him turn sharply left through a breach in a higher, heavier wall.

A sudden shout rattled in her helmet as he disappeared from sight. She threw herself forward in a long bound, and another, until she could see him again. He was struggling to get to his feet again, where he had fallen in another pile of girders and rubble. But just beyond him was the thing that had wrung the cry from him—a vast hole opening in the surface of the vaster floor.

Mythili caught a protruding end of beam, pulling herself up short at Chaim's side. "What happened?" not directing the question at him, but at the hole beyond him.

"It's gone." His own thoughts followed hers to the rim of the pit. "The reactor—it's gone!"

She clung harder to the beam-end, strangling the useless words that tried to form in her throat. *Why? Where? Who?* "How?" She voiced the one question that she could possibly imagine having an answer.

"I don't know. I don't know. . . ." Chaim muttered, drawing himself up. "God help me. But this—" he waved a hand at the blasted wall, "—must've been done on purpose, for a way to get the thing out of here. Maybe the blast was what slowed the rock down enough to trap it here. They must've been in a hell of a hurry to rip it out the hard way."

"Then you think someone found this place after the first attack, and—stole the reactor out of it?"

He grunted. "Yeah."

"But what happened to it? Why wasn't there ever any record of it?"

"I don't know. If it happened during the war, it could be nobody ever knew it happened. Maybe the reactor's in use somewhere in the Demarchy right now. Or whoever stripped it might have got blasted themselves, and the thing was lost forever. All we need to know is that the goddamn thing is gone!" He wrenched loose a piece of metal and hurled it. She watched its slow, graceful arc outward and down beyond the rim of the hole.

She bit her lip, feeling her own emotions stretched beyond the limits of control, beginning to break loose and recoil. "But the rest of the factory is still here!" She threw that undeniable fact in the face of her faltering courage. "There must be other things worth salvaging, that some factory could use—"

Chaim turned back to her; she searched behind his faceplate glass. She heard the long, slow intake of his breath. "Maybe there is. The exterior waldoes we saw as we came across the field; they looked intact. The factory I told you about—its waldoes were damaged. If we can get these clear, we just might be able to sell them for our own ransom. Nobody else's got replacement parts to offer."

"I do." A third voice, a stranger's, filled the captive space of their helmets.

Mythili shook her head in disbelief; she saw the perplexed look that Chaim gave back to her. Together they turned, found a third figure standing, impossibly, behind them. A shudder crawled up her spine as she imagined that she saw a specter from the dead past, a ghostly guardian seeking vengeance on the violators of a tomb.

"What the hell. . . ." Chaim whispered. "Who—?"

"Don't tell me you've forgotten me, Chaim. It wasn't so long ago we met, back on Mecca. I'm your father's friend, and yours, boy."

"Fitch!" Chaim shook his head, uncomprehending. "What in the name of God? How—what the hell are you doing here?"

"Following you. You don't think this was a coincidence, do you?"

"You tracked us all this way." Mythili was already sure of the answer, sure there could be no other explanation. "How? The signal separater you gave us back at Mecca wasn't bugged, I know it wasn't!"

Fitch came toward them, his face still invisible to her. "You're a bright girl," he said mildly. "But not bright enough. . . . How's Lucky doing? And did you ever take a good look at his cage? That's where the transmitter was hidden." He laughed. "You must've paid a fortune for those damned crickets!"

She felt her face flush. "You bastard—" she murmured, hearing Chaim's curse echo her own. She cursed herself, silently; knowing she should have realized that power leak meant something.

As Fitch approached, she saw that he carried something massive at his side, something she couldn't identify. She felt herself beginning to sweat.

"What were you following us for?" Chaim asked, although the answer was as clear to her as the answer to *how;* and probably it was to him, too.

"I told you before, Chaim: I knew your father. I knew he was smart—I knew he'd leave you something, a key, a clue. I knew you weren't going out on this survey without a real goal in mind." She could see his face now, familiar, shining with sweat like her own. "That was smart of you, trying to throw anybody who suspected off by spending so much time in the Main Belt. I almost had to give up on you, I didn't know if my ship could take it; it'll never make the trip back to the Demarchy from here. But I didn't give up. And now after all this time, it's finally paid off . . . I'm going to be a rich man." He pulled the thing he carried forward.

"Look," Chaim said shortly, and she heard an edge of

nervous fear in his truculence, "I told you I'm not taking on more partners. Just because you followed us to this claim doesn't mean we're going to cut you in on it."

"I didn't figure you would." He brought the thing up in front of him; Mythili recognized it at last as a portable laser cutting torch. Her lungs were suddenly tight and aching.

"Fitch—" Chaim raised his hands, placating, surrendering.

"Don't bother with it, Dartagnan. I saw your testimony against Siamang; I know you'd promise me anything now, and try to turn me in later. I'm not giving you the chance to do that to me."

"What does that mean?" Chaim said, knowing what it meant.

"It means he's going to kill us, and pirate our claim." Mythili moved forward a little, painfully aware of the uncertain footing and the pit behind them. "Fitch, listen, *listen* to what I just said. You don't seem like that kind of man, not a murderer, not a thief. We never did anything to you. You're not that greedy. And you said Chaim's father was your friend—" she was amazed at the quiet reason in her own voice, which was somehow functioning without the control of a conscious mind that had gone white with the fear of death.

Fitch laughed once; there was something in the sound as desperate as their own terror, and as unable to believe that he was actually doing this to them. But he shook his head at her, and the quiet torch in his hands did not waver. "We weren't close. Besides, I think he'd understand. He'd understand that a man who's spent his life in space gets old before his time. And when you're getting too old and your ship is, too; when in all your life you've never made a find that's done more than just keep you alive to go on searching; when you know you're born unlucky, you'll die old and poor and alone . . . when you know all that, and you see two healthy young kids get handed a ship and go out to make a rich strike—"

"—you go a little crazy," Chaim finished softly.

"No!" Fitch said. "You finally get sane. You realize the truth, that you're the one you have to look out for. I lived inside the rules all my life, and what did it get me? Nothing! Now I make my own rules. Nothing else matters—you don't.

Don't waste my time with talk," as Mythili tried to speak, "just start backing up." He gestured with the laser.

She glanced over her shoulder. They were less than two meters from the edge of the gaping reactor hole, its lips bearded with overhanging rubble. They would fall into the pit, not a fatal fall, but the rubble coming down on top of them would bury them forever. Her eyes leaped from a piece of twisted metal to a chunk of concrete, searching for a weapon— all the while knowing that there was nothing she could do quickly enough to save herself or Chaim from Fitch's torch.

Chaim moved abruptly beside her, not moving back but toward Fitch, his hands still outstretched. She wondered with sudden disgust whether he was about to beg for his life. But before she could even finish the thought he stumbled, sank to his knees in the broken masonry.

Fitch swore, and the nose of his laser torch dropped slightly, following Chaim down. "Get up." His attention flickered between them.

Chaim thrashed awkwardly, starting a slow cloud of debris. Mythili wondered at his inability to get his equilibrium back, wondered if he was that frightened. But then in the space of a heartbeat he was up and moving—on a collision course with the weapon in Fitch's grasp. "Mythili, get out!" The shout spilled over into movement, impact, a chaos of input, a crack of lightning. She threw herself backwards as the laser flew off-track, firing, slashing through the space where she had been and dazzling her eyes to tears. She heard more grunts and cries; blinked furiously, trying to force sight back into the dark-bright mottled space inside her head as she groped in the debris for a metal bar. She pulled one free at last, pushing herself upward. The periphery of her wounded vision showed her the two men struggling to keep from being overbalanced in the soft sea of rubble. The intermittent, bloody streak of the laser's beam lashed the darkness. Fitch's knee caught Chaim in the stomach, thrusting him backwards, tearing his hands loose from the torch.

As Fitch recoiled from his own thrust, rising in the air, he brought the torch's beam back into line. Mythili hurled the bar, her body's reaction to the movement distorting her aim. But still the bar struck the torch, knocking it out of Fitch's hands, and sent it spiraling lazily into the air. The red beam roved, pointing like the finger of God, and she realized that the dead-man switch had jammed. "Look out, look out—!" She threw her hands up, pressing her helmet glass . . . watched helplessly as Fitch tried to maneuver himself out of its path, and failed. Still in mid-fall, with nothing to give his frantically twisting body support for a counter-motion, he cried out as he saw his own weapon turn against him.

The stream of intensified light stroked down across him in an idle caress, laying open his suit, searing the cloth and flesh beneath it; releasing the captive oxygen, the artificial ecosystem that kept him separate from the vacuum outside. She heard his scream start, lost it in the rush of escaping air that saved her from hearing its end.

Chaim pushed off as the falling finger of light reached out for him in turn, rebounded sideways before it found him—kept on tumbling, as the debris shifted under him, spilling him toward the pit.

"Chaim!" She screamed this time, screamed his name as she saw him slide toward the edge. He clambered over the shifting face of the rubble, a grotesque slow-motion pantomime of a man trying to walk on water. A chunk of cement struck him in the chest, canceling his frantic upward momentum, throwing him back.

She bounded forward as she saw him fall, doubled her own momentum as she landed at the shifting lip of the pit and plunged recklessly out and down. She matched Chaim's free fall, catching frantically at his leg as she dropped past him. Her body wrenched, and together they went on falling through the crest of the avalanching metal and concrete, to a collision with the bottom of the pit. Her feet struck cement with an impact that ground her teeth, and bones grated on cartilege.

"Move! Move—" She didn't need Chaim's garbled shout of warning to go on collapsing over her feet, to push herself off again across the floor of the pit in a blind leap. He followed her through it, and together they came up against the far wall in another jarring impact, as behind them the falling rubble made inexorable silent thunder. She settled at the wall's foot, sank

down in pain and exhaustion, not letting herself turn back to
watch.

"Thank you," Chaim said thickly, crouching strengthless
beside her. "Thank God you didn't run." He laughed, with
shaken irony.

She looked up at him, and suddenly her own body was
trembling uncontrollably. "You fool! You damned fool! What
did you do that for? You threw yourself right at him, it's a
miracle he didn't fry you! What the hell were you trying to
prove?"

More laughter seeped into her helmet, thin and gray; she
listened in disbelief. "I can't do anything that suits you." He
pushed himself up, rested a hand on her shoulder. "I guess I
was trying to prove that—that what happened on Planet Two
would never happen again."

She drew him toward her, felt their bodies touch, suit to suit.
Their faces met, glass to glass, in silence.

They buried Fitch in the abandoned city below the factory:
the only inhabitant in a City of the Dead. She listened with
uncertain emotion as Chaim spoke a benediction, calling Fitch
a symbol of all Heaven's humanity and the thing that had killed
him a symbol of how it had destroyed itself—not through
technology, but through misguided greed.

And then with the ship's salvaging equipment, they cut loose
the waldoes of the ruined factory and lifted them away. Clutching
the prize in spidery arms, the *Mother* began a homeward
course, tracking back through lifeless wastes toward the
Demarchy's still-beating heart. Chaim did not try to force the
closeness between them, although she felt his longing, and she
was grateful. She felt no need either to pull away or to draw
close before she was ready, and yet her gratitude at his
understanding drew her closer in spite of herself. And while the
journey outward had seemed endless in its solitude, their shared
return slipped by her like a soft afternoon, as the past fell
further and further behind.

They made radio contact long before they reached Demarchy
space, reporting their find, anticipating their reception and not
disappointed by the eagerness of the response. But as they

neared Calcutta planetoid Mythili felt her tension rising again, without a clear reason.

"Mythili . . . what's bothering you?" Chaim studied her earnestly across the trays of food on the metal tabletop. The chameleon perched on his shoulder, looking at her too, with one of its independently roving eyes. His own appetite had grown cautiously hearty, while she sat picking at her sticky mixed beans and rice like an unhappy child. "What's wrong?"

She looked away from the droning entertainment tape on the salvaged player they had installed beside the table. "Nothing," she murmured, unable to say anything substantial.

"Don't give me that. Tell me what it is—something I've done?"

The dismay on his face surprised her so much that she laughed without meaning to. "No. No, it's not you, Chaim. It's just . . . I don't know. I just—hate having this end, I think." The laughter flinched. "It's ironic; I hated this trip, this ship," *you,* but she didn't say it, "so much on the way out; and now I hate the thought of it ending."

"Do you?" The absurdness of the emotion on his face didn't change, although the emotion itself did. "But this isn't the end—it's just the beginning. We've got the ship now and forever. We're free—"

"Free to end up like Fitch?" The words burst out of her, and hearing them she recognized at last the source of her unhappiness.

He sat back, grimacing; as though the idea had only just struck him. But he shook his head. "No. It won't be like that. Because . . ." he hesitated, "because it's not so much the money, or the lack of it, that made this trip better, more, than the trip out. It's the fact that we're sharing this one." His fingers pressed the table edge. "Hell, if we have to, we can haul gases with this ship to make a living. But I figure we'll always be able to get by on prospecting, if we want to. And I want to: A find like the one we made this time—it *means* something. Not just to us, but to the Demarchy. It gives everybody a little more time." His eyes grew distant. "If that damned reactor had only been there!"

She felt a shadow fall across her own mind, realized that

after what she had seen in the Main Belt, she was beginning to believe him. "You think it would have saved the Demarchy?"

"No . . . I don't know . . . it would have helped. And with the money we got out of it, I could've done what Sekka-Olefin wanted me to do: sold the Demarchy on moving its people to Planet Two."

"You still believe in that crazy old man's crazy ideas?" Her voice rose slightly.

"It makes a lot of sense!" His sharpness answered her own. "He told me it's no worse than part of Old Earth—no worse than Antarctica, and people live there."

"Antarctica!" She shook her head. "Antarctica's an icecap; don't you know that? He was right . . . Planet Two's just as bad."

"But it's a world, like Earth—" He leaned forward; the chameleon tilted precariously on his shirt collar, and blinked. "You don't need the same sort of artificial environment we need in space—you don't need the technology, you don't have to make everything. Air, water . . . you have all you need. It's a natural environment."

"All the food? The heat?" she said, unable to keep the words neutral. "Do you really think it would be any easier to survive on Planet Two than out here? It's too cold. The only reason people could live in Antarctica was because the rest of Earth had a better climate to support them—no one lived there before Earth had a high tech level."

"How do you know so damn much about Earth, anyway?" His exasperation prickled.

"My books. You've seen them—" She was able to say that, at least, without rancor now. "Remember that ecology book I gave you; didn't you get anything about 'natural environments' out of it?"

"Not much." He looked down uncomfortably. "I had other things on my mind. . . . You really think it's impossible? You think I'd be leading the Demarchy from one bad end to another one? You really think Sekka-Olefin was crazy, he didn't know what he was talking about?"

She nodded. "It was a fool's dream, Chaim. Something to keep him from going mad, stranded there all alone. . . ." She gentled her voice at the sight of his face. "Read the books yourself, if you want to be sure."

His head moved from side to side. "But he wasn't wrong about what's happening to Heaven, to the Demarchy—to us. That we'll all die, in the end. If we can't start a colony on Planet Two, there's nowhere left to run. There's nothing anyone can do to stop it ... only try to hold back the night as long as we can. Doing what you and I are doing: at least that's something. . . ." He turned a can slowly on the surface of the tray, staring down at his hand, at the futile motion.

"Yes." She nodded, feeling a great heaviness settle inside her, knowing that it would never lift again as long as she lived. "I guess—maybe it is worthwhile to go on with prospecting. I guess we can manage together. We do make a pretty good team." Forcing a smile, she found that suddenly it felt real.

An insistent chiming fell like coins down through the well from the control room, signaling their final approach to Calcutta. She unsealed a pocket on her jumpsuit and reached into it, pulling out the jewelry she had found in the nameless planetoid that had turned their lives around. Separating the ring from the necklace, she held it out to him. "Here," she said, speaking with a cheerfulness she barely felt. "A memento. We might as well look like rich SOBs for once in our lives. Even if it is junk, this may be the only time we'll be able to carry it off."

He laughed, grateful for the change of subject. Taking the heavy ring without reluctance, he turned it between his fingers. "Whoever owned this must have massed a ton." He poked a finger through the hole, with room to spare.

"Maybe they wore it over a suit glove." She untangled the necklace's gaudy, jeweled pendants, shaking her head. "Anyone whose taste ran to this sort of thing would be tasteless enough to wear it outside."

"Maybe it's an antique. The Old Worlders were a lot heavier-set." Chaim squinted at the inside of the ring hole. She saw him straighten and shift suddenly, bringing the ring up closer to his eyes. "Myth ... tell me what you see inside here." He passed her the ring, so intently that she wondered whether he was playing a joke on her.

But she took the ring, holding it up into the light. Her own hands froze as she made out the small, worn symbols on the inside. "F-fourteen karat?" She looked up at him, her eyes still straining. "It's real—?" breathless. "Shiva! It can't be—" Fumbling, she picked up the necklace, chose a depending clear-colored stone and pushed it across her watch crystal. She felt it scrape, rubbed her fingers over the furrow it left behind. *Real*. "And there's a whole trunkful of it out there...."

"My God." He struck his forehead with his hand.

"But once we've sold the waldoes, we'll be able to go out again and get the rest." She held the necklace up, watching it wink languorously in the air. "Maybe it's not worth much against the darkness—but there are still enough blind, rich SOBs who'll buy it anyway to keep us bankrolled for a while." The thought gave her a perverse pleasure. She looked at the chameleon making its way down the front of Chaim's threadbare shirt. "Lucky," she murmured, and shook her head, "you lived up to your name, after all.... You're going to eat crickets till they come out your ears when we get home, little one!" She grinned.

Chaim grunted, sharing her irony. "You can count on it." He smiled briefly, stroking the chameleon's speckled green back. His eyes darkened again as he turned the ring on his finger. "All of it real...."

"Chaim?"

He shook his head. "Nothing. Just thinking about fool's gold...and fools' dreams. Mythili—" he put out his hand until it covered one of her own. "Maybe this is too soon. But I have to say it now, before...while I've still got some privacy...."

She looked down at his hand, back at his face, wondering at his sudden inarticulateness. "What is it?"

"Myth...I want to get married."

"What?" She blinked, and blinked. "Married? To whom?"

"You, damn it, who do you think? I know, I know—" he ran on before she could answer, "—it's too soon. I'm not trying to rush anything, it's your choice, it always was...I just wanted you to know, that's all. That I...that I mean it." His hand tightened.

She freed her own hand nervously, curling the edge of her

collar. "You know I'm sterile. I can't ever have children—" A choking knot in her throat kept her from saying more.

"I know. That's fine with me. I don't want any children; I don't want to bring them into a world without a future."

"Then—why? Why get married at all?"

"Because it's a commitment. A promise that I'll remember there's something worth living for right now, even if there isn't any future. Our own lifetime doesn't have to be so bad, if we make the most of it. And because—" he caught her eyes, "—because I guess I love you, Myth." He took a deep breath.

She glanced down, weaving her fingers together, twisting them, testing the fit. She looked up again, her throat aching, still unable to speak the words that had been prisoner too long inside her; hoping that he could read in her eyes the promise he would not hear from her lips. "I'm—not ready to say *yes* now, Chaim. But I'm not saying *no*." She untangled her fingers, and gave him her hand freely.

He grinned. "Damn—I can still sell an idea when I want to."

They left the ship at last, trailing the long guide rope down to the surface of the Calcutta docking field. It was cluttered with corporate mediamen and freelancers; the din of questions blurred into white noise in their suit speakers. But a single figure stood waiting for them as they forced their way through the gauntlet of questions. Mythili saw the insignia on his plain, dark pressure suit, the silver octagonal star enclosed in a teardrop, the symbol of the Demarchy. Chaim glanced over at her, murmuring, "Abdhiamal?"

She nodded. She pictured his self-satisfied smile as they closed with him, imagined the litany of smug congratulations he would be reciting to himself at the sight of their success and their reconciliation.

She frowned abruptly, giving Chaim a light shove. "Keep away from me, Dartagnan. I hope I never see you again, after this!"

He gaped at her. She winked, and the amazement fell away; he smiled feebly, nodded. "The same goes for me, you bitch!

If I ever see Abdhiamal again, I'm going to shove his teeth down his throat.''

"You'll have to wait in line." Vicious satisfaction—"Abdhiamal!"—and mock surprise.

Abdhiamal looked from face to face between them, shaking his head, his own face dour. "Well . . . I only have one question for you, then.''

They stopped, holding murder on their faces. "What is it?''

"Are you going to ask me to witness when you marry?''

They looked at him in silent incredulity, and at each other. Slowly Chaim worked the gold ring off of his gloved finger, and pressed it into Abdhiamal's open hand. Smiling, they passed him by on either side, and moved on across the field hand in hand.

THE
OUTCASTS
OF
HEAVEN BELT

There are more stars in the galaxy than there are droplets of water in the Boreal Sea. Only a fraction of those stars wink and glitter, like snowflakes passing through the light, in the unending night sky over the darkside ice. And out of those thousand thousand visible stars, the people of the planet Morningside had made a wish on one—called Heaven.

Sometimes when the winds ceased, a brittle silence would settle over the darkside ice sheet; and it might seem to a Morningside astronomer, in the solitude of his observatory, that all barriers had broken down between his planet and the stars, that the very hand of interstellar space brushed his pulse. Space lapped at his doorway, the night flowed up and up and up, merging imperceptibly with the greater night that swallowed all mornings, and all Morningsides, and all the myriad stars whose numbers would overflow the sea.

And he would think of the starship *Ranger*, which had gone up from Morningside's fragile island into the endless night: a silvered dustmote carried on a violent invisible breeze across the cathedral distances of space, drawn from candleflame to candleflame through the darkness. . . .

They would be a long time gone. And what had seemed to the crew to be the brave, bright immensity of their fusion craft shrank to insignificance as they left the homeworld further and further behind—as the *Ranger* became only one more mote, lost among countless unseen motes in the fathomless depths of night.

But like an ember within a tinderbox, their lives gave the ship its own warm heart of light, and life. The days passed, and the months, and years . . . and light-years, while seven men and women watched over the ship's needs, and one another's. Their shared past patterned their present with images of the world they had left behind, visions of the future they hoped to bring back to it. They were bound for Heaven, and like true believers they found that belief instilled a deeper meaning in the charting of stars and the tending of hydroponic vats, in their silence and their laughter, in every song and memory they carried with them from home.

And at last one star began to separate from all the rest, centering on the ship's viewscreen, becoming a focus for their combined hope. Years had dwindled to months and finally weeks, as, decelerating now, backing down from near the speed of light, they kept their rendezvous with the new system. They passed the orbit of Sevin, the outermost of Heaven's worlds, where the new sun was still scarcely more than an ice-crowned point of light. Counting the days now, like children reaching toward Christmas, the crew anticipated journey's end before them: all the riches and wonders of the Heaven Belt.

But before they reached their final destination, they would encounter one more wonder that was no creation of humankind— the gas giant Discus, a billowing ruby set in a plate of silver rings. They watched it expand until it obliterated more of this black and alien sky than the face of their own sun had blocked in the dusty sky of home. They closed with the giant's lumbering course, slipping past like a cautious firefly. And while the crew sat together in the dayroom, gazing out in awe at its splendor, the captain and the navigator discovered something new, something quite unexpected, on the ship's displays: four unknown ships, powered by antiquated chemical rockets, on an intercepting course . . . .

"Pappy, are they still closing?"

"Still closing, Betha." Clewell Welkin bent forward as new readings appeared at the bottom of the screen. "But the rate's holding steady. They must be cutting power; they couldn't do ten gees forever. Christ, don't let them hit us again...."

Betha struck the intercom button again with her fist. "It's going to be all right. No one else will get near us." Her voice shook, someone else's voice, not Betha Torgussen's, and no one answered, "Come on, somebody, answer me. Eric! Eric! Switch on—"

"Betha." Clewell leaned out across the padded seat arm, caught her shoulder.

"Pappy, they don't answer."

"Betha, one of those ships, it's not falling back! It's—"

She brushed away his hand, searching the readouts on the screen. "Look at it! They want to *take* us. They must; it's burning chemical fuel, and they can't afford to waste that much." She held her breath, knuckles whitening on the cold metal panel. "They're getting too close. Show them our tail, Pappy."

Pale eyes flickered in his seamed face. "Are you—?"

She half-rose, pushed back from the panel, down into the seat again. "Clewell, they tried to kill us! They're armed, they want to take our ship and they will, and that's the only way to stop them.... Let them cross our tail, Navigator."

"Yes, Captain." He turned away from her toward the panel,

and began to punch in the course change that would end their pursuit.

At the final moment Betha switched the screen from simulation to outside scan, picked out the amber fleck of the pursuing ship thirty kilometers behind them—watched it fleetingly made golden by the alchemy of supercharged particles from her ship's exhaust. And watched its gold darken again into the greater darkness shot with stars. She shuddered, not feeling it, and cut power.

"What—what do we do now?" Clewell drifted up off the seat, against the restraining belt, as the ship's acceleration ceased. The white fringe of his hair stood out from his head like frost.

Before her on the screen the rings of Discus edged into view, eclipsing the night: the plate of striated silver, twenty separate bands of utter blackness and moon-white, the setting for the rippling red jewel of gas that was the central planet. Her hand was on the selector dial, her eyes burned with the brightness, paralyzing her will. She shut her eyes, and turned the dial.

The intercom was broken. They still sat at the table, Eric and Sean and Nikolai, Lara and Claire; they looked up at her, laughing, breathing again, looked out through the dome at the glory of Discus on the empty night. . . . She opened her eyes. And saw empty night. *Oh, God,* she thought. The room was empty; they were gone. *Oh, God.* Only stars, gaping beyond the shattered plastic of the dome, crowding the blackness that had swallowed them all. . . . She didn't scream, lost in the soundless void.

"They're all—gone. All of them. That warhead . . . it shattered the dome."

She turned to see Clewell, his face bloodless and empty; saw their lives, with everything suddenly gone. Thinking, frightened, *He looks so old.* . . . She released her seatbelt mindlessly, pushed herself along the panel to his side and took his hands. They held each other close, in silence.

A squirming softness batted against her head; she jerked upright as claws like tiny needles caught a foothold in the flesh of her shoulder. "Rusty!" She reached up to pull the cat loose, began to drift and hooked a foot under the rung along the panel base. Golden eyes peered at her from a round brindled face, above a nose half black and half orange; mottled whiskers twitched as the mouth formed a *meow?* like an unoiled gate hinge. Betha's hands tightened over an urge to fling the cat across the room. *What right does an animal have to be alive, when five human beings are dead?* She turned her face away as Rusty stretched a patchwork paw to touch her, *mrr*ing consolation for an incomprehensible grief. Betha cradled her, kissed the furred forehead, comforted by the soft knot of her warmth.

Clewell caught Rusty's drifting tail, bloodied at the tip. "She barely got out."

Betha nodded.

"Why did we ever come to Heaven?" His voice shook.

She looked up. "You know why we came!" She stopped, forcing control. "I don't know . . . I mean . . . I mean, I thought I knew . . ." Four years ago, as they left Morningside, she had been sure of everything: her destination, her happiness, her marriage, her life. And now, suddenly, incredibly, only life remained. *Why?*

Because the people of Morningside, the bleak innermost world of a pitiless red dwarf star, had a dream of Heaven. Heaven: A G-type sun system without an Earthlike planet, but with an asteroid belt rich in accessible metals. And with Discus, a gas giant ringed in littered splendor by frozen water, methane, and ammonia—the elemental keys to life. The ore-rich Belt and the frozen gases had made it feasible—almost easy—to build up a colony entirely self-sufficient in its richness; heaven in every sense of the word to colonists from Sol's asteroid belt, who had always been dependent on Earth for basic survival needs. And it had become a dream for another colony, Morningside, hungry now for something more than survival: the dream that they could establish contact with the Heaven Belt, and negotiate a share in its overflowing bounty.

The dream that had carried the starship *Ranger* across three light-years; that had been shattered with the shattered dayroom, by the reality of sudden death. The desolation burned again across her eyes; her mind saw the *Ranger*'s one-hundred-meter spindle form, every line as familiar as her own face, every centimeter blueprinted on her memory . . . saw it flawed by one tiny, terrible wound; saw five faces, lost to her now in darkness, endlessly falling . . . .

Clewell said softly, "What now?"

"We go on—go on as planned."

"You want to go on trying to make contact with these . . ." His hand pointed at the ruin on the screen. "Do you want to lead them home by the hand, to murder all of Morningside? Isn't it enough—"

Betha shook her head, clinging to the arms of her seat. "We don't have any choice! You know that. We don't have enough hydrogen on board to get the ship back to ramscoop speeds. We have to refuel somewhere in Heaven, or we'll never get home." A vision of home stunned her: firelight on dark beams, on the night before their departure—a little boy's face bright with tears, buried against her shirt. *Mommy . . . I dreamed you had to die to go to Heaven.* Remembering her child's sobs waking out of nightmare, her own eyes filled with tears and the endless darkness. She bit her lip. *Goddamn it, I'm not a child, I'm thirty-five years old!*

"Pappy, don't start acting like an old man." She frowned, and watched his irritation strip tens years from his face. Without looking, she reached out to blank the viewscreen. "We don't have any choice now. We have to go on with it." *We have to pay them back,* her eyes flickered, hard edges of sapphire glinting. She tossed Rusty carefully away, watched her cat-paddle uselessly as she drifted out into the room. "We have enough fuel left to get us around the system—but who do we trust? Why did they attack us? And those ships, chemical rockets—they shouldn't have anything like that outside of a museum! It doesn't make sense."

"Maybe they were pirates, renegades. There's nothing else that fits." Clewell's hand hung in the air, uncertain.

"Maybe." She sighed, knowing that renegades had no place in Heaven. Having no choice except to believe it, she forgot that the angry, mindless face that had cursed her on their screen had called her *pirate*. "We'll go on in to the main Belt, to the capital at Lansing, as planned, then. And then . . . we'll find a way to get what we need."

TOLEDO PLANETOID (DEMARCHY SPACE)

+30 KILOSECONDS

Wadie Abdhiamal, negotiator for the Demarchy, stirred sluggishly, dragged up out of sleep by the chiming of the telephone. He turned the lights up enough to make out its form and switched it on. "Yes?" He saw Lije MacWong's mahogany face brighten on the screen, pushed himself up on an elbow in the bed.

"Sorry to wake you up, Wadie."

He grinned. "I'll bet you are." MacWong enjoyed getting up early. Wadie glanced at the digital clock in the phone's base. "Somebody need a negotiator at this time of night? Don't the people even sleep?"

"I hope they're all sleepin' now. . . . Are you alone?"

Wadie glanced back over his shoulder at Kimoru's brown, sleek side, her tumbled black hair. She sighed in her sleep. He looked back at MacWong's image, judged from the disapproval in the pale-blue eyes that MacWong already knew the answer. Annoyed but not showing it, he said, "No, I'm not."

"Pick up the receiver."

Wadie obeyed, cutting off sound from the general speaker. He listened, silent, for the few seconds more it took MacWong to surprise him out of his sleep-fog. "Be down as soon as I can."

He got out of bed, half-drifting in the scant gravity, and went into the bathroom to wash and shave. When he returned he found Kimoru sitting up in bed, the pinioned comforter pulled up to her chin. She blinked reproachfully, her eyelids showing lavender.

"Wadie, darlin' "—a hint of spite—"it's not even morning! Whyever are you gettin' up already; am I such a bore in bed?" A hint of desperation.

"Kimoru." He moved across the comfortable confinement of the room to kiss her lingeringly. "That's a hell of a thing to say to me. Duty called, I've got to leave . . . you know I hate to get up early. Particularly when you're here. Get your beauty sleep; I'll come back to take you out to breakfast—or lunch, if you prefer." He fastened his shirt with one hand, touched her cheek with the other.

"Well, all right." She slithered down under the cover. "But don't be too late. You know I've got to charm a customer for dear old Chang and Company at fifty kilosecs." She yawned. Her teeth were very bright, and sharp. "I don't know why you don't get a decent job. Only a government man would put up with a schedule like yours . . . or have to."

Or a geisha—? He went on dressing, didn't say it out loud; knowing that she didn't have a choice, and that to remind her of it was unnecessary and tactless. A woman who had been sterilized for genetic defects had very few opportunities open to her, in a society that saw a woman as a potential mother above all else. If she was married to an understanding husband, one who was willing to let a contract mother provide him with heirs, she could continue to lead a normal life. But a woman divorced for sterility—or an unmarried sterile woman—had only two alternatives: to work at a menial, unpleasant job, exposed to radiation from the dirty postwar atomic batteries; or to work as a geisha, entertaining the clients of a corporation. It was prostitution; but it was accepted. A geisha had few rights and little prestige, but she did have security, comfortable surroundings, fine clothes, and enough money to support her when she passed her prime. It was a sterile existence, but physical sterility left her with little choice.

Knowing the alternatives, Wadie neither blamed nor censured. And it struck him frequently that in working for the government, he had picked a career that most people respected less than formal prostitution—and one that had left his private life as barren of real relationships as any geisha's. He looked past his own reflection in the mirror, at Kimoru, already asleep again with one slender arm reaching out toward the empty half of the bed. He had no children, no wife. Most of the women he saw socially were women like Kimoru, geishas he met while negotiating disputes for the corporations that used them. He avoided them while he was on assignment, because he avoided anything that could remotely be considered a bribe. But in their free time the geishas liked to choose their own escort, and he had enough money to show them a good time.

But he rarely stayed in one place long enough to get to know any woman well; and the few normal women he had known at all had bored him with their endless insipid conversation, their endless coquetry.

Wadie brushed back his dark curling hair and settled the soft beret carefully on his head. He was a fastidious dresser, even at dawn. It was expected. He picked up a gold ring set with rubies, slipped it onto his thumb. It had been a gift of gratitude, from two people he had helped long megaseconds before, a husband-and-wife prospecting team. He remembered that woman again—a woman pilot, a sound, healthy woman who had chosen to be sterilized in order to go into space. No kind of woman at all, really; because no real woman would willingly reject a home and family. That woman had been a freak—stubborn, defensive, self-righteous; a woman out of her place, out of her depth. And yet her partner had married her. But he had been a kind of freak himself; a mediaman—a professional liar—with scruples. It was no wonder the two of them chose to spend the rest of their lives in the middle of nowhere, picking over salvage on ruined worlds. . . .

Wadie shook his head at the memory, looking into the mirror, into the past. He wondered again, as he had wondered before, what bizarre chemistry had drawn them together, and still kept them together. And wondered briefly, almost enviously, why that chemistry had never worked on him. He shrugged on his loose forest-green jacket, buttoned the high collar above the embroidered silken geometries. Hell, he was eleven hundred and fifty megaseconds old—thirty-eight Old World years—most of them spent solving everyone else's problems, living everyone else's life instead of his own. If he hadn't found a woman by now who would accept him on his own terms, or one who could make him forget everything else, he never would. He wasn't getting any younger; if he wanted a child, he couldn't afford to wait much longer. When he finished this new assignment he would hire a contract mother to bear his child and raise it while he was away. He glanced back one last time at sleeping Kimoru as he left the apartment, closing the door quietly.

Wadie yawned discreetly as he left the building's shadow and started across the quiet square. It was barely daylight now; the glow of the fluorescent lamps brightened like dawn in the ceiling's imitation sky, ten meters above his head. The magnetized soles of his polished boots clicked faintly on the polished metal of the square, added security in the slight spin-gravity of Toledo planetoid. The surface of the square curved along the inside hull of a massive, hollowed chunk of iron, a rich miner's harvest and a solid home, but one that was beginning, ungraciously, to show its age. The silvery geometric filigree of pure mineral iron beneath his feet had been preserved once by a thin bonding film, but it was oxidizing now as the film wore away. He could trace rusty paths, dull reddish brown in the early light, leading his eyes across the square and under the tarnished rococo wall to the entrance of the government center. Symptoms of a deeper illness . . . Something like panic choked him; from habit he took a long breath, and eased back from the edge, from admitting that the disease would be terminal. He went on toward the center, ordering the lace at his cuffs. *Living well is the best defense,* he thought sourly.

Lije MacWong was waiting for him inside. Officially Wadie worked for the citizens of the Demarchy; actually he worked for MacWong. MacWong, the People's Choice. The Demarchy's absolute democracy was an unpredictable water beneath the fragile ship of government, and it had drowned countless unwary representatives. But MacWong moved instinctively with the flow of popular opinion, sometimes even risked diverting that flow to suit his own vision of the people's needs. He did the people's business, and made them like it. Wadie wondered from time to time what MacWong's secret was; and wondered whether he really wanted to know. "Peace 'n' prosperity, Lije."

MacWong glanced up as Wadie entered the office, ice-blue eyes placid in his dark face. "Peace 'n' prosperity, Wadie." He rose, returned a formal bow, and moved reluctantly away from his aquarium.

Wadie peered past him for a glimpse of the fish—three glittering golden things no larger than a finger, with tails of shining gossamer, moving sinuously through sea grasses in the green-lit water. The goldfish were the only nonhuman creatures he had ever seen, and for all he knew MacWong was still paying for them. He pulled off his hat, watched its soft mushroom roundness begin to flatten beside MacWong's on the desk top. "With all due respect, I trust this news about a Mysterious Message from Outer Space is genuine, an' I'm not here because you like to see me suffer." He sank slowly into MacWong's neocolonial desk chair, smoothed wrinkles from his jacket.

"Have a seat." MacWong smiled tolerantly. "The 'message' is genuine. These aren't home movies I'm goin' to show you." He leaned carefully against the corner of his desk, avoiding the fresco of silver animal heads, and flicked a switch on the communications inset. Nothing happened. "Dammit." He picked up a platinum paperweight shaped like a springing cat and dropped it on the panel. The impact was unimpressive, but the Kleinfelter mural projection on the far wall faded, and was replaced by the image of a woman's face. "I don't know what I'll do if this desk quits working. They don't build 'em like they used to." He set the paperweight gently back in place.

"They don't build 'em at all, Lije." Wadie traced the scrolled embroidery on his jacket front; his fingers froze as he looked up at the screen. "A hologram? Where'd you get that, MacWong?"

"We picked it out of the air, or space, anyhow, thirty kilosecs ago. It's a genuine hologramic transmission; it took us ten kilosecs to figure that out. And it's not beamed. Think of the power and bandwidth something like that requires! I don't know anybody who can do that for the hell of it anymore."

"Not many that can do it at all—" He broke off, watching, listening, as the woman's voice rose. Her skin was pale to the point of colorlessness, like her cropped, floating hair; her face was long and angular. She wore a faded shirt open at the neck, without jewelry. In her thirties, he judged, and making no attempt to cover it up; her plainness was almost painful. He put it out of his mind, concentrating on her voice. She spoke Anglo, but with an unfamiliar accent; the most common words seemed to take on extra syllables in her mouth.

". . . please identify yourselves further. We were not aware of violating your space. We are not, repeat *not,* from your system; and we—" She was interrupted by a noise that barely recorded; Wadie saw her pale skin blush with anger, her eyes sharpen like cut sapphire. He glanced at MacWong.

"The Ringer navy," MacWong said. "Their 'cast went the other way. This is all we picked up."

The woman glanced offscreen, and spoke words that he couldn't hear, insulting words, he guessed; but her voice was steady as she faced the screen again. "This is not a Belter ship, we are not 'Demarchists,' and we have committed no acts of 'piracy.' You have no authority over my ship; permission to board is denied. But if you will give us co-ords for your—"

Again she was interrupted; he watched tension grow, tightening her face. "We're not armed—" And resolution: "But we deny your 'right of seizure.' Pappy, get us—" She turned away again, and her image was ripped apart by a burst of red static. For half a second more he saw her, and then the screen went white.

"Well?"

Wadie loosened his hands on the metal frame of the chair. "Did they destroy it? Is that all?"

MacWong shook his head. "The ship took a hit, but it got away from the Ringers—all but one of 'em. We monitored some of their followups; that alien ship is a ramscoop, and when one of the Ringer pursuit craft got too close she just used the exhaust to melt it into scrap. Maybe that indignant Viking Queen isn't armed, but she's dangerous."

Wadie said nothing, waiting.

"We don't know where the ship is now, or even why it's

here. But I have some ideas. She said it was from outside the system, and I believe that. Nobody in the Belt has anything that sophisticated anymore. And a woman runnin' it—particularly a woman who looks like that—''

"Maybe she's an albino . . . maybe she's from the Main Belt. The scavengers don't care who goes into space; they've got no protection against radiation anyhow. Maybe they got very lucky on salvage." And yet he knew that MacWong was right; that the woman and her accent were too alien.

MacWong looked at him. "Nobody gets that lucky. What's wrong, Wadie, the miracle too much for you? This isn't some mediaman's fantasy, believe me. That's a ship from Outside, the first contact we've had with the rest of humanity in over three gigasecs. And the course they set away from the Rings could be taking them to the old capital, Lansing. If that's right, there can only be one reason why that ship is here: they don't know about the Civil War. They've come to Heaven lookin' for golden streets, and when they learn there aren't any left we'll never see 'em again. We can't let that happen. . . ."

"What good would one ship do us now?" He stared at the blank wall screen, against his will felt another question stubbornly taking form.

"*That* ship could do us all the good in the universe." MacWong picked up his platinum cat. "*That* ship is treasure, that ship is power . . . that ship could save us."

Wadie nodded, admitting to himself that the ship's immense fusion reactor alone could give the Demarchy the start to rebuild capital industry. And God only knew what other technology—functioning technology—they might have on board. Just the possession of a ship like that would change the Demarchy's snow dealings with the Rings forever. They could even bypass Discus and the Ringers, set up distilleries of their own out of Sevin's moons. . . .

For as long as he could remember he had lived with signs of a society gradually coming apart at the seams, alone in the wasteland that civil war had made of Heaven Belt. Because of its peripheral location, the Demarchy had survived the Civil War relatively intact. But the Main Belt had been destroyed, and now the Demarchy's only outside trade contact was with the Grand Harmony of the Discan Rings, and the Ringers were barely surviving. The Demarchy was slipping down with them, but because it had so much further to go, he had discovered that no one else seemed to realize the truth. They were blinded by the fierce, traditional self-interest that was the Demarchy's strength— and perhaps, now, its fatal weakness.

He had become a negotiator, hoping to bind up his people's self-inflicted wounds. He had believed that somehow the unifying element, the common bond of need that joined every human being, could be used as a force against disintegration and decay; that the Demarchy would continue, that they would find an answer. And with this ship . . . His imagination leaped, fell back as the question struck him down: Who would control a ship like that . . . and who could control the one's who did control it? "But as you said, that ship will go back home, once they see what's left of Lansing."

"Maybe." MacWong flicked dust off of his cuff. "But Osuna thinks they might need to refuel first. It's a long way home to anywhere from here. They're not likely to go back to the Rings to get fuel, under the circumstances. Which means they might come to us; if they need processed hydrogen, there's no place else to go. So I'm sendin' out everyone I can spare. I want you at Mecca. The distilleries will make it a prime target, and you're more experienced at dealing with—'aliens'—than anybody on the staff."

Wadie accepted the tacit compliment, the tacit distaste, remembered fifty million seconds spent in the Grand Harmony of the Discan Rings, and things it had shown him that he had never expected to see. He stood up, reaching for his hat. "What if they're not in the mood for negotiation?"

"I don't expect they will be. But that doesn't matter; you're paid to put them in the mood. Promise them anythin', but keep them here, stall that ship, until we can take control of it."

Wadie adjusted his beret, looked back from the mirroring wall. "What do you mean by 'we,' Lije? Just who *is* goin' to control that ship? It won't be the government, the people will see to that. And the first kid on the rock to own one—"

MacWong was not amused. "I sometimes wonder if you didn't spend too much time with the Ringers, Abdhiamal.

Dammit, Wadie, I'm not still questioning your loyalty, after two hundred megasecs. But there are still some who do; who think maybe you'd really like to see a centralized government here.'' He stopped. ''There'll be a general meeting to settle the issue once we have the ship.'' He leaned forward across the gargoyled desk. ''The Demarchy has to have that ship, an' no one but the Demarchy.''

''You're the boss.'' Wadie bowed.

''No.'' MacWong straightened. ''The Demarchy is the boss. We give the people what they think they want. Nothing else means anything. Forget that, and we're out of a job—or worse: If I was you, I wouldn't ever forget it.''

And knowing that MacWong never did, Wadie left the office.

RANGER (IN TRANSIT, DISCUS TO LANSING)

+ 130 KILOSECONDS

Betha left the hydroponics lab at last, began to climb up through the hollow silence of the central stairwell. She could no longer remember how many times she had climbed these stairs in the past two days; the duties of a crew of seven were an endless treadmill of labor for a crew of two. She passed the machine shop on the fourth level, kept on, reached their sleeping quarters on the third. One more level above, across the well, the flashing red light over the sealed dayroom door caught her unwilling eyes. She stopped, wrenched out of her fatigue by a fresh rush of grief.

She stepped hurriedly through to the corridor that ringed the stairwell on the third level, that gave access to seven private rooms . . . and all that remained of five human beings who were lost to her forever. To her right, Lara's room; everything in its place, mirroring the precision of Lara's mind. . . . Betha remembered the crisp directness of her voice across an examining table in the ship's infirmary; her graying hair, the warm concern in her gray eyes that denied her clinical detachment. There was a padded stool in Lara's room made from a cetoid vertebra; a *Color Atlas of the Diseases of Fish, Amphibians, and Reptiles*. She had been a medical researcher on Morningside, before their family had become a crew and she had become their doctor; but marine biology had been her hobby, her real love. And Sean, the smartass, had written a song, "Lara and the Leviathan," that swallowed her up in verses about this "cetoid monster," the *Ranger*. . . .

Through the open doorway directly before her, Betha could see a tangle of electronics gear, Nikolai's balalaika laid out on the sleeping bag on the platform of his bed. She pictured him, balding, bearded, brooding; with a voice like an echo escaping from a well. . . . A patient, skillful teacher, an electronics expert—a repairman, at home, serving the entire Borealis moiety. She remembered him laughing, dodging the shoe she had thrown at Sean for calling her *Ranger* a whale . . . .

She turned to her left, moved along the curving hallway against the currents of memory, like a woman wading into the sea . . . .Remembering Claire, placidly moon-faced, curly-haired; plump, fair farmer's daughter . . . Sean, the red-haired kid among them, only twenty-four . . .

Betha hesitated, finding herself before her own doorway. She glanced in, at her cluttered desk, her rumpled bedding. She moved on desperately, as though she would drown herself, to the next room . . . to Eric. Eric van Helsing, social scientist, moiety ombudsman, spokesman. . . .

> You are the rain, my love, sweet water
> Flowing through the desert of my life

The words of the song came unbidden into her mind, with the rushing heart of a desert wind on Morningside, the passion of first love:

> Let me flower first for you
> Let me quench my thirst in you
> Share the best and worst with you . . .

Her hands twisted, unconsciously; six rings of gold slid against one another, circling her fingers, four on the left hand, two on the right.

> Husband, have me for a wife.
> You are the rain. . . .

She sagged against the wooden doorframe, shutting her eyes; pressed her face against the coolness, supported by its noncommittal strength. He was gone; they were all gone: her crew, her family . . . her husbands and her wives. Her strength, the strength that came from sharing, was gone with them, bled away into the bottomless void. How would she go on? Loss was too heavy a burden, life was too heavy a burden, to bear alone—

Something brushed her ankles; she opened her eyes, focusing. The cat wove between her feet, meowing forlornly. "Rusty—" She leaned down to pick the cat up, seeing the day of their departure from Morningside: the squirming, mewing kitten held out to her in the grubby hands of her daughter, Kiki, as all their children solemnly presented their chosen gifts to each and every parent. There had been a dozen grandparents looking on—and siblings, cousins, nieces and nephews, their proud, hopeful faces washed with ruddy light, the Darkside Perimeter's eternal twilight.

All of them were waiting—all of them were a part of her. The children were waiting; she was not alone. But they were all beyond her reach now, across too much space and time; and it was her duty, her responsibility, to get this ship back to them—

She heard a sound in the hall, straightened away from the doorframe with Rusty still nested in her arms. She saw Clewell, wearing only his shorts, standing in the doorway of his own room, watching her.

"Betha—are you all right?"

"Yes . . . yes, I'm just tired, Pappy." *Tired of remembering, and remembering. How can one sudden sorrow turn all my joy to pain?* Watching him back she saw the same desolation, the same wound of loss that tormented her. She felt her fear rise again, *Oh, Clewell; don't let me lose you, too.* "May—I share your room again, tonight?"

He nodded. "Please. I couldn't get to sleep anyway, alone."

She followed him into his room, and in the darkness unbuttoned her plain cotton shirt, slipped out of her shoes and jeans. She settled into the double sleeping bag beside him, into his arms, and put her own arms around him gratefully in a gesture of long familiarity. He had not been her first husband, but he had been her friend through more years than she could remember now. He had been twenty-seven the year she was born, one of many uncles; but from childhood on he had been her favorite among all the relatives of her extended family. He had been an astronomer before he had become navigator on the *Ranger;* he had traveled from Borealis on the chill perimeter of day, out across the Boreal Sea and over the crumpled ice sheet of the darkside glacier, to his observatory under eternal night. Sometimes he had taken her along for a brief holiday of stargazing, free from the duties and clan responsibilities that even a child on Morningside was expected to fulfill.

When she was fifteen she had gone away for her technical training; and then to her first job as an engineer, at a production plant on the desert edge of the subsolar Hotspot. She had fallen in love with Eric, married him; and in time they had returned to the Borealis moiety. She had reentered Clewell's life as a grown woman, and she and Eric had been invited to join his family.

Morningside society grew out of the multiple-marriage family, and bonds of kinship were its strength and security. Marriage among the members of a clan—a parent family, its children, their own children—was socially taboo; but outside the central clan unit, cousins, aunts and uncles, nieces and nephews married freely, their sheer numbers providing the cultural and biological controls. A marriage could be made between a single couple or a dozen people, and each family made its own rules to live by. Special friendships between individuals in a large family were common, and either the group as a whole adapted, or a subgroup split off. Weddings were a cause for general celebration, but divorce was a common, and private, matter for a family group. Three of the members of Clewell's family that Betha had known as a child had divorced the rest, and his first wife had died, before she and Eric had joined the group, and Claire, and Sean, after them.

Betha remembered the brief, fond ceremony of marriage, the immense, freeform family celebrations that had followed. All of Morningside loved a celebration, because too much of the time they had too little to celebrate. And now there would be even less, whether the *Ranger* ever returned or not. . . .

Betha became aware of Clewell's hand moving slowly, tenderly along her side. But the warm instinctive response of half a lifetime died in her. She buried her face against the pillow, smothering the words, "Oh, Clewell, I can't . . . I can't. Not yet. I'm so sorry. . . ."

His arms comforted her again. "No, Betha . . . it's all right. This is all I really need. Just to hold you."

She felt Rusty stir and settle between their feet at the end of the bed. She moved deeper into Clewell's arms, closing him in her own, and fled from memory into sleep.

LANSING 04 (LANSING SPACE)

+ 190 KILOSECONDS

The night stretched like silence beyond their searching eyes; they took comfort in its vast, star-flecked indifference. They were scavengers, picking the bones of worlds; the night gave them shelter because it made no judgments, and they were grateful for its amorality.

Shadow Jack watched the night, or its image on the screen...sometimes in the dim, close womb of the ship his mind blurred, and reality began to merge with image. He stretched his legs and scratched, brushed back the dirty hair that drifted forward into his eyes and was as black as the night before him on the screen. One eye was green and one was blue; both were bloodshot, and his head throbbed with his heartbeat. The carbon-dioxide level in the cabin was well over three percent; he had long ago stopped noticing the smells. He pulled himself back down into his seat, looking at one errant hole pricked in the darkness, the one star that was not a star—that was something infinitely more insignificant, and infinitely more precious.

"I think we're close enough to begin scan."

He heard Bird Alyn's voice, barely audible as always, even in the quiet space between them. He swallowed twice, wetting his throat for words. "Right. Go ahead an' run it through."

She reached forward with her right hand, her crippled left hand resting on air as she typed the order into the reconnaissance-unit computer that would begin one more analysis. Shadow Jack watched the long fingers with the broken, dirty nails move over the shining board. He looked away, for the ten thousandth time, at the cramped squalor of the cabin: still finding no miracle to transform the welded scrap-iron husk into a ship to match the technological beauty of the reconnaissance unit. Almost in apology, he smoothed fingerprints from the coolness of the panel with his frayed sleeve. The recon unit was a prize of salvage, a more precious thing than his own life, because it gave his entire world a chance for survival. Before the Civil War it had been a prospecting unit, programmed for laser and radar analysis of asteroidal metals, organics, volatiles. Now it scanned for the old instead of the new, searching the debris of death for artifacts to stretch the lives of the living. He looked back at the display with Bird Alyn, waiting, watched figures print out on the flat glossy screen—

"Nothin'," Bird Alyn said. "No metallic reflections, no radioactivity, no effluent across the surface... nothin', nothin', nothin'. Nobody ever lived there—"

"It's always nothin'!" He struck at the thick, darkened glass of the port, at a universe beyond his control.

"Maybe next time. Besides, maybe somebody else's found what they need. We're not the only ship..." She faded.

"I know that!" His voice battered his ears, he put up his hands. "I'm sorry. My head hurts."

"So does mine."

He glanced at her. It wasn't a reproach; her red-rimmed eyes were gentle, before they dropped away, fading against her face and the matted cotton of her hair, brown into brown into brown. Freckles splattered her nose, darker brown. "Do you think there's any water?"

"I'll see." He unstrapped and drifted up out of his seat, one bare foot pushing off from the panel. He reached the wall behind them, read the gauge on the still. "Yeah, there's some in it now." He heard Bird Alyn's sigh as he forced the nozzle through the seal on the drinking cup, waited while it filled. "Point four liters." He sighed, too.

They drank, taking turns at the straw, savoring the water's warm flatness; Bird Alyn reached over to turn down the display on the screen. She hesitated, leaned forward. "This's strange ... look, the display's changed. There must be something else out there; we're getting a backscatter analysis of somethin' further on. Metal . . . low radioactivity. . .'' Her voice rose until he could hear her without trying.

Bubbles of water burst against his fingers and slimed his hand as he squeezed the cup too hard. ''A derelict?''

She tapped the controls briefly, and displayed a picture from the Matkusov mirror on the hull. A sun-bright needle threaded stars on the blackness. ''A ship,'' she whispered.

''Oh, reality, look at that. . . .''

''I never saw a ship like that. . . .''

''There's never been one.''

''Not since the War. It's got to be—''

''It's got to be—salvage.'' Shadow Jack leaned forward, touched the ship with a wet fingertip. ''I claim you, ship! With a ship like that . . . we could do anything with a ship like that.''

''It's driftin', no propulsion. That doesn't mean it's dead. . . .To find that, here, so close to Lansing—''

''It is dead, it must be more'n two gigasecs old. What's our relative velocity? Can we intercept?''

Her long fingers asked the questions, the board answered. ''Yes!'' She looked up. ''If we push, in four or five kilosecs.''

''Okay.'' He nodded. ''We push.''

They waited, caught inside webs of private dream, as the needle of light grew into an impossible golden insect: triple antennae bristling ahead, spokes on an invisible wheel, its body stretching behind, filament-fine, and broadening into a bulbous, pearlike tail. A *miracle*. . . .The word shone in his mind, and knowing there were no miracles, he believed, defiantly. A ship that could get them water to fill the marshes, to bring back life to the parched grasses and dying trees . . . to the dying people of Lansing.

His mind's eye looked back into the past, down across Lansing's fields from the limits of the sky, where he had worked suspended cloudlike fifty meters up, spinning the sticky patches to mend the plastic membrane of the world-shroud. Somewhere below him through the fragile canopy of trees, Bird Alyn had worked in the gardens. . . . Like a vision of Old Earth, he remembered her crossing the yellowed fields at dusk to meet him, her footsteps lifting her like a bird. When they

brought back that ship everything would be made right . . .
everything.

He looked over at Bird Alyn, at her hand—three crooked,
nerveless fingers and a thumb; felt her catch him looking. *Not
everything.* He frowned with helpless self-disgust; she turned
her face away as though the frown were meant for her. He
looked out at the night, cracking his knuckles as he remembered
why it would never be all right. He remembered the broken
sound of his father's reassurance, a third of a lifetime before—
as he left his only son sitting in the grass, abandoned to the
fatal light, and went back into the sheltering depths of rock
alone. . . .

RANGER (LANSING SPACE)

+ 195 KILOSECONDS

Betha heard the intruders banging faintly against the *Ranger*'s hull as they moved toward the main lock. "At least they didn't actually decide to cut their way in through the dayroom."

"Their manners don't impress me. You're just going to let them come aboard?" Clewell rebounded lightly from the wall as he pushed a covered cup into a cubby beneath the panel.

She nodded. "Pappy, we've been tracking that tin can of theirs for nearly two hours; it's hardly a warship. They must be in trouble—their drive is leaking radiation. Besides, we need information, and we haven't gotten much trying to monitor Lansing's radio traffic. Letting them come aboard is the safest, fastest way I can think of for getting some facts." She rubbed her eyes, until brightness drove back the vision of all her loves and one love, and the vision of a pursuing ship consumed by invisible fire. *Besides, there's been enough death.*

"And what happens if they happen to be crazy, like the others?"

"You said yourself they can't all be like that." Her hand closed over the bowl of her pipe. "But even if they are, they won't take the ship." She let the pipe drift as she rechecked the override program, a mosaic of lighted buttons on the control board. "Just keep your feet near the floor."

Someone had entered the lock. She felt more than heard them through the wall, felt her body tense as the lights changed above the lock entrance. The door hissed open. Two tall figures, amorphous in suits with shielded helmets, drifted into

137

the room. And stopped short, catching at the handrail set into
the wall. A muffled, accusing voice said, "What are you doin'
here?"

Betha's mouth quivered; helpless with disbelief, she began to
laugh. "W-what are *we* doing here?"

Clewell grunted. "We could ask you the same question; and
it wouldn't be nearly as funny. You're lucky you're here at
all."

"We thought the ship was dead; we didn't even know you
had power till your lock cycled." The taller suit shrugged.
"You've got a hole in you, and—you mean, you run this thing,
you already claimed it?"

"We didn't 'claim' it, we own it." Betha caught her shoe
under a restraining bar and twisted to face them. "I'm Captain
Torgussen. This is my navigator. We let you come aboard
because I thought you were in trouble. Your craft's power unit is
leaking radiation; you're barely mobile. Is that why you intercepted
us?"

The silvered faceplates showed her nothing, only her own
tiny, distorted face. The voice was tinnily indignant. "What do
you mean, leaking? There's nothin' wrong with our drive. We
been out a megasec this trip, already."

Nothing wrong? Betha glanced at Clewell, saw his eyes
widen. A megasecond—a million seconds—nearly two weeks.
Whoever faced her, whatever insanity moved them, their lives
were going to be short and sick spent in a ship like that.

The blind face went on, "We intercepted because we thought
this ship was salvage, and we wanted it. I guess it's not." A
gloved hand rose from his side, threatening, holding something
that glinted. "But we have to have it. So we're taking it
anyhow. Get away from those controls." The hand twitched.

"You'll regret it. The two of you can't possibly handle this
ship." Betha carefully let go of the bar, her feet centimeters
above the rug, her eyes on the panel. When she touched one
button this room would be under an abrupt one-gravity acceleration:
one stranger would fall onto his head, the other one onto
his back. . . . *And break their necks?* She hesitated. "If you
think—"

A blob of mottled fur squeezed out of a plastic port in the

wall; Rusty *mrr*ed pleasantly, circling the knees of the two strangers. Betha herd one of them gasp. He pulled back, bouncing off his companion. "Look out!" Rusty darted sideways eagerly, enjoying the game. "What is it?" Their voices rose. "Shadow Jack, get it off me!"

Betha jerked the computer remote from her belt and threw it. It struck the stranger's arm and his weapon flew out into the room. Clewell moved past her to pick it from the air; the hijackers pressed back against the wall, waiting.

"Rusty. Come here, Rusty," Betha put out her hand, and brindle ears twitched. Slowly Rusty crossed the room to sidle along her waist, purring in satisfaction. Betha scratched under the ivory chin, stroked the brindle back, shaking her head. "Rusty, you make fools of us all."

"Well, I'll be damned!" Clewell began to pry at the weapon; strange shapes bristled along its length. "This is a can opener! Corkscrew, fork . . . I don't know what this one is. . . ." He pulled himself down. "I've heard of ailurophobes, but I've never seen the likes of those."

Betha caught hold of a chair back, unsmiling. "You two. Get out of the suits." They stripped obediently, rising like moths from the cocoons of their spacesuits: a man and a woman . . . a boy and a girl, incredibly tall and thin, neither of them more than seventeen; barefoot, in drab, stained coveralls. She blinked as the smell of them reached her. "You've just committed an act of piracy. Now tell me why I shouldn't send you out the airlock for it, without your suits." She wondered if the threat sounded as credible or as terrible as she wanted it to.

The boy glared back at her, across a muffled fit of coughing. The girl moved away from the wall. "It was a matter of life and death." Her voice was strained in a dry throat.

"We offered you help. That's not good enough."

"Not *our* lives." She shook her head. "We need the ship for . . . for . . ." She broke off, her eyes darted away, searching the room.

"Bird Alyn, they know why we need the ship." Betha saw a terrible, impersonal hatred settle on the boy's face as he turned back. "You know what we are. We're just junkers, we haven't done anything to you. Let us go."

Betha laughed again in disbelief. "You 'just' tried to commandeer my ship. I 'just' asked you why I shouldn't space you for it. But you expect me to let you go? Is everyone in Heaven system crazy?" Her voice almost slipped out of control.

"It doesn't matter." He let go of the handhold, shrinking in on himself. "We'll die anyway. Everybody's dying. You've still got it good, you Demarchists. It's nothing to you to let us go, or let us die."

Betha found her pipe drifting, fumbled in a pocket of her jacket for matches. "We're not 'Demarchists,' whatever they are. We've come from another system to establish contact with the Heaven Belt; and since we've been here we've been attacked twice, with no provocation, near the rings of Discus and by you. Now, maybe you believe you had some sort of 'right' to do it, and maybe you can even make me believe it. Or maybe I'll take you to Lansing to be tried for piracy." She saw surprise on their faces. "But first you're going to answer some questions . . . . To begin with: who are you, and where do you come from?"

"I'm Shadow Jack," the boy said, "and this's Bird Alyn. We come from Lansing." He waited.

"But that's where we're going—" Clewell began.

"*Why?*" the girl said, blinking.

"Because it's the government center for Heaven Belt." Betha looked back at her sharply. "Your capital must have come on hard times."

"You really are from Outside, aren't you?" Shadow Jack folded his legs like a buddha, somehow managing not to flip over backward. "There hasn't been any Heaven Belt for two and a half gigasecs."

"What?"

He stared, silent; Clewell gestured threateningly at the cat.

"There was a war, the Civil War. Everything got blown up, all the industry. Nobody can keep anything going anymore, except the Demarchy and the Ringers. They're the only ones far enough out to have snow on some of their rocks. Lansing is capital of zero, nothin'; most everybody in the Main Belt's dead by now."

"I don't understand," Betha said, not wanting to understand. *Oh, God, don't let our very reason for coming here have been pointless.* . . . "We heard that Heaven Belt had the perfect environment, that it had a higher technology than any Earth colony, than even Old Earth."

"But they couldn't keep it goin'." Shadow Jack shook his head.

Betha saw suddenly the fatal flaw the original colonizers, already Belters, must never have considered. Without a world to hold an atmosphere, air and water—all the fundamentals of life—had to be processed or manufactured or they didn't exist. And without a technology capable of the processing and manufacturing, in a system without an Earthlike world to retreat to, any Dark Age would mean their extinction.

As if he had followed her thoughts, Shadow Jack said, "We'll all be dead, in the end, even the Demarchy." He looked away, forcing out the words, "But our rock is out of water now. Everybody there'll die if we have to go around Heaven again without it. And we don't have a ship left that'll take us to the Ringers—to Discus—for hydrogen to make more. We've got to find enough salvage parts to put one together. That's why we were out here. It's a gigasec before we'll be close enough to Discus to make the trip again."

"You trade with Discus for hydrogen?" Clewell broke her silence.

"Trade?" Shadow Jack looked blank. "What would we trade? We steal it."

"What happens if the—Discans catch you in their space?" Clewell reached under the panel for his covered drinking cup, pulled up on the straw.

Shadow Jack shrugged. "They try to kill us. Maybe that's why they attacked you: they thought you came from the Demarchy. Or maybe they wanted your ship; anybody'd want this ship. Can you run it all with only two people—?" His mismatched eyes wandered speculatively.

"Not two untrained people," Betha said, "in case you still have any ideas. It's not even easy for us. There were five more people in our crew; the Discans killed them all." *And all for nothing.*

He grimaced. "Oh." Betha saw the girl flinch.

"One more question." She took a deep breath. "Tell me what this 'Demarchy' is, that everyone seems to confuse with us."

Shadow Jack glanced away, suddenly oblivious, as Clewell finished his drink. Bird Alyn licked her lips, rubbed her mouth with a misshapen hand.

Out of water. . . . A memory of her own children, too far away, too long ago, dimmed their hungry faces. She looked down at her own hands, at thin golden rings, four on the left hand, two on the right. "Well?"

Shadow Jack cleared his throat, his eyes daring her to offer water. "The Demarchy—it's in the trojan asteroids sixty degrees ahead of Discus. It's got the best technology left now. They made the nuclear battery that runs our electric rocket; they're the only ones who can make 'em anymore."

"If they're so well off, why do they have to rob the Discans?"

"They don't have to. Usually they trade, metals for the processed snow, for water and gases and hydrocarbons. Sometimes things happen, though—incidents. They both want to come out on top. I guess they think someday they'll build up the Belt again. They're wrong, though. Even if they'd quit fightin' each other, it's too late. Anybody can see that."

"Not exactly a cockeyed optimist, are you, boy?" Clewell said.

Shadow Jack frowned, scratching. "I'm not blind."

"Well, Clewell." Betha felt Rusty snuffling against her neck, settled the cat on her shoulder. Claws hooked cautiously into the weave of her denim jacket. "What do you think? Do you think it's the truth? Did we—come all the way to Heaven for nothing?"

He rubbed his face with his hands. She saw his own wedding bands reflecting light, three on the left hand, three on the right. "I guess it's possible. It's so insane, it's the only way to explain what we've been through."

She nodded, glanced at the haggard faces of the waiting strangers: *Not exactly angels.* Victims, of a tragedy almost beyond comprehension; a tragedy that had reached into her own life, and his, to destroy the dreams of another people as it had destroyed its own. This Heaven, like all dreams of heaven, had been a fragile thing; perhaps none of them had ever been meant to be more than a dream. . . . She lit her pipe, calmed by its familiarity, before she searched the two tense, expectant faces. "I'll make you a proposition, Shadow Jack, Bird Alyn. You said Lansing needs hydrogen for water; we need it for fuel. We're going after it now. Come with us and tell us things we need to know about this system, and if we succeed we'll share what we get with you."

"How do we know you'll keep your word?"

Betha raised her eyebrows. "How do we know you've told us the truth?"

He didn't answer, and Bird Alyn frowned at him.

"If you're honest with us, we'll be honest with you." Betha waited.

He looked at Bird Alyn; she nodded. "I guess anythin's better than our chances alone. . . . But what about the *Lansing 04*? We can't junk it—"

"We can take your ship with us. It's possible we can repair your shielding."

His mouth opened; he shut it, embarrassed. "We—can we radio home, Lansing, and tell 'em what happened?"

"Yes."

"Then it's a deal. We'll stick with you, and tell you what we know." They relaxed visibly, together, hanging like rag dolls in the air.

Clewell folded his arms. "Just keep one thing in mind—that the captain meant it when she told you it takes training to run the *Ranger*. We'll be accelerating at one gravity. Even if you took over the ship and contacted your people, they'd never catch up with you. All you'd get out of it would be a one-way journey to forever."

Shadow Jack started to answer, kept silent.

"I'll see to your ship, then. Clewell, will you take them below? Maybe, ah . . ." She looked back; tactfulness eluded her. "They could use a shower."

"A shower of what?" Bird Alyn murmured.

Betha paused, inhaling smoke. "Well . . . water."

"Unfortunately we're out of champagne." Clewell pushed off for the doorway.

Shadow Jack laughed uneasily. "Enough water to wash in?"

She nodded. "Use all you want; please. We have plenty. And soap. And clean clothes, Clewell—"

"With pleasure." He led them eagerly out of the room into the echoing stairwell; Rusty floundered after them. For a moment Betha drifted, listening, her eyes taking in the grass-greenness of the rug, the dust-blue sky color of the walls, that had been designed to keep seven people from going mad during more than three years tau of close confinement. She realized the vast and pernicious emptiness that had filled the room, the entire ship, in the past few days; like the greater desolation beyond its hull. Realized it, now that suddenly it was no longer true. She heard the sprayers go on, and faint yelps of excited laughter.

Clewell reappeared in the doorway, carrying Rusty. "I hope they don't drown themselves . . . though anything would be an improvement."

She looked down at the pipe in her hand, remembering how he had carved it for her during their final days in Borealis. Surprising herself, she began to smile.

RANGER (IN TRANSIT, LANSING TO DEMARCHY)

+ 290 KILOSECONDS

Bird Alyn moved slowly through the green light of the *Ranger*'s hydroponics lab, her frail body twitching with the effort of standing upright in one gravity. She hummed softly, oblivious to discomfort, pulled into the past by the cool constant moistness and the smell of apples, the hum of insect life. Shadow-dapples slid over the tiles, merging and breaking with the drift of canopied leaves, showering sparks of veridian fire over the viscous liquid inside clear, covered vats.

The setting was strangely alien, like everything in the bountiful alien wonderland of this starship. But a fern or a tree were always the same, no matter how gravity or its lack contorted them. They were living things that required her—that rewarded her care and attention with a leaf or a blossom or fruit to give her people life. The only living things that willingly absorbed all the love she could give them, that never turned away from her because she was an ugly, ungainly cripple. . . .

Bird Alyn drew the dipstick out of another vat, studied the readings, shook it down. She sighed and slid down the vat's side to sit on the floor, massaging her swollen feet. They prickled, with the sluggishness of poor circulation. She leaned back, looking up through the shifting green; imagined she saw the milky translucency of the Lansing shroud and Shadow Jack working as a spinner, instead of the banks of fluorescent lights.

She had counted the kiloseconds, the very seconds of every Lansing day, until Shadow Jack came down to join her for the day's one meal. Silent, moody, filled with futile anger—he was still the one person in her world who responded to her, who pushed out of his own shadowed world each day long enough to show her kindness. Sometimes she wondered whether he was kind out of pity; never caring whether he was. She was simply grateful, because she loved him, and knew that love had no pride.

From childhood she had understood that she would work in the surface gardens; through all of her life she had seen why—that she was different, deformed. Her parents had trained her to use a computer, because they had accepted that she would have to work at a job where the radiation level was high; they had equipped her to work on a ship, to do the best she could for the survival of her world. But beyond that they had withdrawn from her, as people withdraw from a mistake that has ruined their lives, as they withdraw from the victim of a terminal disease.

And she had never questioned her own inferiority, because Materialist philosophy taught her that every individual must accept the responsibility for his own shortcomings. She had gone to work on Lansing's surface almost gladly; glad to escape from the world of normal people, glad to lose herself in the beauty of the gardens, solitary even among her fellow defectives.

And then she had discovered Shadow Jack sitting dazed and frightened in the grass at the entrance to the tunnels.... Shadow Jack, who had grown up used to a normal life of security and acceptance. Who had been told, suddenly, that he was not normal, and cast out into an alien world, ashamed, abandoned. She had comforted him, out of compassion and her own need; his need had bound him to her, and made them friends.

But as they grew older she began to want more than just his friendship; even though she knew that it was wrong, and impossible. On the Lansing surface the mores of the tunnels were distorted by neurosis, or by need, until each person became literally responsible for his own actions, and endured whatever consequences followed. She had seen things that would have appalled her parents, and learned to see that they did no one any harm; to see that that was the only real criterion for what was right or wrong. And there were things that had made her afraid, once she understood them, and grateful that Shadow Jack slept beside her every night in the sweet cool grass or between the sheltering pillars of the abandoned state buildings.

But Shadow Jack would never touch her, never let her ease the anger and helpless resentment that never let him go. And helpless in her own futility, she kept her silence, knowing that it was wrong for a defective to want a husband; impossible, that Shadow Jack could ever love an ugly, clumsy cripple....

Bird Alyn saw someone draw aside the insect netting and enter the lab, brushing aside grasping shrubs and vines. She struggled to her feet, trying to make the figure into Shadow Jack... heard a woman's voice call softly, "Claire?"

Bird Alyn stood on tiptoe, fading against the flowers in her green shirt and blue jeans. "What?" She teetered and almost dropped the dipstick. She clutched it against her side with her crippled hand. "Oh, Betha."

Betha stared at her in return; shook her head, bemused and disconcerted.

Bird Alyn smiled, glancing down. "I—I thought it was Shadow Jack. He said he was goin' to come watch me work...." Her smile collapsed.

"Pappy's got him cornered; he's showing him around up in the shop." Betha touched a fern, pulled off a yellowed frond, pulling the dead past loose from the present. She looked back, concern showing on her tired, pale face. "Are you sure you want to do this, while we're still at one gee?"

Bird Alyn nodded. "It's all right. I sit down a lot, and just—watch, and smell, and listen. It's so long since I worked in the gardens. Do you mind?"

"No... no. You don't know how much I appreciate it. There's enough work on this ship for seven people. And—Clewell's not as young as he used to be." The captain's eyes left her, searching the green shadows. "You have the perfect touch, Bird Alyn... I almost took you for a dryad when I came in."

"What... what's that?"

"An enchanted forest spirit." Betha smiled.

"Me?" Bird Alyn twisted the dipstick, laughed her embarrassment. "Oh, not me. . . . These plants take care of themselves, really, it's easy . . . not like Lansing . . . they look so different here, so thick and squat. . . ."

"These?" Betha looked up.

"On Lansing things keep growin' up, they don't know when to quit; it's tricky, the root systems have to go down to bedrock and catch hold . . . and with the mutations . . ." Bird Alyn faded, suddenly aware of her own voice.

Betha sat down on a tiled bench, reached out for the strangely shaped thing half-hidden under a fall of vine. "Claire's guitar. Claire used to run hydroponics, and she used to play for the plants. It's a musical instrument," seeing Bird Alyn's puzzled expression. "We all used to come down here in the evenings, and sing. She used to claim the plants enjoyed the music, and the emotional communion. Of course, Lara would claim it was just the carbon dioxide they wanted . . . and Sean said it was the hot air." Her mouth curved wistfully. "And Eric—Eric would say that it was probably a little of everything. . . ." Her hand rose to her face; Bird Alyn counted four plain golden rings, surprised, before it dropped again.

"How . . . um, how does it work?" She had known a girl once who had a whistle made from a reed. "The—guitar, I mean." She leaned back against a heavy wooden shelf, pushed up onto its edge with an effort.

"I can't really give you a proper idea. Claire was an artist; I only know a few chords. But it's something like this . . . ." The captain settled the guitar across her lap, positioned her fingers on the strings. She stroked them tentatively.

Bird Alyn shivered. "Oh . . ."

Betha smiled; her fingers changed position on the strings and the shimmering water of sound altered. She began to sing—almost unconsciously, Bird Alyn thought—in a warm, clear voice merging with the flow of music:

> "Understanding comes from learning
> No one ever changed a world.
> Live your life, don't waste it yearning,
> You can't change it, little girl—"

Bird Alyn felt her throat tighten, looked down at her twisted hand, blinking hard.

She heard the captain take a long breath, caught in her own memories. "I'm sorry." The clear voice strained slightly. "I should have found something a little more cheerful."

"Please . . . will you—will you do some more?" Bird Alyn looked up.

Betha's face eased. "All right—they aren't much, just some old folk tunes. But it's a strange thing, the effect that everyone singing together had—the bond that grows between you, the feeling of unity. It gives you the strength to carry on, when things are hard. And it's hard to hate anyone when you're singing with them; hard to be angry. . . . .

> "Together we continue,
> Our song will never end.
> Sister, brother,
> Father, mother,
> Share their lives with one another:
> Woman, man and friend. . . ."

Bird Alyn leaned forward, like a flower leaning into the light. "Morningside must be a beautiful place!"

Betha made a sound that was not quite a laugh. "No, it's . . . Yes. Yes . . . in a way. In its own way." Her fingers brushed the strings again.

"I wish I could do that. . . . Do you . . . know any love songs?" The captain looked up sharply; Bird Alyn realized that somehow she had said the wrong thing.

"I'll be glad to show you what guitar chords I know, Bird Alyn, if you want to learn to play. Maybe the plants miss it."

Bird Alyn folded her arms. "I—I don't think I have enough fingers. . . ."

The captain's face froze with a second's embarrassed awkwardness. "Oh. Well, I think I can reverse the strings for you; I've seen a guitar played left-handed before. If you'd like me to?" She smiled again.

"Oh, yes!" Bird Alyn slipped down off of the shelf, left the dipstick hanging absently in the air. It slid through her nerveless fingers and clattered to the floor. Instinctively a long bare foot stretched to pick it up; she lost her balance, and fell. "Lousy luck!" Sprawled on the floor, she fumbled after the rod, shook it and checked the readings, while a familiar hot flush crept up her face.

The captain came to her, caught her arms and lifted her effortlessly to her feet. "Are you all right?" Betha's hand brushed her arm reassuringly, as a mother might have touched her. "It takes a while, doesn't it, to break the habits of a lifetime."

Bird Alyn looked down, confused by her solicitude. "Does anybody ever got used to this? If you're not born used to it, I mean. . . ."

Betha stepped back. "In time. Morningside's pull is less than one gee, but we've been at one gee on the ship for three years, and we don't even notice the difference anymore. I've read some Old World studies on one-gee adaptations from low gravity. It's possible, but it takes about a year—thirty or forty megaseconds—to get back to the minimum endurance you had at zero gee. And there are long-term stress effects on the body. But they decided that you'll last, with good medical care, if you wanted to go through with it."

"I think I'd rather go home," Bird Alyn said.

"Me too." Betha nodded.

But you can't. Bird Alyn glanced down at her, blushing again. "I mean . . . I always say the wrong thing!"

"No. It's all any of us want, Bird Alyn. And we're going to do it." Betha studied the pattern of gleaming rings on her hands; they tightened suddenly.

Bird Alyn listened to water dripping somewhere, thought of tears. She heard someone else enter the lab; recognized Shadow Jack this time.

Betha smiled, a pleased, private smile, following her glance. She turned back to the bench, picked up the guitar. "I'll change the strings for you, when I get the chance. But now I'd better get back to work. We're almost into Demarchy space; you won't have to put up with gravity much longer." She started away toward the door, spoke to Shadow Jack as she passed him. Bird Alyn watched his own gaze fix on her, follow her, with admiration that was almost adoration. Bird

Alyn felt envy stir, turned it inward habitually. Her mouth tightened with pain as though she had turned a knife.

But Rusty struggled in Shadow Jack's arms, meowing with sudden impatience as they caught sight of her. Shadow Jack let the cat drop, still half afraid of its strangeness. Rusty trotted ahead to butt against Bird Alyn's bare ankles; Bird Alyn leaned over and picked the cat up, and a pink tongue sandpapered her chin joyfully. Rusty settled, purring, onto her shoulder. She thought of the embroidered hanging in the room that was hers now: a cross-stitched portrait of Rusty, and the words, A HOME WITHOUT A CAT MAY BE A PERFECT HOME, PERHAPS—BUT HOW CAN IT PROVE ITS TITLE? Bird Alyn let herself imagine an entire world filled with living creatures, and music; not a fruitless dream, but reality. The kind of world Lansing must have been, in the time she had never known; the kind of world it could never be again.

"I thought Rusty was looking for you," Shadow Jack murmured, self-conscious. "I'll bet if there were ten animals on this ship, every one would want to be with you."

She met his eyes hesitantly, forgetting everything in the miracle of his smile.

Raul Nakamore, Hand of Harmony, settled back into the padded acceleration couch, weightless, held down by straps. He wedged the light wire headset into a slot on the panel, through with the radio, through arguing with his half-brother Djem. So he was wasting the Grand Harmony's resources . . . risking his life . . . risking the crews of three ships to pursue a phantom. So he was leaving Snows-of-Salvation unprotected from a Demarchy attack to chase a ship that could run rings around the ships of the Grand Harmony, even this high delta-vee strike force. A ship from Outside . . . a crippled starship, that had left behind a tiny spreading cloud of debris and human remains. A ship that had eluded their grasp once—but that might not be able to do it again. It was worth the gamble. *But Djem never could see beyond the end of his own nose.* Raul half-smiled.

Somewhere five thousand kilometers below him, silhouetted against the silvered detritus of the Discan rings, the lump of frozen gases that was Snows-of-Salvation held the Grand Harmony's chief distillery. It had been constructed with Demarchy aid, and it was crucial to the Harmony's survival, and the Demarchy's. His brother was in charge of Snows-of-Salvation, would do anything to maintain its safety. But if the Demarchy decided to attack here in the Rings, even this "secret weapon" couldn't stop them from doing fatal damage. And in spite of what too many in the Navy believed, the Demarchy would never try it, anyway. Djem would never be able to see that, but Raul would stake his career on it—*had* staked his career on it.

The Demarchy would never attack them . . . unless it had that starship. But if the Grand Harmony took it first—

"Sir." Sandoval, the balding ship's captain, interrupted his pattern of thought diffidently. "Everything's secure for ignition. At your command—"

Raul nodded, unbuttoning his heavy jacket in the unaccustomed warmth of the control room. *Been underground too long.* . . . He sighed. "Proceed."

Sandoval settled back into his own seat, spoke orders into his headset that would coordinate with the crews of two other ships. There was no video communication; video was used only to impress the enemy. Raul studied the complexity of the control board, banks of indicators spreading up the walls in the cramped space around them. Most of it was prewar artifact computing equipment, installed to give these ships superior maneuverability in combat. They were one segment of the Grand Harmony's high delta-vee defense force, specially designed, specially equipped with a fuel-to-mass ratio of one thousand to one. Although Raul Nakamore ranked in the highest echelons of the Harmony navy, he had always maintained that their existence was a pointless waste of desperately needed resources; and for that reason he had never been on board one of these ships before. But now the starship had changed his mind; as it could change the very future.

He sank heavily into the padded seat as the ship's liquid-fuel boosters ignited and thrust grew to a steady two gravities, more than slightly painful on his Belter's frame. He checked the chronometer on the panel. Thrust would continue for thirteen hundred seconds, boosting them to sixteen kilometers per second . . . and in that time, expend seven thousand tons of fuel: the outer stages of the three ships themselves, and of seven drones. And still it would take them over two megaseconds to reach Lansing—and their quarry might not even be there. Raul settled down to wait, trying not to imagine the waste, but rather to remember what had made him so certain it was worth it. . . .

He had been sitting in his office, studying endless shipping schedules, when the confidential report had reached him: a ramscoop starship, origin unknown, had crossed the path of a naval patrol . . . and had destroyed one of their ships before escaping. He had studied the report for a long time, with the warmth of the methane stove at his back and the chill silence of Heaven's future ahead of him. And then he had noticed that a meeting was announced, his presence was required.

He left his office and made his way along the endless dank, slightly smoky corridors from the Merchant Marine wing. The government complex made up the greater part of the tunnel-and-vacuole system that honeycombed the subsurface of the asteroid Harmony, that had been the asteroid Perth in the time before the Civil War, before the founding of the Grand Harmony. The chill began to eat its way through his heavy brown uniform jacket; he pushed one hand into his pocket, using the other to push himself along the wall. He was a short man, barely 1.9 meters, and stocky, for a Belter. There was a quality of inevitability about him, and there had been a time when he had endured the cold better than most. But he was a career navy man, and he had spent most of his adult life on ships in space, where adequate heat was the least of their problems. But for the past sixty megaseconds since his promotion he had been an administrator, and learned that the only special privilege granted to an administrator was the privilege of managing a double workload.

He passed through large open chambers filled with government workers, into more hallways identical to the ones he had just left, into more chambers—as always experiencing the feeling that he was actually traveling in circles. Unconsciously he chose a route that took him through the computing center, guided by past habit while he considered the future. The past and the present surprised him as he became aware of his surroundings: of the crowded rows of young faces intent on calculation, or gaping up at his passage.

He looked toward the far corner of the chamber, almost expecting to find his own face still bent over a slate of scribbled figures. He had worked in this room, twelve-hundred-odd megaseconds ago, starting his career while still a boy as a computer fourth class. A computer in the oldest sense, because the sophisticated machinery that had borne the Discans' burden of endless computations had been lost during the Civil War. After the war, the Grand Harmony had learned the hard way that it would never survive without precise data about the constantly changing interrelationships of the major planetoids. And so they had fallen back on human computation, using the inefficient and plentiful to replace the efficient but nonexistent, as they had had to do so many times.

A bright child could learn to do the simpler calculations, and so bright children were used, freeing stronger backs for heavier labor. Raul remembered sitting squeezed onto a bench with another boy and a girl, huddled together for warmth. His nose had dripped and his lips were chapped, and he had stared enviously at the back of his half-brother Djem, who was one hundred and fifty megasecs older and a computer second class. The higher your rank, the closer you sat to the stove in the center of the room.... By the time Djem made first class, Raul had joined him, and been rewarded with warmth and one of the few hand calculators that still worked.

Their common grandfather had proved Riemann's Conjecture, and become the best-known mathematician—and perhaps the best-known human being—to come from the Heaven Belt; but then the war had come, and made him only one more refugee. He had been on vacation in the Discan rings when the war began, and his loyalties had been suspect. But his mathematical skill had been undeniable—and now, two generations later, the residue of his genius had put his grandsons on the path to success in a new regime.

"Only through obedience do we earn the right to command...." Raul left the computer room, and his youth, behind; the universally colorless moral admonitions from the inescapable wall speakers crept back into his consciousness along with the cold. He wondered how long it would be before the news of the alien starship worked its way into the communal broadcasts, between the Thoughts from the Heart and the lectures on Demarchy decadence—and what form it would take when it did. He did not object to the constant intrusion into his life. He was used to it. It was as much a part of the life he knew as the cold. He realized that it served a purpose, distracting the people from the cold and the endless dreary labor of their daily lives, reinforcing their sense of unity and dedication to the group.

But if he felt no resentment toward the broadcasts, neither

did he take them seriously anymore. He had realized long ago that they were just as much propaganda as the Demarchy's own lurid displays of unharmonious advertising. . . . The Demarchy, that still lived in warmth and comfort—thanks to the distilleries of the Grand Harmony—but which kept the people of the Grand Harmony from sharing that comfort. It refused to sell them the atomic fission batteries that were still the Demarchy's major source of power, for heat, for light, for shipping, for the few factories that still operated. No existing factories operated at more than one percent efficiency in the Grand Harmony—except for the distilleries—and virtually their only source of heat and light came from the inefficient burning of methane (because the Rings had a surplus of volatiles, but that was all they had).

Raul pushed the thought out of his mind, as he pushed aside the more painful truth that his people, all the people in the Heaven Belt, were doomed. Regret was useless. Hatred was counterproductive. Raul faced the truth, and faced it down. He saw the road ahead clearly, saw it grow steeper and more difficult until at last it became impossible. But he moved ahead, one step at a time, strengthened by the knowledge that he had done all that was humanly possible.

There had been a time when he had absorbed every word of the broadcasts, and believed every word. He had hated the Demarchy then, with the blind passion of youth; and because he was young and competent and expendable, he had been sent on a mission of sabotage into Demarchy space. And he had failed in his mission. But to his intense humiliation, the perversity of the Demarchy's media-ruled mobocracy had transformed him into a popular hero, taking his impassioned last denunciation of their own aggression to heart . . . and the Demarchy had sent him home, a shamefaced messenger of goodwill, to open negotiations for the construction of a distillery that would benefit both the Demarchy and the Grand Harmony.

But relations between the Harmony and the Demarchists had never improved past that one act of cooperation, the real purpose of which lay in their shared needs. Independent Demarchy corporations still violated Discan space, and only their overall economic weakness kept them from outright seizure of the Harmony's vital resources. The Grand Harmony still denounced the Demarchy, and blamed them for its own marginal existence.

But because of his experience in the Demarchy, the conviction that good and evil were as easily marked as black and white, that every question had a simple answer, had been lost to him forever. And as he came to see that the Demarchy was not totally evil, he had realized that it was not totally to blame for the Harmony's precarious survival, either. He had come to see the greater, totally amoral and totally inevitable fate that drew the Grand Harmony, and the Demarchy as well, down the road of no return.

And when he had seen that there was no turning back, no turning aside, he had transferred from Defense to the Merchant Marine; to serve where he believed he could function most effectively, and make the Harmony's passage down that road as easy as possible.

Raul reached the hub of the government complex at last, felt the eddies of cold draft catch him as he moved out into the suddenness of open space. Overhead the ceiling was dark and amorphous, but he knew that its vault was a surface of clear plastic, not solid stone. Once it had opened on the stars, and the magnificence of Discus—when the Rings of Discus had been the water-well for the entire Heaven Belt. But now the clear dome was blocked beneath an insulating pack of snow: the dome had become too great a source of heat loss.

He made his way across the multiple trajectories of other drifting government workers, most of them navy men like himself. He returned their raised-hand salutes automatically, his mind reaching ahead of him into the restricted meeting room where his fellow Hands sat in a private conference with the Heart.

Raul settled quietly into his seat, waiting for the meeting to be called to order. He sat at the end of the long table farthest from the position of the Heart, as the newest officer to achieve the rank of Hand. He nodded to Lobachevsky on his right, looked past, identifying the faces of officers and advisers down the table. He noted without surprise that they had split into opposing factions, as usual—the defense faction on one side, the trade faction on the other. He had settled with the trade faction, as usual. Seeing the bare, shining tabletop as a kind of no-man's-land between them, he smiled faintly.

A single word silenced the muttered speculation; Raul turned his attention to the head of the table, rose with the rest, acknowledging the arrival of the Heart—the triumvirate that controlled power's ebb and flow in the Grand Harmony. Chatichai, Khurama, and Gulamhusein: like a many-faceted Hindu deity, indistinguishable from one another, or from their staff, in the drab sameness of their bulky clothing . . . but unmistakably set apart by an indefinable self-satisfaction—and the unharmonious ambition that had taken them to the top, and made them struggle to stay there. Raul knew the kinds of stress that worked on them, and was grateful that he had already risen above the level of his own ambitions.

The three men at the head of the long table settled slowly onto the seat, a sign for the officers to do the same.

"I assume you all read the communications that brought you here"—Chatichai spoke, taking the initiative as usual—"and so I assume that you all know that fifty kiloseconds ago our navy encountered a ship like nothin' that exists anywhere in this system. . . ." He paused, looking down; Raul recognized a tape recorder on the table before him. "This's a report from Captain Smith, who was in charge of the patrol fleet that encountered the craft." He pressed a button.

Raul drifted against the table, listening, and watching expressions change along the table's length. They had taken the intruder for a Demarchy fusion ship violating Discan space, at first. Then, as they began to close and a woman's voice answered their challenge, they realized that what they had come upon was something totally unexpected. The ship had broken away from them, accelerating at an impossible sustained ten meters per second squared; it had destroyed one of their own closing craft almost casually, with nothing more than the deadly effluence of its exhaust. But they had fired on the escaping ship, and they had recorded a small, expanding cloud of debris. . . .

An undercurrent of irritation and excitement spread along the table. "Why the hell didn't Smith give that woman port coordinates, when she asked for 'em?" Lobachevsky muttered beside him. "Damn sight more reasonable than tryin' to take the ship by force. Losin' a ship—serves him right." He glared across no-man's-land at the opposition. Raul kept his own face expressionless.

Chatichai raised his eyes, and his voice. "The question before us now, gentlemen, is not whether Captain Smith acted in the best interests of the Grand Harmony—but what further action should be taken concernin' that ship. I don't think anybody here will disagree that the ship had to come from outside the system. . . ." He paused; no one did. "And I don't think we have to detail for anybody here what a ship like that could mean to our economy . . . or to the Demarchy's, if they get hold of it instead." Another pause. "But is it feasible, or even possible, for us to get our hands on that ship? And in any case, what action should be taken to ensure that it doesn't fall into the Demarchy's hands instead?"

Raul studied the dull sheen of the table's scarred plastic surface, seeing beyond it as he listened with half-attention to the debate progressing along the table's length: The ship was damaged . . . the ship could still outrun anything that Heaven Belt could send after it. The ship might seek out the Demarchy because of the attack . . . there was no reason to believe its crew would trust anyone in the Belt, now. The ship was the answer to the Harmony's survival . . . the ship was a phantom, and pursuing it would only waste more resources they couldn't afford to lose. . . .

Raul glanced up, pushing his own thoughts into order. He rarely spoke out unless he had been able to consider all sides of a question; he had learned long ago that selective silence was a more effective tool than a loud voice. Since his promotion to Hand, he had used it to good effect to earn himself a reputation for getting what he wanted, for building up the efficiency of the Merchant Marine and the influence of the trade faction. Finding a lull, he broke into the discussion: "As you all know, I've been opposed to the development and support of our high delta-vee force from the beginnin'. . . ." He searched the faces along the table, seeing resentment glance along the far side, feeling the gratification that spread from Lobachevsky along his own side. He had believed, along with the minority of others, that the Demarchy posed no realistic threat to the safety of the Grand Harmony, that the resources used to maintain a defense fleet would serve the Harmony's interest better if they were employed to bolster trade within the Rings, and even with the

Demarchy itself. Because he understood that the status quo was
deterioration, and that nothing could overthrow that order. . . .
"But this's a situation I never foresaw. In this situation, I have
to admit I'm glad we have a high delta-vee force available...and I
am in favor of usin' it to pursue that ship—" Voices indignant
with betrayal cut him off; he saw the hostility re-form into
surprise across the table. "I know it's a gamble. I know it's
probably a futile one, and the odds against us capturin' that ship
are damned high. But they're not astronomical: the ship's
damaged, we don't know how severely. It may be that they'll
lie low at Lansing, if Lansing's still alive; it's worth the loss,
worth the gamble, to find out. We've got this damned high
delta-vee force whether we want it or not—let's put it to some
rational use! If we know this much about the starship, you can
count on the Demarchy knowin' just as much—and bein' just as
interested. I don't believe they're any threat without that ship;
but if we don't get the ship, and they do, anything we do is
goin' to be academic from then on.

"I propose that the closest available high delta-vee force be
readied as soon as possible to pursue the starship toward
Lansing. And I request that I be given command. . . ."

The acrimony of the final debate faded from his mind as
acceleration's false gravity abruptly ceased, leaving his body
free in a sudden release from tension. He had won, in the end,
because there was no one in the room who could question his
sincerity, or his determination to achieve whatever goal he set
himself. And so these ships would continue in a drifting fall
toward Lansing. And if the life-support systems held out, they
would find—something; or nothing. The cards had been laid
down; the Grand Harmony had gambled on the last chance it
would ever have.

RANGER (DEMARCHY SPACE)

+ 553 KILOSECONDS

"No, that won't work either. They could see this isn't a prewar ship." Bird Alyn shook her head; her hair, caught into two stubby ponytails, stood out from her head like seafoam.

"Then there's nothing more I can suggest, offhand." Betha glanced from face to face, questioning. Clewell sat firmly belted into a seat; Bird Alyn and Shadow Jack sprawled in the air, totally secure in the absence of gravity. The five-day journey along sixty degrees of Discus's orbit had transformed them, superficially: Their skin and hair were shining clean, their long, gangly bodies forced into dungarees and soft pullover shirts. But the start of one-gee acceleration had left them crushed on the floor like reedflies, and they still winced with the stiffness of wrenched muscles, and the memory. And there were other memories, that shone darkly in their hungry eyes and quick, nervous words; memories out of a past that Betha was afraid to imagine and glad she would never know.

"I still say you should leave the Demarchy alone." Shadow Jack struck out a thin bronze foot, stroked Rusty gingerly as she drifted past. "We should've gone for the Rings. It's a lot safer to steal it from them. If you ask me—"

"I wasn't asking—that." Betha smiled faintly. "I want to trade, not steal. . . . I already know how 'safe' it is in the rings of Discus, Shadow Jack."

"But the Demarchy's worse. They've got a higher technology."

"How much higher? You don't really know. And they aren't looking for us, either. With your ship to ferry us in, we can slip in and out of a distillery before they even think about it. But what do we trade for hydrogen?'' She repeated the inventory again in her mind, struggling with the knowledge that only Eric would know what was right, what to offer, what to say. Only Eric had been trained to know. . . . *Oh, Eric*—

Shadow Jack frowned, pulling at his toes. Bird Alyn caught Rusty, set her spinning slowly head over paws in the air. Rusty caught her own tail and began to wash it. Bird Alyn laughed, inaudible.

"The cat," Shadow Jack said. "We could give them the cat!"

"What?" Clewell straightened indignantly.

"Sure. Nobody's got a cat anymore. But nobody in the Demarchy could know we didn't; Lansing had a lot of animals, once. And it's just what the Demarchists go for: somethin' really rare. The owner of a distillery, he'd probably give you half his stock to own Rusty."

"That's ridiculous," Clewell said.

"No . . . maybe it's not, Pappy." Betha spread her hands, and Rusty pushed off toward her. "I think he's got a point. Rusty, would you like to live like a queen?" She gathered Rusty into her arms, gathered in the precious memories of her children's faces, as they handed her the gifts of love. She felt her throat tighten against more words, wondering what payment would be demanded next of them; knowing that whatever the emotional price was, they must pay it, if it would buy this ship's passage home to Morningside. She saw sharp sorrow on Bird Alyn's face; saw Bird Alyn struggle to hide it, as she hid her own. "Besides . . . we haven't been able to think of anything else that wouldn't give us away. Any equipment we tried to trade would be obvious as coming from outside the system. We'll be taking enough of a risk as it is."

"I know." Clewell looked down. "You're the captain."

"Yes, I am." Betha pulled herself down to the control panel, tired of arguing, tired of postponing the inevitable. There was no choice, there was only one thing that mattered—saving this ship—and she must never forget it. . . . She watched the latest surveillance readouts, not seeing them. The *Ranger* was well within Demarchy space now. They had detected dozens of asteroids and heavy radio traffic. They had identified Mecca, the largest distillery, eight million kilometers away, with a closing velocity of ten kilometers per second—only hours of flight time for the *Ranger*. But it would take the *Lansing 04* two weeks, decelerating every meter of the way, to close the distance-and-velocity gap between them and Mecca. Her stomach tightened at the prospect; the extra shielding they had put on board the Lansing ship cut the radiation levels to one-sixth of what they had been, but the readings were still too high. And yet if the *Ranger* came any closer to an inhabited area, the risk of detection would be too great.

> The road to Morning
> Is cut from mourning,
> And paved with broken dreams. . . .

"I'm going to Mecca, Pappy," she said at last. "I'm going to get us our ticket home."

Clewell sat firmly in his seat as Bird Alyn floated free above his head. They watched together while the *Lansing 04*, a battered tin can with a reactor tied to its tail, fell away into the bottomless night. He looked back from the darkness to Bird Alyn's face, her own dark eyes still fixed on the screen. "I'm glad you're here. There's too much—emptiness on this ship, alone."

She blinked self-consciously, her arms moving like bird wings as she turned toward him in the air. Her eyes rarely met his, or anyone's; as if she was afraid of seeing her own image reflected there. "I wish—I wish she hadn't taken Rusty."

He had to strain to hear her, wondered again if he was getting a little deaf. "So do I. She did what she thought was best. . . . And you wish she hadn't taken Shadow Jack."

She still looked down; her head twitched slightly.

"She did what she thought was best." He thought of Eric, who had been trained to know what was best; remembered Betha's anguished doubt, in the private darkness of their room. "She means everything to me, too."

Bird Alyn looked up at him at last. "Are—are you Betha's father?"

He laughed. "No, child; I'm her husband. One of her husbands."

"Her—husband?" He almost thought he could see her blush. "*One* of her husbands? How many does she have?"

"There are seven of us, three women and four men." He smiled. "I take it that's not so common here."

"No." Almost a protest. "Are . . . the rest of them back on your—planet?"

"They were the crew of the *Ranger.*"

She jerked suddenly. "Then—they're all dead, now."

"Yes, all. . . ." He stopped, forcing his mind away from the empty room on the next level below, where a gaping wound opened on the stars. Deliberately he looked back at Bird Alyn, saw her embarrassment. "It's possible to be in love with more than one person, you know."

"I always thought that meant somebody had to be unhappy."

He shook his head, smiling, wondering what strange beliefs must be a part of the Lansing culture. And he wondered how those beliefs could survive, when a people were struggling for their own survival.

On Morningside the first colonists had struggled to survive, expatriates and exiles fleeing an Earth where the political world had turned upside down. They had arrived in a Promised Land that they discovered, too late, was not the haven they were promised—discovering at last the lyrical irony in the name Morningside. Tidally locked with its red dwarf star, Morningside turned one face forever toward the bloody sun, held one side forever frozen into night. Between the subsolar desert and the darkside ice lay a bleak ring of marginally habitable land, the Wedding Band . . . until death did them part. The fear of death, the need to enlarge a small and suddenly vulnerable population, had broken down the rigid customs of their European and North American past. They were no longer the people they had once been, and now, looking back across two hundred years of multiple marriage and the freedom-in-security of extended family kinship, few Morningsiders saw reason in their own past, or any reason to change back again.

Bird Alyn folded her arms, hiding her misshapen hand. And Clewell realized that perhaps the people of Lansing had had no choice in their customs either. If the radiation levels were as high as those on the *Lansing 04*, even one percent as high, then the threat of genetic damage could force them into breeding customs that seemed strange or even suicidal anywhere else. The whole of Heaven Belt was a trap and a betrayal in a way the Morningside had never been: because Heaven had promised a life of ease and beauty in return for a high technology, but it damned human weakness without pity.

Clewell was silent with the realization that whatever Morningside lacked in comfort, it made up for in a grudging constancy, and that even beauty became meaningless without that. . . .

"How did you and Shadow Jack end up out here?"

She shrugged, a tiny waver of her weightless body. "I can work the computer; my parents programmed the recon unit. And Shadow Jack wanted to be a pilot and do something to help Lansing; he won a lottery."

"Your parents let you go, instead of going themselves?" He saw Betha suddenly, in his mind: a gangly, earnest teenage girl, helping him take the measure of the immeasurable universe...saw his own children, waiting for him across that universal sea. He covered a sudden anger against whoever had sent their half-grown daughter out in a contaminated ship before they would go themselves.

Bird Alyn looked down at her crippled hand. "Well, you can only go if you work outside. . . ."

"Outside?"

"Lansing's a tent world...we have surface gardens, an' a plastic tent to keep in an atmosphere." She ran her hand through her hair, her mouth twitching. "You work outside if you can't have children." For a moment her eyes touched him, envious, almost accusing; she turned back to the viewscreen, looking out over isolation, withdrawing into herself. "I think I'll take a shower."

He laughed carefully. "If you take too many showers, girl, you'll wrinkle up for good."

"Maybe it would help." Not smiling, she pushed off from the panel.

He looked out at the barren night, where all their hopes lay,

and where all the dreams of their separate worlds lay ruined.
Pain caught in his chest, and made him afraid. *Help me, God,
I'm an old man. Don't let me be too old.* . . . He pressed his
hands against the pain, heard the sprayer go on and Bird Alyn's
voice rise like warbling birdsong, beginning a Morningside
lullaby:

> "There's never joy but leads to sorrow,
>   Never sorrow without joy.
>   Yesterday becomes tomorrow;
>   I can't stop it, little boy. . . ."

"There it is," Shadow Jack said, with almost a sigh. "Mecca rock."

Betha watched it come into view at the port: a fifty-kilometer potato-shaped lump of stone, scarred by nature's hand and man's. Mecca's long axis pointed to the sun; the side nearest them lay in darkness, haloed by an eternal corona of sunglare. As they closed she began to see landing lights; and, between them, immense shining protrusions lit from below, throwing their shadows out to be lost in the shadow of the void. She identified them finally as storage tanks—enormous balloons of precious gases. *At last* . . . She stirred in the narrow, dimly lit space before the instruments, felt her numbed emotions stir and come alive. She filled her congested lungs with the dead, stale air, heard a fan go on somewhere behind her, clanking and ineffective; wondered whether she could ever revive a sense of smell mercifully long dead. It was small comfort to know that the claustrophobic misery of their journey would have been worse without the overhauling they had done on board the *Ranger*. Two strangers from Lansing could teach even Morningsiders something about toughness. . . . The *Ranger* came back into her mind, and with it the galling knowledge that they could have crossed Demarchy space to Mecca in one day instead of fifteen, in perfect comfort—if things had been different. "But we're here. Thank God. And thanks to you, Shadow Jack. That was a good job." Her hand stroked his arm unthinkingly, in a gesture meant for someone else. He started out of his habitual glumness, looking embarrassed and then something more; reached to scan the radio frequencies. Static and voices broke across the cabin's clicking silence.

"Did—did you love one of them best?"

She sighed. "Yes . . . yes, I suppose I did. It's something you can't help feeling; I loved them all so much, but one . . ." *Who isn't here, when I need him.* She shook her head, her eyes blurred, and sharpened again as a piece of the real world moved across them. "Out there, Shadow Jack." She leaned closer to the port, rubbed the fog of moisture from the glass. "A tanker coming in."

He peered past her. They saw the ship, still lit by the sun: a ponderous metallic tick, its plastic belly bloated with precious gases and clutched inside three legs of steel, booms for the ship's nuclear-electric rockets. "Look at the size of that! It must be comin' in from the Rings. They wouldn't use that on local hauls." He raised his head, following its downward arc. "Down there, that must be the docking field."

She could see the field clearly now, an unnatural gleaming smoothness in the artificial light, cluttered with cranes and ringed by more mechanical parasites, gorged and empty. Smaller craft moved above them, fireflies showing red: sluggish tows in a profusion of makeshift incongruity. *Another world . . .* She listened, watching, matching fragments of one-sided radio conversations with the movements of the slow-motion dance below them: boredom and sharp attention, an outburst of anger, unintelligible humor about an unseen technicality. "Shouldn't they be receiving our signal?"

He nodded. "They are. I guess they'll call us down when they feel like it."

Rusty stirred in the air above the control board, batted listlessly at the twined cord of his headset. "Poor Rusty," Betha murmured, reaching out. "Your trip in this sauna is almost over. . . ." The rawness of her throat hurt her suddenly.

Shadow Jack twisted guiltily, stroked Rusty's rumpled fur. "Bird Alyn really let me have it for makin' you take Rusty away. She didn't want to lose her. She loves plants, makin' things grow—things that are alive. . . ." His mouth twitched, almost a smile, almost sorrow. "I guess Rusty was about the most wonderful thing of all, to Bird Alyn."

"You miss her."

"Yeah, I . . . I mean, well, she's the only one who can really use the computer."

"Oh."

He glanced back at her, knowing what she hadn't said. "We just work together."

She nodded. "I thought maybe you—"

"No, we don't. We're not married."

She felt her mouth curve up in scandalized amusement. "I admire your self-restraint."

His blue and green eyes widened; she saw darkness settle across them again. "There's no point in wanting what we can't have. It's only keeping alive that matters—everybody keeping alive. If we can't get water for Lansing, then it's the end, and it's stupid to pretend it's not. There's no point in . . . in . . ." He looked down at the control panel. "Those daydreamers! Why don't they answer us? What do they need, a miracle?"

A voice broke from the speaker, "Unregistered ship— what the hell are you doing up there, running so dark?"

Shadow Jack turned back to her, speechless; she smiled. "Now try wishing for hydrogen."

Shadow Jack took them in, cursing in the glare, to a moorage on Mecca's day side. " 'Not registered for main field.' Those nosy bastards! How come we couldn't land in the dark, like the rest of those damn charmed tankers?" He stretched, leaning back, and cracked his knuckles.

"I suppose they don't want some tourist crashing into the distillery." Betha relaxed at last, at the reassuring sound of magnetic cables attaching to the hull outside.

He pushed himself away from his seat. "That doesn't help us. If something goes wrong, we'll have a hell of a time gettin' out of here this way." He moved toward the locker that held their spacesuits.

She sighed and nodded, reaching out to catch Rusty. "We'll

just hope nothing goes wrong,'' thinking that whoever had named him for shadows had named him well.

Betha clung momentarily to the edge of the open airlock, looking down, and away, to where the world ended too suddenly: the foreshortened horizon, like the edge of a gleaming, pitted knife blade against the blackness. And beyond it the stars, scarcely visible, impossibly distant across the lightless void. She saw five torn bodies, falling away into that void where no hand could stop their fall, where no voice could ever break the silence of an eternity alone . . . . She swayed, giddy. Shadow Jack touched her back.

"Go on, push off." His voice crackled, distorted by his feeble speaker.

Behind his voice in her receiver she heard Rusty's fruitless scratching inside the pressurized carrying case; she saw figures coming toward them, moving along a mooring cable fastened amidships. She pushed herself out of the hatchway with too much force, drifted through a graceless arc to the ground. She began to rebound, caught at the mooring line and steadied herself. *A mistake* . . . And she couldn't afford to make another one. She was dealing with Belters, and she'd damn well better act like the Belters did. She felt tension burn away the fog of her exhaustion, as she watched Shadow Jack land easily on the bright, pockmarked field of rubble behind her. Above him she saw the sun Heaven, a spiny diamond in the crown of night, frigid and faraway—bizarre against the memory of her sun's bloody face in a dust-faded Morningside sky. As she turned away from the shadowed hull of the *Lansing 04* she could see other ships moored; the stark light etched the crude patchwork of misshapen forms on her mind, overlaying her memory of the *Ranger*'s ascetic perfection.

"You staying here long?"

She couldn't see the port man's face through the shielding mask of his helmet; she hoped her own faceplate hid her as well. "No longer than we have to."

"Good; your exterior radiation level's medium-high. Not good for the plants."

She looked down at the stained rubble, wondered if he was making a joke. She laughed, tentatively.

"You're the Lansing people?" Eight or ten more figures spilled out from behind him, with bulky instruments she realized were cameras.

"What are you here for?"

"Is it true that—"

"I thought everybody in the Main Belt was dead?"

She shifted Rusty's case, getting a better grip on the cable; their voices dinned inside her helmet. "We want to buy some hydrogen from your distillery." She looked back at the port man. "I hope we don't have to walk to the other side?"

He laughed this time. "Nope. Not if you're paying customers."

Betha noticed that he was armed.

". . . heard you Main Belters mostly scrounge and steal," the voices ran on. "Have you really got somethin' there to trade for snow?"

"How is it that a woman's in your position; are you sterile?"

"What's in the box?"

They surrounded her like wolves; she drew back, appalled. "I don't—"

"That's for us to know, junkers," Shadow Jack said suddenly. "We're not here for handouts. We don't have to take crap from any of you." He caught the guard's rigid sleeve. "Now, how do we get to the distillery?"

Betha's jaw tightened, but the guard raised his hands. "All right, you media boys, get off their backs. Take a picture of the ship; they didn't come from Lansing to pose for you. And be sure to mention Mecca Moorage Rentals. . . . No offense, buddy. Just follow the cable back to the shack; they're holdin' the car for you. Welcome to Mecca."

"Say, is it true that—"

Shadow Jack drifted over the cable and pushed past them to the far side. Betha followed, her motion painfully nonchalant. "Thanks—buddy," she said.

The guard nodded, or bowed, and so did Shadow Jack.

"Christ, who *were* those people?" She glanced over her

shoulder as they boarded the single canister car of the ground transport; behind them someone sealed the door. She heard Shadow Jack mutter, "Unreal." There were two others in the cabin, she saw, wishing it was empty, glad there were only two and hoping they didn't have cameras. Ahead through the plastic dome, the filament-fine monorail track stretched away over the barren brightness. Beyond the platform on her right she saw what looked to be a circular hatchway set into the surface of the rock; above it was a sign: HYDROPONICS CO-OP. She realized that the guard hadn't been making a joke; the chunk of naked stone that was Mecca was a self-sufficient world, riddled with tubes and vacuoles that supported life and all its processes. Too much radiation was bad for the plants. . . .

Her thoughts jarred and re-formed as gentle inertia pressed her against the seatback. Rusty snuffled and scratched in the carrier, making a sound like static inside her helmet; suddenly, painfully, she remembered their destination, and their purpose. And that only Eric could help her now—but Eric was gone. "I wonder if this was built before the war?" She glanced at Shadow Jack's mirrored faceplate, needing an answer.

"Yes, it was." The voice in her helmet belonged to a stranger.

She started; so did Shadow Jack. They turned to look at the two others in the car; one, long legs stretching casually, reached up to clear his faceplate. "Eric—!" Her hand rose to her own helmet, hung motionless, almost weightless.

Curling dark hair, a lean, pensive face; the sudden smile that was almost a child's. The brown eyes looked surprised . . . amber eyes . . . not Eric, not . . . *Eric is dead*. She pulled down her trembling hand, leaving her faceplate dark. "I—I'm sorry. I thought . . . I thought you were someone I knew."

He smiled again, politely. "I don't think so."

"You're the ones who came to trade, from Lansing." The second voice rasped like grit. "They said the car was waiting for you."

Betha winced, unseen. She looked across at the shorter, somehow bulkier figure; wondered if it was possible to find a fat Belter. Her own 1.75 meters felt oddly petite. The woman cleared her helmet glass, showed a middle-aged face, brown skin and graying hair, eyes of shining jet.

"Yes, we are." Betha kept her faceplate dark to hide her paleness, felt Shadow Jack fidget beside her.

"You're the first ones I've ever seen from the Main Belt. What's it like back in there? It's good to learn that you aren't all—"

Rusty emitted a piercing yowl of desolation, and Betha gasped as it rattled against her ears.

"My Lord, what was that?" The woman's gloves rose to her own shielded ears.

"Ghosts," Shadow Jack said, "of dead Belters."

The woman's face went blank with confusion. Betha glanced at the man, saw him smile and frown together; he met her unseen eyes. "Never heard a noise like that. Maybe we passed over a power cable." She realized that not only the cat, but the carrying case transmitter must be an unheard-of novelty in Heaven now.

The woman looked shaken. "I'm sorry. That wasn't gracious of me, anyway. Just that you're such a novelty. I'm Rinee Bohanian, of Bohanian Agroponics." She gestured at the sunside behind them. "Family business, you know."

"Wadie Abdhiamal." The man nodded. "I work for the Demarchy."

"Don't we all?" the woman said.

"The government."

She peered at him with a suspicion edging on dislike. "Well." She looked back at Betha. "And what's your name? You know, I'd like to get a look at a genuine spacewoman—"

"Betha Torgussen. I'm sorry, my helmet's broken." She crossed her fingers; no one showed surprise. "And this is—"

"Shadow Jack," Shadow Jack said. "I'm a pirate."

"Pilot," Betha murmured, irritated, but the others laughed.

"That's a Materialist name." The man was looking at Shadow Jack. "I haven't met one of those in a long time."

"Everybody's one, on Lansing. But it's just wishing. Nothin' left to contemplate." He was almost relaxing, the hard edge softening out of his voice.

The man glanced at Betha, questioning.

"Not everyone." She turned away toward the front of the car, looking for a reason to stop talking. She heard the woman asking the man what he did for the government, didn't listen to his reply. They were nearing the terminator; it ran smoothly to meet them, like a cloud shadow crossing the broken desert lands of Morningside. Beyond the terminator, parallel to the edge of shadow, lay a line of leviathans: stubby poles of steel crowned by rings of copper, strung with serial blinking lights, red and green.

"That's the linear accelerator," the woman said. "It's used to ship cargo that doesn't have to move too fast, or go too far. . . . What exactly does a Materialist think?"

They crossed the terminator, blinking into night as though a switch had been thrown, and passed between the looming towers of the accelerator. The dark-haired man sat listening to Shadow Jack; unwillingly Betha felt her eyes drawn back to his face.

". . . and you're given a word, the name of somethin' material that's supposed to set each of you apart and shape your being somehow. Half the people don't even know what their words mean, now. . . ."

She watched the stranger in silence, helpless, flushed with sudden radiance, chilled until she trembled. . . . Remembering Morningside, the first days of her love for Eric: remembering an engineer and a social scientist ill-met in a factory yard on the Hotspot perimeter, and blazing metal in the unending heat of endless noon. . . . Remembering their last days on Morningside: a film of ice broken in a well in unending dusk, where the crackling edge of the darkside ice sheet, stained with rose and amber by the fires of sunset, shattered its mirror image in the Boreal Sea. Borealis Field, where her family, as the newly chosen crew of the *Ranger*, worked together preparing for an emergency shipment, preparing themselves for the journey across 1.3 light-years to icebound Uhuru.

They had been selected from all the volunteers willing to leave homes and jobs because another world in their trade ring needed help; but they had never imagined the journey that in the end would be assigned to them. Word had come from the High Council that a radio message had been received from

Uhuru, and aid was no longer needed. They had been given a new, unexpected destination, the Heaven system, and a goal that was more than simple survival for another world or their own. She remembered the celebration, their pride at the honor, their families' families' pride.... Remembered Eric leading her quietly from the crowded, fire-bright hall, for one brief time alone before a journey that would last for years. His gentle hands, and the caressing heat of the deserted sauna; their laughing plunge into banked snow ... the heat of passion, the wasting cold of death ... fire and ice, fire and ice.... She cried silently, *Eric, don't betray me now.... Give me strength.*

The car slipped on through darkness.

The car drifted to a stop beneath the slender towers of their destination, among the ballooning storage sacs that glowed with ghostly foxfire—dim yellows, greens, and blues, excited by the ground lights into a strange phosphorescence. Betha shook off the past, looking out into the glowing forest of alien shapes. She heard the woman: "... how your Lansing fields are like our tank farmin'. Of course, there's no shortage of water for us; we have the snow stored below in the old mining cavities. We've got enough to last forever, I expect." A pride that was unconsciously greed filled her smile. The government man glanced at her; Betha saw him show quick anger and wondered why. Shadow Jack pushed abruptly up out of his seat, stabilized himself instinctively. Tension tightened him like a wire again; she wondered what showed on his face.

They followed the man and woman through disembodied radio noise and the impersonal clutter of workers on the platform, came to another hatch set into the solidness of the surface rock. Below the airlock they entered tunnels that sloped steeply downward, without seeming to, into the heart of the stone. Betha felt her suit grow limp with the return of air pressure, making her movements easy. Sounds carried to her now, dimmed by her helmet, as she passed new clusters of citizens, some suited and some not, all mercifully oblivious; she wondered again at the behavior of the cameramen on the field.

They followed a rope along the wall of the main corridor, where the rough gloves of pressure suits had scraped a shallow trough along the pitted surface. Ahead and below she saw the tunnel's end, opening onto a space hung with fine netting. Curious, she drifted out onto the ledge at the chamber's lip.

"Oh..." Her breath was lost in a sigh. She stood as Shadow Jack already stood, transfixed by a faery beauty trapped in stone. Before them a vacuole opened up, a kilometer or more in diameter: an immense, unnatural geode filled with shining spines of crystal growth, blunt and spike-sharp, rainbow on rainbow of strident, flowing color. The hollow core of air was hung with gossamer, silken filaments spread by some incredible spider....

The images began to re-form in her mind; she realized that this was the city, the heart of life in the Mecca asteroid—that the crystal spines were its towers, reaching up from the floor, out on every side...down, from the ceiling. *Why don't they fall*—? Her thoughts spun, falling; she felt someone's hands clutch her arms. Her mind settled, her feet settled softly on the ledge. Angrily she forced her eyes out again into the chamber's dizzy immensity. People drifted, as tiny as midges, along the gossamer threads; light ropes, strung across the wide, soft spaces. The towers grew thickest, probing the inner air, on ceiling and floor, in the direct line of gravity's faint inexorable drag. The buildings that hugged the hollow's curving sides were shorter, stubbier, enduring greater stress. The towers shivered delicately in the slight stirring currents of ventilation; they were not solid crystalline surfaces, but trembling tents of colored fabric stretched over slender metal frames.

"It was a 'model city' before the war." She saw that the government man was the one who had caught her arms; he released her noncommittally. "It used to be a gamin' center. Now we play more practical games; most of those towers belong to merchant groups." The man unlatched his helmet, lifting it off and looking at her expectantly. "The air's okay here."

She reached up only to switch on her outside speaker; her skin prickled, wanting the touch of his eyes. "Thank you" —she tried to sound unsure—"but I'll wait." Shadow Jack, speakerless, stood looking out into the city, sullenly content to play deaf and dumb. "Can you tell us which of those belongs to someone who can sell us hydrogen?"

"Hydrogen?" His wandering glance leaped back to her shielded face. "I thought you'd want air. Or water."

"We do. We need water—we have oxygen. So we need hydrogen, obviously." Rusty yowled; she closed her ears.

"Oh." His face relaxed into acceptance. "Obviously. . . . You know, it's not often that I meet a woman who's chosen to go into space. Is it common on Lansing?"

"Going into space isn't common on Lansing, anymore." Betha remembered suddenly that the stranger's golden-brown eyes belonged to the enemy. "If you could just point out the distillery offices for me?"

"Down there"—he pointed—"that cluster of long greens on the floor; lot of offices for the distilleries in that bunch. Tiriki, Flynn, Siamang . . ."

"Distilleries? There's more than one?" *Should I have known?* She swore under her breath.

"Sure are." But he smiled, tolerantly. "This is the Demarchy, the people rule; we don't like monopolistic practices. It infringes on the people, they won't stand for it. . . . I know— let me take you around."

"No, really—"

"It's the least I can do, when you've come this far." He put two fingers into his mouth and whistled shrilly, three times. She flinched; he turned back to her, surprising her with a quick, apologetic bow. "That's how you call a taxi here, now. Mecca's manners are going to hell. . . . Heaven is going to hell." He laughed oddly, as if he hadn't expected to say it out loud. "I'm from Toledo, myself."

"What—ah—did you say you do for the government?" She looked away uneasily across the ledge. The woman from the train had disappeared. *Why is he staying with us like this?*

"I'm a negotiator. I try to keep things from getting any more uncivilized than they already are." Again the quick, pained laugh. "I settle disputes, work out trade agreements . . . look into unexpected visits."

She almost turned, froze as she saw the cameramen from

moorage emerge from the tunnel. "Shadow Jack!" She caught
his arm. "Stay with me, don't get separated."

The voices closed in on them, ". . . in that run-down ship?"

"Who are you making your deal with?"

"How much—"

"What do you have—"

Mediamen and staring locals crowded them, ringed them in,
jostling and interrupting. She saw the government man elbowed
aside as the air taxi drifted up to the ledge, grating to a stop.
She pushed toward it, gesturing to Shadow Jack. It was
canopied and propeller-driven, steered by hand by a bored-
looking, well-dressed boy. "Where to?"

"To—to Tiriki's. And hurry." She ducked her head at the
edge of the striped canopy, felt the footing bob beneath her in a
sea of air, seeing crystals reflecting above and below. Shadow
Jack followed. The taxi sank outward and down, away from the
grasping mob on the precipice.

". . . Torgussen!" She heard the government man shouting
after her.

She looked back; her hands rose to her helmet, fumbling,
pulled it off. She saw his face change with surprise . . .
recognition . . . loss. . . . *Stop it!* There was no resemblance,
there could be no recognition . . . *Eric is dead!* She clung to a
canopy pole, feeling the air currents stir her pale, snarled hair,
soothe her burning face. *Oh, God, how often will this happen?*
Shadow Jack hung over the edge, looking down, up, sideways,
as they passed the artificial sun caged in glass suspended in the
cavern's center. Slowly she sank onto a seat, forcing her own
senses to absorb her surroundings, jamming the echoes of the
past.

The cavern was filled with sound, merging and indistinct:
laughter, shouting, the beehive hum of unseen mechanisms.
She looked ahead, aware now of subtle differences of richness
and elaboration among the massed towers; of balconies set at
insane angles; of dark hollows in the bedrock walls, tunnels to
exclusive homes. And gradually she became aware of the
mingling of spices that perfumed the cool filtered air; she
breathed deeply, tasting it, savoring it, easing her stuffy head.

Unimpressed, the driver stared through her at the emerald pinnacle of their destination.

They pushed through the soft elastic mouth of the roof entrance, into a long empty corridor stretching twenty-five meters down to the building's base on rock. Betha began to sink toward it, almost imperceptibly, and with no sensation of falling; they began to pass doorways. Shadow Jack unlatched his helmet, pulled it off and shook his head. She heard him take a deep breath. "Where are we?" His hair was plastered like streamers over his wet face; he wiped it back with a gloved hand.

"Tiriki Distillates. The man from the train suggested it." She hesitated, not wanting to tell him what she suspected.

"Bastards." His mouth pulled back. "I'd like to see this place blow up. They wouldn't be so—" Anger choked him.

Betha watched him, feeling sorrow edged with annoyance. She reached out; her glove pressed the soft, resistant covering on his shoulder. "I know how you feel...I know. But so did the people in that train car. Take the chip off your shoulder, right now, or I'll knock it off myself: I can't afford it. I want something from these people, and so do you, and it's a hell of a lot more important than what either one of us feels. So put a sweet smile on your face while we make this deal, and keep it there if it gags you." Somewhere the memory broke loose: "'Smile and smile...and be a villain.'" She smiled, breathing the cool scented air, and willed his eyes to meet hers. Slowly he raised his head; as he looked at her, for the first time, she saw him smile.

Someone pushed through a doorway almost at her side. He caught the flap, looking at her with frank disbelief.

She rubbed her unwashed face, embarrassed. "We'd like to negotiate for a load of hydrogen. Can you tell us who to see?"

A mask of propriety formed. "Of course. Sure. At the far end of the hall, the Purchasing Department. And thanks for doing business with Tiriki." He ducked his head formally and moved past them, pushing off from wall to wall, rising like a swimmer through the brightening sea-green light. They went on down, into the depths.

"Look at this rag." They heard the voice before they reached the doorway. "What do they know about it? They don't know a damn thing."

"No, Esrom."

Betha brushed aside the flaps and they went in, wearing smiles rigid with tension.

"I could do better myself. That's what we ought to do, do it ourselves. We ought to hire some mediamen and put out our own paper—"

"Yes, Esrom."

"—tell them our side. Look here, Sia, 'monopolistic' . . ."

The golden-skinned, ethereally beautiful woman behind the counter looked up at them; her arching eyebrows rose. The golden-skinned, strikingly handsome man with the printout turned. *Brother and sister,* Betha thought, *and . . . impeccable.* They wore soft greens, colors flowing into a background of sea-green light, the woman in a long embroidered gown, the man in an embroidered jacket, lace at his sleeves. She pictured what they saw in return, brushed at her stringy hair.

But the man said, "Sia, did you ever see anything like that? Look at that skin, and hair, together. . . ." His dark eyes moved down her suit, identified it, looked back at her face. "But she's been in space." Interest faded to regret.

The woman tapped his arm. "Esrom, please!" She charmed them with a smile. "And what can we do for you?" She smoothed her sinuously drifting, raven-black hair along her back, tucked strands under her lacy cap.

"We'd like to buy a load of hydrogen from you." Betha felt herself blushing crimson while they watched in fascination. She tried to hide her annoyance. "One thousand tons."

"I see." The man nodded slowly, or bowed, looking vaguely surprised. He reached for a clipboard on a chain. "Do you want it shipped?"

"No, we can move it ourselves."

"Where are you coming from?" The woman's voice was as fragile as her face, but with no hint of softness.

"Lansing." Shadow Jack smiled, tall and thin and genuine, with one blue eye and one green.

"The Main Belt!" Brother and sister looked at them again; silent, this time, with a morbid awe. A newscast appeared on the screen behind them, flashing pictures between lines of print. "That's quite a trip," the man said quietly. "How long'd it take you?"

"A long time." Betha gestured up at worn, dirty faces, not needing to force the grating weariness into her voice. "And it'll be even longer going home. We'd like to get this settled as soon as we can."

"Of course." He hesitated. "What—er, what did you want to offer in trade? We're limited in what we can take, you understand. . . ."

Charity begins at home. She saw Shadow Jack's rigid smile twitch, as she pulled off her gloves. *But who am I to blame them for that?* She balanced Rusty's carrying case against the metal counter top and unsealed the lid, hearing the hiss as the pressure equalized. Rusty's mottled head rose over the edge, her dilated pupils black with excitement, flashing green in the light. Her nose quivered and she wriggled free, rising up into the air like a piece of windborne down. Betha heard the small gasp of the woman, and let the case drift away. "Will you take a cat?"

"An animal," the woman whispered. "I never thought I'd ever see one. . . ." Shyly she put out a hand. Betha stroked Rusty, reassuring, pushed her toward them. Rusty butted softly up against the woman's palms, sniffing daintily, sidling in pleasure along the fine satin cloth of her sleeve.

"I think you've come to the right place." The man's slender hands quivered. "Dad would give you the whole distillery for that animal." He laughed. "But he'd make you pay shipping to the Main Belt."

"Are there many animals left on Lansing?"

"No." Betha smiled, felt it pull. "A load of hydrogen will be fine."

"We have gardens," Shadow Jack said. "Lansing's the only tent rock. We were the capital of all Heaven Belt, once." He lifted his head.

"Sure," the man said. "That's right, it was. I've seen pictures. Beautiful . . ."

Rusty slipped away from the woman, began to jab a paw through the holes of a mesh container for papers. The papers danced and she began to purr, smugly content at the center of the world's attention. Betha's eyes were drawn away to the newscast on the wall; she froze as she saw her own face projected on the screen, realized it was not coverage of their arrival on Mecca. With all her will she glanced casually away, reaching out to scratch Rusty under the chin.

The man caught her motion, turned to look up at the screen. Her eyes leaped after him, saw her image vanish into lines of print. The man looked back at her, puzzled; shook his head, grimacing politely. "Don't mind the screen. We like to get the news from all over, to see what the competition's up to. It's all static anyhow—mediamen'll say anythin' they're paid for." He gestured at the printout settling gradually into a heap on the counter. Rusty pounced, overshooting, and swept it out into the air.

"Here, little thing, don't hurt yourself," the woman murmured, her hands tightening with indecision.

"She'll be all right," Betha said, irritable in her relief.

A small disapproval showed on the woman's face.

"Do you mind if we take a look at your ship?"

Betha looked back at the man. "No . . . but it's at the other end of the ast—of the rock."

He nodded. "Easy to do." There was a small control panel under the wall screen; he moved away toward it. "What's your designation?"

"*Lansing 04.*"

He changed settings, and the news report vanished. "*Lansing 04 . . .*" Betha saw their ship appear, an image in blinding contrasts on the sunbleached field. "I guess it's possible for you to move a thousand tons with a ship that size. How much does it mass?"

"Twenty tons without reaction mass or cargo."

"We like to be sure, you know." He looked up. "It's goin' to take you a lot of megasecs, though, to get back to Lansing."

She watched his face for unease, saw only his easy solicitude. "We'll manage; we have to."

"Sure." His eyes moved from her to Shadow Jack, touching them, she saw, with a kind of admiration. "We'll start processing your shipment."

Rusty crashed against the counter edge in a snarl of printouts and sneezed loudly.

"Hey, now." The man turned away, reaching for Rusty almost desperately. "Dad would kill us if somethin' happened to—" His voice faded, he let her go, catching up a sheet. Betha saw her own face on the page between his hands, not disappearing this time. "...alien starship..." She heard Shadow Jack's soft curse of defeat. She drifted, clutching the counter edge until her fingers reddened.

The Tirikis turned back to her. "It's you," the man said, staring. "You're from the starship."

"And you've come to us," the woman whispered.

An unconscious smile spread over their faces, the look of guileless greed Betha had seen on the woman in the shuttle. "I don't understand," she said stubbornly. "You've seen our ship; we've come from the Main Belt. There were a lot of people taking our pictures on the field—"

"Not that picture." The woman shook her head, her black hair rippling. Betha watched them remembering, reassessing. "We've heard about you ever since you came into the system over a megasec ago."

"And you didn't get from there to here in a megasec in the ship we saw." The man looked at Shadow Jack again. "You are from the Belt; maybe it's your ship. What are you, a snow pirate?"

"We're not pirating anything." Betha caught Rusty, pinned her against her suit. "We offered you a deal, this cat for a load of hydrogen. We've got nothing else that would interest you, wherever we're from. Just let us make the deal and go—"

"I'm sorry." The man looked down at the spiral of paper. "I'm afraid we *are* interested in a ship that can go from Discus . . . to the Main Belt . . . to the Demarchy . . ." Betha saw his mind work out the parameters, ". . . in one and a half megaseconds."

She wondered bleakly what he would think if he knew it had only taken a third of that. "What is it you want from us, then?" Knowing the answer, she knew now that she had failed, because there had never been a way to enter Mecca undetected.

"They want your ship! Let's get out of here." Shadow Jack pushed away toward the door, pulled aside the flaps, froze. Betha turned. Facing him, in a wine-red jacket flawlessly embroidered, was the man who worked for the government. Impeccable . . . The man's eyes fixed on her in return, and on Shadow Jack. He stared, incredulous, and she knew that this time he was staring at wild, filthy hair and streaked faces. Not at her paleness—she knew from his eyes that her face held no surprises for him. "Captain Torgussen," he nodded. "And not from Lansing—obviously."

"You have the advantage of me," Betha said. "I'm afraid I've forgotten your name."

He smiled. It hardened as he turned to the Tirikis, making a bow. "And just what *does* Tiriki Distillates want with the starship?" His hand found the front of Shadow Jack's suit, pushed him back into the room. "I guess you weren't kidding, boy, when you told us what you do for a living."

"Who are you?" the woman asked, indignant.

"Wadie Abdhiamal, representing the Demarchy government."

"Government?" The man made a face. "Then this is none of your business, Abdhiamal. Butt out before you get into trouble."

"That's monopolist talk, Tiriki. And I think you've got the ideas to go with it. I'm here on business—these people and their ship are what I came to Mecca to find. The government has claimed the ship in the name of all the people of the Demarchy."

"Your government claims don't hold air, Abdhiamal." The man glanced down at his reflection on the counter top, readjusting his soft beret. "You know you've got nothin' to back them up. We found these two first, and we're keeping them."

"Public opinion will back me up. Nobody's goin' to let Tiriki have total control of that ship. I'll call a public hearing—"

"Use my screen." The man pointed. "When we tell the people how the government has been goin' behind the Demarchy's back looking for the starship, they're not goin' to hear a word you say. You'll be out before you know what happened, and I mean out of everything.''

"But you'll be out one starship—and that's all that matters to me. Set up a hearing."

The woman moved toward the wall screen.

"Just a damn minute!" Betha turned desperately, caught them all in a look. "Sixty seconds—one minute, where I come from—to mention some things you seem to have forgotten about my ship. One, it is *my* ship. And two, only I know where it is. And three, if you think you'll get it without my full cooperation, you're wrong. My crew will destroy it before they'll let it be taken—and that will destroy any ship that gets within three thousand kilometers of it." Shadow Jack came back to her side, his face questioning. The others were silent, waiting, their frustration and greed sucking at her like flames. "Now, then. You seem to have reached an impasse. But I came here to make a deal, and I'm still willing to make a deal—since I don't think I have any other choice. I doubt if you'll let us leave, in any case.

"So . . . suppose each of you tell me why you want my ship so much, and then I'll tell you who gets it. And it wouldn't hurt if you mention what's in it for me—" Rusty began to struggle, clawing for a foothold on her slick suiting. She saw Abdhiamal watch the cat, smile with irrelevant fascination before he met her gaze in turn. He didn't answer; waiting for the opposition, she thought. "Well?" She turned away, afraid of him, afraid of herself, afraid to let him see it.

The Tirikis spoke softly together. They faced her finally, beautiful and determined. "Your ship would build up our business—and revolutionize the Demarchy's trade. The way things stand we don't have all the snow we need where it's easy to get at; we have to go to the Rings, and it's a hard trip with nuclear-electric rockets. And the Ringers make it even harder, because they know we can't do anythin' that would threaten our allotments of gases. If we had your ship we wouldn't have to depend on them. Your ship would make the Demarchy a better place to live. . . . You could continue to captain it, work for us.

We'll pay you well. You'll be part of the richest, most powerful company in the Demarchy—''

''And when the Demarchy objects, that company will make your ship into a superweapon and take over.'' Abdhiamal held her eyes.

She felt her eyelids flicker; he slipped out of focus as she shook her head, denying. ''No one will use my ship as a weapon. Not even you, Abdhiamal, if that's why you want it.''

''The government wants it so it won't become a weapon and bring on a new civil war. God knows, the old one's still killin' us. Somebody's got to see that the ship is used for the good of the whole Demarchy, and not turned against us. It could be the stimulus we need to revive the whole Belt, the technology you have on board. We might be able to duplicate your ramscoop, build our own, reestablish some kind of regular communication outside the Demarchy. You could help us—''

''Don't listen to him!'' the woman said. ''We're the government, we, the people. He's got no authority to do anythin'. You'd be torn apart by everybody who wants your ship. He can't protect you. Stay with us. We'll take care of you.'' She lifted her hands. ''You've got nowhere else to turn.'' Betha recognized the threat behind it.

''They'll take care of you, all right,'' Shadow Jack whispered. His gloved hand caught Betha's wrist, squeezing until it bruised. ''Don't do it, Betha! They're all liars. You can't trust any of 'em.''

''Shadow Jack.'' She turned slowly, her hand still locked in his, and touched him with her eyes. He let go; she saw the anger drain out of him, leaving his face empty. ''What about the hydrogen—for Lansing?''

''We'll send them a shipment; whatever they need.''

''And you?'' She faced Abdhiamal again. ''Is it true that your promises are worthless?''

''The government only does the Demarchy's pleasure. Why don't we ask the Demarchy? We'll call a general meeting, and let you tell them all about your ship. Tell everyone the location—but warn 'em too, to keep away—tell them what you told us. Then nobody will be at an advantage. I'll tell them what your ship could mean to all of them, to the whole Belt.

Everybody will have a hand in decidin' how to make the best use of the opportunity, the way things were designed to be done. . . . The Demarchy means you no harm, Captain. But we need your help. Give it to us, and you can name your own reward."

"Anything but a ticket home." Shadow Jack searched her face; she averted her eyes.

"All right." She reached down for Rusty's carrying case, forced herself to look at Abdhiamal again. "Abdhiamal, I'll try it your way. . . ."

He smiled, and she couldn't see behind it; she fought the desire to trust him. "Thanks." He turned to the Tirikis. "Set up a meeting."

"No. Wait." Betha shook her head. "Not here. I want to be on my ship when I make the announcement. If everyone has to know where it is, some lunatic will try to take it no matter what I say. I have to be there, to countermand my orders; I don't want to lose my ship now. I'm sure you don't, either?" She looked back at him. "We'll take you to the ship; we can broadcast from there. . . . After all, it's not going to get away from you without fuel, is it?"

"I suppose not. And I suppose you're right." He nodded once, watching the Tirikis. "Okay, I'll accept your terms."

"Go with 'em, Abdhiamal." Esrom Tiriki's voice mocked him. "That'll give us plenty of time to spread the news of this; the mediamen will tear you apart. By the time you call a meetin' you'll be public enemy number one. Nobody will listen to you then. You can count on it." His hand jerked at the counter's edge, chopping down.

She saw Abdhiamal's smile tighten. "Let's get goin', then."

She pushed Rusty, protesting, into the case and sealed the lid. She felt a small joy at a sacrifice refused, and felt the Tirikis' eyes change enviously behind her. She smiled faintly.

"How can you smile now, after that's happened?" Shadow Jack muttered. He picked up his helmet.

Softly she said, "Didn't I tell you there was always a reason to keep smiling?"

Wadie watched the starship grow on the screen in the cramped, stinking cabin of the *Lansing 04*. His admiration grew with it—and his heartfelt gratitude. This was the Ship from Outside, a ship to cross interstellar space at interstellar speeds, with a body streamlined to silken grace as a protection against the corroding particulate wind. It had none of the ugly angularity of the spacecraft he had always seen; it was pragmatic perfection, and there hadn't been a ship like it in the Heaven system in generations. The prewar starships of the Heaven Belt had been converted into the deadliest of warships during the war— and had been destroyed, every one, just as the access to the basic requirements for life, the delicate balance of survival, had been destroyed. In the end the Main Belt had become a vast mausoleum, and now the isolated survivors were disappearing, like patches of melting snow. . . .

He looked down at the back of Shadow Jack's head. His own head ached insufferably. He looked back at the screen again, counting the seconds until they reached the ship. Even if it hadn't been all he imagined, still it would have been a haven, an escape from the past two hundred kilosecs of suffocating indignity in the foulness of this scrap-metal coffin. And an escape from the sullen, hostile boy and the small, blunt woman who might as well have been a man, like all the other women who pushed their way out into space. He watched her as she soothed the cat above the humming control board, the rings shining on her hands. He looked down at the gold-and-ruby

ring on his own thumb, the gift of that other spacing woman
and her man, and wondered wearily why this one bothered to
wear so many rings, when she obviously wasn't interested in
her appearance.

The starship's image blotted out the stars; unobtrusively, he
used his water ration to clean his face and hands.

Not a ship. Wadie pulled back, halfway through the *Ranger*'s
lock, as the room opened before him. *This is a world.*

"This is the control room." The captain moved past him, her
voice husky in her hoarse throat; he heard the clanking as
Shadow Jack still fumbled with a pressure suit in the lock
behind him. He drew a long breath of cool air, coughed once as
his startled lungs reacted.

"Hello, Pappy."

The captain pushed off from the wall, with the indefinable lack
of grace that marked her alienness more than her face and hair.
She moved across the vastness of the control room toward
the instrument panels. He suddenly realized that the room was
not empty, that he was being studied by a girl and a short
pale-skinned man. "Betha—" A smile spread in the man's
grizzled beard—an old man, too old to still be in space, to still
be sound.... The slim brown girl wasn't looking at him at all, but
only staring through him toward the lock. She was a Belter,
ludicrously dressed in faded pants cinched by a flapping belt.

"You mean to tell me this is all you brought back?" The old
man gestured at him, half joking, half appalled. "This—fop?
You traded our Rusty for *this*?"

The captain shook her head, amused, said blithely, "No, not
'Shadow Jack and the Beanstalk,' Pappy. I just said we didn't
get the golden goose . . . and maybe we've been the golden
goose, all along, and didn't know it."

Wadie felt Shadow Jack brush by him with the cat in his
arms. The boy tossed her out into the air, giving her momentum, and she paddled on across the room, perfectly at ease.

"Rusty!"

She made rusty meows of pleasure, moving toward the old
man's familiar hands.

The Belter girl's face startled him, transformed by wild bliss as her eyes found Shadow Jack. He looked away from her, back at the old man. "Wadie Abdhiamal, representin' the Demarchy. And usually better than this. I'm afraid two hundred kilosecs in that deathtrap didn't do much for my appearance." The old man laughed.

Shadow Jack glanced back at him. "Try it for a couple megasecs, sometime."

The captain drifted against the control panel, lines of strain settling on her face again, making it grim. "It was hell, Pappy. I didn't want to make you come into Demarchy space to pick us up, but I don't know how much longer the life-support system would have held up. It wasn't adequate for two—and with three . . ." She rubbed her face, smearing grime. "The past two days were worse than the whole two weeks going in. But we had to bring him along. It was the only way we could get out of there. Their communications network is incredible; they already knew everything about us—everyone did, on every single separate piece of rock. And every one of them just waiting to grab our ship and play God with it—just like the Ringers. We can't trust either of them now; if we want hydrogen we're going to have to take it."

"Captain Torgussen," Wadie said, "the government only wants—"

"I know what you want, Abdhiamal. My ship. You made it clear enough. But your Demarchy will have to catch us first." Her eyes cut him, blue glass. "I'm sorry, Abdhiamal, but you're on our ground now. Consider yourself our hostage."

Shadow Jack laughed, sitting back in the air. The girl moved away from the panel to his side, her face expressionless.

Wadie said nothing, saw the captain hesitate.

"You don't seem very surprised. You didn't believe what I told you at Mecca, and still you let this happen?"

"I didn't know whether to believe you or not. After what you've been through, I figured maybe you really had given orders for the destruction of your ship, and I didn't want to take that chance. And I didn't want to take any chances with the Tirikis. And if you were lying about cooperating . . . well, I'm on your ship; that gives me another chance to change your mind. Heaven Belt needs your help."

"We don't owe you anything; greed and hostility are all we've met in Heaven Belt."

"Why did you come here in the first place, except to trade on the fact that you figured we were ridin' high? Why shouldn't we be as greedy? One hundred million people—most of the Main Belt—died in the first hundred megasecs after the war. And the ones that are left . . ." He pointed at Shadow Jack and the girl. "Look at Lansing. Their people won't last another circuit around Heaven. And we're all headed for the same thing, unless we have your ship."

She frowned, hooked a shoe under the security rail that edged the panel. "The fact remains that we have rights of our own, as human beings—including the right to leave this system if we choose—and you're not willing to give them to us. It's true we came here to trade, because we thought Heaven had things we wanted. But you've got nothing to offer, and we can't afford to waste our ship and the rest of our lives for nothing. Morningside can't afford it. We just don't have the resources to throw away on you."

"I—admit we didn't consider your position—" He broke off, the crassness of it embarrassing him. "We made a mistake, not considerin' your position. It was a stupid mistake. But we aren't the Ringers; we don't just want your ship, we want your cooperation. We might still have some things you'd want. It wouldn't have to be forever. The use of your ship, its reactor, and its shop, for a hundred and fifty megasecs. We'll deal with you fairly." The part of him that had questioned MacWong asked, *Will we?* The Belter kids stared at him, distrustful, more in sympathy with outsiders than with a man from their own system.

The captain moved restlessly. "I don't believe that. Everything I've seen shows me I can't depend on the Demarchy. You can't even depend on each other. Even if you meant every word you said, someone else would make it a lie and attack us. . . . I'm not blind, Abdhiamal, I can see what's happened here, and I know it's true that you need help. If I'd only had some sign to prove to me that at least the Demarchy was worthy of our trust. But I haven't. We can't help you; you won't let us. It's impossible."

"Captain, I—"

"The matter is closed." Something in her voice told him that it was closed, irrevocably, and that the reason went much deeper than a simple betrayal of trust.

Not understanding, he only nodded, his own fatigue and exasperation leaving him defeated. "To what end am I your hostage then, Captain?"

Her eyes shifted, clouding. "I don't know. Whatever end we come to, for better or worse . . . will be yours too, I suppose. You helped us out of a tight spot, Abdhiamal. Inadvertently, but you did help us. I'll try to be as fair to you. If we get the hydrogen we need, I'll find a way to get you back to the Demarchy before we leave the system. It will only be a—temporary inconvenience." She looked at him strangely for a moment; turning away, she reached for the old man's arm. "Oh, Christ, Pappy, I'm so tired. So glad to be back." He pulled her close, too close; held her until she broke away, kissing her once, tenderly.

Old enough to be her father . . . Surprise let a grimace of distaste pull his own mouth down; he covered it as they looked back at him. Only four, in this large, empty room; and two of them were Belters. Too empty. "Where's the rest of your crew?"

The old man glanced at the captain; she shook her head. "It doesn't matter; he'll find out soon enough, I suppose." Her hand gestured at the screen and knotted into a fist. "They all died at Discus. And we're going back. Pappy, get started on a course for Discus. We can't risk staying here any longer. We're going to take what we need from the Ringers, Abdhiamal, any way we can, and that's going to suit me fine." She threw it at him, defiant, before she turned to Shadow Jack and the girl. "I'm going to get us out of here as fast as I can. I want to be sure no one from the Demarchy can touch us. We'll be doing one gee for five or six days, again, to get us back to the Rings."

"It'll be worth it." Shadow Jack cracked his knuckles. The girl's mouth set in a line; she nodded. She moved closer to Shadow Jack, stroking his bare arm lightly. He glanced down at her, irritated, but didn't pull away.

"Thirsty?" she said. He straightened out of his drifting slouch, smiled suddenly, wiping his hand across his mouth. "Yeah!" He pushed off from the wall and they left the room.

The old man was strapped into a seat, working at the panel. The captain moved out into the air to collect a pencil and an unidentifiable metal cube. She pushed the cat into a compartment in the wall.

"Captain."

She started back toward the control board. "What?"

"I'd like permission to use your radio."

"Refused." She reached a chair, maneuvered herself down.

"But I need to—"

"Refused." She turned her back, cutting him off as she began her work at the board. He waited, studying the tasteless combination of pale-blue walls and green carpet. He noticed a stripe of deeper blue on the wall, an arrow, and the word DOWN.

"The Lansing ship is secure. Are the co-ords in, Pappy?"

"They're in. Ready when you are."

"Right. Ignition . . . thirty seconds. Feet on the ground, all of you!" The last of it went over an intercom, rattling off the walls through the empty heart of the ship. Wadie watched her hands move through a sequence on the panel, felt the light, familiar hand of gravity settle on his shoulders. And begin to bear down: His feet touched the floor, the drag against his legs continued, increasing past the point of familiarity, past the point of comfort. He backed up, caught hold of a bar along the wall, remembering thirty seconds of one gee on a Ringer ship, and realizing what it would be like for the next five hundred thousand seconds. Pain wrenched his muscles; the blue-on-blue streaked wall filled his vision DOWN. . . . His hands tightened, and he stood, enduring the pain, ignoring the heart that beat against his ribs like a fist.

He stood—and moved tentatively away from the wall, as the pressure bearing down on him stabilized. Dizziness made him sway, but he controlled it, balanced precariously as the captain and the old man rose from their seats. They looked toward him with expectant pity; the cat struggled out of the wall through a plastic porthole, made a circuit of his legs, licked his booted foot consolingly with her tongue. He folded his arms; looked down, and back at them across the room. He smiled, blandly.

The captain turned and walked out of the room. The cat bounded after her, tail flying like a banner.

"Abdhiamal, is it?" The old man came over to him, held out a hand. "My name's Welkin, navigator on the *Ranger*."

Wadie nodded, shook his hand, wondered at his motive in offering it. He noticed that Welkin's hand was bright with golden rings, like Betha Torgussen's; and that his grip was strong and firm.... But the old man must be tough, if he could take one gee—ten meters per second squared, the gravity of Old Earth. This was what it had been like to live on Earth. A crash and Shadow Jack's pained "Hell!" rose from somewhere below them. *No wonder we called this system Heaven.*

RANGER (IN TRANSIT, DEMARCHY TO DISCUS)

+ 2.25 MEGASECONDS

Fifty kiloseconds later Wadie climbed the empty stairwell, one step and then another—wanting to crawl and knowing there was no one to see it, but determined that he would keep control over something, if only his own dignity. He had investigated the lower levels of the ship's living area: the crew's quarters; the alien lushness of a hydroponics lab adapted to one gravity; the workshop—the last memory was almost a hunger. He had seen everything but the section on the second level, behind a sealed doorway where a warning light blinked red. And everywhere he had been stunned by the incredible waste—of water, of air, of living space—in a matrix of drab austerity that was primitive compared to the Demarchy's sophistication. He contemplated the irony in the idea that the Morningsiders considered themselves poor, when in some ways they were the richest people he had ever seen.

He reached the top of the stairs, leaned against the railing until the dizziness passed and his heartbeat slowed. His muscles ached dully when he stood, and when he moved pain burned in his trembling legs like a hot wire. He did his best to put his new clothes in order before he entered the control room.

The others were already there, watching something on the viewscreen. The captain and Welkin sat in chairs. Shadow Jack and the girl lay on the carpet, spreading their weight over the greatest area. The girl was trying to do pushups, her body rigid from the knees, as he looked in. He saw her elbows tremble, watched her collapse facedown on the cushion. She lay spread-eagled on the floor, defeated. "I can't."

"Then don't," Shadow Jack said, and more gently, "It'll be over soon, Bird Alyn; we don't have to get used to it." He flipped playing cards out into the air, watching their incredibly swift plummet to the rug. "Look who finally woke up." He looked back over his shoulder; the cat sidled past his head and sat down on the cards.

Wadie bowed casually, carefully keeping his balance. No one moved in return, and indignation rose in him until he remembered that he couldn't expect civility here. Pirates . . . He almost smiled, struck by the memory of what it had meant to be called a Belter, once, in the time when the only Asteroid Belt was Sol's. He studied the captain's face, clean now like her fair cropped hair; met something in her eyes that startled him. She glanced down, lighting a pipe. The tangy sweetness of whatever burned stirred memories in him, instinctive, of things he had never seen.

"At least you're a likelier-looking trade this time," Welkin said.

Wadie looked down at the blue cotton work shirt, the blue denim pants that stopped ten centimeters short of his ankles. He had forced the pants neatly into his polished boots. The boots braced his legs, but weighted them down like lead. "At least I'm clean." He stepped carefully over the doorsill and crossed the room, holding his head up, back straight. He reached the nearest swivel seat and lowered himself into it, leaned back easily, breathing again. The girl stared up at him, awed. Shadow Jack looked away with a frown; he muttered and pushed the cat, scattering cards.

"Captain . . ." Wadie turned in his seat, reordering his arguments. He stopped, as he realized what they had been watching on the screen. "You've been monitoring Demarchy communications?" Six separate images showed on the bright screen, each one a different broadcast frequency. He recognized a general newscast, three corporation hypes, two local arbitration debates.

The captain nodded. "It's been—enlightening."

"Has there been anything about your ship from the Tirikis?"

"Yes, news items; and there was a—" She glanced back at the screen, as two of the broadcast segments suddenly disappeared, replaced by an octagonal star caught in a golden paisley, on a field of black. As they watched, the symbol blotted out the rest of the segments one by one. "What is this, Abdhiamal?"

"It's a call for a general meeting; any demarch who wants to participate can monitor the final debate, startin' now, and vote on the issues involved." He remembered uneasily that it had been two hundred and fifty kiloseconds since they had left Mecca, more than two hundred and fifty kilosecs since his last report. "I expect this'll be the debate about your ship, and what happened at Mecca. The Tirikis started to promo the second we left the rock; and nobody's heard a word from me. I'd like to monitor the debate. And I'd like a chance to defend myself, if you'll give me an open channel."

She put her pipe aside. "All right, I'll monitor the meeting. You can listen; but I can't let you speak."

"Why not? Your ship's clear. And they can track you by your exhaust, they don't need a radio fix—"

"I don't need you telling them our plans. I'd rather let them guess."

"Captain, I need to talk to them. This meetin' could mean my job." They all looked at him, unresponsive. He swallowed his irritation. "You—experienced the communications network we've got; it's from before the war, and it still works as it should. It's what makes the Demarchy work—every demarch's got equal priority on it, and anybody with a gripe about anythin' can broadcast it. Everybody who's involved or interested can debate. If they need to, they take a general vote, and the vote is law."

"Mob rule?" Welkin said. "The tyranny of the majority."

"No." He gestured at the slender golden teardrop on the screen, symbol of the hundred-and-forty-million-kilometer teardrop distribution of the trojan asteroids. "Not here. You can't get a mob together across millions of kilometers of space. It keeps the voters' self-interest confined to their own rock. They're independent as hell, and they're informed, and they judge. A jury of peers."

"Then why would you be worried about losing your job?"

"Because I'm not there to defend myself; the Tirikis can claim anything, and if nobody hears different from me, what are they goin' to think, except that it's true? My boss will be answering them in my place, and he doesn't even know what's happened. If I can't tell them, I could take him down with me. The govern ment floats on water, and if you rock the boat you drown."

The captain leaned forward, pressing her hands together. "I'm sorry, Abdhiamal, but you should have considered that before you came with me. I can't afford to let you speak now. . . . Do you still want to listen in?"

He nodded. All the symbols but one were gone from the screen again; as he watched, the time lag closed and the last one faded. The general meeting had begun.

". . . should already have put our fusion craft in pursuit." Wadie rested his neck against the seatback, as Lije MacWong's final argument drew to a close on the screen. "We've done all we can to follow the wishes of the Demarchy. Too many things are still unclear to us, too, because we only know what you do. I'm a civil servant, no more, no less. If the people want to remove me for working in the people's interest, that's your privilege. But I don't feel that I've done anything to betray your trust." A band of color showed at the bottom of the screen, slowly turning violet from blue; voter participation was eighty per cent and rising.

Wadie watched the manicured brown hands fold on the gargoyled desk top, the pale compelling eyes that had chal lenged the Demarchy before and won. They disappeared sud denly; the seconds passed. REBUTTAL: ESROM TIRIKI flashed on the screen. He felt his mouth tighten as Tiriki's serene, golden face appeared, eyes gleaming like metal. "The fact remains that the government . . ."

The captain leaned back in her seat, fingers tapping soundlessly on the chair arms. "He's one of the trolls, Pappy. Handsome, isn't he?" She looked up. "And out for our blood. How does it go again? 'I smell the blood of an Englishman. Be he alive, or be he dead—'" She broke off, took a deep breath. "Screw Jack and the Beanstalk . . . .What was that about fusion ships,

Abdhiamal? I thought you said the Demarchy depended on fission power and fission-powered electric rockets?''

He nodded. ''We have three small fusion craft left from before the war; they're our navy, if you want to call it that. But you've got a big lead on them. They couldn't catch you before you got to Discus.''

''But it could give us less time to maneuver once we're there.''

''. . . the government agent Abdhiamal threatened us and kidnapped the Outsiders who had come to us to negotiate. Two hundred kilosecs have passed without any further word from him. Their knowledge would have benefited the entire Demarchy, it could have saved Heaven—but because of this 'government man' we've lost the crew and the starship forever. Consider that, when you make your final decision.'' The band of light below showed an ever-deepening violet.

Wadie's hands tightened over nothing. FINAL REBUTTAL: LIJE MACWONG showed on the screen.

''I regret to say that, in honesty, I can't deny Demarch Tiriki's final accusation. Wadie Abdhiamal, a negotiator from my agency, has overstepped his authority to a degree I consider criminal. He has in the past been suspect of questionable loyalty, of known Ringer sympathies, and I frankly consider it possible that he intends to aid them in usin' that ship against us. I can only repeat that he was acting without my consent, or the consent of any other person in the government. This agency isn't, and never was, a party to these actions. He alone committed a crime, and like any other criminal, he should be found guilty . . .''

Wadie straightened, felt something grate in his neck.

''. . . of treason against the Demarchy . . .''

''Lije!'' he whispered, incredulous, willing the mahogany face to turn and the pale eyes to meet his own.

''. . . and so, fellow demarchs, I want you to reconsider the basic issue before you make your decision. This should not be a simple vote of no confidence against a government that's served you well; this is a judgment on the fate of the one man who has betrayed the hopes of us all. I ask instead for a bill of attainder against Wadie Abdhiamal, government negotiator, for treason . . .''

You bastard— He pushed himself up and moved through a nightmare to the panel.

''. . . let him never set foot on any territory of the Demarchy on pain of death. He has betrayed us all . . .''

''Let me talk.'' He reached toward the instrument panel.

The captain caught his arm. ''No.''

''. . . I further urge again that all fusion-powered vessels be impressed into the pursuit of the alien ship; we must prevent it from reachin' our enemies. We must have that ship for ourselves!''

PROPOSITION flashed on the screen. BILL OF ATTAINDER AGAINST WADIE ABDHIAMAL, NEGOTIATOR. CHARGES: TREASON. PENALTY: DEATH. NEGATING PREVIOUS CHARGE: GOVERNMENT NEGLIGENCE.

He stepped back from the panel, his fingers twitching uselessly; his hand dropped. He went to his seat, sat down heavily, watching the ballots begin to register, APPROVE, OBJECT, numbers tallying with the passing seconds. Below them the percentage-of-voters band moved through red into orange into yellow. Five hundred seconds until it would reach full violet . . . five hundred seconds for the last votes to record from the outermost rocks of the trojans. An insignificant time lag, by the standards of the prewar Belt, as one hundred and forty million kilometers was an insignificant distance. Their closeness had meant survival for the trojans after the war; it meant death for him, now, letting men vote without hesitation, without reflection. He waited. The others waited with him, saying nothing. The ship's drive filled the silence with vibration, almost sound, almost intruding, the only constant in the sudden chaos of the universe.

PROPOSITION APPROVED. They found him guilty, twenty to one, and sentenced him to die. He watched the death order repeat and merge, like a thing already forgotten, into a new cycle of debate over the use of the fusion ships. He raised his leaden hands, let them drop again, smiled, looking back at the others. ''Now I finally know how MacWong's kept his job for so long.''

The captain cut off the debate, filling the screen with the void of his future.

"I guess I see the distinction between 'demarchy' and plain 'democracy.'" Welkin said quietly.

"Welkin, you don't have the right to make any moral judgments about Heaven Belt."

"He's got the right," Shadow Jack said. He sat up, pulling his feet forward. "The crew of this ship, they were..." He fumbled for words. "They were all married, they were a family; all of them together. And they all died in the Rings, except..." He glanced at Welkin and Betha Torgussen, back at Wadie, and down, twisting his fingers. "They all died."

Wadie watched the captain, her arm resting on the old man's shoulder. "I'm not married," he said, his voice flat. "And now I never will be." She looked back at him, not understanding, useless apology in her eyes, and a surprising sorrow. He got up, resenting the intrusion of her unexpected, and undesired, sympathy. "Well, Captain, you've ruined your final opportunity for a constructive agreement with the Demarchy. For my sake, I hope you have better luck with the Ringers than you did the last time." He went out of the room and down the spiraling stairs. No one followed.

RANGER (IN TRANSIT, DEMARCHY TO DISCUS)

+ 2.40 MEGASECONDS

Betha sat alone at the control panel in the soothing semidarkness, gazing at the endless bright stream of Demarchy television traffic, soundless by her own choice, that still trailed after them, two hundred million kilometers out. Caught in a spell of hypnotic revulsion, she marveled at the perpetual motion of the Demarchy media machine, wondered how any citizen—demarch? —ever made a sane decision under the constant dinning of a hundred different distortions of the truth. And remembering the mediamen on the field at Mecca, she should have known enough to believe Wadie Abdhiamal and let him speak. . . .

She cut off the broadcasts abruptly and put the crescent of Discus on the screen. She saw the *Ranger* in her mind, an infinitesimal mote, alone in the five hundred million kilometers of barren darkness, tracing back along Discus's path around the sun from the isolate swarm of rocks that was the Demarchy. She remembered then that they were not entirely alone. Expanding her mind's vision, she saw the Demarchy's grotesque, ponderous freighters loaded with ores or volatiles, crawling across the desolation; ships that took a hundred days to cross what the *Ranger* crossed in six. It was a barely bridgeable gap, now; and the survival of the Demarchy, and the Rings, depended on it. And someday there would be no ships. . . .

But now, tracing the violet mist of the *Ranger*'s exhaust, she saw what might be three fusion craft, barely registering on the ship's most sensitive instruments.

She cursed the Demarchy, the obsessive veneer of sophistication, the artificial gaiety, the pointless waste of their media broadcasts. Fools, reveling in their fanatical independence when they should all be working together; living on self-serving self-sufficiency, with no stable government to control them, no honest bonds of kinship, but only the equal selfishness of every other citizen.... And their women; useless, frivolous, gaudy, the ultimate waste in a society that desperately needed every resource, including its human resources.

Fragments of conversation drew together in her mind, and she remembered suddenly what Clewell had said about crippled Bird Alyn. Perhaps in a sense they were a resource, sound and fertile women who had to be protected, in a society where radiation levels were always abnormally high; women who had let the protection grow into a way of life as artificial as everything else in their world.... Perhaps the danger of genetic damage lay at the root of all the incomprehensible involutions of their sexual mores. Desperate people did desperate things; even the people of Morningside, in the beginning....

She turned slightly in her seat, to glance at Shadow Jack lying asleep on the floor, lost in a peaceful dream, a book of Morningside landscapes open beside him. She wondered, if those were desperate measures for the Demarchy, what must be true for Lansing. Her hands met on the panel, caressing her rings, as Wadie Abdhiamal entered the room.

"Captain." He made the requisite bow. She nodded in return, watching him cross the room: the proper demarch, compulsively polite, compulsively immaculate. And as awkward as a child taking his first steps, moving in one gravity. His face looked haggard, showing the effects of stress and fluid loss. She remembered seeing him use his drinking water to wash his face on the *Lansing 04*, thinking that no one noticed.... She brushed absently at her own hair. "Have you found everything you've needed, Abdhiamal? Have you eaten?" He had not joined the rest of them when they ate together in the dining hall.

He sat down. "Yes...somethin'. I don't know what." He looked vaguely ill, remembering. "I'm afraid I don't get along well with meat."

"How—are you feeling?"

"Homesick." He laughed, self-deprecatingly, as if it were a

lie. He gazed at the empty screen. Rusty materialized on his knee, settled into his lap, tail muffling her nose. He stroked her back with a dark, meticulous hand; Betha noticed the massive gold ring on his thumb, inlaid with rubies.

"I'm sorry." She pulled her pipe out of the hip pocket of her jeans, quieting her hands with its carven familiarity.

"Don't be." He shifted and Rusty muttered querulously, tail flicking. "Because you were right, Captain; and I made the right choice in comin' with you. The Demarchy can't be allowed to take your ship; nobody in Heaven Belt can. . . . I'm not saying that because of what happened to me—" Something in his voice told her that was not entirely true. "I've known all along, from the first time I heard about this ship, that it would make too many people want to play God." He looked up. "Even if it's not my right, I'd still turn your ship over to the Demarchy if I had the chance—if I thought it'd save them. But it wouldn't. The government *is* too weak, they'd never be able to keep an equilibrium now." His fingers dug into the soft arms of the chair; his face was expressionless. "So I'll tell you this. I'll help you get out of here, however I can. Anythin' I can do, anythin' you want to know. As my final service to the Demarchy: to buy them a little more time and save them from them- selves." His eyes went to Discus on the screen. "If I've got to be a traitor, I'll be a good one. I take pride in my work."

She broke away from tracing his every movement, her face hot. "If you really mean that, Abdhiamal . . . I want your help, whatever your personal motives. I need to know anything you can tell me about the Ringers—especially I need the number and the locations of their distilleries. No matter how primitive they are, it's going to take careful planning to steal anything from them with an unarmed starship. . . . And as you say, I haven't done very well so far at getting what I want. Strategy was always Eric's—was never my strong point."

"On the contrary. You outnegotiated us all, at Mecca." Irony acknowledged her with a smile. "I expect I can give you reasonably accurate coordinates; I spent a lot of time in the Rings about two hundred and fifty megasecs ago, when we helped 'em enlarge their main distillery. As a matter of fact, I—" He broke off abruptly. "Tell me something about

Morningside, Captain. Tell me about the way your people get things done. You don't seem to approve of our way."

She studied the words, trying to find the reason behind his change of subject; certain only that he didn't really want an answer but simply a distraction. *And so do I.* "No, I can't say that I do approve, Abdhiamal. But that's the Demarchy's business, except when it gets in my way. . . . I guess that you could say we emphasize our kinship—as fellow human beings, but especially as blood relatives. You already know about our multiple-marriage family unit." She glanced up, away; his eyes made no comment, but she sensed his uneasiness. "Above it is our 'clan'—not in the Old World technical sense, except that it tells you who you can't marry—your particular parent-family, your sibs, your own children. All your relations stretch out beyond it . . . almost to infinity, sometimes. We all try to take care of our own; everybody on Morningside has relations somewhere. . . . Except that a person who isn't willing to share the work finds that even his own relations aren't glad to share the rewards forever.

"The only formalized social structure above the clan level is what we call a 'moiety' . . ." She lost the sound of her own voice, and even the aching awareness of Abdhiamal's presence, in vivid memories that filled the space between her words with sudden yearning. Borealis moiety: an arbitrary economic unit for the distribution of goods and services. Borealis moiety: her home, her job, her family, her world . . . a laughing child—her daughter, or herself—falling back to make angel imprints in a bank of snow. . . .

"Our industries are independently run, as yours are—but I suppose you'd call them 'monopolistic.' They cooperate, not for profits, but because they have to, or they'd fail. It works because we never have enough of anything, especially people. My parent family and a lot of my close relatives run a tree farm in the Borealis moiety . . . my wife Claire worked there too. Some families specialize in a trade, but Clewell and I and our spouses were a little of everything. . . ." She remembered day's end in the endless twilight, the family sitting down together at the long dark wood table, while their children served them dinner. The soothing warmth of the fire, the sunset that never faded from the skylight of a semisubterranean house. The small talk of the day's small triumphs, the comfortable fatigue . . . the welcome homecoming of a spouse whose job had kept him or her away for days or sometimes weeks. Eric, returning from the arbitration of a long-drawn dispute—

She saw Wadie Abdhiamal, sitting back in his chair in the control room of the *Ranger*. A negotiator. . . *I settle disputes, work out trade agreements.* . . . Abdhiamal looked back at her with a faintly puzzled expression. She shook her head. *Stop it. Stop being a fool!* "I . . . I almost forgot—we have a High Council, too. It's a kind of parliament, made up of ombudsmen from the various moieties, elected to terms of service. It deals with what little interplanetary trade we manage and the emergency shipments. It originated the proposal for our trip to Heaven. It doesn't have much to do with our daily lives—"

"Then in a way you are like us," Abdhiamal said, "without a strong centralized government, with emphasis on independence—"

"No." She shook her head again, denying more than the words. "We're like a family. We get things done through cooperation, not competition, the way the Demarchy does. Your system is a paradox: the individual has absolute control, and yet no control at all, if they don't fit in with the majority. We cooperate and compromise because we know we all need each other just to survive. . . . And considering the position the Demarchy is in right now, I'd say it can hardly afford to go on putting self-interest above everything else, either."

Abdhiamal blinked, as if her words had struck him in the face. But he only shrugged. "Needless to say, we don't see ourselves in quite that light. I suppose your idea of cooperation is closer to the Ringers' Grand Harmony." There was no sarcasm in it. "They emphasize cooperation above all too, because they have to; they weren't as fortunate as the Demarchy, after the war. But they have a socialist state and strong navy; they get cooperation at the point of a gun. And that's no cooperation at all, really; that's why they're anathema, as far as the Demarchy's concerned. They don't trust individual human nature, even it if is backed up by family ties."

Betha struggled against a sudden irrational resentment. "It's worked well enough so far. But then we don't kill any stranger who comes to us in need, either.''

"Maybe you just never had a good enough reason, Captain.''

She stiffened. Apology showed instantly on his face and behind it, she saw a reflection of her own disorientation, the frustration of a stranger trapped in an alien universe. He was a man with no family . . . and now no friends, no world, no future. And she suspected that he was not a man who was used to making mistakes—or used to sharing a burden, or sharing a life . . . *not Eric.*

"I'm sorry, Captain. Please accept my apologies." Abdhiamal hesitated. "And let me apologize for my tactlessness after the general meeting, as well."

"I understand." She saw annoyance begin behind his eyes; stood up, not seeing it change into a kind of need. "If you'll excuse me . . ." She moved away, reaching for an excuse, an escape. "I—I have to see Clewell, down in the shop."

"You mind if I go with you?" His voice surprised her.

She hesitated, halfway across the room. "Well, I—no, why should I?"

He rose, setting Rusty down. The cat leaped away, rumpled, moved across the room to where Shadow Jack still lay asleep, his face buried now in the pillow. Rusty settled on the softness beside his head, one speckled paw stretched protectively over his curled fingers.

"Poor Rusty." Betha glanced down. "She's been so lonely since . . . She was used to a lot of attention."

"She would have had all she wanted at Mecca."

"She would have been worshipped. It isn't the same."

She went down one level on a spiraling stairway, waited for him on the landing. He took each step with dignified deliberateness, his knees nearly buckling and his hand on the railing in a death grip. He stopped with studied nonchalance beside her, peering down over the polished wood banister. The well dropped four more stories, piercing the hollow needle of the ship's hull. The concentric circles of a service hatch lay pooled at the bottom.

"It's good exercise." Betha stood against the wall, avoiding the sight of the drop.

He drew back with an innocuous smile. The doorway in the wall behind him was sealed shut, the red light flashing, throwing their shadows out into the pit. "What's behind this?" His hand brushed the door's icy surface.

"That was the dayroom. That's where everyone died when we took the damage to our hull. It's not pressurized; please don't touch anything." She turned away from him, looking down at her hands. She went on down the stairs, leaving him behind.

She reached the machine shop on the fourth level, heard the rasp of a handsaw. "Pappy!" She shouted, heard the echoes rattle around the hollow torus of the shop.

"Here, Betha!"

She traced the answering echoes, began to walk, the gum soles of her shoes squeaking faintly on the wood. The irregular clack of Abdhiamal's polished boots closed with her; she didn't look at him.

"Jesus, Pappy, why in the world don't you use the cutters to do that?"

Clewell looked up as they approached, on up at the nest of lasers above the work table. "Because it's a hobby."

"Which means you stand there for hours, breaking your back to do something you could punch in and get done in a minute."

"The impatience of youth." He leaned on the saw and the end split off the wooden block and dropped. "Finished." His hand rose to his chest; seeing her watching, he lifted it further to rub his neck.

"Smartass." She looked pained, hands on hips. "I—uh, I thought you were going to check over my estimates on patching that hole in our hull?"

"I did that too. They look good to me. But we can't do anything about it now, while we're at one gee." He looked at her oddly.

Abdhiamal stooped to pick up the splintered end of the block, rubbed its roughness, oblivious. "Say, what is this stuff? It's fibrous."

"It's wood. Organic. From the trunks of trees," Clewell said. "False-oak, to be exact. It's hard, but it whittles well."

"The floor, too? All plant fibers—wood?"

He nodded. "It's easier than turning it into plastic. False-oak grown two centimeters a day out by the Boreal Sea."

Abdhiamal's hand caressed the etched metal of the table top; he glanced up at the cutters and the suspended protective shield. "Lasers?" His hand closed, empty, as he searched the room, loosened to point at the wide doors cut into the hull, opening directly onto space . . . at the electromagnets set into the ceiling. She saw him answering his own unspoken questions. "And what's this equipment for, over here?"

Betha followed his hand, seeing in her mind red-haired Sean at work, dauntlessly clumsy; Nikolai patiently guiding. She looked away. "Repairing microcircuits on our electronics equipment."

"You have your own fusion power plant . . . you really could reproduce any part of this ship right here, couldn't you?"

"Theoretically. There are some I wouldn't want to try. This was a long trip; we had to be prepared for anything." *Except this*.

"God! If Park and Osuna could only see this place."

"Who?" Clewell removed the wood from a clamp.

"They're 'engineers.'" Scorn lacerated the word.

"And what's wrong with engineers?" Betha folded her arms tightly against her stomach, raising her eyebrows.

"What's right with 'em?" Abdhiamal made an odd gesture. "They're a bunch of cannibals. They put patches on patches, tear one thing apart and use the pieces to hold three more together, and then they tear apart one of those—"

"That sounds resourceful to me."

"But they gloat about it! The think it's creation, but it's destruction. If they'd only *read* something, if only they had any imagination at all, they'd know what real creation is. The thing we could do, once . . . nobody did them better. But that's like askin' for life in a vacuum."

"Or maybe you've just got your priorities wrong, Abdhiamal! What should they do, torture themselves over the past because relics are all they have left to work with? At least they're doing something for their people, not living at the expense of everyone else like some damned fop!" Betha jerked the piece of wood out of his hands, felt splinters cut her palm. She turned her back on his surprise, strode away through her echoing anger toward the door.

Clewell smiled at Abdhiamal's astonished face. "Abdhiamal, you just told it all to an engineer."

Abdhiamal winced. "I should never have gotten out of bed . . . two megaseconds ago." He stared out into the vastness of the empty room. "I always seem to say the wrong thing to . . . your wife. I thought she was a pilot."

Clewell listened to Betha's footsteps fade as she climbed the stairs. He wondered what fresh burden she had brought with her from Mecca—that showed in her eyes and her every action, and that she could not share even with him. "She was an engineer on Morningside, before she was chosen to captain the *Ranger*. Parts of this ship are her design; she worked on its drive unit." He saw surprise again in Abdhiamal's tawny eyes. "It's the first starship we've had the resources to build since before the Low."

"Low?"

"Famine . . . emergency." Memories of past hardship and suffering rose in him too easily, drawn by the fresh memory of loss. A bruising weariness made him settle against the table's edge. He set aside the wood; morbidly picturing his own body as ancient wood, storm-battered, decaying. He sighed. "On Morningside small changes in solar activity, perturbations in our orbit, can mean disaster. When I was a boy—in the last quarter of my tenth year—we went into a 'hot spell' . . ." He saw the darkside ice sheet withdrawing, shattered bergs clogging the waters of the Boreal Sea. The sea itself had risen half a meter, flooding vital coastal industries; the crops had rotted in the fields from too much rainfall. He had watched one of his fathers kill a litter of kittens because they had nothing to feed them. And he had cried, even though his own empty stomach ached with need. *Still, after all these years* . . . "It took years for the climate to stabilize, most of my lifetime before our own lives got back to 'normal.' We've entered a High, right now, and Uhuru's stabilized—they're our closest neighbor; this flight was planned to send them aid, originally. That's why we took a chance on risking the *Ranger* to come here to Heaven." He felt the cutting edge of wind over snow on the darkside glacier, where the sky glittered with stars like splintered ice. "That's why we can't afford to stay here. Even if we go back to Morningside empty-handed, at least they'll have the ship."

Abdhiamal nodded. "I see. I told—your wife, Captain Torgussen, that I'm willing to do all I can to help you get back to Morningside—for Heaven's own good. The way things seem to be goin', your remaining here is goin' to tear Heaven apart, not pull it back together again. . . ." For a moment Clewell was reminded of someone, but the image slipped away.

He considered Abdhiamal's words, surprised—more surprised to find that he believed them. *Have we found an honest man?*

> "Together we find courage,
>   Our song will never cease. . . ."

"What's that?" Abdhiamal said.

"Bird Alyn." Clewell heard the faint, halting music rise from the hydroponics lab. "Betha taught her some chords on the guitar; I taught her a few more songs, while we were—waiting." He heard Bird Alyn strike a sour note as she strummed. "I don't know if Claire would have approved, but the plants seem to appreciate her sincerity." He smiled. "It's not what you sing, or how, but how the singing makes you feel."

Abdhiamal smiled politely. His glance touched the scarred surface of the table, the floor, searched the room again; the smile grew taut. "You know, I sometimes have the strange feeling that I'm livin' in a dream; that somehow I've forgotten how to wake myself up." A trace of desperation edged into his voice.

"Bird Alyn said the same thing to me. Except that I think she meant it."

"Comin' from the Main Belt, she probably did. . . . Maybe I do too." Abdhiamal cleared his throat, an oddly embarrassed sound. "Welkin, I'd like to ask you a personal question. If you don't mind."

Clewell laughed. "At my age I don't have much to hide. Go ahead."

Abdhiamal paused. "Do you find it—hard to take orders from your wife?"

Clewell straightened away from the table. "Why should that make a difference to me?"

Abdhiamal looked at him strangely. "Frankly I never met a woman I'd trust to make my decisions for me."

Clewell remembered what he had seen on the monitors of Demarchy society, saw why it might make a difference to Abdhiamal. "Betha Torgussen was chosen to command the *Ranger* because she was the best qualified, and the best at making decisions. We all agreed to the choice." He tightened the jaws of a table clamp, not sure whether he was amused or annoyed. "Answer a personal question for me: What exactly do you think of my wife?" He watched an instinctive reaction rise up and die away before it reached Abdhiamal's lips. *An honest man* . . .

"I don't know." Abdhiamal frowned slightly, at nothing, at himself. "But I have to admit, she's made better decisions since I've known her than I have." He laughed once, looking away. "But then she chose space, instead of . . ." His eyes came back to Clewell; the frown and confusion filled them again.

"Why doesn't the Demarchy have women in space? My impression of Belter life was always that everyone did as they damn well pleased. Men and women."

"Before the war, maybe. But now we have to protect our women."

"From what? Living?" Clewell picked up the piece of wood, shifted it from hand to hand, annoyance overriding amusement now.

"From radiation!" It was the first time he had heard Abdhiamal raise his voice. "From genetic damage. The fission units that power our ships and factories are just too dirty. In spite of everythin' we've done, the number of defective births is twenty times as high as it was before the war."

Clewell thought of Bird Alyn. "What about men?"

"We can preserve sperm. Not ova."

"You've lost more than you know because of that war." Abdhiamal stood silently, expressionless. Clewell unstrapped the leather wristband that had been a parting gift from one of his sons, and held it out. "Do you recognize that symbol?" He pointed at the design enameled on a circle of copper, as Abdhiamal took it from his hand.

"*Yin* and *yang*?"

He nodded. "Do you know what it stands for?"

"No."

"It stands for Man and Woman. On Morningside, that means two equal halves merging into a perfect biological whole. A spot of white in the black, a spot of black in the white . . . to remind us that the genes of a man go into the creation of every woman, and the genes of a woman go into the creation of every man. We're not men and cattle, Abdhiamal, we're men and women. Our genes match; we're all human beings. It makes a lot of sense, when you stop to think about it."

"Odd—" Abdhiamal smiled again, noncommittal. "Somehow I didn't think *yin* and *yang* would have been a part of Morningside's cultural heritage."

"Your people and ours all came from the same Old World in the beginning. In the beginning *yin* and *yang* didn't mean much to us. We had a lot of symbols to separate us, then. We just need one now."

"*Yin* and *yang* and the Viking Queen . . ." Abdhiamal murmured; his smile turned rueful. "And Wadie in Wonderland. Why were there more men than women in your—family?"

Because it happened to work out that way. Clewell almost answered him with the truth. He paused. "Son, if you have to ask me why a marriage needs more men than women, you're younger than I thought you were." He grinned. "And it's not because I'm slowing down."

Abdhiamal drew back, disbelief ruffling his decorum. He held out the wristband.

Clewell shook his head. "Keep it. Wear it. . . . Think about it, when you wonder why we're strangers to you."

Betha reentered the control room; Shadow Jack and Rusty still lay head-to-head on the grass-green rug. She moved quietly past them, sat down at the control board, and pulled Discus

into focus on the screen, a small silver crescent like a thumbnail moon. All that mattered now, and nothing else. She would get
this ship home; this time they *would* succeed. Nothing must get in
the way of her purpose, no man, living or dead, no memory. . . .

Her torn hand burned. She pressed it down on the cold
panel, leaving a spot of blood. Her mind crossed three light-
years and a half a lifetime to a factory yard on the Hotspot
perimeter, where she had burned her hand on hot metal,
inspecting the ideal made real. She had gone outside to see her
first engineering design passing in sequence on the assembly
line—unbearably silver in the blinding noon light, unbearably
beautiful. She was in the third quarter of her twentieth year,
fresh from the icy terminator. The golden rain of heat, the
battering flow of parched desert air on this, the perimeter of
total desolation, dazed her; pride filled her with exhilaration,
and there was a certain student-worker. . . . She waited for him
to stand beside her and tell her that her design was beautiful.
And then he would ask her—Rough gloves caught her arms and
turned her back, "Hey, snowbird, you want to go blind?" She
saw Eric van Helsing's adored, sunburned face laugh at her
through the shield of his helmet, as she caught the padding of
his insulated jacket. "They always said engineers were too
quirky to come in out of the sun. You'd better go back."

"For a social scientist, you haven't learned much about
motivation, Eric van Helsing." Angry because he had ruined
everything—and because, like a fool, she had waited for
him—she pulled away, almost ran back across the endless
gravel yard, escaping into the cool, dazzled darkness inside the
nearest building. She stood still in the corridor, fighting tears,
and heard him come through the doors behind her. . . .

> You are the rain, my love, sweet water
> Flowing in the desert of my life. . . .

Someone entered the room; Betha smelled the scent of
apples. She looked for Claire's smooth moon-round face and
golden tangled curls . . . found Bird Alyn again, thin and brown
and branch-awkward: a dryad in a pink pullover shirt and jeans,
with flowers in her hair. . . . Bird Alyn, not Claire, who tended
hydroponics now.

Shadow Jack stirred as Bird Alyn dropped down beside him, her freckled cheeks blushing dusky-rose. Betha turned back to the screen, hiding her smile.

". . . like some apples?"

"Oh . . . thanks, Bird Alyn." He laughed, self-conscious. "You always think of me."

She murmured something, questioning.

"What's the matter with you? No! How many times do I have to tell you that? Get out of here, leave me alone."

Pain knotted in Betha's stomach; she heard Bird Alyn climb to her feet and flee, stumbling on the doorsill. Betha turned in her seat to look at Shadow Jack; kneeling, he glared back at her as he pushed himself up.

"Maybe it's none of my business, Shadow Jack, but just what in hell is the matter with you?"

"There's nothin' the matter with me! You think everybody has to be like you? Everybody isn't; you're a bunch of dirty perverts!" His voice shook. "It makes me sick." He went out of the room. She heard him go down the steps too fast.

Betha sat very still, clutching the chair arms, wondering where she would find the strength to rise. . . . Rusty sidled against her legs, *mrr*ing. Stiffly she reached down, drew the cat up into her lap; hanging on to meaning, to the promise of a time when Heaven would be no more than one of countless stars lost behind the twilight. "Rusty, you're all the things I count on. What would I have done without you?" Rusty's rough, tiny tongue kissed the palm of her hand twice in gentle affection. "Oh, Rusty," she whispered, "you make misers of us all." Betha got to her feet slowly and looked toward the empty doorway.

Shadows moved silently over the tiles, moist and green, like the waters of a dream sea. Bird Alyn sobbed against the cold hexagonal tiles of the seatback, touched by the fragile fingers of a hanging fern. ". . . not fair, it's not fair . . ." Her love was an endless torment because it fed on dreams. He would never touch her, never stroke her hair . . . never love her, and she would never stop wanting his love.

She heard him enter the lab, and the sob caught in her throat. She pushed herself up, eyes shut, wetness dripping off her chin.

"Don't cry, Bird Alyn. It wastes water." Shadow Jack stood before her, hands at his sides, watching her tears drip down.

She opened her eyes, saw him through lashes starred with teardrops, felt more tears rise defiantly. "We have . . . plenty of water, Shadow Jack." Misery coiled inside her, tightening like a drawn spring. "We're not on Lansing; everything's different here!"

His eyes denied it; he said nothing, frowning.

She turned away on the bench. "But I'm not . . . I know I'm not. Why did this happen to me? Why am I so ugly, when I love you?"

He dropped down beside her on the seat, pulled her hands, one crippled and one perfect, down from her face. "Bird Alyn, you're not! You're not . . . you're beautiful." She saw her image in his eyes and saw that it was true. "But—you can't love me."

"I can't help it . . . how can I help it?" She reached out, her wet fingers brushed his face. "I love you."

He caught her roughly, arms closing over her back, and pulled her against him. She struggled in surprise, but his mouth stopped her cry, and then her struggling. ". . . love you, Bird Alyn . . . since forever . . . don't you know?"

Her outflung hands rose to tighten on his shoulders, drawing him into her dreams, joy filled her like song—

> Let me blossom first for you,
> Let me quench my thirst in you. . .

"No—" He pulled back suddenly, letting her go. He leaned against the cold tiles, gulping air. "No. No. We can't." His hands made fists.

"But . . . you love me . . ." Bird Alyn reached out, astonished by disappointment. "Why can't we? Please, Shadow Jack . . . please. I'm not afraid—"

"What do you want me to do, get you pregnant!"

She flinched, shaking her head. "It doesn't have to happen."

"It does; you know that." He sagged forward. "Do you want to feel the baby growin' in you and see it born . . . with no hands and no arms, or no legs, or no—To have to put it Out, like my mother did? We're defective! And I'll never let it happen to you because of me."

"But it won't. Shadow Jack, everything's different here on this ship. They have a pill, they never have to get pregnant. They'd let us . . ." She moved close, stroked the midnight blackness of his hair. "Even one pill lasts for a long time."

"And what about when they're gone?"

"We . . . we'd always have . . . memories. We'd know, we could remember how it felt, to touch, and kiss, and h-hold each other. . . ."

"How could I keep from touchin' you again, and kissin' you, and holdin' you, if I knew?" His eyes closed over desperation. "I couldn't. If I was never going to see you again . . . but I will. I'd see you every day for the rest of my life, and how could I stop it, then? How could you? It would happen."

She shook her head, pleading, her face burning, hot hopeless tears burning her eyes.

"I can't let go, Bird Alyn. Not now. Not ever. I couldn't stand what it would do to me . . . what it would do to you. Why did we ever see this ship! Why did this happen to us? It was all right till—until—" His hands caught together; he cracked his knuckles.

Softly she put out her own hand, catching his; fingers twined brown into bronze. Because of this ship their world would live . . . and because of it, nothing would ever be right in their lives again. She heard water dripping, somewhere, like tears; a dead blossom fell between them, clicked on the sterile tiles.

Betha left the doorway quietly, as she had come, and silently climbed the stairs.

Discus, a banded carnelian the size of a fist, set in a silver plane: The rings, almost edge-on, were a film of molten light streaked with lines of jet, spreading toward them on the screen. Wadie drifted in the center of the control room, keeping his thoughts focused on the silhouette that broke the foreground of splendor: Snows-of-Salvation, orbiting thirty Discuss radii out, beyond the steep gradient depths of the gravity well. Snows-of-Salvation, that had been Bangkok on the prewar navigation charts, the major distillery for the Rings. It was one of five, but it outproduced the rest by better than ten to one; in part because its operations were powered by a nuclear battery constructed in the Demarchy, in part because it could send out shipments using a linear accelerator, also from the Demarchy but infinitely more useful here where transport distances were short. The Ringers' own primitive oxyhydrogen rockets made hopelessly inefficient tankers.

He remembered Snows-of-Salvation as it had been when he arrived with the Demarchy engineers: endless grayness honeycombing the ice and stone; a chill that crept into a man's bones until he couldn't remember warmth; a small gray population, a people renting space in purgatory. A people fanatical to the point of insanity, in the eyes of the Demarchy. He had been sent to keep demarch and Ringer from each others' throats—sent because no one better qualified had been willing to go. He had stayed to see that two incompatible and suspicious groups never forgot their common goal of increasing the supply of volatiles. And in the fifty megaseconds he had spent in his grim and

218

lonely exile, he had come to know a number of men he could only call friends and had seen more of the Ringers' Grand Harmony than any other demarch. He had come to understand the chronically marginal life that existed for the Ringers everywhere; to see, almost painfully, what made them endure their oppressive collectivist ideology: the knowledge that they must always pull together or they would not survive....

The captain's voice drew him back. His eyes fixed on her where she hung before the viewscreen, her hair floating softly, free from gravity, her shirtsleeves rolled up to the elbow. He stared, the present an overlay on the past. The clean, colored warmth of the control room drove out a dreary poverty that made Morningside's plainness suddenly seem frivolous.

Morningside ... could he ever have come to see its people as clearly as he had seen the Ringers? How long did it take to feel at ease with a people who offended your sense of propriety in every way imaginable? Whose behavior slipped through your attempts to categorize it the way water slipped between your fingers.... Four kilosecs ago he had come to the upper level to get himself some food. He had found the captain and Welkin already in the dining hall and Bird Alyn playing her guitar. They had all been singing; as though in four thousand seconds they were not going to commit an act of piracy or face one more trial whose outcome meant freedom and life for all of them....

> Together we find courage,
> Our song will never cease....

Or perhaps, he had realized suddenly, they sang because they were much too aware and afraid of that fact. *Not what you sing, or how*, Welkin had said, *but how it makes you feel*. Suddenly aware of his own part in that coming trial, he had been drawn across the room to join them by something stronger than curiosity ... only to have Betha Torgussen's face close and lose its warmth as she saw him; only to have her rise from the table, braking the pattern of song, and abruptly leave the room.

"...I can't believe this reading, Pappy. They should be frying down there, but they're not. There's no magnetosphere, no trapped radiation field. . . . Do you know anything about this, Abdhiamal?'' The captain glanced over her shoulder at him, not quite meeting his eyes.

He looked past her at the screen. ''This is Heaven, after all, Captain. Discus's radiation fields are strong enough, but they don't reach much higher than the rings. That was one of the things that brought us to this system—the rocks and snowballs around Discus are accessible as they never were around Old Jupiter.'' He caught her eyes. ''You don't seem very concerned about whether *we* were fryin'?''

''We make good shielding on Morningside, or we'd have fried long ago.'' She broke away, as she always did, now; looked up at Bird Alyn hanging near the ceiling above her head. ''Bird Alyn, find the local talk frequency for me.'' Her voice was calm.

Bird Alyn nodded, braced against the ceiling, and swooped down to the panel to catch up an earjack.

''Where's Shadow Jack?'' Welkin asked.

Bird Alyn stared at the panel, said something inaudibly.

''What?''

''. . .don't know. . .said. . .didn't think he could face. . .'' She shrugged. The room filled with static as she switched on the receiver. The static slurred abruptly into words. The words sharpened as Bird Alyn locked them in. ''Here . . .''

''What are they broadcasting?''

''They're talkin' to a ship, I think; a tanker. I heard 'hydrogen.' ''

''Good—then let's rudely interrupt them.'' The captain reached for the broadcast button. ''You're sure they'll know who we are, Abdhiamal?''

''I'm sure. Even the Ringers have had time to spread word of what happened to that ship by now. And if their propaganda is as extreme as it usually is, they'll expect you to be a butcher. They'll—respect your threat.''

''All right.'' She wet her lips, pushed the button. ''Snows-of-Salvation, Snows-of-Salvation, come in please . . .''

The speaker shrilled irritation; Bird Alyn jerked the earjack away from her head.

''Who is that? Get the hell off this freq! There's a mixed-load dockin' in progress here! Do you—''

The captain's hand on the button cut him off. "Tell them to hold off, we have something more important to say to you."

"Who is this?"

"This is..." She hesitated. "...the ship your Navy attacked two megaseconds ago...the ship from Outside." She released the button.

No answer came.

"You've impressed them." Wadie smiled, humorlessly.

A different voice came through, a voice that was strangely familiar to him, ordering the unseen tanker into a holding orbit. Welkin reached across the comm panel, by Bird Alyn's shoulder, and a new segment of the screen erupted into a blizzard of static now. "We're receiving wideband." He input a sequence on the console; abruptly the screen showed a squeezed triple image. He ordered in a correction, and a single black-and-white picture re-formed. They saw a pinched face squinting from behind wire-rimmed spectacles: a middle-aged man in a heavy, quilted jacket and a thick knit cap. "We're transmitting compatible now, too," Welkin said. The captain nodded, seeming to take the old man's skill for granted.

"What is it you want here?" The familiar voice matched a familiar face, harsh with anger or fear. *With anger*...Djem Nakamore was too stubborn and dogmatic to acknowledge anything else. Wadie pushed out of his line of sight as Nakamore glared at Betha Torgussen.

Her face hardened, staring Nakamore down. "We want one thousand tons of processed hydrogen, sent out on the trajectory I give you to our ship. If you fail to do this, I'll destroy your distillery, and you'll all die." The hardness seemed to come easily; Wadie felt surprised.

He watched their expressions change, the two strangers in the background showing real fear. Nakamore stiffened upright, drifting off-center on the screen.

"You won't destroy us. Even the Demarchy would want you dead if you did that."

"We're not from your system; you're nothing to us. The Demarchy is nothing. I hope you all go to hell together for what you've done to us; but Snows-of-Salvation will get there first unless you obey my orders."

"...they meant it..." a blurred voice said in the background. Nakamore turned away abruptly, cutting off sound. He spoke to the others, their eyes still flickering to the screen, faces tense, their breath frosting in the cold air as they spoke. Nakamore turned back to the panel, out of sight below him, and punched the sound on. "We don't have a thousand tons of hydrogen on hand. We never have that much, and we just sent out a big shipment."

Wadie shook his head. "They'd never let the supply get that low. The output is nearly three thousand tons per megasec, and they have at least four times that as backlog in case the distillery goes off-line for repairs."

The captain twisted to look at him, cutting off sound in return. "You're that familiar with their operation?"

He nodded. "I told you—I spent almost fifty million seconds down there. I saw that distillery put together and saw it go into operation. I know what it can do. And I know that man..." He remembered Djem Nakamore's face, the bald head reddened by the light from a primitive methane-burning stove; remembered the amused face of Djem's visiting half-brother, Raul. He heard the hiss as water sweated from the ceiling to drop and steam on the stove's greasy surface, as he waited while Djem pondered his next painfully predictable move that would lose him his hundredth, or his thousandth, game of chess to Wadie Abdhiamal. Stubborn, didactic, and unimaginative... honest, forthright, and dedicated to his duty. No match, as Djem had told him, often enough and without resentment, for Wadie's own quick and devious mind—yet too stubborn not to go on trying to win. Wadie adjusted the earflaps of his heavy hat, put out a hand to move his queen, *Checkmate....* "I know that man. Push him; he's not—devious enough to know whether you're bluffin'. And he'll do anything to keep that distillery intact." He realized suddenly that it could have been Raul instead who faced them now and was glad, for all their sakes, that it was not. He looked away as he spoke, avoiding the bright image on the screen and Betha Torgussen's eyes.

The captain frowned slightly, then turned back to Nakamore on the screen. "I don't accept that. You have twenty-five thousand seconds to give us the hydrogen or be destroyed."

"That's impossible!...It would take at least a hundred thousand seconds."

"Lie," Wadie said softly, shook his head again. "He's stalling; Central Harmony keeps plenty of naval units in this volume, and he's hopin' some of 'em will get here in time."

Nodding, she repeated flatly, "You have twenty-five kiloseconds. I know you have a high-performance linear accelerator down there. Use it. I don't want any manned vehicles to approach us. Copy coordinates..." She spoke the numbers carefully.

As she finished speaking Nakamore looked past her, angry and beaten, but little of it showing on his face. "Are you there givin' her the answers, Wadie?"

Wadie hung motionless...speechless. He pushed away from the panel at last, out into Nakamore's view. "Yeah, Djem, it's me."

"We picked up the broadcast debates from the Demarchy—how they've outlawed you. I figured maybe you'd—" Nakamore's face set, with the righteous anger of a man to whom loyalty was everything; with the pain of a man betrayed by a friend. "We were fools not to see what you and your...starship aliens would try. Why stop with a thousand tons of hydrogen? Why not take it all?"

"One thousand tons of hydrogen is all we need, Djem. And we need it bad, or I wouldn't put you through this." Without fuel, the starship was trapped, prey to the first group quick enough to take it. And then the Grand Harmony, the Demarchy, and everyone else would be the prey. Then the threats would be no bluff. This was for the best; this was the only choice he could possibly make, the only sane choice. If he could only...He started, "Djem, I—" But no words would come.

Nakamore waited, his black eyes pitiless. At last he leaned forward, reaching for the unseen panel. "Traitor." His face disappeared; and with it the last chance of asylum for a banished man. Discus alone lay on the screen.

The captain sat gazing fixedly at the screen, her mouth pressed together, a brittle golden figurine. Welkin glanced at

Wadie, apologetic but saying nothing, saving him from the embarrassment of a witty response that wouldn't come.

"...think they'll do it?" Bird Alyn pulled at the flapping end of her belt. "What if they don't?"

"They will." He found his voice, and his composure. "In fifty million seconds, Djem Nakamore never won a game of chess from me."

"You were perfect, Betha." Welkin turned back, his faded eyes searching the captain's downturned face. "Eric couldn't have put it more convincingly."

"If Eric were alive, we wouldn't be doing this."

Wadie nodded, relieved. "I almost believed you meant every word of that myself."

She struck a match. "What makes you think I didn't, Abdhiamal?" She lit her pipe, facing him with the same hardness that had faced down Snows-of-Salvation. "What have the Ringers done for us lately?"

"Indeed." He bowed grimly, looked back at Welkin. "I've learned my lesson—I'll never insult another engineer." He pushed off toward the door.

Betha watched him disappear down the stairwell, shaken with the coldness that left her words of apology stillborn.

"Betha...would you...are you really goin' to...destroy the distillery?" Bird Alyn whispered unhappily.

Betha met the frightened face. "No, of course not, Bird Alyn, I wouldn't do that. I'm not really a—a butcher."

Bird Alyn nodded, blinking, maneuvered backward and started for the door.

Clewell rubbed his beard. "Then why act like one, Betha? That was a little too convincing for me, too. Or isn't it an act anymore?"

Shame warmed her face, drove the coldness from her. "You know it is, Pappy! But that damned Abdhiamal—"

Clewell lifted his head slightly, unfastened his seatbelt. "He's not such a bad sort...for a 'damned fop.' He's held up pretty well under one gee...under everything he's been through." Meaning that she hadn't made things any easier.

"He's a phony; he's lucky he didn't cripple himself." She looked away irritably.

"He's a proud man, Betha. He might not call it that . . . but anybody who can stand straight and smile while gravity's pulling him apart—or loyalty is—has my admiration. In a way, he reminds me of—"

"He's not at all like Eric."

His eyebrows rose. "That wasn't what I was going to say. He reminds me of you." He held up a hand, cutting off her indignation. "But now that you mention it, there is something about him . . . a manner, maybe; even a physical resemblance. Maybe it's why I like him in spite of myself; maybe it's what bothers you. Something does."

"Oh, Pappy . . ." She lifted her hand, pressing her rings against her mouth. "It is true. Every time I look at him, anything he does, he reminds me—But he's *not* Eric. He's not one of us, he's one of *them*. How can I feel this way? How can I stop wanting . . . wanting . . ." She reached out; Clewell's firm, weathered hand closed over her wrist.

He smoothed her drifting hair. "I don't know. I don't know the answer, Betha." He sighed. "I don't know why they claim age is wisdom. Age is just getting old."

Shadow Jack moved restlessly, trapped in the too-empty box of the room where he slept, haunted by the ghost of a stranger: manuals on economics, a nonsense song lyric, a hand-knit sweater suspended in midair—a dead man's presence scattered through drawers and cupboards in the clutter of a life's detritus. Rusty clung to his shoulders, her mute acceptance easing the shame of his exile. He stroked her mindlessly, hearing only the ticking of the clock; meaningless divisions marking the endless seconds. He wondered whether they would get what they wanted from the Ringers, wondered how he could face Betha Torgussen again . . . wondered how he would face the rest of his life.

Rusty's small, inhuman face rose from his shoulder, her ears flicking. "Bird Alyn?" He pushed to the doorway, saw Wadie Abdhiamal disappear into another room. He heard Abdhiamal's voice, almost inaudible: "Damn that woman! She'd spit in the eye of God."

Shadow Jack moved along the hall, stopped at Abdhiamal's doorway, staring. "What's the matter, she spit in your eye?"

Abdhiamal twisted, a split-second's exasperation on his face. He smoothed his work shirt absently, smoothed his expression. "Yeah . . . somethin' like that."

"What happened up there? Did we get the hydrogen?"

"Probably. . . . Why weren't you in the control room?"

He grimaced. "I couldn't do it. I—I called the captain a pervert."

"You what?" Abdhiamal frowned in disbelief.

Shadow Jack caught the doorway to move on; desperation turned him back. "Can . . . I talk to you . . . man to man?"

Abdhiamal gestured him into the room, no trace of amusement on his face. "Probably. What about?"

Shadow Jack cleared his throat; Rusty pushed off from his shoulder, rose like a lifting ship, and swam toward Abdhiamal. "How come you never married?"

Abdhiamal laughed, startled. "I don't know." He watched the cat, reached out to pull her down to his chest. "Maybe because I never met a woman who'd spit in the eye of God."

Shadow Jack's eyes widened; and looking at Abdhiamal, he wondered who was more surprised.

Abdhiamal laughed again, shrugged. "But somehow I doubt it."

"I mean . . . you said before, that now you never would get married. I thought there was—some other reason." He reached for the doorframe.

"There was."

He stopped, holding on.

"I've traveled a lot. That means I've been exposed to high radiation levels and potential genetic damage. We have ways of preservin' sperm so men at least can travel and still raise healthy children. But with the bill of attainder, I'm legally dead now. They'll destroy my account." Abdhiamal took a deep breath. "And I've been sterilized."

Shadow Jack looked back, letting the words come, "I'd be happy if I was sterile!" He shook his head. "I didn't mean . . . I didn't mean it like that. But we can't ever get married, Bird

Alyn and me, because I'm not sterile and she's not. We *are* defective. We shouldn't ever have children, but we would...."

Abdhiamal scratched Rusty under the chin. "It's a simple operation. Can't they perform it on Lansing?"

"They could... but they won't." Misery hung on him like a weight. "If you're a Materialist, you're supposed to take responsibility for your own actions. You're supposed to take the consequences, not expect anybody else to do it for you. Like my mother, when my sister was born an' they said she was too defective... my mother had to put her Out.... She wouldn't let my father touch her anymore." He looked down at his hands. "But the medical technology's bad anyhow. Sometimes I think they just don't want to waste what's left."

Abdhiamal's voice was gently professional. "How were you judged defective? You look sound to me."

Shadow Jack's hands tightened on metal. "Maybe I wasn't defective, then. But my sister was. And they needed more outside workers, so they told me I had to work on the surface. That's what you do if you're marginally damaged, like Bird Alyn. That's where I met her...." Where he had discovered what life must have been like once, lived in the beauty of gardens and not the blackness of stone. And where he had discovered that his own life did not end because he had left the shielding walls of rock; that feeling did not, or belief, or hope. But he had spent too many megaseconds mending a tattered world-shroud, too many megaseconds in a contaminated ship.... And there were no miracles to heal a crippled hand or mend a broken heart.

He struck the doorframe. "Everything goes wrong! I didn't mean to call Betha... what I called her. But she had so many husbands; she even has children! When Bird Alyn and I can't even have each other... it just made me crazy. Betha lost so much, and I said—I said that to her. She helped us after we tried to take her ship just like everybody else—"

"You did? And she let you get away with it?"

He nodded, feeling ridiculous. "All we had was a can opener—I guess she thought we were fools."

"And—you said she has children?" Abdhiamal looked down at the wide leather band circling his wrist.

"Yeah. Goin' into space is like . . . like doing anything else to them. It's not the end of anything." He bit his tongue, remembering that it had been for the crew of the *Ranger*.

"If she forgave you for trying to steal her ship, I expect she'll forgive you for callin' her a pervert. Sooner than she'll forgive me for makin' remarks about engineers."

Shadow Jack frowned, not understanding.

Abdhiamal's smile faded. "It seems you and I have more than one problem in common. Like every group in Heaven Belt shares the problems of every other one. And I'm not so sure any more that there's an easy answer for any of us."

Shadow Jack turned away, saw Bird Alyn watching him from the end of the hall. He met her eyes, hopelessness dragging him down like the chains of gravity. "There aren't any answers at all. I should have known that. Sorry to take up your time, Abdhiamal."

Wadie closed the door, still cradling the cat absently against his side. In his mind he saw the future on Lansing, grief and death among the gardens—and saw in Lansing the future of all Heaven. . . . *The future?* Silence pressed his ears, deafening him. *The end.* The Demarchy was only one more fading patch of snow. There was no answer. Nothing he could ever do—nothing he had ever done—would hold back Death. He had made himself believe that his work had some relevance and worth, that a kind of creation existed in his negotiations, a binding force to keep equilibrium with disintegration and decay. But he had been wrong. It had always been too late. He was a damned fop, living at the expense of everyone else . . . and wasting his life on the self-delusion that he was somehow saving them all. Wasting his life: he had thrown away his last chance of ever having a life of his own, a home, a family, any real relationship. And all that he had ever done, been, or believed was meaningless. It had all been for nothing—and it would all be nothing in the end. *Nothing.*

Rusty squirmed in his grasp like an impatient child. As he released her his arm scraped the ventilator screen, his hand closed over a flat, palm-sized square trapped by the soft exit of air. He pulled it down, stared at it. A picture—a hologram—of a man and a woman, each holding a child, flooded in blazing light where they stood before an ugly, half-sunken dwelling. The woman was Betha Torgussen, her hair long, coiled on her head in braids. And the man, tall, with dark hair and a lean, sunburned face . . . *Eric?* Her voice came to him suddenly, from behind a shielding faceplate, in a train car on Mecca. *I—I thought you were someone I knew.* Wadie brushed the images with a finger, moving through them. Ghosts . . .

Betha Torgussen's voice came to him out of a speaker on the wall, telling the crew that Nakamore had acquiesced.

RANGER (DISCAN SPACE)

+ 2.74 MEGASECONDS

"Okay, Pappy, the cables are secured. We really outdid ourselves when we closed with this load! Start us in." Betha raised her chin from the speaker button, hooking her arm under the twisted strength of the steel cable, secure in the crevice between cylinders of hydrogen. She felt the abrupt lurch as the winches started the final shipment of fuel moving in toward the looming brilliance of the *Ranger*.

"This is the lot, Betha." Clewell's voice filled her helmet, smiling. She imagined his smile, felt it through the ship's mirrored hull.

"This is it. We've done it, Pappy! We're really going to make it." Through the shielded faceplate of her helmet she saw the molten silver, the ruby scarab of Discus reflecting on the *Ranger*'s hull, rising above a dull-green horizon of clustered tanks, marred by a tiny spot of blackness. The shadow of Snows-of-Salvation . . . or a ragged hole torn in the metal. She looked away, dizzy, past the small bright-suited figure of Shadow Jack at one end of the fifty-meter-long bundled cylinders. And out into the void; imagined the merciless drag of the Discan gravity well pulling her loose into the endless night . . . like five others before her. She shut her eyes, clung to the cable; opened them again to look down at the solid surface of the tanks, along the dull greenness at Abdhiamal, inept and uncommunicative at the shipment's other limit. They were almost flush now with the *Ranger*'s massive protection; it would be over soon. *One more, just one more time.* . . . Sweat tickled her face; she shook her head angrily inside her helmet. *Damn it! You won't fall—*

"Betha!" It was Bird Alyn's voice, rising clearly for once above the crackle of her feeble helmet speaker. Betha saw her, gnatlike beside the immense holding rack clamped to the ship's skin. "The load's not closing even! . . . Abdhiamal, your end—the end cable's caught between tanks—"

"I'll clear it."

"Abdhiamal, wait!" Betha saw him go over the end, saw the flash of his guidance rocket as he disappeared. "Pappy! Loosen the aft cable, right now!" She pulled her own guidance unit loose from the catch at her waist, pressed the trigger, sent herself after him to the end of the world. Looking over, she saw him hovering near the hub of the wheel of tanks, the cable trapped between two cylinders. She saw him catch hold of the cable, brace his feet, and pull—"Abdhiamal, stop, stop!"—saw the cable slip free . . . watched as the bound tanks recoiled below her and the cable wrenched loose from the hull, arcing soundlessly toward her like a striking snake. She backed desperately, knowing, knowing—

"Clewell!" Her face cracked against the helmet glass in starbursts of light as the cable struck her across the chest, throwing her out and away from the ship. She fought for breath, blood in her mouth, her lungs crippled with pain, saw the ship like a fiery pinwheel slip out of her view, blackness, blood and molten silver, blackness. . . . She fumbled for the trigger of her guidance rocket, but her hands were empty. And she was falling.

No—Betha began to scream.

Wadie felt the cable slip loose as the captain's voice reached him, telling him to stop. He fell back, suddenly unsupported, looking up in surprise—to see what he had done, see the tanks rebound, the cable lash out like a whip and knock her away . . . saw her guidance rocket fly free, tumbling, a spark of light. "Oh, my God—" He heard the cries of Bird Alyn and Shadow Jack, echoing his own, no sound from Betha Torgussen. He waved the others back as he went after her into the night.

The immensity of isolation stifled him, filling the black-and-

brilliant desolation like sand, dragging at him, holding him
back...as the isolation of his own making had cut him off
from the truth all his life. He closed with her spiraling form
slowly, agonizingly, centimeters every second...seeing in his
mind a ruptured suit, a frozen corpse, her pale, staring face
cursing him even in death for the hypocrisy of his wasted
years. Yet wanting, more than he had ever wanted anything in
his life, to close that gap between them, and see instead that it
was not too late....

And after a space as long as his life his gloved hand
clamped over an ankle. He drew her toward him and used his
guidance unit to stop their outward fall. He caught her helmet
in his hands, felt her clutch him feebly as he searched behind
the silent, red-fogged glass for a glimpse of her face. Repeat-
ing, wild with relief, "Betha...Betha...Betha, are you all
right?"

Her shadowed face fell forward, peering out; her chin
pressed the speaker bouton. "Eric...oh, Eric." He heard her
sob. "Don't let me go...I'll fall...don't let go, don't let
go..." Her arms tightened convulsively, silence formed between
them again. He stroked the tempered glass. "I won't...it's all
right...I won't let you go." The plane of the Discan rings
blinded him with frigid glory, as immutable as death; he turned
away from it, started them back toward the diminished ship,
across the black sand desert of the night. She kept radio silence;
he did not search for her face again behind the blood-reddened
glass, granting her the privacy of her grief, feeling the ghosts
of five human beings move with them. And at last he heard her
voice say his own name, thanking him, and say it again....

"What happened?"

"Is she all right?"

"Betha, are you all right?"

The voices of Shadow Jack and Bird Alyn clamored in his
helmet as they met him, their hidden faces turned toward Betha,
gloved hands reaching out.

"She's hurt. Help me get her inside." She scarcely moved
against his hold, silent as they made their way through the
airlock.

They entered the control room, her hands still locked rigidly on his suit. He looked across the room at the panel, looking for Welkin; cleared his faceplate, suddenly aware that nothing moved. "Welkin?" He saw a hand, motionless above the chair arm, and his throat closed.

Betha raised her head as if she were listening, but he could not answer. She released her grip, pushing away from him. "Pappy?" Her voice quavered, she folded into a tight crescent in the air, her arms wrapped against her stomach. "Pappy . . . are you there?" He heard a small gasp as she tried to lift her hands. "Somebody . . . get this helmet off. I can't see. Pappy?"

"Betha—" Shadow Jack began, broke off.

Bird Alyn moved to release Betha's helmet, lifted it slowly, jerked back at the sight of her face filmed with blood.

But Betha had already turned away, shaking her head to clear her confusion, pulling distractedly at her gloves. She froze as she saw the old man's drifting hand. "Oh, Jesus." Her own hand flew out, caught at Bird Alyn's suit, groping for purchase. Bird Alyn put an arm around her, helped her cross the room. Wadie followed.

"Pappy . . ." Her voice broke apart as she reached him.

Welkin opened his eyes as she touched his face, stared her into focus uncomprehendingly, his right hand pressing his chest. She laughed, or sobbed, squeezing his shoulder. "Thank God! Thank God . . . I thought . . . you're so cold . . ."

"Betha. Are you—?"

"I'm all right. I'm fine." She put a trembling hand up to her face, glanced at her bloody fingertips. "Just a . . . nosebleed. What—what happened?"

"Pain . . . in my chest, like being crushed; down my arm . . . must be my heart. Was afraid to move. When I saw . . . what happened to you on the screen—"

"Don't. Don't think about it . . . it's over. We'll make it, Pappy. We'll make it yet. Close your eyes, don't move, don't worry, just rest. We'll take care of you." She managed a smile, new blood blurring on her chin, her hand gently cupping his face.

"Should we get him to the infirmary?" Wadie hesitated near her shoulder, forcing himself to speak.

"No." Welkin shook his head, eyes shut. "Not yet. Finish the job!"

"He's right. We shouldn't move him yet, anyway. Thank God we're in zero gee. . . ." Betha pulled a scarf out of a cubby under the panel, starting a small blizzard of papers drifting. She wiped her face and spat gingerly, wincing. Wadie saw her control slip again, saw pain show, and her body bend as she pushed out of Welkin's sight. Bird Alyn moved back to her side, mouth open; she frowned, straightening, shook her head. "All right. Pappy said it. We're going to finish the job. Nothing will stop us now! I'll start the winch. Bird Alyn, get back outside . . . and make sure the load is secured. Shadow Jack, you'll chart us a course for Lansing. Tell me what you need to know, I'll double-check you. . . . Abdhiamal—"

He met her eyes, bracing against what he expected to see. "Keep the hell out of your way?"

Expressionless, she said, "Go to the infirmary and get me a hypo of painkiller for Clewell. They're prefilled, with the first-aid supplies." She caught hold of a chair back, shook her head. "Make it two hypos. And then"—her eyes changed, clung to him—"keep the hell out of my way, Abdhiamal!"

"... how you intend to explain what your man's done now, MacWong? He must've shown the Outsiders how to get that hydrogen. Now he's made certain we can't catch the starship before it leaves the system." Esrom Tiriki moved incautiously in the overcrowded space of the ship's control room.

"He isn't 'my man' anymore, Demarch Tiriki. He was declared a traitor," Lije MacWong repeated wearily. *He is a traitor, much to my surprise. Why? Revenge? A reasonable assumption...* "In any case, he didn't deliver the starship to the Ringers, either."

"But you said he would."

"It was a reasonable assumption." MacWong felt unaccustomed tension tightening the muscles in his neck—brought on by the discomfort of the ship's acceleration, and by the effect discomfort was having on everyone else, as well. He silently regretted the ill fortune that had made Tiriki Distillates a part owner of this fusion ship, and permitted Esrom Tiriki to be here as its representative. Tiriki—and his company—had suffered considerable embarrassment when their personal plans for the starship had been exposed; even Tiriki's two fellow representatives had begun to let their disapproval show as their tempers shortened. MacWong further regretted that Tiriki did not have the self-control to suffer in silence.

The Nchibe representative drew Tiriki's unwelcome attention again and MacWong drifted away past a yawning, fawning mediaman in Nchibe livery. They had picked up the Ringers' reply to the starship's threats, and it had been sent on to the Demarchy—as all crucial information was, and would be, during their pursuit. The people, the changeable god to whom he had offered up Wadie Abdhiamal and other sacrificial scapegoats, kept watch over him even here. But now for once the people kept their silence, because any response would have reached the starship too, and revealed their pursuit. For possibly the only time in his career he had a measure of freedom in his decision-making; he was not sure yet how much he could afford to enjoy it.

Because the next decision he would make now—and answer for later—was whether to continue pursuing the starship or to return to the Demarchy. And the decision was not as obvious as it seemed. . . . The starship had taken a thousand tons of hydrogen—far more than it needed to escape from the system, from what Osuna had told him. Enough fuel to critically cripple its speed and maneuverability. Had they done that for revenge, too? Somehow he doubted it. They had destroyed a ship before; this time they could have destroyed so much more . . . they could have destroyed the major distillery. But they hadn't. He experienced a curious mingling of fascination and relief.

But the starship had gone to Lansing when it first entered the system; there had been a Lansinger with the woman at Mecca. If its crew had made some sort of deal with Lansing, that could explain a lot of things. And it would mean that the starship would not be heading directly out of the system; that there was still a chance for Demarchy ships to overtake it.

MacWong looked back as the ship's pilot approached Tiriki and the others, to interrupt them deferentially. And what would happen if they captured the starship? He glanced out of the port beside him, seeing the long, intensely lavender thread of a second ship's torch reaching across the night. By then they would be millions of kilometers from the Demarchy—these three armed ships, and the men who controlled them: ambitious men, men who enjoyed power, men like Esrom Tiriki. No matter what the people decided concerning the starship, by then there would be no way that the Demarchy could force these men to obey it . . . and no one would be quicker to realize that. His nearness to Tiriki and his insulation from the people had made him understand what Abdhiamal had known instinctively from the start: that the starship which could be their salvation could instead turn out to be the bait for a deadly trap.

He sighed. *You were always a better man than I was, Wadie; and that was your whole problem....* And maybe that explained Abdhiamal's treason better than any speculation about revenge. He had been more than sorry to make Abdhiamal into a man without a world ... but maybe in the end it would turn out to be the best move he had ever made. And perhaps now he had the opportunity to repay Abdhiamal in part, as the spokesman of the people—by keeping his mouth shut about what he knew.

"Demarchs—" The three company men and the pilot looked up at him together; he watched a mediaman adjust a camera lens. "I think we all know by now that our attempt to seize that starship has failed. But at least it hasn't fallen into enemy hands. It's leavin' the system; we might as well save a further waste of our own resources and return home—"

"Maybe we haven't lost it yet, Demarch MacWong." Tiriki showed him a porcelain smile that was somehow more unpleasant than his former petulance.

"We've just been given some new information about the starship." The Estevez nephew nodded at the ship's pilot. "Lin-piao says that the ship isn't leavin' the system; it's turned back in toward the Main Belt."

"To Lansing," Tiriki said. "They're goin' back to Lansing."

"We still have a chance to take it; Lin-piao says it's only doing one-quarter gee now."

MacWong hesitated, seeing the three of them united, finally, in the purpose of carrying through their mission. And behind them the entire Demarchy watched in silent judgment. It knew what they knew; and it knew that he, MacWong, had instigated this pursuit. The people didn't know everything—but had they already learned too much? He could still press for a retreat ... but would they accept it now? "If the people feel that a further effort to pursue the starship wouldn't be worth the Demarchy's while, I hope they'll let us know." He spoke the words to the waiting cameras with careful emphasis. "In the meantime ..." He felt the intentness of seven sets of eyes, felt the pressure of a thousand more behind them. "In view of this new information, I feel we should continue our mission. I have personal data, concernin' the starship's entry into the system and its fuel needs, that support the theory it's headin' for Lansing now." *Sorry, Wadie.* He watched the faces relax into satisfaction and complacency. *But it's my job to give the people what they want.* He matched them smile for smile, one satisfaction for another.

"Demarchs . . ." The pilot pulled self-consciously at the hem of his golden company jacket. "By the time we've changed course, we still may not be able to catch up with 'em. Even if the starship can only manage one-quarter gee, by the time we decelerate again for Lansing ourselves—"

The pilot broke off, as a frown spread among them like a disease. MacWong weighed its significance like a physician; and prescribed the remedy that he knew would heal any damage to his own credibility: "I think that may not turn out to be a problem, demarchs. If you'll consider the followin' course of action. . . ."

RANGER (IN TRANSIT DISCUS TO LANSING)

+ 2.96 MEGASECONDS

Wadie walked the corridor to Betha Torgussen's private room, slowed by one-quarter gravity and the fatigue of their work in space . . . and by the same tangle of emotion that drove him to face her now. The memory of the Discan sky, hazed with shining flotsam and hung with crescent moons, haunted him: the knowledge of a costly victory won and almost lost again by his own actions; two lives, the last of the Morningside crew, almost lost—and with them the part of himself that he had only just begun to discover. . . .

He reached the open door, stopped as the hallway slipped back into focus, and stepped through.

Rusty's head appeared suddenly from a cocoon of bedding, watched him like a familiar as he looked across the room. The captain sat at her desk, her back to him, her attention lost among scattered displays and printouts. Empty coffee cups littered the desk top; there was a sign above her head on the wall, TEN YEARS AGO I COULDN'T EVEN SPELL "ENGINEER," AND NOW I ARE ONE. He smiled briefly, until he heard her sigh, a sound that was a small groan. The vision formed inside his eyes of her cracked and bandaged ribs, a bruise the width of his arm.

He turned abruptly to leave the room again, found a picture on the wall inside a broad green arrow pointing DOWN: found Betha Torgussen, and Welkin, and—Eric, bearded now and smiling. With them, two more women, two more men, and seven children bundled in heavy clothes; all pale, laughing, waving in three dimensions, joyfully disheveled against a background of snow. A family who knew how to share . . . and somehow, with the fever of futile greed that burned through Heaven, their sharing no longer seemed so alien or so bizarre. . . .

Rusty stirred on the bed, blinking; she *mrr*ed inquiringly. Betha turned across the back of her chair, controlling a grimace, her own eyes suddenly quick and nervous, question his presence.

"Betha . . . I'd like to see you, if you don't mind. There're some things I think I need to say." He crossed the room.

"All right, Abdhiamal." Her eyes went to his wrist, Clewell's wristband. "Yes, maybe you should." Her face changed. "But first, tell me how Clewell is. How is he taking the acceleration?"

"Well enough, I guess. He's very weak, but he's no fool. . . ." *And nobody's fool.* Sudden appreciation for the old man filled him. "I don't suppose I'd have the guts to be here if I didn't believe he was goin' to be all right. . . . But what about you? What are you tryin' to prove? Why the hell aren't you getting some rest—" He broke off, not sure who he was really angry at.

Her bruised mouth tightened. "Because I'd rather be sore than dead. And yes, I am trying to prove something." She gestured at the computer terminal, her expression easing. "I—didn't know whether to let you know about this, but . . . we've detected a patch of hydrogen and helium, Doppler-shifted into the red; I think it's a hydrogen fusion torch pointed away from us. Right now it's still thirty million kilometers behind us—but we're being followed."

"You can detect an averted torch at that range? Your instruments are better than ours." He was impressed again.

"Are they? Good. . . . But with these fuel canisters strapped to the hull, we can't move faster than whoever's behind us. What I need to know is whether the ships come from the Demarchy or Discus; and, if they are from the Demarchy, what you think their mission is. Do they still want to take the ship, or are they out to destroy us?"

He leaned on the desk, the tendons ridging slightly in his arm. "Good question. The ships are from the Demarchy. Nobody else has anythin' like that left; the Ringers have only oxyhydrogen rockets. Our—the Demarchy's—fusion ships are owned by interests in the most powerful tradin' companies, but in times of 'national emergency' the Demarchy commandeers 'em. Which means MacWong's story about my handing you to the Ringers must've been well received. . . ." He stopped. "He knows it was a damn lie; and knowin' him, I'd say that means he did it because he still wants this ship, and that was the only way he could think of to get the ships to follow you."

"But then he must know that we'll still outrun them, now that we've got the fuel; even if we stop at Lansing. If they have to do a turnaround to match our deceleration we'll be long gone before they reach us. If they don't slow down, they'll overshoot . . . and all they could do then would be destroy us in passing." Her fingers tapped nervously.

He nodded. "He'd know that too. But he wants that ship intact for the Demarchy, and he's not the kind to mine quartz and think it's ice. He's got somethin' planned but I don't know what."

"At least we know where they are, and they don't know we know. If they were counting on surprise to close the gap they've lost it." She shifted in her seat, leaning hard on the desk top. "I suppose we'll know more when we begin decelerating and see if they do the same. Even if they don't slow down . . . well, depending on what you can tell me about the range of their weapons, I think we can still stop at Lansing long enough to off-load the extra hydrogen—and then accelerate at right angles to them with enough time to get away. By the time they can change course, we'll be out of this system forever."

"Out of our system forever. And we'll be . . ." He looked down at her strong and gentle face, wondered why he had ever thought it was plain. His hands tightened over a sudden desire to touch it.

Realization colored her cheeks. She looked up at him strangely, almost welcoming, lifted a hand. "Sit down, Abdhiamal . . . Wadie Abdhiamal. You'll be—better off without us, yes."

He sank down on the padded wall seat, pushing aside heaped clothes. "Betha, there're no words to apologize for what I've

done to you, out of my own stupidity... my God, I nearly—
killed you. All the things I said, not meanin'—''

Her hand waved the words to silence. "I never meant to ruin
your life, Wadie.... I owe you as many apologies as you owe
me. More. Is it too late to cancel them out, now?''

He leaned back, resting his head against the wall, eyes on
her. "It's never too late. But I'm not—very good at expressing
my emotions, Betha. I'm not even good at admitting them to
myself.'' He took a long breath. "All of a sudden there are a lot
of things I want to be different. But there's so little time—'' He
broke off; feeling the presence of ghosts. "That picture across
the room: Is that—Eric, beside you?''

Surprise caught her. She nodded, her face composed. "He
was my first husband. He was—a kind of negotiator too, an
ombudsman. We were monogamous for eight years before we
married into Clewell's family.''

"And you have children?''

"The twins, Richard and Kirsten; the boy and girl in front
of me. They're about eleven now...." She smiled. "They're all
my children. But the twins were born to me, they have my
name. All seven of our kids who are still at home are staying
with my family.''

"You left your children—'' He stopped himself before he
hurt her again. *We do change; but change always comes too
fast... and too late.* And there were only one hundred kiloseconds
remaining until they reached Lansing.

She glanced at him, puzzled. "Yes. We left them with my
parents, on their tree farm." And understanding, "Half the
world is your family when you're growing up on Morningside.
They hug you, tell you stories, and make you toys...there's
always someone who's glad to see you. We didn't abandon our
children. But it has been very hard to miss seeing so much of
their lives as they grow. At least Clewell and I will get to see
how they've grown...." She looked down, shuffling papers; he
saw the return of more than one kind of pain.

"Shadow Jack and Bird Alyn... are they why you're risking
everything, to buy a dyin' world a few more seconds?''

She hesitated. "I don't know. I hadn't thought...but I
suppose maybe it is. I wish—I wish I knew how to do more.''

"You know, then? What it's like for them on Lansing?"
She nodded.

"I'm not much lookin' forward to it myself, I've got to admit. But I've talked myself out of anythin' better—literally." He smiled. "I don't regret it. It was in a good cause."

She picked up a cup, set it down aimlessly. "What will you do, Wadie, on Lansing?"

He smiled again, hearing his name; the smile stopped when he remembered. "Sit and watch the world end, I suppose. All the worlds. Not with a bang but a gasp."

"You don't have to, you know."

He felt her touch him as though she had raised a hand. He shook his head. "Maybe I do. Maybe that's my penance for pretendin' there was no tomorrow."

"You don't believe that?"

"I don't know." He shrugged. "I don't know what I believe anymore." Only knowing that he was alive in a vast mausoleum and afraid to look at death. "But I belong here, to Heaven; if that makes any sense. It scares the hell out of me, but I've got to see it through. But thanks." He saw her smile, disappointed.

"You can change your mind."

"Sooner than I could change Heaven. . . . Ironic, isn't it; that we began with everything and Morningside with nothing . . . and look who failed."

"We almost failed too—more than once." Betha stared at the wall, looking through time. "So did Uhuru, and Hellhole, and Lebensraum. But we had help."

"From where?"

"From each other. Planets like Morningside are so marginal any small setback becomes a disaster . . . but they're the most common kind of habitable world; they're all like Morningside in our volume of space. But our worlds are within reach of one another. We set up a trade ring, and when one of us falls flat, the rest pick it up and put it back together. And that's how we survive. That's all we do; we survive. But it's enough . . . it'll have to be enough forever, now that our journey here has failed.

"We have our own ironies, you know. . . . Morningside was

settled after a major political upheaval on Earth. Our nearest neighbor now, Uhuru, was settled by some of our former 'enemies' after their own empire on Old Earth fell. Need makes stranger bedfellows than politics ever did.''

He laughed abruptly. "As the five of us should know."

"Yes." She held him with her eyes, fingers over her lips.

"If you'd come before the war, Betha, maybe the five of us would even be doin' some good. Heaven could have learned somethin' then about sharing. Now it's too late; there's nothing left to share."

She shifted position again, wincing. "Wadie . . . you said the knowledge that put Heaven's technology where it was is still intact. That if you could rebuild your capital industry, you could still make the Belt work again, and it could be everything it once was. You said even the *Ranger* could make the difference. . . . What if—what if we tied you into our trading network? It's feasible; the distance here from Morningside isn't that much greater than the distances we already travel. If we gave you the means for recovery, you could give us what we wanted all along, a richer life for all our worlds—and you'd never have to see this happen again!''

He listened to her voice come alive with inspiration; felt suddenly as though the pain and grief had lifted from her mind only to settle in his own. "That's what I said. But I was wrong."

"Wrong?"

"We've gone down too far. We can't recover now; death is a disease that's infected us all. We'll never work together now, even to save ourselves."

"But if they could understand that there was hope for all of them . . ."

"How could you make them understand? You've seen how well they listen." He slammed his hand down on the bench. "They wouldn't listen!"

"No, they wouldn't. . . ." Betha began to smile, in misery, moving her head from side to side. "Wadie Abdhiamal—how did we come to this? You saying they wouldn't, me saying they would. . . . How did we come to understand each other better than we understand ourselves?''

He shook his head, felt a smile soothe his own mouth, lost his useless anger watching her.

Her hand moved tentatively from the desk to touch her band on his wrist; he caught her hand and their fingers twined, brown and pale. She looked across at him, down at their hands. She drew her hand from his again, said quietly to no one, ''And not one of them lived happily ever after. . . .''

A raid. While he, Raul Nakamore, had been chasing the phantom Ship from Outside, it had run literal rings around him and raided the very distillery his borrowed ships had been set to defend. While he was still locked into his initial—futile—trajectory toward Lansing, without fuel enough to make an attempt at further pursuit anything but a joke. Raul drummed irritably on the arm of his seat, having no better way to vent his frustration.

And yet, the reports he'd received indicated that the starship had not headed directly out of the system; indicated, in fact, that the ship might be tracking his own course and returning again to Lansing. Raul glanced at the instrument board, seeing twenty-seven hundred kiloseconds elapsed, only twenty-three kiloseconds remaining before they reached Lansing. Like the fable of the tortoise and the hare—slowed by the stolen hydrogen, the starship would never reach Lansing before then, if Lansing was its destination. But why should it be? Why would these outsiders play pirate for Lansing, when they'd suffered losses in the Rings already? Revenge? But they could easily have destroyed the distillery, and instead they stole one thousand tons of hydrogen: too little to cripple the Grand Harmony, too much for a ramscoop's drive.

And showing them how to steal it had been Wadie Abdhiamal . . . Wadie Abdhiamal of the Demarchy. Outlawed by the Demarchy, Djem had said, voted a traitor by his own people for helping the starship escape them. And if there was one thing he, Raul, was sure of, it was that Abdhiamal was no traitor.

Why had he betrayed the future of his own people, then? He might not be a jingoist but he wasn't insane. Why would he threaten Snows-of-Salvation, when he knew better than any other demarch what it meant to the survival of both their peoples? Why would he betray his friends? Because they had been his friends; and by betraying them he had cut himself off from the only haven he would have found in his exile.

Maybe he'd been forced into it. But Djem hadn't thought that Abdhiamal had acted like a man who had been forced. . . . Raul knew that Djem would never forgive Wadie Abdhiamal— for the betrayal of their friendship, if for no other reason. What was it about that ship, or whoever ran it, that would make a man like Abdhiamal willing to sacrifice everything? Maybe he would never know. But if that ship was following them to Lansing . . .

Raul stretched and turned to look at Sandoval. Sandoval sat with an expression of uncompromising boredom on his hawk-nosed profile, rereading a novel tape. A good officer, Raul thought. If he believed this use of his ship and crew was fruitless or pointless, he never let it show. Raul kept his own doubts and speculations private. Twenty-three kiloseconds to Lansing. And maybe they wouldn't be disappointed after all. . . .

The sight of Discus, shrunken almost to insignificance, greeted Raul as he pushed off from the hatch, drifting down to the stony surface of Lansing's docking field. He remembered looking up into a Demarchy sky, long ago, where Discus had been only a bright starpoint, one of a thousand scattered stars, and as unreachable as the stars. He remembered the feeling of isolation and desolation that had struck him then. But this time, invisible now but much closer at hand, there was the ship that he had left in low orbit above Lansing to ensure their safety. He moved cautiously as he waited for the handful of crew from the two docked ships, easing tension and unused muscles; grateful, after nearly three megaseconds, for the return of normal gravity. Across the field lay three other ships. He studied them with a fleeting curiosity, realizing that even Lansing had the nuclear-electric rockets that the Grand Harmony didn't have; but realizing too that these ships were so deadly that even the Harmony would be better off without them. Below him (the angle of gravity's feeble drag put the term into his mind), the semitransparent plastic that shrouded nine-tenths of Lansing rock showed muted patches of green and gold, pastelled by the angle of his sight. He thought of drifted snow, the pastels of impure gases crystallized by cold.

This was Lansing, the once-proud capital of a once-proud Heaven Belt, the only world of its kind. Its self-contained ecosystem had re-created Old Earth, and that was why its population had survived the war; and because, as a capital, it had been a showplace and nothing more. He knew that Lansing had been reduced to piracy at the time of their last close pass with Discus; he wondered what they had been reduced to by now. His crew were nervous and hostile. He had given orders for them to remain suited even inside the asteroid, to isolate them from any contagion—and to isolate them from any other incidents that might come out of a face-to-face confrontation with the locals.

They started toward the single airlock visible in the hillside above the ships. Raul glanced on up at the solitary radio antenna on the crest of the naked hill. It was half-illuminated by the cold light of the distant sun, sinking into shadow as the planetoid tumbled endlessly, imperceptibly. No lights blinked along its slender stalk as a warning to docking ships. His radioman had been unable to detect any broadcast response from Lansing. He wondered whether their communications had failed entirely, whether they even knew his ships had landed . . . whether—like an unpleasant premonition—they might all be dead.

One of his men turned the wheel on the hatchway sunk into the rock; he watched it begin to cycle. The men behind him waited, without eagerness, without relief, without any sense of triumph at having reached their goal. He heard only broken whispers, an uneasy muttering, picked up by his suit radio. Their silence surprised him until he realized that it was an extension of his own; as if isolation and the pall of death that shrouded the Main Belt like a tent shrouded this world had affected them all. The airlock hatch swung out. With a sudden vision of the yawning pit, the gates of hell, Raul entered the underworld.

The lock cycled again, replacing vacuum with atmosphere in the crowded space between. Raul felt his suit lose its armor rigidity, glance back to be sure that no one disobeyed him by loosening a helmet. After nearly three megaseconds of uncertain reprocessed air, he knew well enough how strong the temptation was. He checked his rifle, settled it in the crook of his arm.

The inner hatch slid open. He looked through—into the staring faces of half a dozen men and women, frozen in disbelief. They had not, he gathered, been expecting him. He pushed through into the corridor, searching the frightened faces for a sign of leadership; taking in the filth, the patched and piecemeal clothing. He heard the startled curses of the men behind him, raised his own voice. "All right, who—"

A woman who might have been young or old moved away from the rest toward him, carrying something bundled in rags; he saw a sheen of tears filming her cheeks, her dark eyes fixed on him with peculiar urgency. He heard her voice, trembling, ". . . a miracle, it's a miracle . . ." Before he could react she had forced the bundle into his arms; she pushed off and disappeared down the sloping tunnel. Taken aback, he looked down at the ragged bundle and found himself holding a newborn child. The baby made no sound; when he saw why, he turned his face away. "Whose baby is this?" His voice hardened with anger, with denial.

One of the men moved toward him, fear still on his face, a kind of desperation dragging him forward. "It's mine . . . ours. Please . . . please, let me have it." Something in his tone made the baby a thing. He stretched his arms; one sleeve flopped free, torn up to the elbow. His nails were outlined with black dirt; dirt filigreed the lines of his hands.

Raul held the child out slowly, uncertain. The father took it, almost jerked it from his arms. Abruptly the man pushed through the circle of armed crewmen and caught the edge of the hatchway. He thrust the baby inside, his hand found the control plate, his fist struck it and started it cycling.

Raul saw Sandoval leap forward, but the man pressed himself against the wall, covering the plate, as the door began to slide shut. Sandoval's gloved fist caught him by the front of his shirt, ripping the rotten cloth; the man pushed him away with a foot. The hatch sealed shut as Sandoval tried to force his fingers into the gap. The light blinked red from green above their heads. "Why you—" Sandoval turned back, as two of his crew pinned the man between them.

"Sandoval!" Raul raised a hand. "That's enough. That's enough... It was a—mercy killing. Let him go."

"Sir—" He saw Sandoval's rage trapped behind helmet glass.

Raul shook his head, putting aside the memory of his own three daughters and two sons, all grown now and sound. He watched the father sag against the wall in slow motion as the crewmen released him. The man plucked mournfully at the drifting edges of his torn shirt, as though the tear were a death wound.

Raul glanced back down the tunnel, saw that the rest of the onlookers had disappeared. He moved toward their prisoner through the crew's muttered anger, through a ring of set faces. The man cringed and put up his hands. "I had to... I had to. Somebody had to do it; she knew that, but she wouldn't admit it! Everybody said so. It would've died anyway—wouldn't it? Wouldn't it? You saw it, it was defective...." He lowered his hands, reached out to grasp Raul's suited arm. "You saw it?"

Raul's fist tightened against the urge to slap the hand away. He took a deep breath. "Yes, I saw it. It wouldn't have lived."

The man began to whimper, clinging to his sleeve. "Thank you... thank you..."

Raul shook him roughly, caught somewhere between pity and disgust. "Who are you?"

The man looked at him blankly, stupidly.

"Your name," Raul said. "Identify yourself."

"Wind... Wind Kitavu." The man straightened, letting go of Raul's arm as reason came back into his eyes; aged eyes in a young man's face. "Who—what are you doin' here?"

"Askin' the questions. First, is anybody in charge here, and if so, can you take us to 'em?"

Wind Kitavu nodded, staring distractedly into the muzzles of half a dozen rifles. "The prime minister, the Assembly. I know where the chambers are. I'll take you. . . ." His fingers searched the tear in his shirt again, drew the edges together nervously. "You aren't the—" Raul watched the question form on his lips, saw him swallow it. "You want me to take you?"

Raul gestured his men aside; letting Wind Kitavu pass, he followed, and the crewmen fell in behind him. He noticed that one of the prisoner's legs was shorter than the other and twisted. *The gates of hell; the capital of Heaven.*

They were not led out onto the surface as he had expected. Wind Kitavu kept to the subterranean hallways, where dull-eyed men and women with stringy hair watched them pass, showing mingled fear and wonder, but mostly confusion. *No threat.* He felt his wariness settle into a bleak feeling of depression. A woman pushed out from the wall, moving with Wind Kitavu, ". . . starship . . . ?" Wind Kitavu shook his head, and she drifted free, her face tightening. Raul saw despair in her eyes as he passed, and his spirits rose.

On his orders Wind Kitavu pointed the way to the communications center, and he sent Sandoval with two men to investigate. With the others he continued on, wondering what they would find when they reached the assembly chambers.

Whatever he had been expecting could not have prepared him for what he found. Someone had sent word of their arrival ahead: seven figures stood waiting, tiny in a vast rough-walled chamber that he somehow instinctively knew must have been intended for storage and not as a meeting hall. And like gem crystals in a matrix of barren rock, the five men and two women shone, resplendent in robes of state. One man, Raul noticed, was still adjusting the folds of a sleeve tangled by haste. The nearest of them started forward, his drifting progress a ceremony, his face set in expressionless formality. Raul studied the intricacies of layer on layer of brocade as the official approached: the fibers absorbed and enhanced light, sent it back at his eyes in a shower of scintillating fire. He began to see, as he probed the wash of gemlight, the patches where it dimmed and faltered. The garments were stained and frayed, eaten by time. The man wore a soft, turbaned head covering of the same material; his seamed face and gnarled hands, fading darkly against the brilliance, were clean.

Raul waited silently until the official reached him. The six assembly members, their own threadbare splendor muted, clustered slowly behind him. Their group stare rested on Raul's weapon rather than his face. At last the man lifted his gaze, searching Raul's helmet glass to meet his eyes. "I am Silver Tyr,"—the voice surprised him with its unwitting arrogance—"President of the Lansing Assembly, Prime Minister of the Heaven Belt—"

The man broke off, as laughter rattled in Raul's helmet; for a long second he didn't realize that it was not his own bitten-off laugh, that it had come from one of his crewmen. He raised a hand to stop it, hearing mentally the clattering mockery the chamber would make of the sound.

"And you are—?" The prime minister forced the words with rigid dignity—demanding respect not for an aging shadow man, ludicrous in the rags of lost richness, but for the undeniable fact of the lost dream-time, of what they had all been, once, before their fall from grace.

"Raul Nakamore, Hand of Harmony." And almost unthinkingly he held out a hand, gloved against contamination but open in friendship, in recognition. "We mean you people no harm; we only want your cooperation while we're here."

The prime minister extended a hand, with the hesitancy of a man who expected to have it lopped off. "And what have you come here for, sir?"

Raul shook the hand, let it go, before he answered. "We've come huntin' pirates, Your Excellency." He dredged the unaccustomed title up from a half-forgotten history lesson. He noted the ill-concealed start of guilty knowledge on more than one face.

Seeing him observe it, the prime minister said, almost protesting, "But that happened almost a gigasec ago, Hand Nakamore—and it was an act of need, as you must know. Surely you haven't come all this way, after all this time, to punish—"

"I'm not speakin' of your last raid on the Rings, Your Excellency—I think you know that. I'm speakin' of a starship from outside the Heaven system, that destroyed one of our Navy craft and raided our main distillery—and is passin' by Lansing on its way out of the system—''

"Sir—'' Raul heard Sandoval's voice, turned at the sound of more men entering the room.

Sandoval and the two crewmen joined his group, escorting an angry, thin-faced woman. Brown skin, brown eyes, brown hair graying at the temples: Raul assessed her as she assessed him. He felt her anger flick out in a lash of wordless contempt as she glanced at the robed figures of the assembly. Her gaze returned to him, the anger cooling; he thought of a fire banked, controlled, still burning underneath.

"Sir, we found this woman in the radio room. She claims their comm's out of order.''

He nodded; turned back as the prime minister said, "We know nothin' about a starship. You saw the only ships we've got. They can't reach Discus anymore—''

"Face reality, Silver Tyr!'' The sharp edge of the woman's voice slashed his words. "He can see you're lyin'; all of you, you couldn't cover the truth any more than those robes cover your rags. If he didn't know the truth before, he knows it now. The best we can do is cooperate, the way he says, and hope maybe he'll be willin' to bargain—''

"Flame Siva! Would you betray the only people in the universe who care enough to help us? And your own daughter—''

"No cripple, no defective, is a child of mine.'' Her voice betrayed her. Raul felt the heat of bitter disappointment in the ashes of her words. The sagging figure of crippled Wind Kitavu tightened in a flinch. "But that's irrelevant, anyway, under the circumstances.''

A frown settled into the lines of the prime minister's face. "Two of our people are on board the starship. They say the Grand Harmony attacked the starship first. It had a reason and a right to retaliate against you, and you have no legal claim on it, in our judgment. We have no intention of cooperatin' with any attempt to seize it.''

"I see.'' Raul matched the frown, realizing that there was nothing he could really do to these people, because he had already destroyed their only hope. "Fortunately for you, we don't really need your cooperation . . . but we won't tolerate any interference. We intend to wait here until that ship arrives." He studied their responses; knew, with certainty and a kind of callous joy, that it would. "One of my ships is remainin' in orbit above Lansing; if we encounter any resistance, the captain has orders to hole your tent. If you want what time you've got left to you, don't get in our way."

"Even on Lansing we don't run to meet Death, Hand Nakamore." The prime minister looked down at his gun.

"Especially on Lansing," Flame Siva said. "We're Materialists, Hand Nakamore, realists. At least we're supposed to be." She paused. "Just what are you plannin' to do to that ship and its crew? Will you seize it intact?"

Raul laughed shortly. "That's what we'll try to do. But I'd disable it permanently before I'd let it get away from us again. And we want the crew alive, to show us how to run it. But if they refuse to let us board—piracy is a high crime by anybody's law, punishable by death." He saw the assembly members shift, glittering.

"She's lost most of her crew to you already," the woman murmured, almost to the floor.

"She?" Raul said, surprised. "That's right"—remembering a detail of alienness and the detection of human remains— "she: a woman pilot. So her crew is shorthanded?"

"Two of our own people are with them," she repeated. He realized that it was more than a simple statement of fact: *her daughter*, the prime minister had said. Her hand rose, agitated; she brushed her neck, her matted hair, controlling a gesture he recognized as threatening. "The captain promised us the hydrogen we need to survive, if they helped her get it for her own ship . . . the hydrogen you wouldn't share with either of us, unless we took it from you by force."

He waited, not responding because she hadn't made it a challenge.

"What would you give us if I helped you secure the ship intact?"

Surprised again, he asked, "What could you do to guarantee that?"

Thin hands crossed before her, locked around her thin arms;

sleeves that were too long and too wide slid back. "Allow me to finish repairs on the radio . . . give me parts for it if you have them." She glanced up, her eyes hard and bright. "Let me make contact with the ship when it approaches, to reassure them that it's safe to come in close, so that you can take them easily."

"We could do that ourselves."

"No, you can't. My—our people on the ship know the radio here and its problems, and they know my voice. A stranger's voice would make them suspect somethin' was wrong . . . and so would radio silence."

"You may have a point." Raul nodded.

"Will you leave us the hydrogen if I do that?" No fire showed this time.

"If the ship escapes, they can come back with the hydrogen!" Wind Kitavu burst out. "Don't take away our only chance—"

She turned; her face silenced him. Raul wondered what showed on it. She turned back. "Will you?"

Knowing how easy it would be to lie, he said, "I'll request permission. Maybe I'll get it; maybe I won't." He waited for her reaction, was puzzled by a kind of exasperation, as if she had wanted him to lie, wanted an excuse to perform treason. Or was it something else? He thought of Wadie Abdhiamal.

"But the crew, then? If you . . . take the ship intact."

"If I take them alive?" *Her daughter*. . . finding in that sufficient explanation at last. "So she does matter to you?"

Flame Siva started; her eyes were cinders, her voice lost its strength. "Yes . . . of course she matters . . ." And suddenly defiant, "They all matter! They're tryin' to save us!" She stopped, biting her lip.

Raul shifted lightly. "If they don't resist us, we'll release your daughter and the other one here; if that's what you want." *That'll be punishment enough.* "For the rest—there's a Demarchy traitor on board, who gave 'em the information to hit our distillery. I don't think he's left himself much of an option." *But I still want an explanation.* "And the outsider crew, what's left of it—they'll cooperate with our navy, one way or another, I expect."

"You'll never let them go." Not a question.

"I don't think either the crew or our navy will ever be in a position to negotiate about that."

She nodded, or shook her head, a peculiar sideward motion. "We do what we can, here . . . and take what we can get. We're responsible for our own actions." Again the defiance, the spite, the fire . . . she faced the ghosts incarnate of the Lansing assembly. "We take the consequences."

"Sandoval." Raul signaled him forward. "Take her back, let her work on the radio. And whatever happens, don't let her broadcast anythin', repeat, *any*thin', until you get the word from me."

"Yes, sir." Sandoval saluted smoothly and led her away, her head high, flanked by guards.

Raul delegated two more men to guard the airlock, keeping one with him. The prime minister and the assembly members waited, aware once more—as he was aware—of their lack of consequence, their loss of control.

The prime minister turned to Wind Kitavu, his robes opening like a blossom. "You. What are you doin' down here like this?"

"You know what I was doin'." Wind Kitavu jerked into an arc away from the wall. "The baby. You all know, don't act like you didn't!"

The prime minister drew back, an undignified motion. "Then don't expect anythin' from us! You knew what would happen. Accept your own mistakes . . . get back to work." He stretched his arm.

Raul saw dirt still crusting it from wrist to elbow as his sleeve moved. He heard one of his crewmen laugh out loud again, seeing it; did nothing this time to check it. He turned away. "Wind Kitavu."

Wind Kitavu halted his sullen drift toward the door.

"Are you goin' out onto the surface?"

A nod, faceless. "Got to tell my—wife. Tell her about the baby."

"Then we'll follow you up. I want to see those damned gardens."

"Damned gardens . . ." It echoed, someone else's voice;

Wind Kitavu moved toward the exit. Raul did not turn to acknowledge the Prime Minister of all Heaven Belt.

Raul followed his unresponsive guide through more tunnels, this time feeling the upward slant. Brightness grew from a point of light ahead of him, widening as he rose to meet it—an intensity of light that could only be the sun's. But this time he approached day in the way that had been natural for the human species through the countless years of its existence, a way that for him was entirely novel and unexpected: he crossed into the daylight freely, easily, unhindered by any barrier.

And stopped, absorbing, absorbed by the blinding greenness that enfolded him as he emerged from the hillside. He had a sudden, vivid memory of the hydroponics greenhouses of the Harmony, the heat and humidity that made them a sweltering hell to the average citizen. His crewman retreated into the tunnel's entrance behind him; he ordered him back sharply. Periodic hydroponics service was required of all citizens, a shared trial. He had done hydroponics service in his youth; but as a Hand of Harmony, it was no longer required of him. *Maybe rank does have its privileges.*

But the handful of ragged workers clustering now didn't look any more uncomfortable than the ones in the tunnels behind him. Insulated by his suit, he would never experience the reality of the gardens, of how life had been on Old Earth. Two futures waited here with him, in the balance of life and death—and either way, he would never have this opportunity again. . . .

He looked back at the shifting knot of sullen, dirty faces, at the genetic deformities that marked them like a brand. Above them all, latticed and embroidered by the fragile looming trees, the roof of the sky was a transparent membrane, disfigured too by blotches of clumsy patchwork. Once there must have been something more, a shield of force to protect them from solar radiation . . . a protection that had long since been lost. In the Grand Harmony permanent hydroponics duty was given as a punishment. Here it was a punishment too, in a different way; for the crime of having been a victim. . . . He left his helmet on, the idea of contamination back in his mind again: not the contamination of disease but a more pernicious contamination of the spirit. It was not a place he wanted to get the feel of, after all.

"What is it now?" One of them clutched at Wind Kitavu's sleeve, pulling his torn shirt halfway off his shoulder. "Are they wearin' *suits* to come out an' preach at us now?"

Wind Kitavu worked free, jerking his shirt back up his arm. "No . . ." His voice dropped, his hand gestured at them as he explained. Raul lost the words as an atmosphere in gentle motion hissed sibilance. He watched the lithe motion of the reaching trees, watched an expression that was growing too familiar spread from face to face in the group of workers, the desolation so complete that it could not even re-form into anger.

Wind Kitavu asked something in return, and the man who had stopped him pointed vaguely away. Without asking permission, without turning even to look back, Wind Kitavu left them, disappearing between the shrubs, loosening a slow shower of pastel blossom petals where he passed. *The baby.* Raul made no move to stop him, remembering what it was he went to do and having no desire to be a witness to it. The other workers began to drift back and away, still watching him warily as their bare feet pushed off from the springy mat of trampled vegetation.

Raul glanced back into the tunnel, still empty behind him. He noticed for the first time that the overhead lamps that illuminated the underground were flameless. Electricity . . . somewhere these people still had a functioning generator, probably an atomic battery from before the war—or even from some later trade with the Demarchy. He considered again the fact that the Grand Harmony had none at all because of the Demarchy. If not for their bounty of snow, the Grand Harmony would be in a worse position than Lansing—and the only worse position was death.

The Demarchy made him think of Wadie Abdhiamal and the mystery that lay behind their impending meeting. He had seen Abdhiamal function as a negotiator at Snows-of-Salvation: inexperienced, unsure of his own position, but wringing cooperation out of both sides with an instinct for fairness that dissolved cultural biases the way a heated knife sank through an ice block. And as a ship's captain he had transported Abdhiamal to meetings in Central Harmony and half the inhabited rocks of the Rings. He had seen the man ignored, insulted, actively threatened, but never losing patience. . . . And he had been surprised, suspicious, and finally pleased when Abdhiamal questioned him about matters of Harmony governmental policy. Pleased, in the end, because he saw Abdhiamal actually listen and learn and make use of what he learned to help them all.

The only weakness he had found in Wadie Abdhiamal was his inability to deal with one thing—the inevitability of Heaven's end. He had found that Abdhiamal believed some answer still existed; while he, Raul, like the people of Lansing, had seen long ago that the only answer was death. And yet he began to suspect that Abdhiamal's obsessive optimism covered a conviction as certain as his own that Heaven was doomed . . . but more than that, it covered a deep, pathological fear: Abdhiamal was not a man who could accept that all he accomplished would mean nothing in the end. He could not continue on that road, knowing its end was in sight; he would stumble and fall, crushed by the burden of his own knowledge. And so some part of Abdhiamal's mind had shut the truth away, buried it in a lie that let him continue. Raul had envied Abdhiamal the Demarchy, where comparative richness helped him protect his illusions. And he had wondered whether anything would ever force him to admit the truth. . . .

But the starship—even he, Raul, had discovered hope again in what it could offer Heaven . . . and, specifically, the Grand Harmony. Why would Abdhiamal, of all people, try to make sure that neither of their governments got its hands on the ship? Abdhiamal was a fair man—but was he fair to the point of insanity, of genocide? And the woman who piloted the ship . . . why would she run such risks to keep a promise to a place like Lansing? Were they both insane, were they all? Or was there something he wasn't seeing? . . . Too many things that he couldn't see. But *if* she kept her promise, if that ship was falling right into his hands . . . that was the only answer that he would ever need. Ever.

"Can't you raise Lansing, Pappy?" Betha moved stiffly up from the rendezvous program on the control board.

Clewell pulled the ear jack away from his head wearily. "No. I've got the ship monitoring all up and down the spectrum. If anyone talks to us we'll hear it."

"Maybe the transmitter broke down," Shadow Jack said. "It's out about half the time, seems like. They have a hard time keepin' it repaired." Bird Alyn floated beside him above Betha's head, gazing at the magnified image of Lansing on the screen. Betha watched the cloudy, marshmallow softness of the tent passing below: a shroud for a dying people, who would live a little longer because of the *Ranger*.

Discus hung above and to the left, tilted and indistinct, a tiny finger's jewel. And somewhere in the closer darkness: three fusion ships from the Demarchy. Not one of them had begun deceleration to match velocities with Lansing and the *Ranger*. Their mission was one of murder. . . . Betha glanced at the latest tracking update; less than ten minutes left to off-load the hydrogen.

"Well, our time is a little limited . . . I'm sure that Lansing won't mind if we drop you and the tanks into low orbit, and then get ourselves out of here." She smiled up at Shadow Jack and Bird Alyn, forcing warmth into her voice. "They should be glad to see you two coming home with eight hundred tons of hydrogen."

"They will," Shadow Jack said. They nodded, their faces shining clean and smiling bravely above the collars of their

260

pressure suits. "But . . . are you sure you're goin' to be all right when we go?" An odd longing edged his voice, and a secret shame. "Just the—two of you?" He glanced away at Clewell's drawn face, cracking his knuckles.

From the corner of her eye Betha saw Wadie look at her. . . impeccable Abdhiamal, in embroidered jacket and faded dungarees. She smiled in spite of herself. "We'll be all right," she said, managing a confidence her own aching, battered body did not really believe, for his sake. She would not play on his guilt to make him change his mind. They had come this far; they would find a way to do the rest, somehow. Later . . . she'd think about it later. "Don't crack your knuckles, Shadow Jack. You'll ruin your joints."

Shadow Jack grinned feebly and stuffed his hands into his gloves.

Wadie touched her shoulder. "Look."

As they spoke the *Ranger* had slipped a quarter of the way around Lansing. On the near horizon, they saw a blunt protrusion of naked stone, the tent lapping its slope like clouds below a mountaintop.

"The Mountain," Bird Alyn said. "There're the radio antennas, an' the moorage . . . there's one of our—"

"Hey." Shadow Jack tugged at her arm. "That's not one of our ships! I never saw anythin' like that; where'd it come from?"

"Maybe it's salvage."

"No, look, there's another one."

Betha increased the magnification. "Pappy, those look like—"

"—Ringers! Ringers, go back, it's a trap, a—" A woman's voice burst out of the speaker, was choked off.

"Mother!" A small cry escaped from Bird Alyn.

"Those look like chemical rockets down there." Clewell finished the sentence, his voice like dry leaves rattling.

Wadie's hand tightened on her shoulder. "My God, those are Ringer ships; fifty million kilometers from Discus. . . ." His voice sharpened with disbelief. "The Demarchy knew the Harmony had a couple of high-mass-ratio strike forces, but nothin' like this. To be here now, with only chemical rockets, they must've started right after they first attacked you. And even then they'd need a mass ratio of a thousand to one—''

A new voice came over the speaker: ''Outsider starship! This is Hand Nakamore of the Grand Harmony. Maintain your present orbit. Do not activate your drive or you'll be fired upon. One of my ships will approach you now for boarding.'' Betha looked down on the airless mountain, at three cumbersome Ringer craft, each hardly more than a mass of propellant tanks surrounding a tiny crew module. At last she saw one of them begin to rise, its invisible backwash kicking up clouds of surface rubble. *Trapped.* . . . Her hands knotted at her sides. The best the *Ranger* could ever do was one gravity; and now she could only get one-quarter of that, with the load strapped to its hull. The Ringer chemical rockets could do several gees for more than long enough to close with them.

The seconds passed; the Ringer ship rose slowly, almost insolently, toward them. The minutes passed . . . and with them, the *Ranger*'s last hope of avoiding the Demarchy fleet as well. *Christ, why must we lose now, when we're so close!*

Wadie hooked a foot under a rail along the panel, steadying himself. ''Betha, that was Djem Nakamore's half-brother, Raul, on the radio. He's a Hand of Harmony, an officer in their navy. A high-ranking officer. Let me talk to him. He probably knows what I did at Snows-of-Salvation, but we were friends, once.''

''Better wait, Abdhiamal,'' Clewell said quietly. ''We've got more company, sophisticated wideband.'' He touched the panel and another segment of the screen brightened.

''Lije MacWong,'' Wadie said; Betha saw the easy grace tighten out of his body.

''Captain Torgussen: If you're receiving this, you must realize that the Demarchy has pursued your ship. The distance-velocity gap between us is small enough now so that you can't outrun our missiles; do not attempt to leave Lansing space.'' Behind MacWong's self-satisfied face Betha could see a control room half the size of the *Ranger*'s and a ship's officer in a sun-gold jacket. Farther back in the room she saw cameras trained on the screen, saw a cluster of demarchs, like bright-painted wooden dolls—company representatives overseeing their interests. She saw Esrom Tiriki, felt her mouth tighten.

She signaled at Clewell to transmit. "I hear you, MacWong. And I'm impressed. Have you actually come all this way to destroy my ship? You can't take us now; all you can do is destroy us in passing. . . ." She hesitated. MacWong's startling blue eyes still stared blindly from the screen. She realized, chagrined, that even closing at eight hundred kilometers per second the Demarchy ships were still millions of kilometers away; light itself took half a minute to bridge the gap.

At last MacWong reacted, looked past her to Wadie. For an instant she saw apology and regret; another second, and she saw only triumph. "On the contrary, Captain Torgussen. We have no intention of destroyin' your starship—if you obey our instructions. Our ships will pass through your vicinity in about four thousand seconds. You have that much time to dismantle and deactivate your drive. If, by that time, you haven't satisfactorily proved that your ship will be immobilized till we return for it, you will be fired on and destroyed. The people want your ship intact, Captain, but if they can't have it, they don't intend to let it go to anybody else."

Betha pushed back, her arms rigid against the panel. "Wadie . . . he's no fool after all." The *Ranger* lay in the jaws of a trap; and each jaw was unaware of the other. When the jaws closed on her ship they would have to destroy each other too. She let go of the panel, forcing a smile. "Then I'm afraid you have a problem too, MacWong. We would have been gone before you arrived, except that someone else is already holding us here . . . Hand Nakamore, I'm sure you've been monitoring. Would you care to comment?" She waited, savoring the bitterness of useless satisfaction.

Clewell grunted. "The Ringers are transmitting video, not to be outdone. . . ." A new patch of screen brightened with a black-and-white image. The Ringer control room was small, the crew strapped down to padded couches crowded by equipment: an image from the earliest days of space travel. A thickset Belter in a helmet with the Discan rings for insignia sat nearest the camera, his face grim behind a stubble of beard. "This is Hand Nakamore of the Grand Harmony. My forces have seized the Outsider starship, and if it attempts to comply with your demands, we'll destroy it. We have several prewar fusion bombs in our possession. If you attempt to keep us from takin' that ship we'll do our damnedest to destroy you too.''

Betha glanced at Wadie, questioning.

"He could have the bombs; salvage from the war.'' Wadie studied the embroidered whorls on his jacket front. "If he could maneuver into MacWong's path with them, he wouldn't have to be too accurate, even if it took the Demarchy crews a megasec to die of radiation poisoning. Things like this happened during the war, crews of dead men fighting their final battle. That's how we got three fusion craft intact. . . .'' He raised his eyes. "Nakamore will never let the Demarchy take the *Ranger*, even if it means he has to die too.''

Betha saw the trace of consternation that betrayed MacWong at the sight of Nakamore; the obvious disbelief on the ruddy face of the ship's officer and on the face of Esrom Tiriki. She watched them change again to hatred and defiance, heard MacWong begin an angry response.

"And so we're all going to die, and so are they . . . and so is Heaven.'' Her voice rose. "And for what? This is insane—''

"Don't you think they know that?'' Wadie moved toward her, almost touched her again. "They know it as well as we do. But they're trapped here just like we are; all that's happened in the last two and a half gigasecs since the war, all the frustration and fear, has been leadin' down to this. . . . It had to end like this. Your own song says it—'No one ever changed a world.'''

She drew away from him. "It's the people who have to be willing to change! It didn't have to end like this. If they could have seen that there was still a future . . . There could still be one now, but even you can't see it; you won't see it. You're right, death *is* what you want. . . . Suicide is the ultimate selfishness, and I've never seen a people more ready to commit it.'' She unstrapped, pushing up out of her seat and away from him, her breath catching at the punishment of sudden movement. "You deserve it. Damn you all!''

He caught her wrist. Furious, she felt Shadow Jack move out of her way, staring, as Wadie pulled her back to the screen. "MacWong, Raul, this is Abdhiamal. I want to talk to you.''

Nakamore acknowledged him and Betha thought she saw a smile; she waited, saw MacWong break off his speech: "Sorry, Abdhiamal. You're a dead man. You've got nothin' to say to the Demarchy." MacWong glanced sideways, barely turning his head. Betha looked past him at Tiriki.

"We're all dead men unless you listen to me! Because of this ship, which you don't have any more right to than Nakamore does, or I do. For God's sake, MacWong, there were seven people on this ship, who came three light-years from another system to Heaven; and five of them are already dead because of it. And now you're goin' to destroy the rest of them, along with the best ships left to the Demarchy and the Rings? You're all that's left of Heaven Belt, and your own greed is ripping your guts out. You're killin' yourselves because you're scared to die. Taking the starship won't save Heaven, and it's goin' to finish you off instead, if you let it.

"But you don't have to let it happen." He nodded at Betha waiting beside him, silent with surprise. "These people came to trade with us because they wanted a better life. And in spite of what we've done to them, they're still willin' to trade. There's a whole trade ring of worlds out there, holding each other up so that they never fall into the kind of trap we've put ourselves in. They can save us too. Heaven Belt can be all it ever was if we join them." He waited, searching the screen for a response. "Let the starship leave Heaven, instead of destroyin' it. You'll accomplish the same goal but you'll have everything to gain and nothing to lose."

"You always could convince Djem that cold was hot, Wadie." Betha looked for mockery on Nakamore's face, was surprised when she didn't find it. "But this time you even make sense to me. . . . I don't *want* to destroy the starship or my own ships. If I could get out of this bind by lettin' the ship leave the system, I would. The way things have turned out, it'd be enough just to put the ship beyond everybody's reach. . . . And the point's not lost on me that the only reason we've got you now is that this woman, this Captain Torgussen, came back to Lansing as she said she would." Nakamore found Betha's eyes, curiously respectful. "I think you would come back to help us too."

Betha frowned in sudden pain, bit her lip.

"I'm willin' to let you go, Captain. But is MacWong?"

Betha saw MacWong surreptitiously rolling the lace on his shirt front, still listening to Nakamore's transmission. Behind him the mediamen transmitted his own every move, his every word, to the waiting Demarchy: MacWong was pinned under the public gaze like a bug under glass. At last he said, "Your suggestion violates the Demarchy's mandate for this mission. I only have the authority to seize the ship or destroy it; I can't let it go."

"Even though you want to! Even though we may all die if you don't." Nakamore's words burned with contempt; his taciturn face was abruptly transformed, as though he were making a speech. Betha realized suddenly that he must be well aware that there was an audience waiting to receive it. Wadie began to smile, almost wonderingly. "You puppet. You call the Harmony a 'dictatorship' but we give more freedom to the individual than your people's mobocracy ever did or will. I have the power, the freedom of choice, to stop this stupidity. But you don't. Your people don't trust a man to use the judgment he was born with; they pick the words every time you open your mouth.

"But how are they goin' to tell you what to do this time, MacWong? They never imagined needing second-to-second control over hundreds of millions of kilometers, across a comm lag like this. By the time the whole Demarchy hears this and debates and amends and votes, things will be all over for us, and whatever they wanted won't mean a damn thing.... But you won't take the decision in your own hands because you're too afraid of the system, and of those pretty-boy anarchists behind you. The basic weakness and inefficiency of your self-servin' mob rule will make the Demarchy destroy its own ships, and mine, and destroy this system's last hope of survival. I've always known your 'government' was a farce...an' even you can't deny that now. I'd laugh if it wasn't such a tragedy. Because that's what it is, a tragedy."

Betha watched impotent rage fracture MacWong's mask of complacency, saw real emotion for the first time on the faces of the listening demarchs behind him...saw the mediamen recording it all, so that the entire Demarchy could see and share their indignation. MacWong covered his anger. "Captain Torgussen, our ships will pass you in thirty-six hundred seconds. If you intend to follow our instructions, I suggest you get in touch with us soon." His image vanished abruptly.

Betha said softly, "Try to monitor MacWong's communications with the Demarchy, Pappy; let me know how much worse that outburst makes things."

Nakamore loosened the upturned collar of his stiff, bulky jacket, the anger flowing out of his eyes and voice. "He'll be back, I expect."

"My congratulations on . . . your promotion to Hand, Raul." Betha watched Wadie bow, inscrutable.

"My duty, to accept; my desire, to serve." Nakamore gestured the honor aside, oddly embarrassed. "I wish I could say the same to you, Wadie. But I don't know the Demarchy's etiquette for its traitors."

Wadie smiled bleakly. "There's not any."

"You're the only reasonable demarch I ever met, and that's probably why the mob went after you. I don't approve of your act of piracy against the Harmony . . . but I think I finally begin to see why you did it; why you want to help these people. I doubt if Djem'll ever understand it—"

"I know . . . and I'm sorry. There wasn't any other choice. It would never have happened if—"

"If we hadn't attacked the starship when it first appeared? You're right. It was stupid of us. If we'd had sense enough to direct 'em to one of our bases instead, the Grand Harmony'd have its own starship now. But we didn't, and all we got was death. But we knew the ship was damaged, and Central Harmony figured it was worth the gamble I could catch them here."

"That was a long chance," Wadie said. "You'd have been a long time gettin' home if what we saw is all the propellant you've got left."

"I know. Even without a battle, it would take us twenty megasecs to get back to Outermost—if our life-support systems held out. And then we'd freeze our asses off on that snowball, waitin' for a fuel shipment to get us to the inner Harmony."

Nakamore scratched his chin, looking tired. "But we took on food and air down on Lansing."

Shadow Jack pushed past Betha's shoulder to the camera. "Why didn't you just rip the tent and kill 'em quick, you bastard?"

Nakamore shrugged. "Boy, you're all pirates to me. But we didn't take that much. Look on it as a trade for the hydrogen you stole from the Harmony."

"Where's my mother?" Bird Alyn cried suddenly, shrill with anguish. "What did you do to my mother?"

Nakamore peered at her blankly; Betha saw comprehension come to him. "So . . . your mother's goin' to have a stiff jaw for a few hundred kilosecs. But aside from that she's better off than you are—or we are—right now. Speakin' of which: Captain Torgussen, you have my permission to off-load those gas canisters into a low orbit around Lansing. Then I recommend all our ships move out a few hundred kilometers into space. When the Demarchy forces arrive the fireworks'll be lethal over quite a volume; there's no reason why Lansing should be part of it. Somebody might as well get somethin' out of this." He turned away, issuing soundless orders.

"Thank you," Betha said. She saw the curious smile still on Wadie's face as he watched the screen. "What is that man? I don't understand him."

Wadie turned toward her, and the smile grew gentle. "Sanity hasn't entirely disappeared from Heaven, Betha. Not even from the Rings. . . . Raul is a decent man; but more than that, he's not stupid. I told you his brother never won a chess game from me. In all the time I spent in the Rings, I won only two games from Raul. He may still have some surprises left."

Betha rubbed her arms. "All I know is that he intentionally infuriated the Demarchy to the point where they'll never be satisfied until they see us all in hell. Whatever he thinks he's doing, I don't like being his pawn."

The *Ranger* moved slowly out from Lansing. Betha watched it growing smaller below them, a world of elvish beauty, rising and falling in soft undulations beneath a transparent film of plastic spotted with milky patchwork. Trees reached upward toward the tent like sprays of lace, fragile fountains of leaves spilling over fields of ripening grain . . . and fields of dying grass. She saw the velvet green of parklands, still well watered . . . and the peeling mud of dried marshes. The people below moved in a dream ballet among airy minarets and pillared buildings of state, on the world that had once been the symbol of Heaven's splendid extravagance. The last world she would ever see. . . . She glanced at Clewell's still face, his closed eyes, where he drifted in his seat listening for the Demarchy's response. Afraid of the stillness, she looked away again, stroked Rusty's purring, clinging form while she tried to picture the other beloved faces already lost to her and the homeworld none of them would ever see again. There was no comfort now, no satisfaction, in this ultimate revenge that Heaven would inflict on itself in retribution for their deaths and her own. A terrible weariness settled over her, the futility of the last few weeks, the last four years.

"Betha . . ." Wadie kept his eyes on the screen. "I don't know how to save this ship. But I think I know how to save our lives. We can leave the *Ranger*, use the *Lansing 04* to take us down to Lansing. All Nakamore wants an end to is the ship, not our lives. If we use our suits we can all make it."

"No." Betha wrapped her arms across the aching muscles of her stomach. "I won't leave the *Ranger*. But yes, the rest of you, get into your suits and go. There's no reason for you to stay; at least save yourselves."

"What do you mean, you won't leave this ship?" Wadie pushed back from the screen, caught her chair arm. "It's just a ship, Betha; it doesn't control your life. You aren't chained to it."

She shook her head. "You still don't understand, do you? After all this time. This is *my* ship. I was part of its design, and part of its construction. Its crew were the people I loved; this journey meant everything to us, the future of our world. . . . Everything about it binds me to my people, my past, my home. I can't leave it. I don't want to lose everything, I don't want to live forever in the place where it happened. I don't want to live like that."

"Now who's indulging in the ultimate selfishness?"

Her mouth tightened. "It's not going to hurt anyone but me"—realizing, as she saw his face, that that wasn't true.

"Well, what about . . . what about Clewell?"

"What about me?" Clewell opened his eyes, irritably, at the communications board. "I have no intention of leaving the *Ranger* for that overgrown cinder down there."

"Dammit, you're just makin' her more stubborn. Why the hell don't you tell her she's wrong?"

"She's my wife, not my child. She has a right to make her own decision. And so do I. . . . I've lived too long already if I've lived to see this day. My body already knows the truth." He closed his eyes again. "Now let me do my job; monitoring the Demarchy is hard enough as it is at this distance."

"May it do us some good." Wadie pulled himself back to the panel, massaged the cramped muscles of his neck. "All right, then. . . . I'll stay too. I guess I've earned the right. I lost everythin' I ever valued because of this ship."

Betha froze her expression, willed emotion from her voice. "You won't blackmail me into changing my mind, Wadie."

He bowed solemnly. "Not my intent. Allow me the privilege of making my own decision, since you expect me to accept yours. I'd rather die a martyr than a traitor."

She sighed, her nails digging into the palms of her hands. *Thank you.* "All right, then. So only two will be going to Lansing."

Bird Alyn raised her head from Shadow Jack's shoulder, drifting, cradled in his arms. "No. Betha, we're not goin'."

"Now, listen—"

"No," Shadow Jack said. "We did what we wanted to do for Lansing. But there's nothin' anybody can do for us. We'd rather be—together—now, for a little while, than be apart forever." He glanced at the doorway.

"I see." She nodded once, barely hearing her own voice. "Come here, then, both of you." They drifted forward obediently. Betha worked a golden band from one finger of each of her hands. Reaching out, she took their own left hands, one at a time, slipped a ring over a thin straight finger, a thin crooked one. She joined the hands to keep the rings from floating free.

"By my authority as captain of this ship, I pronounce you husband and wife. . . . May your love be as deep as the darkness, as constant as the sun."

Their hands clung to her own for a moment; she felt Shadow Jack's trembling. She turned away, heard them leave the room. Clewell's eyes touched her face in a caress. "Pappy, get off the radio a minute. We've got to leave those people some hydrogen. . . ."

There were seventeen hundred seconds until encounter.

Three hundred kilometers away now, Lansing was a greenish, mottled crescent on the darkness. Far enough away, Betha hoped, to survive whatever fires must burn across Heaven. On all sides emptiness stretched, filling the light-years to the distant stars. And the *Ranger* had been built to bridge those distances, at speeds close to that of light itself. But it would never cross them again . . . it lay stranded like a beached cetoid on the desolate shores of Heaven, trapped by primitive ships with primitive weapons in the ultimate irony of defeat.

"Five hundred seconds," Wadie said. Rusty curled serenely in the crook of his arm and washed a protruding foot.

Betha lit her pipe, inhaled the familiar, soothing odor of the smoke. "That's when the first ship will pass; they're strung out at about one-hundred-second intervals. But it doesn't matter . . . we can't comply with MacWong's demand now."

Clewell chuckled suddenly, oblivious.

"God, Pappy, what in hell are you laughing at?"

He shook his head apologetically. "At the Demarchy reacting to Nakamore's speech—their righteous indignation at being named for what they are."

"Well, put it on," Wadie said, strangely eager. "I want to hear that."

A burst of static mixed with garbled speech filled the room. Clewell lowered the volume. "Sorry; even with enhancement, it takes some practice to make sense out of that."

Four hundred seconds.

He pulled off his ear jack. "My God, Betha, I think they're actually trying to take a vote . . . a vote on whether to let us go."

Betha pushed up out of her chair, caught herself on the panel edge with a gasp. "Pappy! Can't you clean up the transmission?"

"I'll try. MacWong's ships are close enough now; we may be in the tight beam from the Demarchy." He put an image on the screen; Betha saw print, illegible through snow, recognized the format of a Demarchy general election. A band of golden yellow brightened at the bottom.

"It takes about five hundred seconds for a full tally."

"Five hundred! Christ." She felt Wadie move close, his sleeve brush her arm. "Pappy, raise MacWong's ship."

"I've tried. They're not talking."

She could almost see the numbers, almost see them change. And beside the static-clouded picture, the *Ranger's* displays projected the track of three closing ships on a star-filled sky. Three ships that stood out like flares now, their torches extended ahead of their flight, decelerating at last. She searched their brilliance for a smaller track, a seed of blossoming destruction. *Give us time, MacWong.* . . . Clewell left his seat, moved slowly along the panel to her side; she took his arm. The digits on the chronometer narrowed like sand in an hourglass, eroding their lives. One hundred seconds until the first ship passed . . . sixty . . . fifty . . . She realized she had stopped breathing. "They're holding off! Forty seconds; that first ship can't fire on us now."

MacWong's face appeared below the tally. "Captain Torgussen." They saw the stress on his face and on the faces that ringed him in. "We're just now receivin' the results of a vote from the Demarchy. The majority accepts your aid to Lansing as evidence of your goodwill, Captain, and favors a modification of our mission. . . . I hope you're listenin', Nakamore; you've just seen a demonstration of the real flexibility and strength of the people, the wisdom and fairness of the Demarchic system." He looked away, into the media cameras, and back.

"Captain Torgussen, the Demarchy will allow you to depart— if you will assure us that the Demarchy will be the center for distributin' your aid when you return to Heaven." His eyes asked her to promise anything.

On the center of the screen Betha saw the second Demarchy ship fall past them.

Nakamore's image came onto the screen. "You know I can't

accept that, MacWong.'' His voice was even, no longer reaching out to goad an entire people. ''I don't demand that control go to the Harmony. But it's not goin' to you.''

Betha froze, realizing that Nakamore might still let them go. A promise at knifepoint was no promise at all . . . and no solution. There had to be a way to reach both sides, or the next Morningside ship to come to Heaven would fall into the same deadly trap of greed. She heard someone come up behind her, turned to see Shadow Jack and Bird Alyn, peacefully hand in hand.

''What happened?'' Bird Alyn brushed her soft floating hair back from her eyes and blinked at the screen.

Betha turned back to the screen, saw MacWong's pale eyes search her face for an answer. ''It's going to be Lansing! Tell your people, MacWong, Nakamore. Those are Morningside's terms: our aid will be distributed through Lansing, the capital of the Heaven Belt. Neither of your governments will be shown favor, everyone will be treated equally.''

They stared at her, unreal images; she saw Tiriki come alive, saw his mouth move soundlessly: ''. . . a trick . . . want that ship destroyed . . .''

Wadie leaned past her. ''Lansing's harmless, Lije! The Demarchy will accept it; you know they will.''

MacWong moved back from the screen as Tiriki caught his shoulder; Betha read Tiriki's hatred. She looked at the computer plot. ''That last ship will pass at only thirty kilometers; they can fire on us almost point-blank.'' She nodded at the screen. ''If we don't see that ship pass by, we'll be stardust. . . .''

Behind her Shadow Jack said solemnly, ''You mean we'll be dead.''

MacWong broke away from Tiriki's grasp. She couldn't see his face, only that he faced the media's glaring eye and gave an order. . . .

Nakamore began to laugh. ''Thank you, you son of chaos!''

A barely visible streak of palest violet lit the darkness on the screen before them for the length of a heartbeat, and was gone. The third ship had passed.

> "Crops may wither on the plain
> Sun may parch us, rain turn wild—"

Clewell strapped himself into the navigator's seat, feeling new strength and satisfaction fill the hollow weariness of his limbs. He looked down at the running reflections on the panel, Shadow Jack holding Bird Alyn in his arms as she serenaded the long-suffering cat floating in midair across the room,

> "Sharing brings us help for pain..."

The representatives of Heaven Belt. . . . Clewell smiled, seeing them many years older and wiser, many years into the future, returning again to Lansing. "I never thought I'd be saying it, but I may just live another sixty years."

Bird Alyn braced her feet against the wall to peer sideways at him. "I can't believe it's real, Pappy. How did it happen? How did it all come out like this?" Shadow Jack kissed her cheek; she giggled.

Wadie pushed away from the viewscreen, where Lansing lay before them on the now-empty night: a chrysalis waiting for rebirth into a new life cycle. "Nothin's gone right in Heaven Belt for two and a half billion seconds, Bird Alyn. There are a hundred million corpses out there and God knows how many people who've gone through living hell. . . ." Bird Alyn's smile faltered; Shadow Jack held her tighter, the past darkened their eyes.

Wadie shook his head. "We must have paid for our mistake by now, a thousand times over. It's about time we had some good luck, dammit! It's about time."

Their faces eased. Clewell saw Betha look up from the panel, covering other memories, other sorrows. "Yes, it is. Pappy"—her voice was even—"everything's secured, the sky is empty. Start charting our course; it's time to go home." Wadie moved back to her side; Clewell saw his hand lift, hesitate, and drift away, still uncertain. He had been beside her for days: helping, learning . . . watching Betha Torgussen with an intentness that had nothing to do with starship technology. The man who would be a hero someday when their ship returned, MacWong had said; but who for now was still a traitor . . . and the only trade consultant who would satisfy both the Demarchy and the Rings. A good man, Clewell thought; the right man. Like another good man who had loved his wife and been his friend.

Clewell felt Betha's eyes touch him once more, as blue as field flowers, still shadowed by memory and pain. *Time heals all things* . . . and they would have the time they needed now. She changed the image on the screen. It showed him numberless stars; and one among the millions—shrunken, red, and constant—that would guide them home.

Laughter floated out of the room and down the stairwell as Bird Alyn and Shadow Jack, unknowing and unconcerned, put the past behind them forever.

Rusty settled onto his shoulders, purring in soft harmony with the memory of song:

> Sharing brings us help for pain,
> For nothing's easy, oh my child.

He saw the faces of his other children, who he hoped would live to see the better world that had cost so much and been so long in coming. "Rusty," he said quietly, "it's about time."

ABOUT THE AUTHOR

Joan D. Vinge has had stories published in *Analog*, *Orbit*, *Isaac Asimov's SF Magazine*, and various anthologies, including *The Crystal Ship* (title novella) and *Millennial Women*. Two of her novellas have been published as a book entitled *Fireship*.

Joan has a degree in anthropology, which she feels is very similar to science fiction in many ways because both fields give you an opportunity to view human relationships from a fresh and revealing perspective. She's worked, among other things, as a salvage archeologist, enjoys horseback riding and needlecrafts, and is married to Vernor Vinge, who also writes science fiction.